RUST OR RIDE

Lost Kings MC #22

AUTUMN JONES LAKE

USA TODAY BESTSELLING AUTHOR AUTUMN JONES LAKE

COPYRIGHT

Rust or Ride (Lost Kings MC #22)

Copyright 2023 Autumn Jones Lake
All Rights Reserved
Digital ISBN: 978-1-943950-98-0
Paperback ISBN: 978-1-943950-89-8
Alternate Paperback ISBN: 978-1-943950-94-2
Alternate Hardback ISBN: 978-1-943950-95-9
Cover Model: Camden
Photographer: Wander Aguiar
Cover Designer: Shanoff Designs
Alternate Cover Design: Shanoff Designs
Edited by: Creating Ink
Proofreading: Julie Barney

ALSO BY AUTUMN JONES LAKE

- SLOW BURN (LOST KINGS MC #1) – *free ebook!*
- CORRUPTING CINDERELLA (LOST KINGS MC #2)
- THREE KINGS, ONE NIGHT (LOST KINGS MC #2.5)
- STRENGTH FROM LOYALTY (LOST KINGS MC #3)
- TATTERED ON MY SLEEVE (LOST KINGS MC #4)
- WHITE HEAT (LOST KINGS MC #5)
- BETWEEN EMBERS (LOST KINGS MC #5.5)
- MORE THAN MILES (LOST KINGS MC #6)
- WHITE KNUCKLES (LOST KINGS MC #7)
- BEYOND RECKLESS (LOST KINGS MC #8)
- BEYOND REASON (LOST KINGS MC #9)
- ONE EMPIRE NIGHT (LOST KINGS MC #9.5)
- AFTER BURN (LOST KINGS MC #10)
- AFTER GLOW (LOST KINGS MC #11)
- ZERO HOUR (LOST KINGS MC #11.5) – *free ebook!*
- ZERO TOLERANCE (LOST KINGS MC #12)
- ZERO REGRET (LOST KINGS MC #13)
- ZERO APOLOGIES (LOST KINGS MC #14)
- SWAGGER AND SASS (LOST KINGS MC #14.5) – *free ebook!*
- WHITE LIES (LOST KINGS MC #15)
- RHYTHM OF THE ROAD (LOST KINGS MC #16)
- LYRICS ON THE WIND (LOST KINGS MC #17)
- DIAMOND IN THE DUST (LOST KINGS MC #18)
- CROWN OF GHOSTS (LOST KINGS MC #19)
- THRONE OF SCARS (LOST KINGS MC #20)
- RECKLESS TRUTHS (LOST KINGS MC #21)
- DEEPER YOU DIG (LOST KINGS MC #21.5)
- RUST OR RIDE (LOST KINGS MC #22)

THE HOLLYWOOD DEMONS SERIES (LOST KINGS MC WORLD)

KICKSTART MY HEART (HOLLYWOOD DEMONS #1)

BLOW MY FUSE (HOLLYWOOD DEMONS #2)

WHEELS OF FIRE (HOLLYWOOD DEMONS #3)

STANDALONES IN THE LOST KINGS MC WORLD

RENEGADE PATH (LOST KINGS MC WORLD)

BULLETS & BONFIRES (LOST KINGS MC WORLD)

WARNINGS & WILDFIRES (LOST KINGS MC WORLD)

ABOUT RUST OR RIDE

Lost Kings MC #22

No matter how hard he tries, the road captain of the Lost Kings Motorcycle Club can't resist falling in love in this captivating installment of the Lost Kings MC series by USA Today bestselling author Autumn Jones Lake

Dixon "Dex" Watts has traveled a road full of painful twists and turns. He found love young, lost it, and swore to never give his heart to another woman. He's devoted his life to the only family he needs—the Lost Kings MC.

Emily isn't just another woman. She's the best friend of a brother's wife. Not someone who should spark emotions he thought had rusted out years ago. But when he finds Emily stranded in a cemetery his hardened heart starts to thaw.

Tragedy has followed Emily like a shadow. She's committed to protecting and raising her teenage sister on her own. Dating and relationships don't fit into her carefully constructed world. Besides, no man has ever met her high standards or earned her trust.

But Dex isn't just any man. He's obscenely hot, overprotective, a bit mysterious, and has a moral compass that spins in a different direction. On the outside, everything about him should scream danger. But Emily slowly discovers the truth is more complicated.

No matter how hard they try, neither of them can ignore their burning attraction. They may be complete opposites with painful pasts and incompatible lives but once the spark ignites between them, the flames can't be extinguished.

GLOSSARY OF CHARACTERS AND TERMINOLOGY

The Lost Kings MC™ World © Autumn Jones Lake

Dex's story could be read as a standalone. While he's appeared in the Lost Kings MC series since the beginning and plays a major role in Renegade Path (Lost Kings MC World) this is his first book. We've seen and heard about him through other people's eyes throughout the series but this is the first time we're in Dex's head and get to learn how he sees the Lost Kings MC World!

The following may contain spoilers if you are not caught up on the series or have skipped books.

Please note, this glossary only pertains to my romantic fictionalized motorcycle club world. It should not be construed as applicable to any other fictional club or a real-life motorcycle club.

THE LOST KINGS MC: UPSTATE, NY ("EMPIRE," NY)

President: Rochlan "Rock" North. Leader of the Upstate NY charter of the Lost Kings MC.

Sergeant-at-Arms: Wyatt "Wrath" Ramsey. Protector or enforcer for the club.

Vice President: Blake "Murphy" O'Callaghan. Murphy was the road captain up until *White Lies (Lost Kings MC #15)*

Treasurer: Marcel "Teller" Whelan. Handles the money and investments for the club. In After Glow (Lost Kings MC #11) Rock and Teller discovered they were father and son. In *Reckless Truths (Lost Kings MC #21)* they let the whole club in on their secret.

Road Captain: Dixon "Dex" Watts (newly appointed to the position in White Lies)

THE LOST KINGS MC: DOWNSTATE, NY ("UNION" NY)

President: Angus "Zero" or "Z" Frazier. As of *Zero Apologies (Lost Kings MC #14)*, Z is the president of the Downstate, NY charter of the Lost Kings MC.

Vice President: Logan "Rooster" Randall: Rooster's story is told in *Swagger Sass (Lost Kings MC #14.5)*, *Rhythm of the Road (Lost Kings MC #16)*, *Lyrics on the Wind (Lost Kings MC #17)*, and *Diamond in the Dust (Lost Kings MC #18)*

Sergeant-at-Arms: Grayson "Grinder" Lock as of *Throne of Scars (Lost Kings MC #20)*

Treasurer: Hustler

Road Captain: Jensen "Jigsaw" Kilgore; Jigsaw, Rooster's best friend from childhood, will have his own book in late 2023 or early 2024.

THE LOST KINGS MC: PORT EVERHART, VA

President: Cypress "Ice" Caldwell
   Vice President: Farmer
   Sergeant-at-Arms: Pants
   Treasurer: T-Bone
   Road Captain: Boots

THE LOST KINGS MC: DEADBRANCH, TN

President: Squiggy
   SAA: Steer from the Downstate NY charter moved to TN in *Throne of Scars*.
   Retired President: Digger, we first met him in *Lyrics on the Wind*.

OTHER LOST KINGS MC MEMBERS

Thomas "Ravage" Kane: We've gotten to know Rav and his snarky humor a little bit better in each book. Ravage is a general member who helps out wherever he is needed.

Cronin "Sparky" Petek: Sparky is the mad genius/hippie stoner behind the Lost Kings MC's pot-growing business. He is rarely seen outside of the basement, as he prefers the company of his plants.

Elias "Bricks" Serrano: We have seen Bricks and his girlfriend Winter throughout the series. He's one of the few members who does not live at the clubhouse.

Sam "Stash" Black: Lives in the basement with Sparky and helps with the plants.

Hoot: We've seen glimpses of him since Slow Burn when he was a lowly prospect. He finally got his full patch, but still gets a lot of the grunt work.

Birch: We also met him as a prospect. He's been voted as a full-patch member but shares in a lot of the grunt work with Hoot.

GLOSSARY OF CHARACTERS AND TERMINOLOGY

Priest: The Lost Kings MC's national president. We first met him and his wife, Valentina, in After Burn.

Malik: Prospect for the Lost Kings MC. Helps out at Crystal Ball. Owns the Lucky Duck pawnshop in Ironworks.

Sway: Former president of the downstate charter of the Lost Kings MC. We've seen Sway and his wife Tawny off and on in the series since *Strength From Loyalty*, usually annoying Rock in some fashion. After some legal troubles in *Throne of Scars*, Sway disappeared to Florida and has not been seen or heard from since.

THE LADIES OF THE LOST KINGS MC

Hope Kendall North, Esq.: Nicknamed First Lady by Murphy in *Corrupting Cinderella (Lost Kings MC #2)*, Hope is the object of Rock's love and obsession. Their daughter is named Grace after Rock's mother.

Trinity Hurst Ramsey: Wrath's angel. Former caretaker of the club. She now has her own photography and graphic design business. She is married to Wrath, fiercely loyal to the club, and best friends with Hope. Although she loves her niblets, Trinity and Wrath are happily childfree by choice and intend to *stay* that way.

Heidi "Little Hammer" O'Callaghan: Murphy's wife and Teller's little sister. Heidi just graduated from college and works at Empire Med. Murphy officially adopted her daughter, Alexa Jade. In Reckless Truths, Heidi and Murphy had another daughter, Brittany, affectionately nicknamed "Bit-Bit" by her big sister.

Charlotte Clark, Esq: Teller's sunshine. Often credited with taming the brooding treasurer of the Lost Kings, Teller. As of *Reckless Truths*, she is pregnant with twins.

Lilly Frazier: Z's brave and devoted siren. The new queen of the Lost Kings MC's downstate charter. One of Hope's best friends. Z and Lilly's son is named Chance.

Shelby Morgan: Rooster's sassy little chickadee. Country music singer from Texas. We first met Shelby in *Swagger and Sass*.

Serena Cargill: Former downstate club girl. Abused by Shadow, the former VP of the downstate charter. Found love with her Grinder, her "murder daddy" in *Crown of Ghosts*. She is currently pregnant with their son Lincoln.

Emily C. Walker: Serena's best friend. Smitten with Dex since they met in *Throne of Scars*.

Liberty Isabel Walker: Libby is Emily's teenage sister. The Walker sisters have no other family. Grinder is protective of them.

Willow: Bartender at Crystal Ball, but once or twice we've caught her sneaking in or out of the basement with Sparky.

Swan: Lost Kings MC club girl and dancer at Crystal Ball. Swan has found a new calling as the yoga teacher for the old ladies of the Lost Kings MC and is slowly moving away from dancing at Crystal Ball.

OTHER RECURRING CHARACTERS IN THE LOST KINGS MC WORLD

Roman "Vapor" Hawkins: *Renegade Path* is his story. He is married to Dex's "niece" Juliet.

Remington "Ruthless" Holt: Owns "The Castle" with his best friend, Griff. An underground fighting ring Murphy used to participate in. We've seen him most recently helping out the club in Crown of Ghosts. Guardian of his younger sister, Molly. Considering forming a support club for the Lost Kings MC with Griff, Eraser, and Vapor.

Griffin "Stonewall" Royal: Remy's best friend and business partner. Helped Grinder out in *Crown of Ghosts*. Extremely protective of his best friend's little sister.

Dawson Roads: Famous (fictional) country music singer in the Lost Kings MC world. He's been mentioned here and there since *One Empire*

Night, but we didn't officially "meet" him until *Rhythm of the Road* when Shelby was on tour with him.

Carter Clark: Charlotte's goofy, often inappropriate, younger brother. Most recently rescued by the club in *Reckless Truths*.

Loco: Business associate of the Lost Kings MC. He covers the Ironworks area of the Lost Kings MC's territory. He has appeared throughout the series and become a strong LOKI ally.

Eraser: Owns Zips, a racetrack near the Lost Kings MC territory. Married to Ella. We first met him in *Renegade Path*, and again in *White Lies*.

Margot Cedarwood: The mortuary cosmetologist at the Cedarwood Family Funeral Home, a business the Lost Kings MC invested in as of *Reckless Truths*.

Lynn Morgan: Shelby's mother. May or may not have hooked up with Jigsaw or Steer at some point.

Russell "Chaser" Adams: President of the Devil Demons MC in Western NY. (The Hollywood Demons series contains his story.)

Mallory "Little Dove" DeLova-Adams: Chaser's wife. Daughter of mafia boss Anatoly DeLova.

Angelina Adams: Mallory and Chaser's daughter

Linden "Stump" Adams: Chaser's father. Former president of the Devil Demons MC.

Sullivan Wallace: Jake's brother, and the owner of Strike Back Fitness. He's a significant character in Bullets and Bonfires and has his own book, Warnings and Wildfires.

Jake Wallace: One of Wrath's business partners in Furious Fitness. Jake has appeared off and on throughout the series since Tattered on my Sleeve. He sometimes holds self-defense classes for the ladies.

The mysterious "Quill" who we met in *Diamond in the Dust* and again in Crown of Ghosts. He is Chaser's newly discovered half-brother.

Anatoly DeLova: Mallory's father. Leader of the Russian mafia. Sometime business associate of the Lost Kings MC.

Stella: Pornographic film actress. The downstate charter is the sole investor in her production company. Ex-girlfriend of Z. Current... something of Sway. Her Sex in Every City series sometimes requires members of LOKI to work as bouncers on her film sets.

Inga March: Porn star, and former dancer at Crystal Ball. Sued the whole club for paternity of her son in After Burn (Lost Kings MC #10) Has not been seen since then.

Tawny: Sway's ol' lady. The former "Queen B" of the downstate charter of the Lost Kings MC.

Anya Regal: Porn princess of the Lost Kings MC, Virginia charter.

Shonda: Club girl from the Lost Kings, MC Virginia charter.

Lala: Club girl from Downstate NY.

OTHER MCS: FRIENDLY CLUBS:

Devil Demons MC: Based in Western NY. Long-time friend of the Lost Kings MC. Their clubs are intertwined and share a lot of history. More of this is explored in the *Hollywood Demons* series.

Wolf Knights MC: Mostly an ally of the Lost Kings. They used to run Slater County but said they were dissolving their charter in White Lies and turning it over to the Lost Kings. As of *Reckless Truths*, Slater County is officially Lost Kings MC territory.

Iron Bulls MC: (From the Iron Bulls MC series by Phoenyx Slaughter): Southwestern outlaw club. Meets up and does business with LOKI once in a while.

Savage Dragons MC: (From the Iron Bulls MC series by Phoenyx Slaughter): Texas outlaw club.

ENEMY CLUBS:

Vipers MC: Used to run Ironworks until the Lost Kings took over that territory. Still active in other parts of the country.

South of Satan MC: Vermont MC who has stirred up trouble for LOKI in the past.

LOST KINGS MC TERMINOLOGY

LOKI: Short for LOst KIngs

War room: Where the Lost Kings hold "church."

Property patch: When a member takes a woman as his old lady (wife status), he gives her a vest with a property patch. In my series, the vest has a "Property of Lost Kings MC" patch and the member's road name on the back. The officers also place their patches on the ol' lady's vest as a sign that they always have her back. Her man's patch or club symbol is placed over the heart. Rock's patch is a crown. Wrath's is a star. Murphy's is a four-leaf clover. Teller's is a dollar sign. Z's is the letter Z. Rooster's patch is a rooster wearing a crown. As a joke, Wrath gave Rock and Hope a "product of" patch for baby Grace.

PLACES IN THE LOST KINGS MC WORLD

I use a mix of real and imaginary names to describe the places in my series. Again, I bend and shape geography to my needs as this is a fictional world that I have created.

Empire, NY: The territory run by the Lost Kings MC upstate charter. This is a fictional version of Albany, NY, the capital of New York State. Many of the Lost Kings MC's businesses are located in and around Empire.

Slater, NY: Loosely based on Schenectady County. Until recently it was the Wolf Knights MC's territory.

GLOSSARY OF CHARACTERS AND TERMINOLOGY

Ironworks, NY: Loosely based on Rensselaer County (Troy, NY). At the beginning of the series, it was run by the Vipers MC. It is now considered territory of the Lost Kings MC.

Union, NY: A fictional area two hours south of Empire, NY, where the "downstate" charter is located.

Crystal Ball: The strip club owned by the Lost Kings MC and one of their legitimate businesses. They often refer to it simply as "CB." Located in Empire County.

Furious Fitness: The gym Wrath owns. Often just referred to as "Furious." Located not far from Crystal Ball.

Strike Back: Owned by Sullivan Wallace but members of the Lost Kings MC have worked there in the past.

Johnson County/Johnsonville: Fictional area where Heidi grew up. About an hour west of "Empire." Where Strike Back Gym, The Castle, and Zips are located. Possibly the new home of a Lost Kings MC support club? We'll see!

Zips: Racetrack owned by Eraser where all the illegal gambling/racing in the area happens.

The Castle: Formerly a juvenile detention center. The building is now used to house the underground fighting ring run by Remy and Griff. Murphy used to fight here. Other LOKI members also blow off steam in the cage here from time to time. Located in the middle of nowhere, NY, it once-upon-a-time housed Griff, Vapor, Eraser, Sully, and possibly Teller during their "troubled youth" days.

Kodack, NY: Another fictional NY area located in Western New York. Somewhere near Buffalo, perhaps. This territory is run by the Devil Demons MC.

Empire Medical Center: Local hospital where all the Kings receive medical treatment. Heidi also works there now.

OTHER MC TERMINOLOGY

Most terminology was obtained through research. However, I have also used some artistic license in applying these terms to my romanticized, fictional version of an outlaw motorcycle club. This is not an exhaustive list.

Cage: A car, truck, van—basically anything other than a motorcycle.

Church: Club meetings all full-patch members must attend. Led by the president of the club, but officers will update the members on the areas they oversee. (Some clubs refer to the meeting room where they hold church as the "chapel." My club refers to it as their "war room."

Citizen/civilian: Anyone not a hardcore biker or belonging to an outlaw club. "Citizen wife" would refer to a spouse kept entirely separate from the club.

Cut: Leather vest worn by outlaw bikers and adorned with patches and artwork displaying the club's unique colors. The Lost Kings' colors are blue and gray. Their logo is a skull with a crown. The Respect Few, Fear None patch is earned by doing time for the club without snitching. Brother's Keeper patches are earned by killing for the club. Loyal Brother is for a brother who's spent more than five years with the club.

Colors: The "uniform" of an outlaw motorcycle gang. A leather vest, with the three-piece club patch on the back, and various other patches relating to their role in the club.

Fly colors: To ride on a motorcycle wearing colors.

Muffler bunny or "bunnies": A girl who hangs around to provide sexual favors to members. Old ladies in my series will sometimes refer to them as "friends of the club," depending on the girl in question. Some clubs refer to them as club whores, patch whores, or cut sluts. These terms are not regularly used in my series. Sometimes simply referred to as a "club girl."

Nomad: A club member who does not belong to any specific charter, yet has privileges in all charters.

Old lady/ol' lady: Wife or steady girlfriend of a club member.

Patched in: When a new member is approved for full membership.

Patch holder: A member who has been vetted through performing duties for the club as a prospect or probate and has earned his three-piece patch.

Road name: Nickname. Usually given by the other members.

Run: A club-sanctioned outing, sometimes with other chapters and/or clubs. Can also refer to a club business run.

I'm sure I'm forgetting something! But this should be enough to get you started!

CHAPTER ONE

Dex

FIRST RULE OF LIFE: *Never let anyone get the jump on you.*

Especially in a cemetery.

I take another look around. Rows and rows of headstones. Not another person in sight.

Above me, a crow circles and lets out a mournful *caw*.

"Me too, buddy," I whisper, and I sink to my knees on the hard ground.

Cool air drifts over my face—another cruel reminder of all the things we've missed. Fall, then the holidays, riding down to Florida for the worst of winter. So many things.

Cold, damp earth soaks through my jeans, chilling my knees and shins. The familiar itch to outrun bad memories tingles in my hands—the urge to twist the throttle, ride the wind, and remind myself that *I'm* still alive.

After this visit, it's time to hit the road. Concentrating on the pavement ahead always eases the pain of my past. Quiets the noise in my head. Never quite fills the hole in my heart, though.

"Dex?" A soft voice breaks the silence.

Like a tornado, I jump to my feet, reach under my cut to grab my pistol, and face the intruder.

Short, wavy red layers fall past her chin, dusting her shoulders to frame her perfectly heart-shaped face.

Emily.

1

A violent wind sweeps through the air, picking up the long skirt of her dress and tossing it around her legs. She slaps her hands against her thighs, halting the material's wild dance. A hesitant smile lifts the corners of her mouth. So unlike her. Every other time we've run into each other, she's been confident and unafraid to speak her mind. An undercurrent of darkness that calls to my own always seems to flow under her words and actions, though.

"Didn't anyone ever tell you not to sneak up on a biker in a cemetery?" I growl, irritated by the fondness I seem to have for this woman who should be off-limits to me.

I shove my pistol back in its holster and fake a smile to take the sting out of my violent reaction. Emily's important to a brother's ol' lady. She's under my club's protection. I need to reel in my irritation. It's not her fault I'm so agitated.

Why is she here of all places? Why today of all days did I have to run into her?

"I...well. . ." Her anxious words are almost swallowed by another sudden gust of wind.

My gaze slides over her curvy figure without my permission. The long, black dress seems out of character for her bold personality. Then my brain kicks in. We're standing in a cemetery, for fuck's sake.

"What happened? Are you okay?" I ask.

"Yes. Well, no." She glances down at her dress as if she'd forgotten what outfit she chose this morning. "It's my parents' anniversary." She sweeps her arm toward the long rows of grave markers behind us. "I didn't mean to interrupt you." Her nervous gaze slides to the headstone where I'd been paying my respects. I shift to block it with my body.

"What's wrong?" I hate the sharp, impatient bite to my question but can't seem to control my mouth this morning.

"I...I'm so embarrassed. My car won't start." She waves her phone in the air between us. "I was walking around trying to get a signal. I saw the motorcycle...thought I recognized you..." Her voice falters as if she wishes she'd never started this conversation. "God, I'm so rude. Please forgive me."

Guilt prickles over my scalp. Grinder would kick my ass up and down the Thruway if he knew I was being so disrespectful to Serena's best friend.

I swallow the agony and anguish that wrapped around my throat the

2

second I rode through the cemetery gates. "Let me take a look at it," I offer.

"No hurry. Take your time," she says in a nervous rush. "I'm way over there." She waves wildly toward the dirt path that serves as a road through the cemetery.

"I'm done." I jerk my chin. "Lead the way."

"Oh. Okay. Thank you." She twists a loose chunk of hair around her finger then tucks it behind her ear. Again, she tries to peer over my shoulder and again, I block her view.

Pink spreads over her cheeks and she turns. The bottom of her dress sweeps over the too-long blades of grass. Someone needs to cut the grass, show some damn respect for the dead.

The burst of wind dies down, now only a ruffle through the trees. I scan the rolling green hills. We seem to be the only people here.

Suddenly, Emily tips to the side, arms flailing in the air. I hurry to steady her with a hand at her waist.

"Careful," I warn.

Gingerly, she wiggles her foot and tugs the heel of her shoe out of the soft earth.

Against me, she's warm and soft. Her head barely reaches my shoulder. She turns to peer up at me, the ends of her hair sliding over my leather cut. A hint of sugary vanilla tickles my nose.

"Stupid heels," she murmurs, taking slower steps. "Dumb choice, I know."

"You look nice." The urge to slide my hand over hers strikes me and I release her as fast as I'd toss a lit match. What's wrong with me? This isn't the time or place for a hand-in-hand stroll. Even if it was, she's not the woman I should be walking with.

"Thank you."

My bike's parked at the end of the row and she quickens her steps as it comes into view.

"How far away is your car?" I ask.

"Over there." She points, and in the distance I make out a dark red sedan parked half on the grass, half on the gravel. The only other vehicle in the area. "Do you want to meet me?" She nods to my bike.

That *would* make more sense, but she almost fell once. I scuff my boot against the hard-packed dirt and gravel path. Hate to see her twist an ankle on the uneven ground. And I'd ask Rock to strip my road captain patch if I let her ride on the back of my bike the way she's dressed—even a short distance.

"No, I'll come back and get it."

"I really am sorry I interrupted you." She ducks her head and powers forward.

"It's fine. Cell service sucks out here."

She lets out a nervous chuckle. "It does."

As we approach the car, I catalog its details. It's an older model but probably still not something I can easily repair. I carry a bare minimum of tools with me. Enough for a quick fix of my bike and that's about it.

"Can you pop the hood?" I ask.

"Sure." She dips inside the car and pulls the lever.

I prop the hood up and study the engine. Nothing obvious sticks out.

Something brushes against my side, and I glance down. Emily's standing next to me, hands on her hips, staring at the car like she's ready to roll up her sleeves and assist.

Cute. The corners of my mouth turn up.

"Is it terminal?" She peers up at me with wide, serious eyes. Are they green? Brown? Some sort of in-between?

Doesn't matter.

"I'm not sure yet," I reply. "Why don't you try to turn it over for me, so I can see what it does."

Her anxious gaze darts to the open driver's-side door.

"You in a hurry?"

"I'm late for work," she admits.

"I'd give you a ride"—I nod to her dress and heels— "but you can't get on a motorcycle like that."

She stares down at her dress and fists her hands in the material, swinging the long skirt around. "Why not? In the movies it would just flutter in the wind behind me." She flaps her hands in the air to punctuate her sentence.

I snort with laughter. "This isn't the movies, sweetheart. You could get all that loose fabric caught in the rear wheel." The smile slides off my face. "Knew a couple who thought it'd be fun to ride off into the sunset on their wedding day. Dress tangled, bike crashed, neither of them made it."

Her jaw drops and she stares up at me. "Well. Aren't you full of cheerful tales."

That *was* a bit much. Why'd I have to bring up something so awful?

"Can't help it." I tap the road captain patch stitched onto my cut. "Safety first."

"Good to know." Her eyes stray to the car again. "What if I swap the dress for pants?"

"Are you Superwoman? Ready to change into your cape in an emergency?" I was aiming for a teasing tone to make up for the wedding horror story but my words come out more accusatory than amusing.

"Hardly." She frowns, then rolls her eyes. "I work in a lab. I keep extra clothes in my car in case I get chemicals or something on me."

"Smart."

"Thanks." Sarcasm creeps into her words.

"I didn't mean it—"

"It's fine." She holds up her hand. "Promise not to look."

"At what?"

"Me. While I change." She hurries to the car and pulls a bag from the back seat. "Although, could you come stand here and maybe give me some cover? I think it'd be rude if I flashed my butt to all the dead folks."

"I doubt they'll mind." But I walk over and stand between the two open car doors, doing my best to form a fourth wall for her makeshift changing room.

"You have such nice, broad shoulders," she murmurs behind me.

I resist the urge to turn around. "Uh, thank you."

Her elbow pokes into my back and she mutters an apology. Fabric rustles. A stronger whiff of warm vanilla tickles my nose. Her dress hits my arm, then flops over the car door. I turn slightly. In the side mirror, I catch a flicker of bare skin hidden under black lace.

Fuck.

I tear my gaze away and aim it at the trees in front of me. I manage a strip joint, for fuck's sake. Naked skin doesn't hold much interest for me anymore. No need to creep on a friend of the club when I can go to work and see all the lace-covered tits my heart desires.

She bumps into me again.

"You're awfully violent when you get dressed," I say over my shoulder.

"Nah, I just have a big butt. Gets away from me sometimes."

I smother the urge to tell her everything looks good to me. Besides, it's her quick wit and razor-sharp tongue that interests me even more than her curvy body.

"Ta-da. All done," she announces.

I back away from the car and turn, taking in her jeans and sweatshirt imprinted with *wander with purpose,* the words scrawled around an image of a compass. A sense of déjà vu washes over me.

"That's my symbol." I tap the compass patch stitched onto my cut. "And a very Lost Kings kind of saying."

She glances down at her shirt and a wry smile twists her lips. "Well, it's full of shit because I haven't had much chance to wander. With purpose or without." Her expression softens. "But I like the sentiment." She lifts her head and stares at my patches. "I thought your club's symbol was the skull and crown?"

"It is. But we each have our own patch." I'm not in the mood to give more details to a civilian.

"Ah, right." She nods as if things are clicking into place for her. "Grayson's symbol is the lock and key."

"Right." I pull out my phone. After a few attempts, I manage to get a signal and send a text. "I'm having a friend tow your car—"

"What? Where?" She crams in closer to peek at my phone. "How'd you get a signal?"

"Better service?" I shrug. "I just sent a text." Another whiff of vanilla fucks with my need to keep my hands off Emily.

If life's taught me anything, it's to temper my desires. Emily's not meant to be mine. She's forbidden fruit—too full of life to be swallowed by *my* darkness.

CHAPTER TWO

Emily

THIS MAN IS sex and sin wrapped in a tantalizing package. He towers over me in a protective, reassuring way. Well-defined, inked arms could easily pick me up and toss me over those broad shoulders.

Get a grip, Emily.

The heat of embarrassment clings to me as Dex texts his friend for a tow. I can't believe I interrupted him in a *cemetery*. While he was kneeling in front of a headstone. I was so relieved to see another human being, once I realized I knew him, I threw caution, courtesy, and common sense to the wind and ran to him for help. Ignoring the fact that, given our location, he might be in mourning. I was only concerned about my own selfish needs to flee this place I hate but feel compelled to visit at least once a year.

"How long do you think he'll be?" I ask.

He stares straight ahead and stuffs his phone in his pocket. "Not sure."

Damn. I pull out my useless phone again and try to send a text to my boss.

"I'll get you to work."

I glance up and find Dex watching me so intently, heat sears my cheeks. "Thanks. I really appreciate this. I'm sorry if I'm holding you up." I wave my hands around. "Do *you* have to be at work or something?"

"Not until later." He runs his gaze over me. "You got a jacket?"

"Yes." I hurry to the car and open the back door, crawling halfway across the seat to snatch my heavy canvas coat. As I back out of the car, my butt collides with something hard and unmoving.

"Sorry." Dex's boots scrape over the gravel as he backs away.

I slip my coat on and zip it up. "This okay?"

He slides his gaze over me again. Why does it feel like fingers tracing a path over my skin? "It'll do."

The weight of my keys weighs heavy in my palm. Should I hand them over to Dex now? Or wait until his friend shows up? What's the protocol for this situation?

As if he's read my mind, Dex nods to my palm. "Got your house keys on there?"

"I do." I quickly work my car key loose and hand it over. "Thanks." That's safety 101. Why does this man render me speechless and stupid every time we're in the same space? It's not like I want to date him. I don't have space in my life for a relationship. Two more years until my sister graduates from high school. Then I'll worry about dating.

The bump and scrape of truck tires rolling over the dirt road stops any further conversation.

One corner of Dex's mouth twitches. "That was fast."

The old red-and-white tow truck pulls in front of my car and stops.

"You remember Griff?" Dex asks.

I nod. "He's come with you to do yard work a few times. I feel bad he keeps getting roped into odd jobs for me."

"For the club. Not you."

He doesn't say it in a mean way—he's just stating a fact, so I don't take offense. I'm still confused, though. "But I'm not part of your club."

"No, but you're important to a brother's patched ol' lady."

I don't have a chance to ask what the heck *that* means. I know he's referring to my best friend, Serena. It's the *patched ol' lady* part that trips me up.

"Since when do you drive a cage, Dex?" Griff calls out as he jumps from the cab of the truck.

"It's not mine." Dex walks over and shakes Griff's hand. "Thanks for getting here so fast."

"No problem." Griff leans past Dex's shoulder and lifts his hand in a quick wave. "Hey, Emily."

"Hi. Thanks for this." I sweep my hand toward my traitorous vehicle.

The two of them walk over to the front of the car, discussing what could be wrong with it. I take the time to grab my purse and the lunch I packed and check inside for anything else I might need. Who knows when I'll see my poor car again?

Bang! The hood drops closed.

I jump so high my head hits the ceiling. "Ow. Fuck," I mutter, rubbing the top of my head.

"Sorry about that." Dex leans in my open door and offers his hand.

His concern burns away my embarrassment. "I'm good."

I rest my hand in his and let him tug me out of the car. My stomach flips as our bodies briefly touch. He rubs his fingers over my scalp, intensifying the swoony sensation. Such a gentle touch for such a big man.

"You okay?" he asks in a deep, soothing voice.

It's not the bonk to my head that has my body demanding I fall into his arms. It's *him*. Electricity seems to crackle in the air. Probably one-sided on my part. Usually indifference surrounds him like a cloud of steam. Although, once or twice I've thought I detected a glimmer of interest. "I'm good." Nervous laughter flutters past my lips and I pull away.

"I've got this." Griff waves Dex and me away. "Don't make her even later for work."

"Wait. Where are you taking it?" I ask.

"Do you have a dealership it should go to?" Griff asks.

"I'm not that fancy," I scoff. "I'm not even sure the mechanic my aunt used to go to is still in business."

"Well, we mostly do classics." Griff glances at my car again. "But my shop can probably handle this. If not, we'll get you sorted."

"Thanks."

Dex echoes my gratitude and shakes Griff's hand again, then leads me toward his bike.

"I'm sorry I'm causing you so many problems this morning. I'm sure you had other things to do," I say as we begin the long trek to his bike. At least now my sneakered feet are more stable walking over the gravel that threatened to trip me in my heels.

He opens his mouth as if he's about to deny it, then shakes his head. "Stop apologizing, Emily. I'm glad I was here to help. Who knows how long you would've been waiting around otherwise?"

"Thanks."

Behind us, there's a scuffling over the rocks. "Dex!" Griff calls out. "Wait up."

We turn and Griff's jogging toward us with a helmet tucked under his arm.

"She might need this." He stops and holds out the helmet to me, but he's looking to Dex for confirmation. "I assume you're not running around with a spare."

For a second, Dex's expression turns hard, maybe even angry, but then it's gone. "You're right. Thanks."

I accept the plain, black helmet. It's heavier than I'd expected.

"It's Molly's," Griff explains. "But it should fit."

My thumb rubs against something rough and I take a closer look. Someone's stuck a clear sticker with *Support your local LOKI* in dark blue letters on the back of the helmet. I turn it toward Dex. "LOKI is short for Lost Kings, I assume?"

He stares at it for a second, then frowns.

Griff holds up his hands. "Trinity gave it to Molly, so she thought it was okay to wear."

I hold up the helmet toward the sunlight. "You can barely see it."

"That's the point," Dex says under his breath.

Griff winks at me.

"Will it keep my head from bouncing off the pavement?" I ask.

One corner of Dex's mouth curls up. "Yeah."

"Good. Thanks, Griff."

"No problem." He gives a quick wave, then takes off toward the tow truck.

"Everything okay?" I ask Dex.

"Yeah, just, Molly's a kid. I worry about her wearing our stuff."

"That's Remy's sister, right? She goes to Libby's school." Realization hits me. "Damn, I totally forgot. I have to pick Libby up after practice tonight." I twist, throwing a helpless glance toward my disloyal car.

"Can she catch a ride with a friend?" Dex asks.

"Probably. I hate asking the other parents. And I'm not wild about her driving with any of her friends, you know? I remember how, uh, easily distracted I could be at that age."

He snorts.

"I'll worry about it later. Maybe Griff will have good news about my car." I stop dead. "Wait, how will he reach me? I didn't give him my number."

"I'll take care of it," Dex assures me, then marches ahead, waving his hand to hurry me along.

12

We stop at his bike. He stares at the seat, then me. "Have you ever ridden before?"

Warmth spreads from my cheeks to my forehead. "One of my exes used to ride. He took me out a few times."

Is it my imagination, or did Dex's jaw tighten when I mentioned an ex?

"Sorry, did you want to be the one to give me my first ride?" I tease.

A hint of a smile twitches at the corners of his mouth. "No, just your last."

"That's either really sweet or kind of ominous."

"Well, I didn't mean it to be ominous." He flicks his gaze toward the sky. "And few people have ever called me sweet."

The heat in my face spreads to my ears. "You've been sweet to me today."

"Better put that on." He nods to the helmet, ending our casual banter.

Mushy time over. Got it.

I strap the unfamiliar headgear into place, then sling my purse across my chest. "Let's ride."

Another hint of a smile. Dex is a hard man to crack.

He effortlessly slings his leg over the bike and I try to stop the drool from rolling down my chin. My ex certainly hadn't looked this good straddling his skinny motorcycle with the high-pitched, whiny engine. Dex seems completely confident he can handle the giant machine. Like he's one with his motorcycle.

He straps on his helmet and pulls black leather gloves from his pocket that he carefully works onto his big hands. Damn, since when do I find a man's hands so enticing?

At this point, I should probably look for a towel to wipe my chin.

"You getting on?" he asks.

"Uh, yeah." *How do I mount this thing again?* It seems so much bigger than anything I've been on before.

"Put your hand on my shoulder," Dex instructs.

As if I'm moving too slowly for him, he reaches for my hand, guiding it to his shoulder.

I lightly rest my palm against the leather of his vest.

"Harder than that, little firecracker. I won't break," he encourages.

"That's for sure. You're sturdy. Like a tree." *Come on. You can do this.* I grip him tighter and toss my leg over.

"Watch the pipes," Dex warns.

13

"Okay."

He reaches back, grabbing my calf. I dig my fingers into his shoulders.

"Relax. I've got you." He runs his hand over my sneakers. "Wish these had a heel or something. They might slip off the pegs, so hold tight."

"That's not reassuring."

"Hold tight," he repeats. "Lean when I lean. Okay?"

"Got it." I give him directions to where I work. He nods as if he knows the place.

The engine roars to life. A deep, throaty rumble. So much louder than I'd expected. I cling harder to Dex's shoulders.

He reaches for one of my hands, sliding it down to his waist. "Ready?" he asks.

"Yes."

He opens the throttle and we take off, bumping over the gravel at a slow speed that must make it difficult for Dex to control the bike, but he makes it seem effortless.

When we reach the highway, we shoot forward. I shriek and wrap my arms tighter, cinching his waist like a human belt.

"Is this okay?" I shout. What if I'm squeezing so hard he can't breathe?

"You feel good," he says, a shade louder than the engine. At least that's what it sounds like.

My heart races as he increases the speed. The cool morning air whips against my hands, and I tuck them under Dex's shirt.

Mistake.

He's hard everywhere. Not just his strong shoulders.

Do not molest the operator of the vehicle moving at sixty-five miles an hour.

After a while of steady riding, the tension running through my body uncoils. I loosen my death grip on Dex and carefully shift my body back. A rush of euphoria races over me. Freedom and an odd sense of *peace.* Everything seems so alive and close—like I could reach out and grab a handful of wildflowers on the side of the road if I wasn't afraid I'd plummet to my death.

The vibrating beast between my thighs intensifies the swoony sensation I've been dealing with from being around Dex. Except it's stronger than a swoon and heading south fast.

Oh, no. Now isn't the time.

Work. Focus on work. Reports are due at the end of the month. I'll be slammed with testing and sending results. Chemicals. I need to call and order chemicals today.

The bike slows and gently swerves to the right. I open my eyes. Relief that I'm almost at work fills me, followed by dread. I'm not ready for our ride to end.

I like Dex. A lot more than I should. This is the first time we've been alone together. Yet, spending time with him without our friends around feels natural.

I doubt he feels the same way.

In the distance, I spot my building and tap Dex's shoulder. "It's up there on the right."

He nods to acknowledge the direction and the bike slows.

All too soon, he's pulling into the parking lot of the small brick building where I spend my days. He stops at the curb a few feet past the entrance, plants his feet on the ground, and shuts the bike down. The loss of the buzzing between my legs disorients me for a moment. Like a weirdo, I hug Dex one last time, then brace myself on his shoulder and reverse what I did to get on the bike.

Whoa. My legs quiver like I've punished them with a hundred squats. I stumble backward. Dex reaches for me, curling an arm around my waist to steady me.

"Thanks. My legs are like jelly." I unstrap my helmet. "But I loved the ride."

Unsure of what to do—give the helmet back or keep it and give it to Griff next time I see him—I tuck it under my arm.

"Any time you want, I'll give you a ride," he answers.

Not the kind of ride I'm thinking of.

As if he's heard my unspoken desire, the smile slides off his face. He's all business again. "What time are you done?"

"Usually five." Damn, how am I going to get home? It's not like Ubers or Lyfts are easy to find or cheap in my neck of the woods. I have a few people I'd feel comfortable asking to give me a ride but it doesn't solve my problem of getting to work tomorrow and the next day. "Think my car might be ready by then?"

He shrugs. "Don't know. I'll check in with Griff, and I'll be here at five to pick you up."

"Wait. You don't have to do that."

The shroud of seriousness that seemed to surround him at the cemetery disappears. A playful, almost flirty smile flickers over Dex's mouth. "Nah, little firecracker. That's not how it works."

Why does my heart thump faster every time he calls me "firecracker?"

"How *what* works?"

He fires up the bike, the loud rumble shaking the pavement and forcing me to lean in to hear his answer. "Biker code: I rescued you, so now you're mine."

CHAPTER THREE

Dex

Five o'clock.

I'll be waiting at the curb for Emily.

Why am I stupidly looking forward to seeing her again?

And why the fuck did that *now you're mine* comment have to spill out of my mouth? Way to scare the woman.

Must be from having her on the back of my bike. Girl tried her best to squeeze my insides out my ass, but damn, it felt good having her there. Other women have been in that seat since my wife died but not for long, and none ever felt so *right*.

As I pull out of the parking lot, I try to ignore the way my body tingles in all the places Emily touched me. And all the places I *wanted* her to touch me. Having her on the back of my bike was heaven and hell rolled into one. Like a masochist, I'll be doing it again in about six hours.

And I can't wait.

At the next stoplight, I flick the radio on and turn up the volume to drown out the memory of Emily's voice in my head.

The music doesn't work. Irritated with myself, I note Emily's job isn't that far from Crystal Ball.

What do you think you're going to do? Stop by for lunch dates?

It's too early to open the club. I could go in and start inventory before Willow's shift, but it'll be easier if she's there to help. Before running into Emily, I'd planned to drop by Furious Fitness for a workout. Maybe I'll get lucky and Wrath won't be there to harass me into "one more rep" or hound me about the evils of processed sugar.

No such luck. My brother's massive blue GMC pickup is in its usual spot. At least I'll be able to razz his ass for taking his cage to work instead of riding. A black Ford's parked next to Wrath's monstrosity— Murphy's old truck that Grinder's been using since he got out of prison. Fucking hell. I'm not in the mood for one of the old man's lectures today.

Inside, it's quiet. Seems I missed peak workout time for all the local housewives. *Good.* I won't have to deal with Wrath trying to set me up on a fucking date.

Wrath's office door is closed. Maybe his wife paid him a visit. Trinity's photography studio is right next door so she's at the gym a lot.

I shove the locker room door open harder than I intended, almost smacking into Grinder. He drops his brush into an open can of white paint and scowls. Looks like he was trying to touch up the walls where the door handle often hits the drywall.

"What's the hurry?" he grumbles. The irritated expression slides off his bearded face as he turns and realizes it's me. "Morning, Dex."

Guess my fucking luck just ran out.

"What are you doing here? Don't you have a pregnant ol' lady to be watching over?" My question comes out harsher than intended. Annoyance over the lecture Grinder had given me at Teller's wedding must still be stirring in my brain. Thankfully, Grinder ignores my attitude.

"She's with Lilly," he explains, picking up his brush again and tapping off the excess paint.

"They seem to have gotten tight." Z's wife always liked Serena. Now that Grinder's the SAA at our downstate charter, the four of them probably double-date for all I know.

He nods. "I think Lilly's as excited about the baby as we are."

Uncomfortable with the subject, I blurt out, "I ran into Emily this morning. Had to give her a ride to work. Her car broke down."

Grinder frowns and sets his paint brush on the edge of the can. "She all right?"

"She's fine. Griff's gonna take a look at the car and let me know what it needs." I hold up my hands to ward off any questions. "Don't worry. I said I'd give her a ride home from work tonight. I won't leave a friend of the club stranded."

"Didn't think you would." His hard eyes drill into me. "Sounds like you'll be spending some time—"

"Easy, Grinder. It's just a few rides. Out of necessity. Nothing more."

He shrugs. "Great relationships have started with less."

"Great relationships?" *Who is this man?* "What are you, a dating coach now?"

He grumbles something and shakes his head. "Thanks for doing that for her."

"No need to thank me, brother." I shift from foot to foot. "I couldn't leave her stranded in a cemetery, for fuck's sake."

"Where did...?" His question dies as he realizes what that means.

"Let it go," I warn, not that he gives a fuck about a warning from me. "It's not that big a deal."

"You know what they say about rusting or riding?" Grinder asks. He doesn't bother waiting for an answer. "You can either rust out from doing nothing or wear out from living life."

"I've heard variations of that line forever," I answer cautiously. "Usually from *you*."

"It's deeper than that," he continues. "You know what destroys iron? Itself. Rust. People aren't that much different. Loneliness is a rust on the heart."

"Who's lonely? I'm surrounded by people all day, every day." I narrow my eyes and cock my head. "My life is full of nosy-ass brothers who dissect my life whenever I voice a thought."

One corner of Grinder's mouth twitches. "I've known you since you were a boy, Dixon."

"Hardly." I snort.

"My heart, all our hearts, hurt for you when Debbie died."

My entire body stiffens. Pain prickles over my scalp.

"It wasn't your fault," he adds.

"The fuck it wasn't," I mutter.

"You were a prospect, so I didn't know you as well as I could have—"

"It was a fucked-up time for the club in general," I add, praying to steer him off the conversational path he seems determined to forge.

"But Debbie seemed like a sweet girl." He tilts his head, inviting me to follow him away from the door in case it swings open again. "You two were young, but anyone in your presence could feel the love you had for each other."

"What's your point?" I spit, nearing the end of my patience.

21

"Would she want you to live like this? Alone?"

"Again," I answer with exaggerated patience, "where did you get the idea that I'm *alone?*"

"You're not a pump, dump, and run kind of guy. Never were."

"People change. I don't need complications in my life. Just a warm body every now and then is enough."

"Complications." He scoffs. "You don't want to love someone and risk losing them again."

"Fine. Yeah. You got me. What's wrong with that?"

"It's gonna put you in an early grave."

"Good," I blurt. My eyes widen. It's a thought I've never spoken aloud before. Only I know that each time one of my brothers gets hurt or injured, I ask the universe why the fuck it won't take me instead.

He nods. "You wanna punish yourself for Debbie's death."

"And our daughter's," I rasp. People always forget. Two scars are etched into my soul. Not one.

He winces then reaches out to clasp my shoulder. "No one should have to suffer that kind of loss, brother."

I swallow hard but a response eludes me. Tumbling back in time to those memories pounds a nail through my heart. Not as sharp as it once was, but still painful.

"From what I understand, Emily has had her own losses." His shoulder hitches. "Maybe—"

"What?" I sneer. "We can heal each other?"

"Don't be so dismissive." His phone buzzes and he pulls it out, checking the text. A faint smile crosses his face.

I could make a crack about how much more comfortable he seems with technology since he got released from prison and discovered you could hold the whole wide world in the palm of your hand in the form of a smartphone. But as much as he's pissed me off today, that seems like too much of a low blow.

"Baby's kicking," he says, slipping his phone into his pocket. "Who would've thought something so simple would make me so damn happy?"

Dull pain throbs behind my ribs. An aching loneliness for myself followed by joy for my friend who lost so many years of his life paying for a crime he didn't commit. I force a smile. "Brother, you deserve all the happiness in the world."

His gaze returns to the cold and calculating one I know so well. "So do *you.*"

CHAPTER FOUR

Emily

"WHAT? No cute little outfits today, Emily?" my coworker George ??? with a sneer as I pass his desk on my way to my own.

Har. Har. Jokes about my clothes never get old. As if dressing nicely for work is some sort of crime.

"My car broke down. I had to change." That's the only explanation I'll be giving for my lateness and clothing choices. I slip a lab apron over my head, reaching behind me to tie it. "What have you got for me?"

He gestures toward the white plastic shelf that lines one wall of our small office. Rows and rows of water samples wait for testing.

"Take your pick. Although, Johnsonville's already called twice this morning to ask about their results."

"Great," I grumble. "Bet they suspect the test will show their BAC is out of compliance."

"Bunch of clowns out there," George mumbles, throwing a handful of corn chips in his mouth.

"True story." I don't feel like dealing with any calls from Johnsonville's water department today, so I pick up their samples first. Irritated that I'm giving in to the squeaky wheel syndrome, I plunk the plastic container on the counter harder than necessary.

"Easy, redster." Behind me, George chuckles.

Redster—for my red hair. How original. My jaw clenches. I hate every single one of those cutesy nicknames. I reach for my earbuds and look

25

through my phone for my favorite true crime podcast. That should be enough to drown out George's munching noises and annoying commentary.

By the end of the day, I'm twitching to leave more than usual. Why am I so excited to see Dex again?

Five minutes before quitting time, the distinctive rumble of a motorcycle shakes the walls.

Dex.

He's early.

I can't go running out the door. Not after showing up late this morning.

My feet strongly disagree with my decision to wait. I tap my toes as I finish sending the last of my test results.

Finally, I'm able to leave. I step outside, lifting my arm to shield my eyes from the sun. A flash of silver to my right catches my eye. Dex's bike. I hurry toward him, not caring if I resemble an eager puppy.

"You're here," I say breathlessly when I reach his side.

He turns and his serious expression shifts into something resembling a smile. "I always keep my word."

"I didn't think otherwise," I mutter. Why does something dumb always seem to fly out of my mouth around him?

"Hop on."

I strap my helmet into place and arrange my purse across my body, then grip his shoulder and swing my leg over the bike. Out of the corner of my eye, I catch George standing on the sidewalk gaping at me. I squeeze Dex's shoulders. "All set!"

The furious thunder of the bike's engine drowns out everything.

"Hold on," Dex shouts.

I wrap my arms around his waist. For a brief second, his warm, leather-gloved hand rests over mine. As if he wants to reassure himself that I'm secure. Or maybe to reassure me that I'm safe with him. Whatever the reason, I'm giddy from his touch.

The bike rocks backward then lurches forward. I close my eyes and hold tight.

Much too soon, the bike slows to a stop. I open my eyes. Disappointment washes over me. My driveway. Usually, I relish a few minutes home alone before Libby returns in a whirlwind of chatter and chaos. Today, I want to spend more time with Dex.

He shuts down the bike. My heart kicks. He's planning to stay?

"Do you want to come inside?" I ask.

"Just for a minute. To give you an update on your car."

My car. Right.

I dismount the bike with all the grace of a baby giraffe, wobbling for a second. Dex reaches out, clasping a hand around my thigh to steady me.

"Easy," he murmurs.

Shocked, I stare down, surprised my pants aren't on fire from the contact. Jesus, his hands are big. My not-at-all tiny thigh almost looks itty-bitty under his massive hand.

As if my skin burns through the layers of denim and leather between us, he yanks his hand away.

"Takes time to get used to riding," he says.

"I feel safe with you," I blurt out. "I mean, motorcycles always seemed like two-wheeled death traps. But you make the ride seem effortless." Heat sears my cheeks. What the hell am I babbling about?

"Thanks."

I back up so he can get off the bike but stand there, staring at him like he's a juicy prime rib I can't wait to shove in my mouth.

What's wrong with me? Hot men don't usually render me stupid.

My boycott on dating must be clouding my manners.

I turn and march up the sidewalk to the low front porch and pull out my keys.

"Good locks." Dex's low, rumbling voice right behind me sends a shiver of pleasure down my spine.

"Oh." Nervous laughter bubbles past my lips. "Funny, Grayson said the same thing when Serena was staying with us. Are you all security experts or something?"

"I'm not surprised." Dex huffs a frustrated laugh. "Nothing goes unnoticed by the old man."

"You've known him a long time?" I ask, setting my purse on the entrance table. He follows behind me, his large frame making my foyer feel small. I nod to his vest. "Through your club?"

"I was only a prospect when he went to prison but he was an early influence."

I'm not sure what to make of that.

"We kept in touch and I tried to visit him over the years," he adds.

Dex's loyalty to a man he didn't seem to know all that well impresses me. "That must've been hard."

He shrugs. "He's a good man. Didn't deserve to be there."

Serena said something similar when she first told me about Grayson, and I had questions about him being recently paroled. It's nice to hear it from someone who isn't smitten with him.

Dex remains by the front door, his back toward the solid wood as if he's going to try to slip out when I'm not looking. "Are you a vampire?" I tease. "Do I need to officially invite you inside?"

"What?" He raises his eyebrows, then glances behind him. "No. I just can't stay long."

"Oh. Sure." How do I ask to see him again without seeming desperate? What if he says no?

Don't let fear rule your life.

Isn't that what I'm always preaching to the people I care about the most?

"Dex, would you like to come over for dinner?" I force the words out quickly before I lose my nerve. I can't believe I'm breaking my number-one rule and asking a guy on a date.

No. Not a date. I'm inviting him over for dinner. To thank him for helping me out. That's all.

But offering to cook for a man I barely know breaks another one of my rules. What is it about Dex that makes me want to shred my rule book into confetti?

He stares at me for a few beats before finally answering, "I can't."

Oh. Wow. I hadn't even suggested a day or time. But it's an immediate "no" from him. "Uh. Okay. I just wanted to thank you for today and all the lawn mowing and…"

Shut up, Emily.

Is it my wishful thinking or is that regret in his eyes?

"I'm headed out of town for a bit," he explains. "So I won't be here Friday."

"Oh." A normal person would ask where he's going but I'm still too stung from his rejection.

"But I don't…" He stops and runs his fingers through his hair.

Is he as flustered as I am?

"Nothing is set in stone. I don't have to leave for my trip right now," he continues. With more conviction in his tone, he adds, "I *should* wait a day or two and make sure Griff gets your car back to you in one piece."

My eyes widen. "You're going to postpone your trip to check on my car?" I ask slowly.

"My dates are flexible." He turns and stares at the heavy drapery covering the windows. "Just an annual ride I take."

"Must be nice to come and go as you please." Any time off I'm able to schedule is spent with Libby at home.

Too late, I realize my comment sounded bitter. "I don't get a lot of vacation time," I hurry to add.

Who cares if he thinks you're a bitch? He said no to dinner.

"How about Friday night?" he asks.

"What about it?"

He raises his eyebrows, his gaze straying toward the kitchen behind me. "Dinner? You don't owe me anything, though. We can go out."

Gee, when you say it so enthusiastically...

"You're my hero." I force a smile. "You literally saved my day."

"Trust me, I'm no one's savior."

Awkward. What am I supposed to do, argue that he is indeed a hero?

"Well, I definitely owe you a meal," I say in a cheery tone to smooth over the uncomfortable silence. "Is there anything you don't like? Or you're allergic to?"

"Nope." He backs away. "What time works for you?"

"Seven? It'll give me a chance to change and start cooking."

"Really, Emily, you don't have to—"

"I want to." Suddenly, the awkward way we met this morning returns to mind. "Today was hard for me. Even before my car crapped out and left me stranded. I really appreciate all you've done to make it easier."

Several emotions seem to ripple over his expression—longing, sadness, and maybe guilt all make an appearance. "It was no problem, Emily."

We stand there, staring at each other. For someone who said he couldn't stay long, he doesn't seem to be in any hurry to leave.

"Oh. Your car." He pulls out his phone. "Griff says it's the starter. He can fix it but it's going to take a day or two to get the part."

"Damn." I bite my thumbnail. How the hell am I going to get to work again tomorrow?

"He's stopping by in a few minutes to drop off a car for you to borrow."

"What? Don't I need to fill out some paperwork? Give him my license or something?"

"It's not like that. He's not a rental agency. It's just a car his shop loans out." He coughs and looks away. "To friends and family."

"But I'm neither."

"You're a friend of my club. Close enough."

"You really take this *club* thing seriously."

He cocks his head, studying me. "It's everything."

"But I never see Griff wearing a vest like yours." I point to one of his Lost Kings MC patches.

His piercing eyes never leave my face. "He's affiliated… Helps us out when we ask."

That explanation is as clear as mud.

"Well, I'll pay him for the car, obviously."

"Don't worry about it." He shoves his hand in his front pocket and pulls out his phone. "They're here."

I follow him outside, not sure what to make of how my evening is playing out.

At the curb, two cars are parked—a vintage black muscle car with a unique set of purple and red pinstripes, and an older tan Volvo station wagon. "I didn't picture Griff driving a Volvo."

Dex laughs and ducks his head. "The Chevelle is his. I think the Volvo belongs to the shop."

"Ah, that makes sense."

Dex uses a few hand signals to whoever's driving the Volvo. The car glides up the gentle slope of my driveway and stops.

Griff swaggers over the lawn toward us. A tall, broad guy wearing a faded red plaid flannel shirt slams the door of the Volvo.

Dex smiles broadly at the stranger. "What're you doing here, Vapor?"

"I made the mistake of stopping by—"

"To use my garage," Griff adds.

Ignoring him, Vapor continues, "And somehow that turned into driving a station wagon."

I bite the inside of my cheek to stop myself from laughing.

"Emily." Dex rests his hand between my shoulders and my stomach flutters. "This is my…" He glances at Vapor as if seeking information. "Nephew-in-law?"

Vapor shrugs. "Close enough." He holds out his hand and I take it for a quick hello shake. "The car's for you, I take it?"

"Apparently." With Dex's hand still resting on my back, I'm incapable of conversation. If I were a cat, I'd purr and rub myself against him.

"How's my girl?" Dex asks Vapor.

"She's out with Ella. But she wanted me to say hi and tell you to get your ass over to dinner at our place soon."

Griff scratches the side of his head and turns toward Vapor. "How come Juliet never invites *me* over for dinner?"

"Because you're at our place all the time," Vapor answers slowly, as if he's explaining it to a child.

"Oh, here, Emily." There's a jingling and Vapor holds out a set of keys with a yellow tag hanging from them.

"It's nothing fancy but it runs," Griff explains. "If you have any problems, call the shop. Number's on the tag."

"Thank you so much for this." I take the keys, squeezing them tight in my hand. There's no viable public transportation out here, and it would take me half the day to walk to work. The car really is a lifesaver.

Griff's gaze shifts toward Dex, lingering on Dex's hand still resting on my back. One corner of his mouth kicks into a flirty smile and he meets my eyes. "Not a problem, darlin'."

"All right." Dex shoves Griff toward the driveway. "Thanks for stopping by."

Griff and Vapor exchange matching smirks.

Vapor reaches for Dex, wrapping him in a quick hug and thumping him on the back. "Talk soon, yeah?"

Dex nods and returns the back thump. "Tell Juliet I'll stop by."

"You got it."

Griff and Vapor both say goodbye to me then take off, laughing and shoving each other all the way to the black car.

Then I'm alone again with Dex.

He turns to face me. "Let's check out the car before I go."

"They drove it here, so it must work," I point out. "My aunt actually had a car very similar to that when we moved in." I jerk my thumb over my shoulder toward the house. "So, I've driven one before."

"All right."

He's stopped from saying anything else by pulsing music and a small, yellow convertible screeching to a stop at the curb.

"Dammit," I mutter.

"This Libby?" Dex frowns at the yellow car.

"Yeah, it's her friend's car. The girl's a menace."

My sister bolts from the passenger side and barely slams the door shut before her friend races away, honking her horn loud enough to wake a corpse. Great, the neighbors will love *that*.

"Mackenzie was your ride?" I fold my arms over my chest and aim my big sister stare at Libby.

She scowls, her obstinate eyes briefly clashing with mine. Despite our wide age gap, we're alike in so many ways. Stubborn to the point of self-destruction. "I didn't have tons of options."

Damn, if that doesn't stab a knife of guilt into my stomach.

Her gaze strays to the station wagon. "What's with the boxy thing? Reminds me of Aunt Kimmy's old beast."

"It's a loaner," I explain, relieved she's not going to argue with me in front of Dex.

Instead of verbal combat, my sister rakes her gaze over Dex, then actually smiles. "Is it lawn day already?"

Dex chuckles. "No, I picked your sister up from work." He casts a glance my way. "Lucky we ran into each other this morning."

"I don't know what I would've done if you hadn't saved me." Internally, I cringe at how pathetic that sounds. I'm resourceful. I would've figured something out. Eventually.

Libby's done with this conversation. She shouts, "Homework," and speed walks into the house. "Later, Dex."

"Later," he calls after her.

The door slams shut, and he shifts his full attention to me. "How long has it been just the two of you?"

Pain lodges in my throat. In some ways, it feels like our parents just died. And in others, it seems so long ago, I have trouble remembering their faces. "Nine years—well, eight. We moved in with our aunt after our parents died, but she wasn't in great health. She died about a year later," I finish in a small voice. Too many complicated, painful memories are tied up inside me to explain to someone I barely know.

His serious expression could've been carved out of granite. "Raising your sister was a big responsibility to take on. You must've been pretty young."

I bristle at the observation. How many people told me to put Libby into foster care so I could "live my life" without the "burden" of a much younger sister to raise? Too many to count. "There was no way in hell I was going to give her up to the state to put into foster care. Who knows what would've happened to her?" I flare. "We get by just fine."

"Hey, easy. I wasn't criticizing. You're absolutely right." He jerks his head toward the Volvo. "Roman—Vapor—grew up in foster care. He doesn't talk about it a lot. Not to me anyway. But it was rough."

My throat's too tight to do anything other than nod.

"She's lucky to have you."

"We're lucky to have each other." I let out a sad laugh. "She sort of forced me to grow up and stop making bad life choices, you know?"

"Not everyone's capable of that kind of growth. Lot of people would take the easiest route possible." He glances at our house. "You've done well."

"It's my aunt's place," I admit. "*Was* hers. She didn't have any kids."

He nods thoughtfully, but it's pretty much a conversation killer.

"I should get going." Dex taps my shoulder, then lets his fingers trail over my arm. One of his fingers briefly curls around my pinky before he snatches his hand away. "Friday?"

"Right," I whisper, shaken from his touch. "Seven," I confirm in a stronger voice.

"Seven," he repeats.

And I'll be thinking of nothing but him until then.

CHAPTER FIVE

Emily

LIBBY'S IN THE KITCHEN, picking at a peanut butter and Fluff sandwich when I go inside.

"Wooo," she sings. "My big sister has major heart eyes for Dex."

"Shut up." I walk over to the stove and flick the flame under my tea kettle. "Is that all you want for dinner? I defrosted chicken. I was planning to try that pecan crust we read about and pop 'em in the air fryer."

"Can we do that tomorrow?" she asks. "I'm already feeling crispy around the edges, and I wasn't lying about homework."

I chuckle at her teenage description of burnout. "Yeah, of course." I pull out the chair next to her and sit while I wait for the water to boil. "Anything I can help with?"

"Not really." She jams the rest of the sandwich in her mouth and jumps up, knocking the heavy wooden chair backward with a screech against the tile.

"Easy."

She leans in and slaps a sweet peanut-scented kiss on my cheek. "Study sesh on Zoom with Mackenzie and Caroline."

"Studying or giggle-fest?"

She rolls her eyes and twirls out the door, wiggling her fingers goodbye.

The whistle on my kettle blows. I stand and fix my tea. Stillness creeps through the old house. I push the kitchen door open and lean into the living room, listening for signs my sister's safely tucked in her room. Distant giggles reach me and my lips curve up. She must already be online with her friends.

I return to the kitchen and grab my teacup, then walk to the wide windows overlooking the backyard. The urge to talk to *someone* about today needles me. Most of my friends have settled into relationships. I glance at the clock. Celia's one of my last single friends, but she's probably still at work.

Serena should be home. And she actually *knows* Dex. Maybe she can give me some insight.

She answers on the first ring. "I was just thinking about you."

"Your room's still available if you want to return." *Ah, crap. Why'd I say that?* I miss having her here, sure. But I want to be a supportive friend, not a desperate, clingy one.

"Aww, I miss you guys. How's Libby?"

"Good," I say absently, unsure of how to ask about Dex. I take a quick sip of my tea, searing my tongue.

"Sooooo," Serena prompts, "what's up?"

"Serena…" I pause for dramatic effect. "I think I'm in love."

"What?" She gasps and giggles at the same time. "With who?"

"Grayson's friend or brother or whatever. Dex."

"Is he still mowing your lawn?"

"Sometimes. I think his friend is taking care of it now. Listen," I demand. I need to tell her this before I lose my nerve. What if she repeats this to Grayson, and he tells Dex, and Dex thinks I'm a nutjob? No, Serena wouldn't do that. She already holds plenty of my secrets.

"I'm listening," Serena says so warmly, I can picture her eager-to-hear-my-story smile.

I relay the day's events, leaving out the bit where I was so nervous riding on the back of Dex's bike, I probably cracked a few of his ribs.

When she finishes laughing, she sighs. "Dex has always been really nice. I'm not surprised he helped you out."

"I'm sure it's just out of obligation to your fiancé, or ol' man— whatever you call your Silver Wolf Murder Daddy."

"Wow, what a mouthful. I can't wait to tell Gray you called him my—"

"Don't you dare tell him I said that." My cheeks heat. "I'm kidding, anyway."

"You're on point, though," she says with a gentle, dreamy laugh.

"Please don't regale me with stories of all the sex you're having."

"I would *never*," she gasps in mock indignation.

"Anyway, I invited Dex over for dinner Friday." I plow ahead with my story, needing her thoughts on the situation. "But he was kind of weird about it."

"Wait, what? You invited a guy to your *house?*" Her voice rises a few octaves to punctuate her surprise. "Why, Ms. Walker, that's a violation of rule number three," she teases.

"That rule is for dates I meet *online*. To avoid inviting strangers into my house. It's a safety precaution," I argue in my haughtiest tone. "Dex isn't a stranger."

"All right. That's fair. Rule four is no cooking on a first date, though."

"This isn't a date," I insist. "Trust me. Dex was very clear on that. I just wanted to thank him for being so nice to me today."

"What do you mean he said it wasn't a date?"

"At first, he made up some excuse about going on a trip? But then said he'd postpone it until my car is ready. That's weird, though. Right?"

"I'm stumped. But Dex has always been a bit of an enigma."

Enigma. That's a good word for him. "Hey, enough about me and my lonely libido. How are you feeling?"

"My ankles are three times larger than they used to be, but it's okay because I can't even see my feet—"

"Then how do you know your ankles are bigger?"

"Shut up. I'm serious. I need this baby out of me *now*." She sniffles. "I've been reduced to wearing Crocs."

Do not laugh. To my beauty-blogger best friend, Crocs must be the ultimate style indignity. "Are they at least in a cute color?"

"They're pink with a fuzzy lining."

"Sounds cozy." I sip my tea and try not to laugh.

She grumbles something I can't make out.

"How's Grayson?" I ask, to steer her away from the shoe crisis.

"Wonderful. Spoiling me rotten. He was up in Empire earlier, working at the gym one of the brothers owns. He stopped to get me my favorite butter pecan ice cream, though."

"That's sweet."

"It was. Unfortunately, I wanted strawberry by the time he got home."

I already know the answer, but I ask anyway. "Did he turn around and go get it?"

"He did. I don't know where he gets his patience."

"He loves you," I say gently. "And you deserve to be loved like that, Serena."

"Thank you," she whispers. She clears her throat. "So, what are you going to wear for your non-date?"

"A dress?"

"You have the cutest dresses." She sighs. "And you probably fit into all of *your* shoes. Now, what are you cooking?"

Anxiety thrums through me. As much as I like cooking, doing it for other people always stresses me out. "I haven't thought that far ahead yet. Nothing complicated."

"Well, we can always jump on Zoom or something if you want to go over your outfit, makeup, or menu."

"Jeez. Relax. It's not a date."

Her laughter calls me a liar. "Okay. Whatever you say, Emily."

CHAPTER SIX

Dex

FRIDAY IS the day of the week working stiffs usually look forward to the most. Crystal Ball is busiest on the weekends, especially Friday nights, so it's usually nothing but another work night to me.

Not this week.

Friday can't get here fast enough. Work is something to endure until I have the privilege of being in Emily's aura again.

I groan and lean back in the sturdy leather chair, propping my feet on the wide wooden desk in the back office at Crystal Ball. Something about one of the invoices Willow left for me seems off. I'd rather gnaw on glass than ask Teller to look at it though. I'll figure it out on my own.

My phone rattles against the desktop. I set my feet on the floor and grab it. I recognize Z's number and answer.

"Hey, traitor," I say. "How's Downstate treating you?"

"Like a puppy who's finally learned to pee outside. Who you calling a traitor?"

I chuckle at his description of his downstate crew. Without Rooster, Grinder, and Jigsaw as his officers, Z would be fucked. Hustler can barely count up a week's worth of socks let alone balance the club's books. Without Teller overseeing Downstate as well as Upstate's finances, Downstate would probably go bankrupt.

"You're missed, that's all," I explain. "Not only did you leave us, you abandoned Crystal Ball too. Girls ask me when you're coming back every day."

"Who you tryin' to bullshit? You're the cuddly big brother. I'm the one always yellin' at them."

As if Z's ever yelled at one of our girls. "Yeah, I'm real fuckin' cuddly."

"Where you at?" Z asks.

"In the office. Thinking that we should've burned this desk the last time we remodeled the place."

"That's a new desk, asshole," he laughs. "Everything good there?"

"I'm looking over some invoices. Stuff we're getting from Empire Beverage seems to be running out quicker than usual, but they're charging us the same."

"They're shady as fuck."

"So are we."

Beyond my closed office door, I hear the back door open and slam shut. Must be one of the girls arriving to spread sunshine and bad vibes.

"You're about to get your wish, brother," Z says.

"World peace?"

"Such a romantic. No, I'm on my way up there. I'll go through the paperwork with you."

Z's got enough on his plate, so I wouldn't ask him to stop by to help but if he's offering, I won't turn him down. "Appreciate it. Been too long since I've seen your pretty face."

"Aw, shucks. I'm blushing, Dex."

We trade a few more sarcastic jabs, he promises to be here in an hour, and we hang up.

As I'm setting my phone on the desk, someone knocks on my door.

"Come in."

The door opens so slowly, I almost yell for whoever's there to come in again. But finally, a head of shiny black curls appears. Kamryn? Kynslee? Kaylin? Something with a K and an oddly placed Y. Always on time. Never any trouble. What the fuck's her name? I should know it by now. She's worked for us for at least six months.

Gee, who'd you meet about six months ago?

Is Emily the reason I can't remember an employee's name? Or is it because dozens of dancers come and go through Crystal Ball every year?

"What's up, Kyra?" *I'm ninety-nine percent sure it's Kyra.*

"Kyla," she corrects.

So close.

"Kai-*luh*." She repeats each syllable in slow motion.

"Kyla. Yes. What's on your mind?" I curl my fingers, motioning her closer.

She shuffles into my office, closing the door behind her. Threads from the hem of her tight, flared jeans trail over the floor. Those, combined with her snug brown turtleneck, hint that she's not planning to grace the stage tonight.

"Swan told me to come see you."

I stand and walk around the edge of my desk, stopping to lean against the front of it. Swan's moved on to teaching yoga instead of dancing, but she still works here as a sort of "den mom" for the other dancers. She could've sent Kyla to me for a number of reasons. I glance at my phone. No texts.

A heads-up would've been nice, Swan.

I cross my arms over my chest and run my gaze over Kyla's small, thin frame. She squirms and shifts her feet, her sneakers squeaking against the industrial-tile floor.

My gaze lands on a patch of blue skin near her eye. Something she didn't quite cover with her heavy makeup.

I stand straighter and lean toward her. "Come here."

Hesitant, she steps closer. I rest my hand on her shoulder. She winces. My gaze drops to a ring of purple around her wrist, and she quickly tugs her sleeve down.

Gently, I pick up her hand, push the material out of the way, and study the mark. Someone gripped her hard for a period of time. I release her hand and touch a finger to her chin, turning her head slightly. Jesus fuck. This close, bruising on the whole side of her face is visible.

Her bottom lip trembles and I feel like an utter asshole for treating her like a bug under a microscope. "Who did this to you?"

She jerks away. "No one."

"Does 'no one' have a name?"

"Leave it alone, please." She folds her arms over her chest. A flash of pain crosses her expression. More than her wrist is injured.

"How you planning to work like that tonight?" I ask in what I hope is a milder tone. Swan keeps saying I have to work on not being so "intimidating" or whatever.

"I'm fine," she insists.

"Yeah? You gonna climb the pole with your arm hurting the way it is?"

"I'll ice it. Please don't send me home," she pleads. "I need the money."

"Do you need the money to leave this loser?" I gesture to her face. "Or is he a bum who's living off your hard work when he's not knocking you around?"

Her gaze slides to the floor. "It's none of your business."

"Everything that goes on in here"—I stab my finger toward the floor—"is my business. That's the deal if you want to dance for this club. Don't ever forget that."

"What do you want from me?"

"I want you to tell me who did this so I can pay him a visit."

Her eyes widen. "You wouldn't do that."

"Ask anyone in this club if I make *house calls.*" Unfortunately, it happens more often than I care to think about.

She clamps her lips into a firm, stubborn line.

"Fucking hell." I pinch the bridge of my nose. I can't let her on stage if I know she's injured and could hurt herself worse. But I don't want to send her home so she loses money either. "Go help Willow behind the bar tonight." I gesture to her arm. "How bad is it? Did you see a doctor?"

Seen plenty of dancers keep right on working with injuries that would make most men cry. I doubt she sought any medical help.

"No, it's just strained. I told you, I'm fine," she insists.

I stare at her.

"But I'll help Willow tonight. No problem," she adds in a more respectful tone.

"Thank you." I lift my chin toward the door, indicating she can go. I'll find out who put his hands on her some other way.

Poor Kyla can't get away from me fast enough. She slips out of the office, leaving the door open a crack.

"Sorry, darlin'," someone says in the hallway.

Kyla responds but too low for me to hear the words. A second later, my door flies open and Z fills up the space.

"Honey, I'm home!" He throws his arms up in a wide "V" shape, smacking his wrist against the metal doorframe. "Fuck." He shakes it off and swaggers into the office. "Am I getting older or are they getting younger?" He jerks his thumb over his shoulder. "She looks like she should be climbing on a school bus, not a pole."

"She's legal," I grumble. Does he think I don't know how to check I.D. or something?

"Aw, don't get frowny with me, Dex." He grabs me in a big bear hug, thumping me on the back. "Missed your serious face, brother."

I squeeze him hard and release him. "Missed you too. Did Lilly come up with you?"

"Not this time. She's helping Serena decorate the nursery. I can't tell if Grinder appreciates all the help or wants to slit my throat."

"I'm sure he appreciates it." I hold out my hand, indicating he should take one of the chairs while I slide into the seat behind the desk. "It's what he said he always wanted. Ol' ladies who got along."

"Certainly makes our lives easier." He sits up and taps my desk. "So what's got you all glum and Dex-y over there?" He waves his hand in front of my face and I slap it away.

"I'm not glum." I lift my chin toward the door. "Someone roughed that girl up. Swan sent her to me so I could be the bad guy and tell her she can't go on stage tonight."

Z punches his fist against his palm. "Blanket party? Let's go."

"You itching to give someone a beatdown? Thought you were all mellow house-daddy now?" I sit back and grin.

"Fuck you," Z laughs. "I'm always game to give someone what's coming." He sits forward, leaning his elbow against my desk. "I think it's what Lilly likes about me the most."

"Yeah, all your most annoying traits seem to make Lilly swoon." I roll my eyes, but he grins even wider.

"So, where we headed?"

"Nowhere. She won't tell me anything."

"Talk to the other girls." He waves his hand behind his head toward the hallway.

"Gee, I hadn't thought of that, President Obvious." I roll my eyes. "I'm not sure any of them know much about her."

"Where'd you send her?"

"To help Willow behind the bar. I can't have her on stage like that. She'll fall off the pole and hurt herself even worse."

"She give you shit about making less in tips?"

"No, she was just glad I didn't send her home, I think."

He gestures toward the industrial-size safe in the corner behind him. "Make up the difference outta there."

"I was planning to." I bite off the rest of my words. Z's trying to help, not undermine me. I don't know why I'm so fucking prickly tonight.

"Well, if you get a name, let me know. Don't want you paying him a visit by yourself."

"I usually take Vapor on those jobs. He knows to keep his mouth shut."

A feral smile flashes across Z's face. "It's nice when we get to train them young. You making progress on the support club?"

"I don't think it's mine to 'make progress' on. Murphy's got as much connection to the guys as I do."

He throws a what-the-fuck frown at me. "Vapor's your family. Murphy just used to bop around in Remy and Griff's fighting ring. I'd say it's more *your* project than anyone else's."

I open my mouth to protest again, but there's no point. "I'm sure Rock will bring it up in church soon. Griff was a big help this week. I know Wrath still has doubts, but I think they're ready for something more official."

One corner of his mouth twitches. "I think I heard something about Griff helping you with a car…"

"Jesus Christ, Grinder's supposed to be your enforcer, not your gossip buddy."

"You've been patched too long to be that naive, Dex. Nothing happens without everyone talking about it."

Tapping at the office door stops our conversation. Z leans his chair back on two legs and stretches his arm toward the knob, catching it and twisting just as the legs of his chair start to wobble and threaten to throw him to the floor. He rights the chair with a hard thunk.

Willow strolls in, hands on her hips, irritation rippling over her usually placid face. "Why is Kyla in my shit, Dex?" She flicks an annoyed glance at Z, as if he might have had something to do with screwing up her night.

Z covers his smirk with a hand at his chin and swings his impish gaze my way. "I don't miss *this* at all," he mutters.

Willow smacks his shoulder. "You miss me and you know it."

He grabs her hand before she can whack him again and shakes it. "Yeah, I miss you. Lilly keeps begging me to entice you into moving downstate."

"Don't you dare," I warn. One of the only constants at Crystal Ball over the years has been Willow's presence.

"Nah, bro." Z flashes another devilish grin. "I think the stoner brothers would slit my throat if I tried."

Willow's cheeks turn pink, and she snatches her hand away. "Don't call them that."

"Ooo!" Z's eyes widen like a shark who scents blood in the water. "What's going on, Willow?"

She throws me a pleading look. "Dex, really?"

"Knock it off, Z." I nod at Willow. "Keep an eye on Kyla. See if you can find out who she lives with."

The playfulness slides off her face and her mouth settles into a grim line. "Is it MC business or personal?"

"Both," Z answers. "Their personal shit *is* the MC's business."

Willow ignores him and focuses on me, as if I'll be the reasonable one on this subject. "You can't help someone until they're ready," Willow says.

"The fuck I can't," I mutter.

A faint smile ghosts her lips. "I wasn't trying to challenge you."

"Yeah, I know." I run my palm over the back of my head, frustrated. "The girls work so hard. Put up with all those gross, sweaty fucks." I wave my hand toward the door. "I hate the thought of any of them leaving here and going home to *that*."

"Dex," she sighs, dropping into the chair next to Z. "You're such a gem. The girls don't know how lucky they are to work for you."

"Rock and Z handled things the same way." I wave my hand at Z, who nods like a first-time rider who's managed to keep both wheels on the pavement. "Where do you think I got it from?"

"Oh, I know." She holds her hands in the air. "You're all so cut from the same cloth, you might as well all be blood brothers."

"People put too much importance on blood relationships," Z grumbles.

Exasperation purses her lips. "Fine. What do you want me to do?"

"What you're good at. Listen. Find out if she lives with a boyfriend, parents, I don't know. Someone roughed her up. I can't have her working the pole with her arm fucked to hell." Normally, I wouldn't spread someone's business around. Willow gossips more than she should sometimes, but deep down under her tough exterior, she's got a kind heart, and I don't think she would share *this* with anyone.

"Shit." Willow chews on a thumbnail. "Fine. But if she gets in my way…" She doesn't finish the threat.

"Come talk to me. I'll handle it," I promise.

"Okay." She stands and runs her hands over her legs. "What are you going to do when I find out who banged her up?"

Z and I share similar bloodthirsty smiles. But I'm the one who answers.

"What we do best, sweetheart."

CHAPTER SEVEN

Dex

FRIDAY NIGHT'S FINALLY HERE.

I'm thirty-fucking-four years old. Why the fuck am I...nervous? It's been so long since I experienced the feeling, it takes a second to identify it.

I step onto Emily's small, concrete front porch. Bright yellow lights illuminate every inch. No place for anyone to hide. I jab the doorbell, hear the chimes inside, and wait.

A few seconds later, a shadow bobs behind the curtain covering the small glass window in the front door. The hinges creak as Emily pulls the door wide.

"Hi," she says in a low, breathless tone.

Struck dumb, I stand and stare at the beautiful firecracker in front of me. Loose, spiral curls brushing her shoulders, her lips a glossy dusky pink. I want to squeeze her face between my palms and smash my mouth against hers.

My gaze travels lower to the dark blue dress with a row of buttons from her chest to her shins, highlighting all her curves. The red belt at her waist is like a damn neon sign pointing to where my hands belong. Everything about her is so vibrant and *real*. Not just beautiful. I encounter plenty of pretty women in my business. Emily has an inner glow that can't be bought, taught, or surgically enhanced.

Genuine happiness to find me on her doorstep seems to light up her eyes.

"Hi, Emily." Damn, I even like the way her name sounds in my mouth.

She smiles and opens the door wider. "Come in."

Even though the house is one of those large, old rambling structures with high ceilings, I feel like a giant towering over her as I step inside.

"Do you want something to drink?" she asks, turning toward the kitchen.

You. I stop and slip off my cut, hanging it on a rack outside the hallway closet, right next to her coat.

The scents wafting from the kitchen make my mouth water, and I head toward the door Emily disappeared behind. "Whatever you're making smells amazing."

She's standing by the stove, and she throws a quick smile over her shoulder. "It's nothing fancy. Roast chicken."

"I like chicken." I step behind her as she transfers half a chicken from a roasting pan onto a platter. "Do you need help?"

She jumps and turns. "Oh!"

"Didn't mean to startle you." I should back up. Give her room. But I can't convince my body to move an inch away from hers. "You look pretty tonight." Fuck, that's weak and not even close to fully describing what I see in front of me.

"Th-thank you." She tucks her hair behind her ear. "You wear that T-shirt quite nicely." Her hand flies up to cover her mouth. "Oh my God. I can't believe I…"

One corner of my mouth shifts to the side. "I don't mind hearing it. Glad you approve." I lift my chin, indicating her dress. "For a minute, I was worried I was underdressed."

"Not at all."

I cock my head toward the kitchen door. "Is Libby joining us?"

"No." Her forehead crinkles. "Why?"

Shit, I probably sound like I want to maul her in private or something. Which I do. But that's not why I asked. "I could probably eat that whole platter of chicken by myself."

"Oh!" She lets out a nervous laugh. "There's more. I promise. She's at her friend's tonight."

"The speed racer?" I lift an eyebrow.

"It's supposed to be a sleepover. So, hopefully no racing around town."

"That's good."

The timer on the oven dings. I back up to give her room but keep my gaze glued to her ass as she bends over and pulls a pan of stuffing out, setting it on one of the burners. Her movements are quick and jerky. Am I making her nervous?

"How do you...how should we?" She blows out a frustrated breath and slaps her hands against her thighs. "I don't entertain a lot. Do you mind filling your plate at the counter?"

This is why I didn't want her to go to so much trouble for me. "Whatever's easiest, Emily. I'm not fussy."

She gestures toward the cozy round table in the center of the kitchen. "Libby and I usually eat there, but we can eat by the windows if you want." She waves her hand at the large windows at the back of the kitchen where there's a long wooden table and several stiff dining chairs.

"Right here is good." I nod to the round table. "So we can talk easier."

She nods quickly and hurries to the refrigerator, gathering several items. Her quick, jerky movements jostle the glass bottles she's loading into her arms.

"Relax, Emily." I take a butter dish and bottle of lemon juice out of her hands. "I'm just happy to spend time with you."

Her eyebrows shoot up.

Why does she seem so damn surprised?

A shy smile curves her lips. "I like having you here."

Her gaze drops to my hand, and her smile falters. "Your knuckles look bruised. Did you hurt yourself riding?"

That *would* be an easier explanation, but I like her too much on the back of my bike to give her a reason to be afraid of it. "Work-related injury." At least that's *almost* the truth.

"I never asked what you do for a living?"

I don't normally waste energy being ashamed of anything I say or do, but for the first time, I'm hesitant to tell someone where I work. "The MC owns a nightclub and I manage it." *Nightclub. Good one.*

"Oh, that must be fun. No wonder you're a night owl." She scrunches her nose. "Does Empire still *have* nightclubs? I thought a lot closed down over the last few years?" She shrugs. "I don't go out much anymore. What's the name?"

I cough to clear the stranglehold my common sense has on my throat. "Crystal Ball."

She tilts her head in the most adorable way. "Nope. Doesn't sound familiar."

Christ, she's never heard of the only strip club within a fifty-mile radius of Empire County? Of course she hasn't. Why would she?

I don't belong here.

But I'm not giving up that easily.

To move away from this topic, I hold up the cold bottle of lemon juice. "Where am I putting this?"

"That can go on the counter and the butter on the table."

"You got it." I drop the bottle on the counter with a low clink and the butter on the table.

After we dish everything onto our plates and sit, Emily seems to finally relax.

"For 'nothing fancy,' this is really good," I say, taking another bite of stuffing. "Like Thanksgiving but not as heavy."

She beams, and damn if I don't feel her smile in my bones. "The sage gives it the 'Thanksgiving flavor' but I think the lemon helps keep it crisp and light." She takes a sip of water. "I like lemon in everything."

"Interesting for such a sweet person." What a line. I couldn't come up with anything better than that?

"Obviously, you don't know me that well. I'm not sure if anyone else in my life would describe me as *sweet*." She shrugs. "But I have my moments."

"I know you're a good sister and a good friend."

"Being a good sister definitely means *not* being sweet sometimes."

I chuckle and lift my glass. "I can imagine."

"If I can help Libby not make half the dumb mistakes I did when I was younger, I'll be happy."

"Spoken like a good parent. One who wants to set their kids up to do better than they did."

"I guess so. I still don't feel like I know what I'm doing half the time."

"I don't think you're alone there."

She runs her gaze over my arms, and I have the goofy, adolescent urge to flex for her. "You seem like someone who's extremely capable in every situation. For example, I was running around the cemetery like a loon the other day and you just, *poof*, calmly sent a text and sorted it out. Had your friend bring me a loaner car. All of it." She rests her hand over mine. "Thank you, again."

"You're welcome." I rub my thumb over her knuckles. "Griff says he should be able to drop your car off in the morning."

"Did he say how much it'll be?"

"Don't worry about it." It's an amount I can easily cover.

"Dex," she protests. "I can't—"

"It's fine."

Her jaw ticks but she drops it. For now.

CHAPTER EIGHT

Dex

"THAT WAS INCREDIBLE. THANK YOU, EMILY." I stand and pat my stoma.
"Let me help you clean this up."

Her cheeks flush, like she's pleased or embarrassed by the compliment
—I can't tell. "Thanks. It's usually just me and Libby, and she's happiest
with a fluffernutter sandwich or pizza."

"Fluff, huh? I haven't had that since I was a kid."

"It's sticky and gross and gets all over everything." She shrugs. "But
Libby loves it, so whatever."

I don't know my way around her kitchen, so I mostly watch as she
pulls out plastic wrap and organizes what's left over to store in the fridge.
Once she's finished, I grab a plate and follow her. She leans over, her dress
gaping in the front just enough to flash a glimpse of blue satin and lace
against pale skin. My free hand curls into a fist at my side so I don't palm
her breast. I shift a few inches to the right. This angle's worse. Now I'm
staring at her perfectly round ass hidden by thin fabric.

I've held myself in check all night. I can restrain myself for a few more
minutes.

"Other one?" She holds out her hand without looking at me.

I pass her the plate.

It would be so easy to drag that dress up over her legs. See if her
panties match her dress too.

She backs away from the fridge, closes the door, and turns. I'm so busy fantasizing about exposing her ass that I'm blocking her path. Her elbow hits me in the chest and my control snaps. I barely feel the impact. But it seems to be the cue for my baser instincts to take over.

I curl my hands around her waist and yank her closer.

"Sorry," she squeaks.

"Don't be." I tip her chin up and slide my fingers into her hair. "I'm not." That's the only warning she gets. I lean down and brush my lips over hers. A quick taste. Long enough to know I need more. "I was trying to be a polite guest, but I've wanted to do this all night."

This time she meets me halfway. Leaning up on her tiptoes, she slides her arms around my neck. Our lips fuse together, soft and tentative at first. She makes a noise in the back of her throat, like a primal call for more. I squeeze and lift her against the front of my body and shoulder my way into the living room. Where the fuck is her bedroom? Probably upstairs.

Couch.

Couch is good.

Our connection flares to life and pulses around us. She drags me down onto the cushions, barely breaking our kiss. Our legs tangle and she almost slides off the edge of the couch to the floor. I pull away and she scoots into the corner then curls her hand in my T-shirt, drawing me closer. I fit my hand over her hip, tucking her under me, and keep kissing her. My thumb brushes against the wide belt at her waist and I splay my hand over her stomach, searching with my fingers for a way to undo the contraption. Maybe it's welded shut? Giving up on the belt, I slide my hand up over her ribs. I reach the top button of her dress and tease it between my fingers.

"May I?" I stare down at her and tug on the button.

She nods quickly, her eyes glued to my hand working the button free. I've never unfastened anything so quickly in my life. I work each one loose until the belt—that seems to be cemented into place—stops me.

Eager to see her, I push the sides of her dress out of my way. I rub my knuckle over the swells of her breasts. "Your bra matches your dress. I like that," I rasp, staring and burning every inch of her into my brain.

She laughs, low and husky. "I swear I wasn't planning to show it off tonight."

"I'm not complaining."

She curls her fingers around the back of my head, pulling me in for another kiss. All logic and reason slip away. Desire demands I touch and taste every inch of her. I drag my lips down her neck, smiling against her skin as her breathing speeds up.

Anticipation thrums through my veins. My cock strains against my jeans, wanting freedom. I slide lower, kissing the valley between her breasts, stopping to tease my tongue over her lace-covered nipples. Twisting my hand in the long fabric of her dress, I tug it up over her legs. The second I touch her thigh, her body freezes.

"Too much?" I ask.

"No." She parts her legs. "Keep going."

Don't have to tell me twice. I skim my fingers along her soft skin until my knuckles brush against damp satin.

She gasps. Her hand shoots down, grabbing my wrist. But she doesn't push me away. My heart thuds while I wait.

"Um, it takes me a minute or two…usually," she whispers.

Unreasonable jealousy blazes to life—fury at the thought of anyone else touching what's *mine*. "Just relax. I'm not going anywhere," I answer with a lot more calm than I actually possess.

"Are you sure?" she asks.

Am I sure? I'm drowning with the need to touch her. To find out exactly how long it takes to set her off.

I drop one kiss on her shoulder, then another, kissing my way to her mouth, and finally her body relaxes. "I'm sure."

I slide my hand under her dress again, teasing the soft flesh between her legs. Fighting the urge to rip her panties off and bury my fingers inside her, I run my knuckles over slick, wet fabric. Up and down, slowly increasing the pressure.

"Oh!" Emily's whole body jerks. She lifts her leg, resting her foot on the coffee table to give me more room.

"That's it," I encourage. "Show me what you like."

"I…" She bites her lip and arches her back. "That. Right there."

"Perfect," I murmur, stroking over and over. It doesn't take long to have her writhing and panting under me. I slip my fingers beneath her panties and hiss at the searing wetness.

"Oh God," she whimpers.

That's the sound I'm after. I spear her with one finger, groaning at how incredible she feels, trying to rein in how much I want her wrapped around my cock. But fuck if the unsure way she implied it would take too long to make her come doesn't fire up all my stubborn instincts to prove her wrong. She's beautifully responsive to every single touch.

"Dex," she whispers, her voice full of longing. "Please?"

I trail my tongue along her neck, stopping to suck at a spot below her ear that seems to drive her wild. "Please, what?"

She rolls her hips, trying to explain with her body what I want to hear with words.

"No, Emily." I slide my thumb over her clit and circle it with long, slow strokes. "Tell me what you want."

"Don't stop." She lets out each word with a desperate, panted breath. "Oh my God. I think I'm—I think I'm...close."

I smile against her neck. "Close to what?"

"Don't be mean." She lets out a frustrated sob.

"This?" I work a second finger inside her and twist the angle of my hand a bit. She's so wet and hot. "You want me to make you come on my fingers?" I help her with the words.

"If you can."

Why does she sound so unsure? She's halfway there already. I explore her slowly, seeking the magic combination of touch and pressure to set her off. She gasps and bites her lip, squeezing her eyes shut.

"That's it," I encourage her, driving deeper, pressing the heel of my hand against her clit, giving her more friction. Teasing her has been fun, but I need to see her go off. To know I'm the one who made her unravel.

She moans, low and ragged. Her hips work faster, fucking my fingers.

"Let go for me. I've got you," I whisper.

My other hand's trapped under her body, and I don't want to do anything to disturb her momentum. She's a firecracker, so close to exploding. Using my teeth, I tug at the flap of her dress, baring her lace-covered breasts again. Tight nipples strain against the dark blue lace and I close my mouth over one.

"Ah!" she gasps, her body jerking against mine.

I suck harder and work my fingers faster.

Her breathing turns harsh and desperate. Then finally, she tips over the edge, squeezing my fingers.

I groan with her, imagining how good she's going to feel wrapped around my cock. Soon. That needs to happen soon.

"That's it." I kiss her neck. "That's a girl. Come for me."

"Dex," she whispers with a frenzied urgency. "I can't—I can't *stop*."

Low laughter rumbles out of me. "Good. Keep going. There's no hurry." As if I'd ever try to stop her. We haven't even gotten our clothes off and I'm craving the slide of her skin against mine, her taste on my tongue. That's definitely where I'm headed next.

Finally, her body relaxes. I slow my relentless thrusting, bringing her back to reality with slow, gentle touches.

Emily

"Wow, I never…" I'm not sure how to finish my thought. Everything that comes to mind seems inappropriate. No one's ever been able to make me come that way. In fact, I'm not sure what I've experienced in the past were actually orgasms now.

Dex's serious expression melts into a smile that hits me like a sunbeam, leaving me tingling all over.

I glance down at my dress, open from neck to waist and shoved up around my hips. Dex's hand is inside my underwear, still lightly cupping me.

It was the best orgasm ever, and we didn't even get our clothes off.

Dex kisses my chest and slowly slides off the couch to kneel in front of me. He lifts an eyebrow, silently asking permission as he skims his hands over my legs, up under my dress, anchoring the material at my waist. He leans in and kisses my inner thigh. Unease skitters over me, and I squirm.

"You don't have to." I try to press my knees together but his hands are wedged in there tight. This has already been amazing—let's not jinx it.

"I'm not really a fan…" *Of being disappointed*, I try to explain.

He flicks his gaze up. Desire and challenge glitter in the blue depths of his eyes. "Can I have a few minutes to change your mind?"

What a question. Not a macho challenge—just a devastatingly simple inquiry. Shivers of desire prickle over my skin. How can I say no?

"Okay."

He leans in and gently rubs his chin against the inside of my leg. Light stubble grazes my sensitive skin. "Thank you."

Is he thanking me for the opportunity to go down on me? Dear God. I slide lower and part my legs.

"Hmm." He hums with approval and slides his hands higher, hooking his fingers in my underwear.

Our eyes meet again. A clear question burns in his eyes.

God, that's hot.

I nod and lift my hips. He slides my panties down my legs. For a second, he balls them in his fist, like he's planning to stuff them in his pocket for a trophy. Then he tosses them on the couch next to me.

Just the focused way he concentrates on my bared skin has me hot all over. He presses his hands against my thighs, spreading me farther apart, then dives in, sliding his tongue from my entrance to my clit in one firm lick. Then another. And another.

My legs quiver and I rest my head against the cushion, closing my eyes.

How is he so good at this?

No. No. No. I squeeze my eyes tighter, willing the question to go away. I can't handle the implication of his talented tongue. How much practice did it take for him to get so good? With whom?

Nope. Stop it.

Dex's blissful torture stops. "Emily? Are you with me?"

"I'm here," I answer in a detached voice. "You're so good at that."

He lets out a wicked laugh and wiggles his tongue around my clit.

"Oh my God!" I shriek and curl my fingers into the nubby couch cushion. "Holy shit."

Pleasure coils inside me, tighter and tighter until I'm ready to burst. The slow but determined attention to my clit drives me higher and higher.

My body seizes like a bolt of lightning racing down my spine. I arch my back, bucking my hips wildly against his face, too consumed by my climax to be concerned with anything but chasing this incredible sensation. He keeps at it, licking and fucking me with his mouth. Dear God, he's relentless.

"Oh my," I chant over and over as I float back to earth. I run my fingers through his hair. My brain fuzzes, and my limp body settles like an overcooked noodle.

What was that?

"You really are my little firecracker, aren't you?" Dex kisses my inner thigh, then a ticklish spot near my hip.

"You...you are incredibly talented," I answer, running my fingers through his thick hair.

His kisses travel lower again. I don't know if my body can handle more.

Ding. Ding.

My hazy brain slowly recognizes the sound.

"Dex?" I tap his shoulder. Good Lord, the last thing I want him to do is stop. "I have to"—I gasp— "get that. It's Libby."

He groans, like he can't tear himself away from pleasuring me, but he stops to kiss my thigh, brushing my wetness over my heated skin.

"I'm so sorry," I whisper, twisting to reach my phone on the end table next to the couch.

He smooths my skirt over my legs. *Such a gentleman.*

"I understand." He lifts his chin. "Is everything okay?"

My hands don't seem to want to work. I fumble my phone into my lap, pick it up, and try again.

Finally, my sister's text lights up my screen.

House emoji. Bird emoji.

"What does that mean?" Dex asks, peering over my shoulder.

I click my phone off and sit up, quickly buttoning my dress. "It's code for 'I don't like what's going on here but don't want to seem uncool to my friends by complaining, so please come pick me up and be the bad guy,'" I answer.

"All that from two images? Clever." One corner of his mouth curves to the side.

He's impressed? He doesn't think I'm an overprotective weirdo?

I file that away for later.

"Thanks." I dial Libby's number, anxious to hear her voice.

"Hey, Em," she answers in a flat tone.

Everything in me wants to fire off a series of questions but I put a muzzle on my big sister mouth and calmly ask, "Hey, did you forget to take out the trash before you left?"

"Yup, sorry about that."

"That means you're grounded. I'm on my way to pick you up."

"Aw, come on, Em, really?" she whines in her best stubborn teenager voice. "Can't I do it tomorrow?"

"Nope. You know the rules. I'll see you in ten minutes." I finish our script, designed so that if one of her nosy friends overhears her conversation, it just sounds like her bitchy big sister has laid down the law.

"Fine," she huffs. Then in a lower voice she adds, "I'll be, uh, waiting right inside."

"Got it." I end the call and scoot to the edge of the couch, grabbing my underwear and searching for my shoes. "I'm so sorry, Dex."

When he doesn't answer, I look up, not finding him anywhere.

"Dex?" *Where'd he go?*

He pushes through the kitchen door and flashes a panty-melting smile. "Wanted to clean up before we leave." He holds up his hands.

Heat sears my skin from scalp to toes as I try to discreetly pull my panties into place underneath my dress. Then my brain processes his words. "You don't have to come with me."

His smile slips. "It's almost midnight. Do you know what spooked her so bad she wants to come home early?"

I glance at my phone. "No. We used our sister code."

"Well, then just in case, I should go with you." He waves his arms toward the door in a *let's move* gesture.

"I have a baseball bat in the car," I protest, slipping my shoes on.

"Great. I'll keep it in mind." He motions toward the front door again.

I'm torn between wanting his company and wanting to prove I can do everything all by myself, just like I've been doing since my parents died. The stubborn part of me wants to deny how much I'd like his company.

"I'll be okay," I try again.

"Emily," he says, exasperation weighing down my name, "we can argue about it and then leave, or we can leave right now. Either way, I'm coming with you. If something upset Libby, I'd rather not keep her waiting."

I can't quibble with his logic. Libby's only used our emoji code a handful of times. She'd been looking forward to tonight's sleepover, but something big must have happened for her to want to come home already. I pull my purse off the hook by the door and grab my keys. "Let's go."

Outside, I'm too anxious to appreciate the cool, crisp evening. I hustle to the car, unlocking the doors. Dex hesitates at the passenger side, then folds his large frame into the seat.

I toss my purse in the back seat and slide behind the wheel. Glancing over, I wince at Dex's knees rammed into the dashboard. "Sorry about that," I mutter.

"I'm fine." He leans over to adjust the seat, giving himself a few extra precious inches. "Do you know where you're going?"

"Yup. I've been there lots of times."

It's not far but we have to pass through a seedier part of the town to get there. Thank God Libby didn't storm off in a huff and decide to walk home.

Worry for my little sister keeps my foot pressed against the pedal harder than prudent.

"Easy," Dex warns when I roll through a stop sign. "If you get pulled over, it's going to take even longer to pick her up."

"I know," I mutter, easing off the gas.

Finally, I turn onto Mackenzie's street. Darkness and shadows conceal most of the houses. Then, a bright circle of light filters through a row of hedges. The faint thump of music drifts through the air.

"Someone's having a party," Dex says.

"That's Mackenzie's house." Either Libby lied about the parents being home tonight or she didn't know what Mackenzie had planned.

Too many cars crowd the narrow street. Kids have jammed their vehicles into any random available spot on the sidewalk and on the lawns as well.

"Surprised no one's called the cops yet," Dex mutters.

I hadn't thought of that. Now I'm even more eager to find Libby and take her home.

"Pull over here." Dex gestures to a spot not quite large enough to fit into. "I'll run in and get her. Text her so she knows to look for me and not you."

I slam the car into park. "Okay."

"Lock the door behind me," he orders, shutting it with a hard thump.

I hit the locks and scrabble for my phone, then send Libby a quick message.

Dex is coming to get you.

Anxiety bubbles in my chest as my gaze scans the shadowy lawn, searching for any sign of Dex or Libby. Two drunk guys puking in the bushes. A couple making out in the shadows next to the house. It's too dark to tell if any of them are friends of Libby's that I recognize.

A few seconds later, I spot her bright yellow shirt bobbing toward me. A whoosh of relief passes my lips and I unlock the doors. Dex's larger figure looms behind her like a lethal, high-priced bodyguard. He opens the back door and Libby throws herself across the seat.

"Thanks, Em," she says breathlessly.

Dex slides into the passenger seat, reaches over, and curls his hand over my thigh, giving me a gentle, reassuring squeeze.

I shift the car into drive, check my side mirror, and pull onto the road again. "Everything all right, pudding?" I ask Libby.

She groans at the nickname. "I'm fine."

I flick my gaze to the rearview in time to catch her crossing her arms over her chest and a pout pursing her lips. "Mackenzie said she was just having a few people over," she explains. "Then more and more kept showing up. And then a bunch of older guys who graduated a few years ago came and brought alcohol. They were so gross and creepy."

"You get their names?" Dex asks.

"I dunno."

I side-eye Dex, but he's stone-faced and staring straight ahead.

"I'm glad you texted me," I say.

She sits forward, resting her arm on the back of my seat. "I'm sorry if I ruined your night."

"Your safety's more important," Dex answers in a low, no-bullshit rumble. "That's a neat system you set up with your sister."

Libby presses her hands together and flutters her fingers like wings. "It means I'm ready to fly the coop."

I chuckle.

"And I can blame having to go home on my mean big sister, so my friends don't think I'm being a baby," she adds.

"Happy to be your bad guy anytime." I reach behind me, and she tickles two fingers against my open palm.

She sits back and stares out the window. Did she give me the whole story? Is Dex's presence making her too uncomfortable to talk to me freely?

I slow the car and turn into my driveway then stop in front of the garage.

"I'm going to crawl into bed." She tugs at a strand of her long hair and sniffs. "Eww, I reek of beer. I'll be in the shower." Libby flings open her door and darts up the sidewalk before I have a chance to respond.

Shaking my head, I reach for my purse and step out of the car. Dex meets me by the trunk.

"I'll walk you inside, then head out," he says. "You should probably talk to her one-on-one."

"I plan to." I lift my gaze to his and cock an eyebrow. "This isn't my first rodeo."

"That came out wrong." He curls his fingers around mine and rubs his thumb over my knuckles. "It's obvious you've got it handled. I meant, I'm probably in the way." He tugs me toward the front door.

Tired, I bump into him and he wraps his arm around my waist. What I wouldn't give to wake up next to his strong, solid presence in the morning.

But that's a luxury I can't afford at this stage in my life.

CHAPTER NINE

Dex

I HATE like hell leaving Emily. Still worked up from earlier, my cock cursing me out, but that's not the only reason I want to stay.

I'm worried about Emily and Libby.

I must be getting old. I'm not Emily's boyfriend or Libby's dad, so I don't know why it bugged me to find her huddled in a darkened corner of her friend's porch so damn much. Maybe it was the relieved way Libby jumped and grabbed my hand like a lifeline that prodded all my protective instincts awake.

The front door squeaks as Emily opens it and steps inside. Here's where I should kiss her good night and leave.

Too bad I can't convince my body to turn around and go.

Emily sets her purse on a table in the entryway and walks over to the staircase, cocking her head. The faint screech of old pipes and water running drifts downstairs.

"She's already in the shower." Emily frowns. "Did she say anything to you?"

"No. I found her sitting in a dark corner all by herself, looking pretty miserable, though." My gaze shifts toward the stairs. "Our MC throws some wild parties and I gotta say, those kids could give us a run for our money." Looked like a group of them had been trying to reenact scenes from their favorite pornos. But I keep that part to myself so I don't scare the shit out of Emily.

"Dammit." Emily chews on her thumbnail. "I miss her hanging out with her little nerdy thespian group."

"Is Mackenzie a new friend?"

"No, but they seem to have vastly different interests lately."

I'll say.

She throws one more glance at the stairs then walks closer to me. "Thank you."

She's within reach. All I want to do is get her closer. Pull her into my arms and taste her mouth again. I close the small gap between us and curl my arms around her waist. Heat flares in her eyes, and she slicks her tongue over her bottom lip.

Then somehow, I'm pressing her body up against the wall. Or is it the hallway closet door? It doesn't matter. I grab her ass, lifting her slightly. Our lips meet and she opens for me. Her hands fist into my T-shirt, then slide underneath. Soft, warm fingertips tease along my lower back and it's like a live wire spreading sparks over my skin.

She moans into my mouth and I snap, yanking her dress up. She releases me, fumbling with something behind her, then drags me into the hall closet.

Am I really making out with a girl in a closet? Brings back my own high school days. Who the fuck cares? Closet, back seat of a car—I'm game for anything as long as it's Emily's body pressed up against mine.

We fall against a pile of coats hanging from a hook. Emily bats them away and then I'm pressing her against the wall again. She raises her knee to my hip. Fuck, I'm dying. It would be so easy to free myself and fuck her into oblivion, but this isn't quite how I want our first time to be. A hurried, quiet quickie in a closet—no. I need time to spread Emily out and explore every inch of her body. Listen to her go wild, screaming my name.

Why does this woman feel like she was made for me? Her body fits against mine perfectly. This long fucking dress is driving me nuts, though. I fight my way through the endless fabric of the skirt and finally cup my hand over her searing heat. I shove the damp satin out of my way, not taking the time to pull her underwear all the way off this time.

"I need to feel you come one more time," I whisper against her ear. "Can you do that for me?"

Her body shivers against mine. "I don't know."

I cup her breast, stroking my thumb over her nipple as it strains against her bra and dress. God, I want my mouth on her. With my other hand, I slide my fingers through her wetness until she gasps.

It's hard to see in the darkened closet but I press my forehead to hers. She stares straight into my eyes as I slip one finger inside her and use my thumb to press and roll her clit. Her breasts rise and fall faster. She pulls her bottom lip between her teeth. But she never stops staring at me.

She gasps, "Dex, please. Harder."

I add another finger, moving quicker. Deeper. Her body grinds down on my hand, chasing what she needs.

"That's it," I encourage her. "Take what you want."

She curls her hands over my shoulders, using me for leverage while riding my hand. I'm burning for her. The closet's like an oven with our combined heat. Sweat rolls down my back, but I can't stop until she comes apart.

"Oh, God." Her body shakes, her eyes squeeze shut.

I seal my mouth over hers, drinking in each little cry of pleasure.

Finally, her body slumps against mine, breaking our kiss. She pants and clings to me. I withdraw my hand, tugging her dress into place, and curl my arms around her quivering body.

"How are you so amazing at that?" she whispers.

It's not me. It's her. *Us.* "There's something about you, firecracker."

"But I've never." She shakes her head, disbelief rippling over her face. "Not like that."

Well, don't I feel like fucking Thor, God of the Orgasm, now.

Emily steps out of the closet first, poking her head around the corner and checking if the coast is clear. There's something so weirdly innocent about it that I can't help laughing.

While it felt like we were wrapped up in each other for an eternity, in reality, only a few minutes have gone by. I step closer to the front door, resting my hand on the knob.

"I really will head home now," I promise.

There she goes, biting her lip again. If she asks me to stay, there's no way in hell I would say no.

"I…" She gestures toward the stairs, then shakes her head.

I lean in and kiss her cheek. "Go make sure she's okay."

"Thank you." Her eyes sparkle with humor. "For all the orgasms. I don't know how I'll ever repay you."

"We'll think of something." I open the door and step onto the porch.

"Dex?" Emily's voice is hesitant, almost shy. Odd, since she was coming on my fingers only a few minutes ago.

I turn and lift an eyebrow. The harsh yellow porch light only emphasizes Emily's smooth skin and reddened lips. She scrapes her teeth over her bottom lip but stares straight into my eyes.

"Can you... Will you...?" She clears her throat and pulls her shoulders back. "Will you text me when you get home? To let me know you're safe?"

I stare at her, processing the question. Only my brothers ask me to check in like that. Can't remember the last time a woman worried about me arriving anywhere. Safe or not.

Not since Debbie. I always let her know where I was, and what I was doing. We used to fall asleep talking on the phone every night.

Not now. Not here.

"Yeah, Emily." I step closer and curl my hand around hers, lifting it to my mouth. "I can do that." I brush my lips over her knuckles.

"Thanks," she whispers.

Damn, I really don't want to leave. "What are you doing tomorrow?"

She stares at me.

Shit, too soon to see each other two nights in a row? Not enough notice to ask her out? Fuck it, I don't believe in rules. I want to see Emily. No point in fucking around.

"I usually run errands, catch up on laundry, that sort of thing on Saturdays," she answers.

Saturday. Fuck, my brain's so scrambled I forgot what day it is. I shouldn't take more time off from Crystal Ball. Especially on one of our busier nights.

"Sunday?" More than twenty-four hours. Can I wait that long to see her again?

"I go over Libby's schedule with her." She touches two fingers to her forehead. "Then I spend the rest of my day mentally preparing myself for the workweek ahead."

The words are meant as a joke but there's an underlying seriousness that rings my overprotective bell. "Everything okay at your job?"

"It's not my dream situation but it's a steady paycheck and has decent benefits."

"They treat you okay?" I didn't miss the punk who stared at us when I picked Emily up the other day.

She crosses her arms over her chest and leans against the wall. Her lips slide to one side. "Why? You going to come beat 'em up if they don't?"

I step closer and rest my hand on her hip. "Yeah, maybe I will."

"Violence is never the answer."

I strongly disagree but it seems like a sour note to end the night on. Instead, I lean in and kiss her forehead. "I have something Sunday morning. But after that? Have you and Libby ever been to Origin Park? It's like an hour and a half south of here."

"The place with all the rock sculptures and stuff?"

"Yeah, it's nice this time of year. Libby might like it—there's a whole stage made out of stone."

"You remembered she likes theater?"

"Uh, yeah." Does she think I don't listen to her?

"Well, I'm in. I don't know if Libby has something else planned but I'll ask her." She reaches out and touches my arm. "Thank you for wanting to include her."

I'd give anything to know what's going on behind Emily's thoughtful eyes. I lean down, touching my forehead to hers. Maybe I can absorb the information that way. "Yeah, of course. I'll get my hands on a cage."

She raises her eyebrows.

"You're not both going to fit on the back of my bike."

"Oh." She wrinkles her nose. "Cage?"

"Never heard that before? Bikers don't like being caged in. Anything that's not a motorcycle is a cage."

"Cage," she repeats. "Interesting."

From her tone it's hard to tell if that's a *good* interesting or a *you-must-be-psycho* interesting.

I can't wait to learn everything about her.

CHAPTER TEN

Emily

I SIGH as I watch Dex back his bike out of my driveway. He waits until he's rolled it into the road before firing it up. The rumble reaches the house and can be heard long after he's left my quiet street.

I drop the curtain, turn off the lights downstairs, and head toward Libby's room. Her door's slightly ajar but it's dark inside.

"Libby?" I whisper, tapping lightly.

"I'm awake," she mumbles.

"Do you want to talk?" I ask, crossing the room to sit on her bed.

She lets out a long, dramatic sigh and rolls to her back, staring at the ceiling. "There's nothing to talk about." She glances at her phone. "Mac hasn't even bothered to text and ask where I am or if I'm okay. She probably doesn't even realize I left."

"I'm sorry. So, what happened? Were any of your other friends there?"

"Caroline but she was all over the creepy older guys who brought the booze." She tugs the covers up to her neck. "One of them kept trying to put his arm around my shoulders and talk to me, but he stunk like beer and cigarettes. I dunno. He kept trying to give me an open beer and he was gross."

My heart thumps with fear. Did some asshole try to roofie my sister tonight? "You know not—"

"To ever take an open container from a stranger or leave my drink unattended. Yes, I know, Em." She sighs. "I could tell Mac was getting mad at me and Caroline thought I was acting like a baby, but everything about it felt *icky*."

"That's your intuition. Don't ever ignore it, okay?" I'm in a tough spot. If I shit-talk her friends too much, she'll just want to defend them and probably hang out with them more. But I can't help adding, "And real friends don't pressure you into doing things you're not comfortable doing."

"Ugh. I know."

"Sorry." I hold my hands up in the air. "I'm proud of you. You listened to your gut. Didn't let your friends bully you. And you got out of what sounds like a bad situation in a smart way."

"Thanks," she mumbles.

"I mean it. I didn't always listen to my inner voice. You know, Dad was so strict with me, I was afraid to call Mom and Dad when I was in a bad situation." I swallow hard and look away, my gaze landing on the bright-pink, gauzy curtains that have covered her windows since she was a little girl. Maybe it's time to update those. "You can always talk to me about anything, Libby."

She shoots upright and throws her arms around me, squeezing tight. "Thank you, Em," she whispers against my hair.

Emotion tightens my throat. I love my little sister so much and want to protect her from every bad thing in the world. "You're welcome, pudding."

"Ugh." She flops back against her mattress. "Was that Dex's bike I heard leaving?"

"Yeah."

"He didn't have to go because of me." A sly smile twitches at the corners of her mouth. "He could've stayed over."

"I don't sleep with a guy on a first date." *No, you just let him finger-bang and eat you into oblivion.*

Thank God Libby's room is too shadowy for her to see that my face is probably bright red.

"Well, my class trip to the city is coming up soon. You can have the whole house to yourself."

"Thanks, I'll keep that in mind. Oh, that reminds me—Dex asked if we wanted to go to Origin Park on Sunday."

"We?"

"Yes, he invited both of us."

She's quiet for a few seconds. "I don't want to be like a little kid tagging along."

"It's not like that."

"Will you be mad if I say no?"

"Of course not."

"I really just want to chill on Sunday." She twists the sheet between her fingers. "Study for a test I have and maybe read a little."

"Okay."

"Will you still go?" she asks.

"Do you want me to? I don't have to. We can binge-watch *Devil in Ohio* again."

"We can watch that anytime. You should totally go. He seems to like you."

"I like him too," I admit. *God, do I like him.*

A wistful smile ghosts over her lips. "You should've seen him when he showed up at the party." She shakes her head slightly, almost like she still can't believe it. "He looked ready to torch the place. Asked if anyone hurt me. I think if someone had, he would've ripped off their arms."

Now I like Dex even more. "He's kind of intense."

One corner of her mouth slides up. "So are you." She lets out a loud yawn.

I pat her arm and stand. "Night, kiddo."

"Night."

I run downstairs and methodically check to make sure each door and window in the house is locked. I grab my phone. No message from Dex yet.

Upstairs, I quickly change and slide into bed. I'm almost asleep when my phone softly dings.

Dex: Home.

In the dark and in my sleepy state, I'm not sure what to write back. Then it comes to me.

Thank you for tonight.

CONSCIOUSNESS SLOWLY CREEPS into my brain the next morning.

My phone blinks, announcing I already have a text.

Serena: How was dinner?

The answer requires a phone call. Not a text.

Serena's quiet, musical laughter greets me. "Oh boy, Emily. The answer must be good if you had to call to tell me how your not-a-date went."

I briefly close my eyes, thanking the universe for the happiness in Serena's voice. When we first met, she always seemed so unsure and fearful. Now, she's confident and glows like a damn light bulb every time I see her. I love it.

"First, how are you feeling?" I ask.

There's more laughter, then a rustling sound, like she's shifting to get comfortable. "Tired. Uncomfortable. Ready for this baby to make his grand entrance. Please talk to me about something other than babies."

"Serena." I take a long, dramatic pause. "The man made me come *three* times without either of us even taking off our clothes."

"Whoa." She chuckles softly. "Impressive."

"It was. He's just…"

"Wait a second," she gasps, and I roll my eyes, anticipating what she's about to say. "What happened to waiting six months to get to know him before things get physical?"

"Technically," I say with all the dignity I can gather, "I *have* known him for a few months, so it's not like I let some random dude in my panties."

"True," she agrees.

"And he's a friend of your husband-to-be, so theoretically, he's been vetted to a certain degree." Even though she can't see me, I lift my chin in indignation.

"Also true." She's quiet and in the background, I detect a *tick, tick, ticking,* and I can picture her tapping her nails against the phone as she contemplates what she wants to say. "Gray has a very high opinion of Dex. He seems to like the two of you together. A lot." She snorts. "Although I have a feeling he'll warn Dex that if he hurts you, there will be hell to pay."

"Aw, really?" Why does that make me feel all mushy inside? "Well, I guess I'll forgive him for moving you so far away from me."

"I'm not that far, Em. Once the baby's here—"

"You'll be too busy with new mom stuff."

"I'm never too busy for you," she corrects me, in her quiet but firm way. "You and Libby are always welcome here. Once I get the hang of the *new mom stuff*, I'll feel more comfortable driving up to visit more often."

Sure you will. But I don't want to guilt Serena for her happiness. I'm an adult. I can accept that things change. People move on.

Maybe one day, I will too.

CHAPTER ELEVEN

Dex

BY SUNDAY I'm like an addict who needs his fix of Emily. Usually, I look forward to weekend church at the clubhouse—sitting down and catching up with my brothers. Afterward, everyone—ol' ladies, kids, friends of the club—shares a meal together. Most weekends, Z and the guys from his charter join us and it's like an extended family reunion.

This week, I jog downstairs early, dressed and ready to leave as soon as Rock declares the official meeting over. Sparky and Stash are sprawled across the sectional—looks like they never made it to their basement cave last night. Random girls—some I recognize, some I don't—are draped over furniture or curled up in bundles of blankets on the floor. Some of my brothers really need to learn to sleep with their clothes on in public spaces. No one needs to see this shit in the morning. I toss a blanket over Hoot's junk as I navigate my way through the maze of bodies.

Shaking my head, I walk to the dining room for a cup of coffee before church.

Bright light streams through the uncovered windows. To my right, the bar counter's been set up better than a Starbuck's.

"Perfect," I mutter, grabbing a mug and pouring steaming black brew into it.

"You missed a wild night at Crystal Ball Friday," a soft voice says behind me.

"Morning, Swan." I turn and force a tight smile. Not a lick of guilt touches me for taking the night off. "I could say the same about *you* last night. Cece and Mona got into a fight over their lockers."

She crosses her thin arms over her chest and rolls her eyes. "I wouldn't have gotten in the middle of that, anyway."

Grinder pushes through the dining room door and heads straight for the coffee. Inwardly, I groan, not in the mood for another lecture. I scan the area. Too late to escape. He already saw me. But maybe there's someone else I can sic him on.

"Morning, Grinder. Is Serena with you?" Swan asks.

He gestures toward the hallway. "In the living room with the girls. I didn't want her walking all the way down here."

"I'll bring her some tea," Swan offers, scurrying behind the counter to search for supplies.

"Thanks, sweetheart." Grinder takes a quick swallow of coffee. "Seems mean to have my coffee in front of her at this stage. I'm gonna finish this here."

Lucky me.

Swan chuckles. "You're a good man."

As soon as she leaves, Grinder focuses his attention on me.

"Don't start," I warn. "I'm not in the mood."

"Are you ever?" he asks. "What are you afraid I'm gonna start?"

"I don't need any life advice today."

His lips quirk into a knowing smile. "Guess not. From what I hear, you're quite...*skilled.*"

I don't want to contemplate the implication of his statement.

Then it hits me. Did Emily give Serena details about the other night?

I glance down at my boots, trying to wipe the smirk off my face.

"Glad things are going well," Grinder says. "But I'd be remiss if I didn't warn you."

Here we go again. "Warn me about what, old man?"

"Keep calling me old, you little shithead. You're gonna be my age one day. Ain't gonna be so funny, then."

I bite the inside of my cheek to stop myself from laughing. "You'll *still* be older."

He pokes me in the chest. Older or not, Grinder's got some weight behind the gesture.

More people pour into the dining room but Grinder ignores the increase in noise.

I glance down at his finger and raise an eyebrow. "I have too much respect for you to kick your ass, Grinder. But don't push your luck."

He grunts and drops his hand. "I know you'd never intentionally hurt her but if you break Emily's heart, I'm gonna break something of yours." He slides his gaze over me as if he's picking out which body part he'll snap in half.

"Overstep much?" I cross my arms over my chest.

"That girl's had it rough. And she's been a good friend to Serena. So yeah, I've got strong feelings on this subject."

"Correct me if I'm wrong, Father Time." I tap my finger against my chin in a slow, dickish way. "But haven't you been busting my nuts for months about the need for me to *rust or ride*? You encouraged me to spend time with Emily and now you're *threatening* me when I'm taking your advice?" I'm more annoyed than angry. Maybe a little amused by the seriousness of his lecture. "You going senile already?"

He ignores the dig and holds up his hands in an unconvincing show of surrender. "I said what needed to be said. Just because she doesn't have any family besides her sixteen-year-old sister doesn't mean no one's looking out for her. That's all."

"I'm aware." I hold my hands up to my eyes like a pair of binoculars. "*I'm* the one you asked to stake out her house when we were worried Grillo might harass her, or did you forget that?"

"I didn't forget shit." He glances at the coffee cup in his hand, sets it on the counter, then claps my shoulder. "You're right. I'm sorry. That was harsh. I worry about Emily. She and her sister are all by themselves. I feel guilty I moved Serena so far away from them."

I stand there and blink. Pre-prison Grinder apologized to no one for anything. And I'm shocked he's even acquainted with guilt let alone able to identify the emotion out loud.

"Whoa." Rav sneaks up behind Grinder and wraps an arm around his shoulders. "You threatening a brother? Over a civilian woman? What's this club coming to?"

"Mind your business," Grinder growls, shaking off Rav's arm.

Rav's like a perv with a porno when he butts into a conversation. He scratches his head and a devious smile flashes over his face. "Emily's that banging redhead, right? She's who you two are beefing over?"

"There's no beef, jackass," Grinder says.

"Didn't she wear a dress that went down to her ankles to Teller's wedding?" He cringes. "Girl that uptight needs a good yank on her ponytail." Rav grabs a fistful of air and jerks his fist to demonstrate.

Blind fury shoots through my veins, propelling my hand into Rav's chest, slamming him into the wall next to the bar. "Watch your mouth when you talk about her."

"Christ, Ravage, you got a damn death wish?" Grinder asks.

Rav giggles like an idiot hopped up on helium. "You don't understand, G." Rav slaps my arm. "Our boy Dex is a monk." He bites his lip and flicks his gaze toward the ceiling. "Or maybe a groundhog. Pokes his head out once a year to get his dick wet then goes back in his cave."

Grinder all but snarls at him. "The grown-ups are trying to have a conversation here. Fuck off."

I release Rav. Getting pissed will just encourage him to be a bigger asshole.

"Just tell me it's a fling," Rav pleads with me. He throws a scowl at Grinder, then one at Wrath, who has his back to us while he pours his own cup of coffee. "I can't handle another brother handing his balls over to a female."

"Stop obsessing about everyone else's balls, Rav," Wrath warns without glancing our way. "I'd light my nuts on fire before I ever let you suck on them."

Grinder chokes. "That's an image I didn't need in my head."

"Same, brother," I mutter.

"I'm not..." Rav sputters, "I don't... That's not..."

"*Yeaaaah.*" I draw out the word to a painfully mocking length. "The more you protest, the more I'm thinking Wrath's onto something."

"Fuck this." Rav grabs a can of Coke off the bar and stomps away. "You'll be sorry one day," he calls over his shoulder.

Wrath grins wide and smug as he approaches us. "That was fun." He claps Grinder's shoulder. "You're not harassing my road captain, are you?"

I doubt Wrath's really concerned Grinder might be pestering me. More like Wrath wants to join in on the harassment.

"Can't two brothers have a private conversation?" Grinder asks.

Wrath takes a long, slow, sarcastic look around the dining room. "In a public space? No."

Ignoring Wrath, Grinder points at me. "I said what I needed to say."

"So did I."

"I'll see you at the table," Grinder says.

Wrath watches him walk away, then turns to me. Amusement flickers in his eyes. "So, what'd I miss?"

"Nothing. I was at Emily's the other night and now he wants to play father protector."

Wrath's forehead wrinkles into a skeptical frown. "Wasn't he trying to set you two up a few weeks ago?"

"Yep." I brace myself for the barrage of annoying comments Wrath's about to lob at me.

But he stands there and sips his coffee.

"What?" I prompt. "No witty commentary on my life?"

He raises one blond eyebrow. "Nope."

Christ, I almost think I'd prefer some of Wrath's snark. His indifference feels too close to pity.

"Think you'll go out on the road as part of Shelby's security team again next summer?" he asks.

The question stops me for a second. I haven't thought that far ahead. "If Rooster needs me, yeah. Rav and Bricks can handle Crystal Ball for a few weeks." At Rooster's request, I'd toured with Shelby most of last summer. CB hadn't been as much of a disaster as I'd expected when I returned. "It really depends on what Rock needs around here, though."

He nods.

"Are you and Trinity thinking of riding with them again?" I ask.

"Shelby asked if Trin would be her official photographer." He glances over his shoulder. "And I think Trinity would prefer to stay for the whole tour."

"That's a good idea. Can Furious spare you for that long?"

He shrugs. "With the new baby, Murphy and Heidi aren't going on the road. He and Jake can handle Furious by themselves."

"Look at you," I joke. "The big boss leaving your minions in charge."

"It's good to be king." More seriously he adds, "I'd do the same for them if they asked."

"I know you would." As much as he enjoys being obnoxious, Wrath's never let a brother down.

As if he'd been summoned, our ginger VP muscles into the dining room and claps his hands loud enough to get everyone's attention. "Let's go! Church in five."

"Is Rock even here yet?" Wrath shouts.

Murphy scowls in our direction. "Just get your big ass to the table."

I choke on a laugh. A couple of years ago Murphy wouldn't have dared to throw attitude at Wrath.

Wrath turns toward me with an amused smirk on his face. "He seems to be growing into that VP patch. I'm torn between being proud of him and wanting to punch him."

"You can be both. He's doing good." *I* was damn proud of Murphy. Being a good husband and father came naturally to him. Stepping out of Teller's shadow, standing up to Wrath, and filling Z's shoes as our VP— none of *that* was easy. Yet, he was doing it and still found time to help me adjust to my position as the club's road captain. He'd be pissed if I complimented him out loud, but I hold a lot of respect for my younger brother. Wrath does too, even if he hates to admit it.

Wrath takes his time finishing his coffee. While he loves to irritate Rock, I don't. I slap his shoulder. "See you in there."

I nod and say hello to brothers from Downstate as I pass them. In the living room, the old ladies have taken over the corner sectional, laughing and catching up with each other. Serena's resting with her head on Shelby's shoulder. Lilly's holding Rock and Hope's daughter on her lap while Trinity plays with Z and Lilly's son. I flick a quick wave their way. Watching them makes me wish I'd invited Emily up here today.

Too soon.

I run into Teller outside the chapel. "Hey, brother." I tilt my head toward the girls. "Charlotte okay? She didn't come up with you?"

"She's over at Heidi's." He flashes a quick, tight smile. "Going through baby stuff."

"That's good." I try to fake some interest. "Twins will be here before you know it."

"That's what I'm afraid of." He laughs and tilts his head toward the war room. "Rock's in a mood. We better get to the table."

"What'd you do now?"

Teller throws me a wounded smirk. "Now, why do you assume it's my fault?"

"Seems you enjoy pushing his buttons these days."

"Isn't that what I'm supposed to do?"

"As his son?" I lift an eyebrow. "The treasurer? Or his club brother?"

The smirk slides off his face.

I rest my hand on his shoulder. "I get that it's probably still complicated. But try not to push him too hard."

He nods slowly. "Thanks, brother."

Is he sincere? Hard to tell with him sometimes.

I make my way to my seat at the table. Murphy's already across from me. Teller slaps his buddy's shoulder as he takes his chair next to him. Bricks, Stash, and Sparky all take their seats on the other side.

A heavy hand drops on my shoulder and the chair on my right jerks out from under the table. I don't have to tip my head to know it's Ravage. He lands like a heavy sack of potatoes, kicking his feet out in front of him.

"You ditching me again today?" he asks.

Please don't say I'm needed at Crystal Ball. Not today. "Can you get by without me?"

"Just surprised you trust me so much lately, that's all."

"No one's more surprised than I am," I mutter.

Grinder taps Ravage's shoulder and waves his hand in a get-the-fuck-out-of-my-way gesture. Rav heaves a heavy sigh, picks his big frame out of the chair, and flops into the next one down. "Only for you, old man," he grumbles.

I side-eye Grinder. "If you're going to offer more advice, you might as well move on down to sit next to your prez." I lift my chin at Z all the way at the end of our long wooden table.

Z nods at me. "You need me to reel the old man in?"

"I'll reel you the fuck in," Grinder snaps. "Don't talk about me like I ain't sittin' right here."

As Z opens his mouth to respond, the door behind me slams shut. Wrath drops into his chair on my left and Rock takes his place at the head of the table.

"Simmer down," Rock says, his voice carrying above the chatter like a sledgehammer.

Things settle quickly. Rock nods to Teller first.

Teller sits forward. "Nothing exciting to report. The market's taken a dip but I have the club's assets spread around enough that we shouldn't feel it too much." He slides a sheet of paper into the middle of the table. "I can stay to discuss it in depth with anyone who has questions after church."

No one ever takes Teller up on this offer. And I'm not surprised he isn't going into more detail, since Z's whole crew is here.

Hustler, the downstate treasurer, raises his hand. "You mind if I pick your brain after church?"

"You got it, brother," Teller answers with a quick nod.

Poor Hustler. Brother could dig around in Teller's brain for years and still never figure out complex financial strategies. Few MCs are lucky enough to have someone with a knack for investing the way Teller does. It's benefited our charter mightily, especially in the last few years. Probably one of the reasons he gets away with running his mouth so often.

"Dex?" Rock taps the table as if this isn't the first time he's asked me a question. "CB?" he prompts.

"Good."

He raises an eyebrow, waiting for me to continue.

"Uh." I sit up straighter. "Amateur night is still popular. We had an issue with one of our girls—"

"You track the guy down?" Z asks.

"Not yet."

"Don't forget to invite me." Z throws me a wounded puppy face.

"You won't go alone," Rock says to me as if he expects no argument.

"Probably take Vapor with me." I glance at Z. "If it's something time sensitive and I can't wait for you to get up here."

"I'm two hours away, not on the moon," Z grumbles.

"You have enough to do," Rock says to Z. "Smaller jobs like this are the whole point of the support club."

Z taps his president patch. "Prez or not, I'm okay with gettin' my hands dirty."

"We don't need to know what you and your ol' lady do in the dark, Prez," Butcher says.

"Shut up," Z laughs.

At least Z's antics take Rock's interest off of me. He moves to Wrath next, then Murphy, then turns the meeting over to Z.

I perk up when Rooster goes over numbers for their porn production company.

"Has Stella gotten over her snit?" I ask. "We could use her as a featured dancer at CB again."

Z groans.

"I'll ask," Rooster promises. "But I wouldn't get your hopes up." He slides his gaze to Z and back to me. "She hasn't exactly gotten easier to deal with since Sway took off."

"I'm not surprised." I shrug. "It was just a thought."

"You got a thing for our girl?" Butcher asks.

"No." Christ, Stella's the last person I'd want to be involved with. But she brought a different clientele to Crystal Ball.

"Anything else?" Rock asks.

No one raises their hand, so Rock dismisses us.

I press my hands against the table and push my chair back.

"Dex?"

I glance at Rock. Concern seems to be brewing in his eyes. But he's almost cautious as he asks me to stay. "Got a minute?"

Not really. But I can't exactly say no to my president without a solid reason.

"Sure." I stand and push in my chair, moving past Wrath. Rock takes a few steps away from the table, toward the window. Usually, he stays at the table for these after-church talks with us. "What's up, Prez?"

"How's everything going?"

"Uh, fine." I sweep my hand toward the table. "Like I said—"

"With *you?* How are things?"

"Good," I answer immediately. For the first time in years, it doesn't feel like a lie. "I'm supposed to go pick up Emily." *So could we hurry this up?*

He lifts an eyebrow. "Yeah?"

For some reason, his interest sends unease coursing through me. "Yeah. Thinking of taking her out to Eraser's place one night." Might as well assure him that I'm not letting my club responsibilities slide.

"She into race cars?"

"Don't know yet. But I need to check up on those guys if we want them to be our support club."

"Think we'll make them official soon?"

Soon would be nice. I've never been able to get a read on how Rock really feels about the support club. Whether he's doing it to keep Priest, our national president, off our backs, or he thinks it's the next logical step in securing our upstate New York territory now that the Vipers MC and Wolf Knights MC are no longer in the area.

"I think they're ready," I say with conviction.

"Have they come up with a name, colors?"

I snort. "I think I know what name they're going with." It was truly perfect for many reasons.

A smirk twists his mouth. "Surprise me."

"Will do."

"Go on." He cocks his head toward the door. "If anyone's earned a day off, it's you."

"Thanks." I don't know why that makes me feel guilty, but I shake it off.

Time to see Emily.

I can't remember the last time I looked forward to seeing someone this much.

CHAPTER TWELVE

Emily

"Does this look okay?" I ask Libby, hating the awful example I'm setting for her. I want to project strength and confidence to my little sister. Not a woman who worries about her appearance. Why am I so damn nervous about my date?

"You look great." Libby squints at my leggings. "I'm just surprised you're not wearing a dress on a date."

I glance down at my tight, black hiking leggings. "We're going to be walking around a bunch of rocks." I reach into my closet and grab a teal half-zip sweatshirt and slip it over my tank top. "Are you sure you don't want to come with us?"

A hint of her sneaky smile curves her lips. "No way. I don't want to be the third wheel."

"You wouldn't be a third wheel." I wish she'd change her mind but I don't want to beg. Not that I don't want to be alone with Dex, I just hate leaving Libby alone to go on a date. It's not like me.

She's sixteen. She can be alone for an afternoon. It's okay.

I trust *her*. I don't trust the rest of the world.

"Em, I'm fine. Honest." She holds up her hands. "I have plenty of homework and television to keep me occupied. I won't throw any wild parties."

I roll my eyes. "I know you better than that, Libby."

It still feels wrong to choose a date over my sister.

91

The doorbell chimes.

"I'll get it." Libby flashes a devilish grin.

"No way." I rush past her, my socks sliding over the hardwood floors. Damn, my hiking sneakers better be in the hall closet.

Libby's hot on my tail all the way down the stairs but throws herself onto the couch in the living room. With her back against the arm, she faces the front door with an evil little grin.

"Well, go on." She sweeps her hand toward the entryway. "Don't keep the man waiting."

Gritting my teeth, I check to make sure it's him, then practically twist the knob off in my eagerness to open the door.

And there he is. Casually standing on my porch with a small, white paper bag in one hand. Black jeans that fit perfectly and a tight, plain black T-shirt stretched over his chest under an unbuttoned fleece-lined, blue plaid, flannel shirt. No leather vest today. His serious expression melts into a warm smile as soon as our eyes meet.

"Hey, Emily," he says in the deep, rumbling voice that turns my insides to lava.

"Hey," I murmur, stepping back to let him inside. "Come in. I just need to find my shoes."

With his free hand, he reaches out and curls his arm around my waist, drawing me closer. "Let me say hello properly, first."

I open my mouth to answer but he presses his lips against mine, stealing my words and breath. Caught off guard, I rest my palm against his chest, almost falling against him.

"That's better," he says against my lips, pulling away slightly.

"Yes, that's better," I mimic, feeling like a cartoon character with love birds chirping and circling my head.

"*A-hem.*" Libby clears her throat—loudly.

Dex briefly closes his eyes, an amused smile flickering over his face. He tilts his head, staring past me. "Hey, Libby."

"Hello, Dex. How do my sister's tonsils taste?"

"Libby!" I whirl around, staring daggers at her.

Dex rumbles with laughter. "Are you sure you don't want to come with us today? I brought an SUV. There's plenty of room."

I can't believe he'd still ask after her tonsils comment.

"No, I'm good." She pats her laptop. "Full day."

He holds up the white paper bag. "In that case, how about some study snacks?"

Libby sits up, eyebrows raised, eyes blazing with interest. "You have my attention."

His free hand curls around mine and he drags me into the living room, stopping at the back of the couch to pass the bag to Libby. "Emily said you like fluffernutters. I saw these and had to get them for you."

She frowns as she accepts the bag and rips it open. Inside, there's a small, shiny white box with the label of a local, family-owned candy store. Pricey place. My parents used to fill our Easter baskets with chocolate bunnies and lambs from there every year. I doubt Libby even remembers. I haven't been there since they died.

My pulse thunders though my ears, blocking out everything else for a moment.

"Ohmygod!" Libby squeals, pulling me into the present. "What the..."

"They're marshmallows, covered in peanut butter and chocolate," Dex explains.

Inside the white box, six fat chocolate-covered marshmallows sit in two neat rows. Libby plucks one out of the box, biting it in half.

"You may have my sister for the afternoon, Dex," she mumbles around a mouthful of the treat.

"I have something for you, too," Dex whispers in my ear.

Tears sting my eyes. I couldn't care less about treats. Dex remembered an off-handed comment about my sister and went out of his way to bring her something he knew she'd like. He could have brought me two dozen long-stemmed roses and I'd still find *this* more romantic.

Who is this man?

"I'll be home by dinner." I glance at Dex to confirm.

"We can pick up dinner on the way back." He glances at Libby. "Any requests?"

She raises two hopeful eyebrows. "Pizza?"

"There's a great place right off the Thruway," Dex says. "We might have to throw it in the oven by the time we get here, though."

"That works," Libby says. "Em and I are masters at reheating pizza."

While they discuss toppings, I search for my hiking sneakers. "*Aha!*" I find them hiding under a fallen sweatshirt and shove them on my feet.

"I'm ready." I return to the couch, leaning over the back to wrap my sister in a hug. "Call me, if anything..."

Anxiety churns in my stomach. Am I really leaving my baby sister alone for the afternoon?

She wriggles out of my hug and pats my arm. "I'll be fine, Em." Her serious eyes meet mine. "Really," she whispers. "Go. Have fun."

Dex grabs a notepad off one of the end tables and scribbles something, then rips off a page and hands it to Libby. "That's my number. And that's my niece's number—Juliet. She and her husband don't live too far from here. We'll be about an hour away, so if anything urgent comes up, don't hesitate to call them. Okay?"

Libby stares at the paper. Several smart-ass remarks seem to form on her lips but finally she nods and looks up at Dex. "Okay. I will. Thanks."

That's it. I'm done. If I thought I was smitten with Dex before, I was dead wrong.

It may seem like a few small gestures, but they mean *everything*. His thoughtful actions prove he understands how important Libby is to me.

Dammit. I'm already falling in love with him.

CHAPTER THIRTEEN

Dex

OUTSIDE, the cool air slaps me in the face. Maybe it's too cold for outdoor activity today? Nah, it'll be warmer downstate. Hopefully.

We stop at the truck and I open the passenger-side door.

Emily leans up on her tiptoes. "Thank you," she whispers in my ear.

"For?"

Her eyes seem to search my face, like she can't put her thoughts into words. "You seem to understand…my situation." She tilts her head toward the house. "Thanks for giving her someone nearby to call. Just in case. I…I worry a lot."

"Hey." I rest my hand on her shoulder. "I get it. We don't have to go far if you're not comfortable. We can do something more local."

"No. It's not that far. Like you said, an hour." A quick smile flickers over her glossy pink lips. "I've been looking forward to this."

"So have I." Every second I've been away from her has left me craving her more and more.

I help her into the truck, then jog to the driver's side.

"This is nice." She runs her hand over the carbon fiber dashboard.

"Thanks." I slant a look her way. "I prefer two wheels but four gets the job done sometimes, too."

"Well, I appreciate it. Trying to include Libby, I mean."

The wobble in her voice seems like she's close to crying.

My hand hesitates over the ignition. "Are you sure you're okay?"

"What? Yes." She flashes a quick smile, then reaches over, brushing her hand over my leg. "I'm more than okay. I'm with you."

What's that warmth sliding through my chest? Affection?

I clear my throat and start the truck. "Good."

Emily

As we drive away from the house, Dex's gaze sweeps over the yard and driveway. "A lot of house to take care of."

"Tell me about it." I sigh. "I'll probably sell it after Libby leaves for college. But after everything...well, I want her to have a stable home."

"I can understand that. You said it was your aunt's house? So you didn't grow up here?"

"No, but my dad and his sister were close. We spent all our holidays here when I was a kid." I smile fondly as warm memories return. "We moved a lot when I was little. So, Aunt Kimmie's place was always a constant."

"Was your dad in the military?"

"No." I swallow hard. "My parents were high school sweethearts. First love. All that. Accidentally got knocked up their senior year. I was the *oops baby* that derailed their futures." I let out a nervous laugh. "Libby was the kid they planned for and were excited about."

Wow, I've never been able to express those feelings to anyone before.

Dex is silent.

Shit. Why'd I have to expose emotional scars within the first twenty minutes of our date?

His hands remain so tightly wrapped around the steering wheel, his knuckles are white.

"Sorry, was that too much info?" I shift my gaze to my pants, focusing on a stubborn piece of lint that just won't come off no matter how hard I pluck at it.

"No." He clears his throat. "*I* married my first...my high school—"

"Wait, you're married?" My heart thuds. Why am I just learning this now?

"No," he says in a dull voice. "She died years ago."

"Oh. Jesus. Oh my God. I'm so sorry." How is it possible this keeps getting worse and worse? I made it sound like getting married young was the worst thing in the world. Probably offended him. I won't be surprised if he turns this thing around and drops me off at the curb.

"Sorry. It just hit a little close." He glances over. "Continue. I'm sure you didn't derail their lives."

So many follow-up questions I'm burning to ask. But it feels like he just slammed the lid closed on the subject of his marriage. And I've already stuck my foot in my mouth; I'd rather not eat my entire leg.

"That's how they made me feel. I'm sure it wasn't intentional," I say quietly. "They wanted Libby so bad. Were so excited about her." I let out a sad snort. "At least I was old enough to be the perfect built-in babysitter."

"So you were taking care of Libby long before your parents died?" he asks.

"I didn't mind," I say quickly, hating to sound like I'm complaining. "I loved her the second I saw her."

"I bet she was a cute kid."

"Oh yeah." My lips curve at the memory of the first time I held her. "The cutest. I didn't resent her until I was a teenager."

"Why's that? I'd think you'd be even more protective of her."

"I was," I say slowly. "But my mom made me take Libby everywhere. If I wanted to hang with my friends, I had to take Libby. I guess she thought having to look after my sister would keep me out of trouble."

From the corner of my eye, I catch him frowning. "Depending on what kind of teenager you were, that could've been dangerous for your sister."

I sense of note of disapproval and have the urge to defend my mom. "Well, for a while it worked." I snort at the memory. "Especially once Libby was old enough to tattle to my mom whenever I spoke to boys."

Now, it's a cute, funny memory. Back then I wanted to strangle my little sister.

A thoughtful frown still creases his forehead.

"They kept me busy taking her to all the after-school activities they couldn't afford for me when I was little—ballet, piano, singing lessons." Damn, why do I sound so bitter about it?

I open my mouth, dying to ask him about his wife but unable to think of anything that won't be rude or invasive. And in the back of my mind a thought tries to form that I have to push away.

I don't want to exist in the shadow of his first, dead love.

There it is. And now that it's a complete thought, it won't go away. It takes on a life and shape of its own.

Why is it, the more I try *not* to think about something, the more it taunts me?

Dex

Telling Emily about Debbie doesn't feel as awful as I expected. I *want* her to know something about my past that I rarely share with anyone.

Emily's silence on the subject is also a relief. I may not mind sharing that bit of information with her, but the details are too much.

My chest aches listening to her try to make light of being her sister's caretaker since she was a kid.

"So, all those activities, and she settled on theater?" I ask to keep the conversation centered on Emily.

For the first time in a long time, I'm focused on the road ahead instead of the wreckage behind me. I'm enjoying time with someone outside of work or my club and I want it to remain that simple.

"Oh yeah. All those classes were good preparation."

She falls quiet again. Maybe that's a topic I should quit poking at.

"Did you get the full story of what happened at that party?"

"I think so. Some older boys brought beer. One kept trying to get her to drink it. Her friends were annoyed with her, etc."

"She doesn't give in to peer pressure easily, huh?"

"No, thank God." She blows out a relieved breath. "I've been drilling it into her head to think for herself and listen to her intuition since she was little."

Her story of caring for Libby from such a young age only increases my affection for her. Emily's loyal. Fiercely protective. Qualities I admire.

"How's the car been running?" I ask.

"Tip-top. Whatever Griff did to it, I think it's running better than before."

"He's a gearhead. Wouldn't surprise me at all if he tweaked a few other things besides the starter."

"That was awfully nice of him. And you," she adds quickly.

I shrug off the comment. I didn't do anything special. Listening to Emily helps the drive go by fast. Before I know it, I'm signaling for the exit.

Emily

"Sorry I babbled so much." I rub my hands over my pants. Why is it so easy to open my mouth and say all the dumb things that come to mind around him?

"I like listening to you," Dex says.

"Thanks," I murmur, heat searing my face.

He turns onto a narrow dirt road. Branches smack at the windshield and he curses under his breath.

"They don't seem to keep up on the grounds maintenance very well," I joke to lighten up the mood a little.

"I guess not."

He stops short, jolting me forward a bit.

I take my eyes off him and stare at the rusty chain blocking the rest of the road. A small metal sign reads "closed" in big, orange letters.

Dex huffs a cynical laugh. "Well, shit. In all my planning, it never occurred to me to make sure they were actually *open* today."

He says it jokingly but I sense he's genuinely upset. "Don't feel too bad," I say. "I did look up the place and *still* didn't notice they weren't open."

"Were you worried I was dragging you off into the middle of nowhere?" he teases.

"No." I glance at my sneakers. "I wanted to dress appropriately."

"You're perfect." He shifts the truck into park and glances over his shoulder. "Well, where should we go now? I have lunch in the back. Picnic in the woods okay with you?"

I glance around. We're surrounded by woods. Majestic pines, maple trees, oaks, and others I can't name. Some stand stark naked, their branches pointing at the sky and their leaves scattered on the ground. Not a person in sight.

Beyond the trees, what looks like a house breaks up the scenery. "What if a werewolf tries to eat us?"

"Werewolf?" He chuckles. "I'll protect you."

Dex shifts into drive and eases the truck off the road, parking under a large maple tree.

"Do you think we'll get yelled at for trespassing?"

"If we do, we'll leave." He shrugs, completely unconcerned.

"I'm a bit of a rule follower."

"And I'm a bit of a rule breaker." He opens his door and steps out. "We make a good pair."

Peering inside the cab, he studies me for a moment. "We're not going to wreck anything. We're not even sneaking into the park. Just two would-be visitors turned away at the gate, looking for a lunch spot."

He's right. I'm being silly. "Okay."

He shuts his door with a quiet *thump*. I reach down and grab my purse, digging through it for a lip balm and quickly swipe it over my lips, then tuck it in my pocket.

My door opens and Dex holds out his hand. He's so sweet. In a scowling, wide-shouldered, protective hero sort of way. Strength and confidence always seem to radiate from him.

His big, warm hand closes over mine and he guides me down from the truck. "So where is the picnic?" I ask.

His gaze roams over me, like I'm the one on the menu for the afternoon. Then he meets my questioning stare. The corners of his mouth lift. "Right here."

He opens the back door and pulls out what looks like a backpack and a fuzzy, red-and-black plaid blanket. He slings the bulky pack over one shoulder and holds out his hand. "Tell me when you see a place that looks comfortable."

I'm still worried we're going to get yelled at for sneaking onto someone's property, so I search for a clear spot close to the truck.

"There?" I point to a large gray rock, covered in moss. A beam of sunlight stabs through the canopy of branches, lighting up the area.

"Looks good," Dex agrees.

When we reach the rock, Dex spreads out the blanket, and I realize he's actually brought two blankets. He folds the other one into a square for us to sit on. "Extra padding," he explains.

"Smart move." Even with the layers of blankets, my butt feels every bump of the cold, hard ground beneath us. I tip my head back and stare at the light-blue sky through the branches. "It's so pretty. And peaceful here."

"You'd like our main clubhouse." He scans the trees and grass around us. "It's on a lot of acreage. Kinda like this place."

"Why didn't we picnic up there?"

"I wasn't sure you'd want to. Everyone would be in our business, for one thing." He reaches for the backpack and unzips it.

One by one, he pulls out sub sandwiches wrapped in white paper, side salads, utensils, paper plates, and a bottle of sparkling water.

He twists the cap off the water and hands it to me, then pulls out a lemon.

"You remembered I like lemons?" I ask, trying to force the awe out of my voice and failing. It's a small thing, really. I don't know why I'm making such a big deal out of it, but I'm touched. No one's ever paid attention to my likes or dislikes before.

"You said you like them with everything." He pulls a pocketknife from his jeans and neatly cuts a wedge from the fruit, holding it out to me.

"Thank you." I take it and squeeze the juice into my bottle.

"And for dessert," he announces, carefully sliding a clear, square box out of the bag, "lemon-lavender cream cake."

"Oh my God." I stare at the box, my mouth already watering. "That sounds amazing."

He grins as if he's happy he chose the right cake. "I wasn't sure about the lavender part—"

"No. It sounds really good." It's just a piece of cake but the care he took in choosing everything touches me. I haven't been on a lot of thoughtful dates. Well, any dates recently.

"I wasn't sure if you're a wine drinker or not, but I brought a bottle of white wine, too," he offers.

"Sometimes, I do."

He reaches inside the bag again and pulls out a bottle, then two stemless wine cups.

"These are pretty." I pick up one of the cups, admiring the holographic shine in the sunlight.

He chuckles softly. "Trinity told me the color is 'unicorn skin.'"

"Trinity..." I blink, recognizing the name. "I met her at Serena's baby shower. She's hilarious. You asked her for help with our picnic?"

He shrugs. "I don't necessarily have to *ask*. Everyone always knows what you're up to." Any annoyance he might have about his nosy family is negated by the smile on his face. "I'm glad you get along with the girls."

The way he says it almost sounds as if I passed some sort of test with his brothers' wives. "They were all really nice." I flick my gaze to the sky and smile. "And of course, my sister *adores* Shelby."

He rumbles with laughter and hands me one of the sandwiches. "She's hard not to like. Spent most of last summer out on the road with her. Rooster had a bunch of us working security for the tour. She's genuine and down-to-earth. On and off the stage."

Maybe other women would be jealous of the affectionate way Dex talks about the women in his life but the respect he has for his brothers' wives and girlfriends shines through his words. Nothing weird or sexual about it. It only makes me like him more.

"That must have been a blast." I slowly unwrap my sub, catching pieces of lettuce that try to escape and tucking them back inside. "Spending time in all those different cities."

"We had fun. But it was work. Not a lot of time to explore each location when you have to keep to a schedule."

"Ah, yeah. That would take a little of the fun out of it. I'm just jealous you got to see so much of the country."

"You've never left New York?" he asks, biting into his sandwich.

"No, I have. We went to Disney when Libby was like five. I was a teenager, so not my first choice of vacation." I huff out a sad laugh, remembering what an absolute bitch I was to my parents that summer. Wishing so much I could rewind time and…

"Where'd you go, Em?" Dex rubs his thumb over the back of my hand, drawing my attention to the present.

"Nowhere. Just remembering how much I fought with my parents that summer. And…I really wish I hadn't now."

"You must have some good memories?"

I stare straight ahead, allowing a few events to come to mind. "I do."

"Focus on the good times." In a lower voice he adds, "Regret will eat you alive if you let it."

"It sounds like you know from firsthand experience."

"You could say that." He focuses on his lunch, and I take that as a cue not to probe for more information.

And enjoy our day together instead.

CHAPTER FOURTEEN

Dex

Is it wrong to be this fascinated by one woman? One minute she's confident and breezy. The next, she looks so damn sad and vulnerable, I want to pull her into my arms, swear to protect her, and heal all her past hurts.

"Ready for cake?" I ask, wanting to see her eyes light up again.

"Ooo, yes please." She folds the wrapper from her sandwich and tucks it in an empty paper bag. A woman with a neat streak wider than my own. Is there anything I don't like about her?

She holds out her hands, eagerly wiggling her fingers. I pass her the box and a plastic fork.

"What about you?" she asks as she pops the lid open with a loud, plastic crackle.

"Nah." My gaze roams over her face, dipping to her neck and lower. "I prefer a different kind of sweet."

Pink rushes over her cheeks and she drops her gaze to the cake, poking her fork into the soft, light-yellow frosting. She lifts a big chunk to her mouth, slowly taking a taste.

"Mmm." She closes her eyes. "Perfect blend of tart and sweet."

Now I'm happy I took the extra time to check out the desserts when I picked up our lunch. I'm going to give her a complex from watching her lick every crumb and dot of frosting off that damn fork.

"You have frosting on your cheek." I reach over and brush my thumb over the spot. Without thinking I lick the frosting from my finger.

"Is that how I have to convince you to try it?" she teases, smearing frosting over her bottom lip.

"Yeah, that works." I grab her by the hips, dragging her into my lap so she's facing me.

She digs into the cake and offers me a bite. Sweet sugary flavor explodes in my mouth, followed by a sharp tartness. "It's good."

We finish the cake like that. Her forking bits in my mouth, then taking a bite for herself. I tug the zipper of her sweatshirt down, licking stray crumbs from her chest.

After lunch, Emily helps me pick everything up and pack it away. I stand and then offer her my hand to pull her off the ground.

"See, it's like we were never even here," I say, bending over to fold the blankets.

"Thank you for this." She clutches her stomach. "Everything was so good, I don't know if I can move."

"Well, I *thought* we'd be walking it off in the park," I grumble, still mad at myself for not checking to make sure the damn place was open.

At least I got the menu right.

"It's fine." Emily steps closer, brushing up against my arm. "This turned out really nice. Maybe we can try to come back another time?"

The hopeful lilt in her voice reassures me that I didn't fuck up too bad. "I'd like that. I'll call ahead to be sure they're open."

Her lips twist as if she's trying not to laugh. "Deal."

Wind rustles through the trees, picking up her hair and tossing it around her face. It reminds me of the day we ran into each other in the cemetery. Feeling conflicted, I try to push the thought away.

I brush the wild strands of hair from her cheek and lean down, focusing on Emily here and now in the present. Her eyes widen a second before I press my lips to hers. She gasps and braces her hand against my shoulder, drawing me closer.

The bag and blankets in my hand hit the ground with a muted thud and I wrap my arms around her, lifting her slightly off the ground.

She sighs and sinks into the kiss. She tastes like lemon and sweetness.

After a few surreal moments, she pulls away, breathing hard. She smiles up at me and adjusts her arms around my neck. I realize I'm still holding her and set her down.

"That was better than dessert," she says, sliding her tongue along her bottom lip. "And I really liked that cake."

Laughing, I grab our stuff and take her hand. "Better than cake, huh? I'm flattered."

She laughs, a honey-sweet, raspy chuckle, and bumps against me as we walk to the truck. I can't seem to get enough of her touch or the sound of her voice.

At the truck, I open the back door and toss the bag and blankets inside. Emily stands by her open door watching me.

"You all right?" I ask.

She ducks her head and shrugs. "I just like watching you *do* stuff."

It's sweet and strokes my ego at the same time. "Oh yeah?"

"Is that weird?"

"Nope."

We settle into the truck. I'm about to start the engine when she says my name.

I glance over.

"Thank you."

I lean over to kiss her. A quick "you're welcome" kiss. But she meets me halfway. Our lips touch and it's a spark lighting a fuse. She moans and twists her body, draping half her body over the console in the middle, but doesn't break the kiss. I grip her under her arms and half pull, half drag her to my side.

It's a tight fit but I can't force myself to stop and suggest we move this somewhere else. I slide my hand in the crack between my seat and the door, searching for the button that will move my seat back. I hit the wrong one and end up reclining a few inches instead.

She rolls her hips, pressing herself right into my growing erection. I let out a groan, breaking our kiss, but she doesn't stop the relentless movements.

Fuck, she's killing me. I can't. Emily deserves better than a quick, sloppy fuck in the front seat of my truck.

"Emily," I groan, pushing her back enough to see her face. "Not in the truck. Not the first time, anyway."

The corners of her mouth twitch and she bites her bottom lip. "That implies there will be a second, third, and fourth time."

I lean in and brush my lips against hers. "Definitely."

She shifts herself back just enough to slip her hand between us and palm my erection.

I groan and suck in a breath.

"You want something?" I ask, raising an eyebrow.

She stares straight into my eyes and rubs even harder. "I've been fantasizing about sucking your cock since the other night."

Those are some interesting words out of Emily's usually proper mouth. But fuck do I love unlocking new things about her. I try to hide my shock. "That right?"

"Yes." She flattens her body against mine, then slowly slides down until her knees hit the truck floor. I reach for the lever on the telescoping steering wheel and push it back as far as I can, giving her some room. "Although, I'm not sure I'm as talented as you are."

I'm absolutely certain her mouth on any part of my body will be fucking heaven.

A rough chuckle spills out of me. I hate having her on the floor of the truck, though. "Are you sure you want to do this here? Now? Are you okay down there?"

She drops her gaze, her lashes fluttering against her pale cheeks. "Just don't let me get stuck down here."

I reach again for the button that will move the seat back. This time, I get the right one. Too bad it only gives her another inch of room.

"That's better." She wriggles closer and rests her hands on my belt buckle. "May I?" she asks in a low, husky voice.

Why is that question so fucking hot coming out of her mouth?

Everything she does is sexy as fuck.

My mouth's too dry to respond. I nod.

She stares at my belt for a few seconds. My stomach muscles tense as she works the buckle loose, then attacks the button of my jeans, tugging and pulling.

"Let me," I offer when she gets to the zipper.

She moves to the side, giving me room. I lift my hips, letting her work my pants lower. My cock's so fucking excited to join us, he springs up tall and proud, smacking her cheek.

"Careful, you could put my eye out with this beast." One corner of her mouth slides into a sly smile and she wraps her fingers around my cock, letting out an appreciative sigh. "My goodness."

As if I need my ego inflated even more.

Fuck, her soft, warm hands feel good. Her hot breath against my aching cock even better.

Then her wet, velvet mouth closes over the tip and I've died and entered heaven.

"Oh fuck." Blindly, I slap one hand against the door.

Her tongue slides into an evil, beautiful, wicked dance along the sensitive underside.

"Em—" My head falls back against the seat.

"Hmm?" The sound vibrates down my dick and I squeeze my eyes shut, then force myself to open them so I can watch every move she makes. She feathers her lips over the tip again. Her tongue darts out, teasing the slit.

This wasn't what I planned or expected this afternoon.

But I'm certainly not complaining.

She keeps working me with soft, wet pulls, each time taking more of me into her mouth, until I hit the back of her throat.

"Fuuuck!" I pound my fists into the roof of the truck. *Nothing, nothing, nothing* has ever felt this amazing.

She lets out a choking sound and backs off.

"Easy." Am I saying that to her or myself?

She moans again, then wraps her hand around my shaft, working it in time with her mouth.

I'm done. My head falls back against the seat. I thread one hand into her hair. Not to guide her movements—she doesn't need my help—rather, to stay connected.

My hips jerk and she nods quickly, halting her explorations. I'm going to die if I don't open my eyes and watch every wicked thing she's doing. I shift my hand to the back of her head, slowly thrusting into her mouth, careful not to give her more than she can take.

Intense pleasure burns me from the inside out. Pressure builds at the base of my spine.

"Em," I warn. "I'm going to—"

She flicks her gaze up, staring at me, *daring* me. I thrust again and again until I'm teetering on the razor's edge of pleasure and pain. She sucks harder, then slides her hand lower.

Every muscle in my body tightens as my release catches me, scalding and hot. I have to see her. I peer down at her worshiping me with her hands and mouth. My hips buck in erratic thrusts. She coughs and sputters but keeps taking everything I have to give.

A wave of dizziness forces my eyes closed. Completely spent, I focus on my breath and the shaking in my legs. Emily strokes her hands over my thighs and stomach. She kisses and licks my spent cock, like she's trying to soothe a wild animal.

I haven't lost control like this since I was a teenager.

You better think of another way to compliment her.

"Thank you," I breathe out, pulling her up off the floor and against my body. She stretches, her legs trembling against mine.

"Mmm." I run my hand down her back and over her ass. "This is nice."

She hums a little noise that sounds like agreement and brushes her lips against my cheek. One of her hands strokes down my chest. God, I can't get enough of her touch.

"I've never enjoyed that so much," she whispers in my ear. "Feeling your body straining so hard not to come. That was quite a rush." She lifts her head, staring at me. "Thanks for not trying to jam your cock down my throat."

The jealous, possessive asshole in me doesn't like the implication that anyone else has been near her sweet, perfect mouth. Or treated her with anything other than the reverence she deserves.

I run one finger over her bottom lip. "You were made for me."

I can't come up with anything better than that? Did she suck my vocabulary out through my dick?

My brain might not be operating at full capacity, but my arms still work, so I wrap them around her, holding her close. She keeps kissing and nuzzling my neck. So fucking sweet. Then her sneaky fingers slide under my T-shirt, tickling my skin.

"What're you doing, firecracker?" I ask.

"Exploring."

Someone taps on the window.

Emily shrieks and ducks.

I jump like someone poured ice water over my head.

"What the fuck?" Through the foggy glass, I make out someone standing right outside the door.

"Don't move," I whisper to Emily. "My cock's still out and I don't want to give this guy a show."

"Who is it?" she hisses, pressing her face so tight against my chest, it's like she's trying to crawl inside me to hide.

"Don't know."

She carefully shifts her body to cover me. I reach for the window and tap the button, only lowering it a fraction.

"Sir, you can't park here," a man in a green jacket with the logo of the park says. "This is private property. The exhibit is closed."

"Yup," I answer in a *no shit* tone. "We're leaving."

He stares at me for a second, then tries to peer into the truck. "Miss, are you okay?"

Without lifting her head, Emily raises one hand and waves. "I'm fine. Thank you, sir."

"We're leaving," I say again and punch the button for the window to raise it.

The guy stalks a few feet in front of the truck and glares.

"Jesus, fuck. We're going, asshole," I growl.

"Oh my God," Emily mumbles against my shirt.

"I think he's going to watch us until we leave." I nudge her arm. "But he's a few feet away now."

She slowly peels herself off my body. The absence of her warmth makes me want to jump out of the truck and beat the intruder bloody. Instead, I zip and button my jeans. I'll worry about my belt later.

"Damn. I think I'm stuck." Emily peers over her shoulder. "Your steering wheel is holding my butt hostage."

Laughing, I twist and shift, untangling our bodies and easing her into a position where she can crawl over to the passenger side.

She throws herself into the seat and grabs the belt, quickly clicking it into place. "Yikes. I hope he didn't see or hear us."

"I hope he did," I grumble, twisting the key in the ignition. "Nosy fuck."

Emily reaches behind the seat, grabbing a bottle of water and taking a long swallow.

I glance over. "You okay? You didn't have to—"

"I'm fine." She offers me the bottle and I take it from her, finishing it.

"I think that was the last one. I'll get you another when we stop at the pizza place."

"Shoot." She slaps her hand against her forehead. "I forgot that we promised to bring home pizza."

I reach over and squeeze her leg. "You were occupied."

"I sure was."

She sounds so damn pleased with herself. As she should. She's fucking amazing. I chuckle and shift into reverse, backing away from the angry guard who doesn't seem to be in a hurry to move.

When we're far enough away from him, I execute a three-point turn and head for the main road.

"Phew!" Emily opens her window and fans herself. "I hope he didn't grab your plate number. We might go on some sort of naughty visitor list."

"Won't be the first list I'm on." I reach over and tap her leg. "You want to text Libby and see if her order is still the same?"

"Sure." She pulls out her phone and swipes over the screen while I try to remember which way to the pizza place.

She really did scramble my brain.

Left. It's gotta be left.

I make the turn and press down on the gas, wanting to get the hell away.

"Yup," Emily announces. "She's thrilled someone else wants to eat ham and pineapple pizza with her."

I grin. "Not your first choice, I take it?"

"Nope. We usually get half-and-half, but a piece of pineapple always seems to make its icky way onto *my* side." She gives her whole body a disgusted shake that I catch out of the corner of my eye. "This way, you two can enjoy your abomination and I'll have my sausage, mushroom, and olives like a civilized person."

"I didn't think pineapple belonged on pizza before I tried it," I admit.

"I've tried it. It's the devil's pizza topping."

"Okay." I raise my fingers off the steering wheel in surrender. "More for us."

I turn into the parking lot and drive around the building, claiming a spot close to the door.

"You know your way around this place," Emily says.

"It's almost halfway between our upstate and downstate clubhouses so we meet up here once in a while." I gesture toward the larger building in front. "They have a sit-down restaurant too."

"Downstate is Grayson's club now, right?" she asks.

I don't know why I'm happy she pays attention to stuff like that. Or that she cares enough to ask questions. But I am.

"Yup. Z stole him from us." It's supposed to be a joke but damn if it doesn't feel like Downstate's robbed us of a lot in the last couple years. But Emily doesn't know that.

"You're all club brothers, though, right?" she asks. "So, still part of the same club."

"Right." I lean back and buckle my belt. "You know how you can love a family member but not always *like* them? That's kind of what the relationship between Upstate and Downstate was for years." I stare straight ahead out the windshield. "Z taking over as president has brought the two clubs back together in a lot of ways."

"But a little of that competitiveness still remains?"

Damn, she's perceptive. "You could say that. Things are a lot better down there with Z in charge. In the past, our clubs didn't always see situations the same way."

She seems to turn that over in her head. "Serena's very tight-lipped about club stuff. But I know her ex was part of your...part of the... downstate club."

My jaw tightens at the mention of Shadow. He's dead and buried for betraying the club. I need to tread carefully when I talk about him.

"Yeah," I answer slowly. "He was one of the brothers who didn't operate within our code. Guys with his outlook didn't stick around after Z stepped into the president's role."

She blows out a slow breath. "Thank you for being honest. I like Grayson. I really do. But when she told me he was part of the same club, I worried about her a *lot*."

I rest my hand over hers. "You're a good friend."

"She's a good friend." Emily sighs and seems to shake off the seriousness of the conversation. "We better order those pizzas, or we'll be here all night."

"Damn, I meant to call before we left the park." I slant a look at her. "Someone distracted me."

"Careful, Dex. I wouldn't mind *distracting* you again. Right here. Right now."

God damn, what did I do to deserve this woman?

CHAPTER FIFTEEN

Dex

LIBBY POUNCES on us as soon as we step inside the house. "I'm starv[ing] She grabs one of the pizza boxes out of my hands and unwinds the plas[tic] bag from my wrist, then hurries into the kitchen.

Emily chuckles and sets her purse on the table. "You better hurry if you want that pineapple."

In the kitchen, Libby's busy setting the table for the three of us. I drop the other boxes on the counter. "Your sister said I should hurry or you'd eat all the pineapple."

She stops and a devilish smile spreads over her face. "Well, you're our guest. I don't want to be a total animal in front of you."

"I doubt you're that much of an animal."

"Don't be so sure," Emily says, coming up behind me. She gives me a playful hip-bump.

Libby grins, then sticks her tongue out at her sister. "By the way, those marshmallow things were the greatest ever." Libby touches her fingers to her lips and blows a kiss. "Feel free to bring them by any time."

"Libby!" Emily scolds.

"I'll remember next time I'm over that way," I promise.

Dinner with them is easy. Comfortable. Quieter than what I'm used to. Nothing like the pandemonium of family dinner nights at the clubhouse.

What would Emily think, listening to Ravage rib the married couples about their boring sex lives? Or Charlotte teasing Ravage about never pleasing a woman? Or Sparky coming to the table high as a kite and asking Heidi to refill an order of buzzy cock rings? Would Emily be uncomfortable? Would she want to keep her sister far away from all that chaos?

I've never worried about what anyone thinks of my family before. My attitude is usually fuck 'em. Then again, I've never tried to make a relationship work with someone outside of the club. Plenty of bikers have citizen wives, who never earn a property patch. They keep the worlds separate. I can't fathom splitting myself in two like that.

I want a woman who loves my club family as much as I do.

Rock and Z managed to bring two complete civilians into our world and make it work. Hope's the queen mother to our whole charter now. And Lilly's the benevolent queen of our downstate charter. Emily's younger than them, but I can already picture Hope taking Emily under her protective wing.

Get ahead of yourself, much?

I bite into another slice of pizza, catching a string of cheese before it lands on my shirt. Libby's busy filling her sister in on the play her theater club is working on. I just enjoy listening to them.

"Will you come to my play, Dex?" Libby asks.

I set my slice down and grab a napkin. "Sure. I heard from Grinder that you're a natural-born star."

She beams at me, then turns hopeful eyes on Emily. "Think they'll be able to come again?"

"I don't know." Emily shoots a look my way. "Serena's getting close to her due date, and I doubt she'll want to bring an infant to the theater."

Libby pouts for a second. "You can send her video."

"Sure," Emily says in a tone meant to pacify her sister, not commit herself to filming an entire high school play.

After dinner, Libby clears the table, then heads upstairs to give us "alone time."

Emily watches her sister leave with an expression I can't figure out.

"I can go," I offer, even though it's the last thing I want to do.

"Do you want to watch a movie?" she asks.

Who knew Emily likes horror movies? She chooses an ominous-looking one that starts off unsettling. The characters are so utterly stupid, it's borderline offensive to the human race.

"Girl, no!" Emily yelps, startling me.

"Listen to your gut! What are you thinking?" Emily squeals and presses her hands over her eyes. "Someone needs to buy this chick a copy of *The Gift of Fear.*"

I chuckle and wrap my arm around her, pulling her closer. She snuggles up against my side, still lively and animated. Only now I can feel her every movement.

Emily watches movies the way she does everything. With passion and lots of keen observations.

"Why do they always have to make the girl the dummy?" she sighs.

"She's too nice," I agree. "She needs to get the hell back in her car and *leave.*"

"Right?" Emily's cheek slides up and down against my chest in agreement. "Nooo, why is she going in the basement with him? Now I'm just getting mad." Instead of anger, she bursts into giggles, her whole body vibrating against mine. "Nooo, this is *so* wrong! No woman with a functioning brain would do that."

Her laughter's a balm, healing all my inner scars. I love her voice. Her snarky comments. So many times, she blurts out the same thoughts running through my brain.

"Sorry." She presses her fingers to her lips and sits up, turning slightly to face me. "I'm always a chatterbox when we watch something. Libby won't go to the movies with me anymore." She rolls her eyes. "I'm too *embarrassing.*"

"I enjoy your commentary." I rest my hand on her knee. "You're smart. You have a way of expressing almost exactly what I'm thinking."

"Hmm." She snuggles close to me again. "Does that make me *smart* or someone who confirms your already existing biases?"

I snort and rumble with laughter, jostling her against me. "Why can't it be both?"

"Oh, you're good." She tips her head and peers up at me. Perfect kissing range.

I lean down. Her eyes widen but her lips curve. She lifts her hand, touching my cheek. "Weird movie to make out to," she whispers.

"I haven't even kissed you yet."

Laughter dances in her eyes. "Oops, getting ahead of myself."

I cup the back of her head, running my thumb over her jaw. "I'm good with that." This time, I don't give her a chance to respond. I press my lips to hers. She slides her hand into my hair. Shivers race down my spine as she rakes her nails over my scalp. I groan at the pleasurable sensation, and she answers with a hungry little kitten noise.

The angle's awkward and I need her a hell of a lot closer. I slip one arm behind her back, pulling her up.

"Where do you want me?" she whispers against my lips.

Everywhere and anywhere.

"In my lap." I pat my leg.

She eagerly sits up and straddles my thighs, resting her butt on my knees and her hands on my shoulders. "Like this?"

"Closer." I thread my fingers through her hair and drag her to me. She wiggles and shimmies until her center's snuggled up to my dick.

"Perfect," I praise.

She smiles against my mouth. "You feel good."

"So do you." I tug on the ends of her hair. "Now, keep kissing me."

"You're so demanding," she teases.

"You have no idea."

She swoops in and kisses my cheek, then finds her way to my mouth again.

From my left there's a steady thud-thud-thud but I'm too wrapped up in Emily to figure out what the sound is. Or rather, *who* the sound is coming from.

"Wowza," Libby says. "Five-alarm fire in the living room."

Emily jumps and throws herself out of my lap onto the couch, almost kneeing me in the nuts.

"Hey, what's up?" she squeaks.

Libby stays in the archway between the hall and the living room. "Sorry, I didn't mean to interrupt. It was so quiet down here, I thought you'd left."

"I wouldn't leave without saying goodbye, Libby." I flash a quick grin at her that she returns.

"Aw, Em, did you watch this without me?" Libby asks, stepping into the living room and staring at the television.

Emily coughs into her fist. "I missed some of it so, uh, I'll watch it again. Not sure you'll like it though, the female main character does a lot of dumb shit in the first ten minutes."

Their easy banter is enough to cool me off so I can stand. "I better head home. It's late."

Emily's gaze darts between Libby and me.

"Sure. I'll walk you out." She picks up the remote and clicks the movie off.

"Night, Dex." Libby wiggles her fingers at me. "Thanks for the treats. And dinner."

"No problem, Libby."

She holds out her fist to me and, pleased she initiated it, I tap my knuckles against hers.

Once we're outside, Emily wraps her hand around mine. "Libby likes you."

"I like her. She's a good kid."

"She is. Most of the time."

I stop her at the steps. "Want you to go inside before I leave."

"I will." Her gaze searches the small, quiet street. "It's a safe neighborhood, but you never know…" Her voice trails off into a whisper.

I brush my knuckles against her cheek. "Thank you for today."

"Thank you. For everything." I lean in and kiss the tip of her nose.

A faint smile ghosts her lips, then she turns serious again. "I don't mean to be pushy…" She bites her lip and a vision of her sweet mouth wrapped around my cock flashes before my eyes. Jesus Christ. *Pay attention for fuck's sake.* She's trying to say something important.

"…It's just a long drive. Late at night. Deer jumping in the road. I know you have the truck tonight so it's safer than your bike. But I still worry."

She must've asked me to text her when I get home again. "I like that you worry about me." I stare past her at the house. "*I* worry about you and Libby here all alone by yourselves."

"We're used to it."

I curl my hand around hers and pull her toward me. "What if I moved closer?" Without waiting for a response, I plow ahead with my thought. "I'll ask Grinder if I can take over the lease to his apartment."

She frowns at my brother's road name for a brief second. "Oh. Grayson. Serena said his place was close when she was staying with us."

"Would you worry less if I didn't have to go so far?"

"You'd do that…for me?"

I'm starting to think I'd do almost anything for her.

CHAPTER SIXTEEN

Emily

WORK HAD BEEN A SLOG. Or it would've been if I didn't have a memora...
afternoon and evening with Dex to replay in my head over and ov...
again.

Reliving those moments certainly helped when I had to notify one of
our clients that their ammonia levels were out of compliance. I had to
endure minutes of verbal abuse over the phone regarding the quality of
my testing methods and equipment. To my annoyance, I ended up
retesting the sample just to shut them up. And what do you know? The
result was the same. I let them know by email.

Happy to be leaving work behind me for the next fourteen hours, I
pull into my driveway, noting the warm glow from the living room lights
around the edges of the window. Libby's already home.

*Hmm...*Which version of my sister will I encounter tonight? The sweet
one or the sassy one? Living with a teenager sure keeps life exciting.

I unlock the front door and push it open. Libby's on the couch with
the television on but she's staring at her phone, endlessly sliding her
thumb over the screen.

"Hey, Libby," I call out.

She turns away from her phone to utter the briefest, "Hey, Em."

Sometimes I miss the little girl who would come running to greet me
at the door, throw her skinny arms around my legs, and plead for hugs.

"How was your day?" I ask.

"Meh." She shrugs. "I heated up some of the leftover pizza for you." She points toward the kitchen without looking away from her phone.

My stomach rumbles. "Thanks." My sister may not be excited to see me but at least she won't let me starve.

I set my purse on the entry table and take out my phone, sliding it into my pocket. "Did you eat?"

"Yup."

I open my mouth to ask what's so interesting on her phone that she can't hold a conversation. Nah, that sounds too much like the kind of nagging a mom might do.

Sighing, I head for the kitchen, stopping to ruffle my hand over the top of her head on my way. She grunts and slaps at me in protest.

In the kitchen, two cheese slices about thirty seconds from being reheated into charred cardboard wait for me in the toaster oven. I grab a paper plate off the counter and tug one of the slices out, burning the tips of my fingers in the process.

"Ow! Damn." I grab a knife and poke it into the other slice and drag it out slowly, plopping it onto my plate.

My phone buzzes in my pocket.

I set the plate on the table and grab a can of lemon seltzer out of the fridge, popping it as I sit down. I pull out my phone and flick the screen on.

Dex: Get home safe?

I smile wide. How'd he know this is almost exactly when I usually get home?

Me: Yup. Sitting down for leftover pizza now.

Dex: Miss you.

My thumb hovers over the phone. I'm so close to tapping out an invitation. But won't that seem sort of desperate and clingy? Too easy?

Me: Miss you too. What are you up to tonight?

There. That's honest. But not too needy.

Dex: A minor bit of mayhem.

Huh. I don't know what to make of that.

I bite into one slice, searing the roof of my mouth. Dammit. How long does a slice of pizza need to cool off?

Knowing I'll just burn my mouth again if I stay put, I stand and wander to the corner of the counter where we usually stack the mail. I sort through the junk—why do companies still waste money sending paper when everyone just looks things up online now? Stuff we don't need, I tear into shreds and toss in the trash. Bills I set aside to take care of later.

I stop my mad tearing spree at a plain white envelope addressed to me by hand.

Ashport Correctional Facility.

Tremors run down my arms, rattling the envelope. No fucking way. *Why?* He's not supposed to send us anything.

Fury replaces my fear and I rip open the envelope. I yank out the grimy piece of notebook paper, staring at the neatly printed block letters.

DEAR EMILY,

This letter is long overdue. At first, I hesitated to write it because I do not want you to think I am asking for anything. Not your pity or forgiveness. It has been years and I do not want to reopen old wounds. I recognize that saying sorry will not bring your parents back or change what I did.

I started a life of crime at a young age. Back then, I didn't see any other options and didn't have any influences to steer me in a better direction. I never planned to hurt anyone. But looking back, I now see because of the choices I made, tragedy was inevitable.

If you find it in your heart to visit me, I would like to share the truth of that night as well as tell you in person how sorry I am for the hurt and pain I've caused your family. This isn't a plea for help or forgiveness. I am where I belong and I will never leave here alive. I hope that gives you some peace.

Sincerely,

Zach Snell

MY ENTIRE BODY'S shaking by the time I finish reading the letter. Like hell would I ever visit that fucking monster.

I crumple the letter in my hand, then stop myself. Leaning over the counter, I smooth the paper flat, neatly refold it, and tuck it in its envelope. Maybe one day Libby will want to read it?

Libby. Shit, did she see this? It was jumbled in with all the other mail, so I doubt she noticed. I jam the envelope in my back pocket.

Even from behind prison walls, someone else's sins still cast a shadow over my life. And I hate it.

I've lost my appetite, but I return to the table and bite into my pizza.

Slowly, I push the short letter out of my mind. I won't give him power over me. He's taken enough already.

I sip my seltzer and check my phone. No more messages from Dex. Maybe I *should* invite him over?

No. Libby and I have done just fine on our own all these years. I can't call a man to come over just because a letter jangled my nerves. That's unacceptable.

Libby pushes through the kitchen door and I set my phone facedown on the table to set a good example of what civilized people *should* do when someone walks into a room.

"Join me?" I ask.

"Sure." She plucks an orange out of the refrigerator and drops into the chair next to me. "What's up?"

"Nothing." I force a cheery smile. "I just like seeing your angelic little face."

She fakes a big, wide smile.

"What's wrong?" I ask, setting my slice down. "You seem sort of down."

"Just tired." She sighs and flicks her gaze toward the door. "I got a sixty-seven on my math quiz. No matter how hard I try, I just don't understand it."

Ugh, I remember those days. "Do you want me to find you a tutor?" That's what I wish my parents had done for *me* at Libby's age.

She wrinkles her nose and purses her lips like she's about to protest, then seems to stop herself. "Maybe. I dunno. Troy Lamb said he'd help me study for the next quiz."

I fight the urge to tease her about studying with a boy. "That's nice. How does he do in the class?"

"Perfect." She digs her nails into the orange peel and rips it apart. Juice squirts out and runs down her fingers. I hand her a napkin.

"Thanks." She wipes her hands and continues peeling the orange.

A cloying citrus-scented mist hangs in the air. Doesn't exactly go with my pizza but I don't want to tell Libby to eat her orange somewhere else. I want her close.

"Have you heard from Serena?" she asks.

"We've talked a couple times. She specifically wanted me to say hi to you."

A quick, eager smile flashes over her face. "Did she drop that little goblin, yet?"

"Please don't call her baby a goblin," I warn, suppressing a laugh.

"*Pshh*. She called him that first." She taps her fingertips together. "Ooo! I hope he's one of those cute, pudgy babies. Not the kind that comes out looking like a wrinkly thumb."

I choke and sputter on a chunk of burned pizza crust. "I thought you weren't interested in babies?" Dear God, I can*not* have my little sister getting baby fever right now.

She shrugs and pops an orange slice in her mouth. "It's Serena's baby, though. I'm excited for *her*," she says around a mouthful of orange pulp.

"Me too." I blow out a relieved breath.

"How was work?" she asks.

"Blech." I pull an annoyed face. "I had to report test results the client didn't like, so they complained until I ran the test again."

"And I'm guessing it came back with the same result."

"You got it." I bite into my pizza with a hard crunch.

"Hurry up." She waves her hand in my face in case I don't know what *hurry* means. "Season two of Chucky just dropped. We have to watch it."

"I heard it's not as good as season one," I say, dabbing the napkin over my lips.

"Awww," she grins, "don't tell me you're scared of little ol' Chucky?"

"Nah, he reminds me of you when *you* were little," I tease.

Her mouth drops in outrage, but she's laughing too hard to protest. "Come on. Stop stalling."

I finish my dinner. Then, the two of us make popcorn with lots of salty butter.

In the living room we nestle into our respective corners of our couch, letting our feet touch in the middle. Libby grabs an afghan our aunt Kimmy made for us and throws it at me. "Here, in case you get scared and need to hide," she teases.

I toss it back, laughing when it falls perfectly over her head. "Nah, you need it more than I do."

She bats it away. "Nope. The Walker sisters don't scare easily."

"That's right."

A knife-wielding doll doesn't scare us one bit.

We've survived enough real-life horrors.

CHAPTER SEVENTEEN

Dex

ALTHOUGH VAPOR SAID Juliet wanted me to come over for dinner, his niece doesn't look pleased to see me when she first opens the front door to their modest brick ranch.

"Uncle Dex, it's been a while," she says, opening the door wider to allow me inside.

Vapor must've told her I was taking him on an assignment tonight. She's never been part of my MC life and the few brushes she's had with the MC didn't exactly endear the world to her.

The couple of times her husband's been inside, I made damn sure my club took care of him—lawyers, bail, whatever was needed. Even if he isn't a patched brother, we take care of our own and anyone who gets in trouble conducting business on our behalf. Juliet prefers to have her husband stay out of trouble—period. The two of them are hyper-protective of one another. I'd rather keep them closer to the club, so I know they're safe. But I also know when not to push. Juliet's stubborn.

I lean down and kiss her cheek. "How've you been, peanut?"

A bit of the frost in her expression melts. "Good. Busy." Her lips flicker into a teasing smile. "Roman says there's a special lady in your life."

"Special lady?" I raise an eyebrow. "What are you two, sixty-year-olds?"

"Stop it. You know what I mean. When can I meet her?"

I can easily picture Juliet and Emily getting along. "Give it a minute, Juliet."

"Hmm." She nods. "Secretive. Must be something real."

I've never introduced her to anyone I've "dated" before, so I'm not sure what she thinks she's confirmed. Technically, Juliet and I aren't related. My wife was Juliet's older cousin. I've tried to maintain a relationship—look out for Juliet—since my wife died. With varying degrees of success or failure, depending on how you look at it. I have a lot of regrets about not being there when she needed me. Introducing her to a woman I'm seeing feels weird and disloyal, no matter how many times Juliet's said she wishes I'd find someone.

"Where's your husband?" I ask, ending the conversation about my love life.

"Right here, Mr. Taskmaster. Settle down." Vapor enters from the hallway, carrying their son.

"Jesus, what're you feeding this kid? He's huge." I grin as Vapor sets Atlas down and he wobble-walks his way over to me.

"Welllll," Juliet says, drawing out the word in her sweet but sarcastic way, "you haven't seen him in a while."

"Nah," Vapor says. "I swear sometimes he's bigger when I get home from work than he was when I left in the morning." He slips his arm around Juliet's shoulders and pops a kiss on her forehead.

I crouch down and Atlas runs right into my arms for a hug and lets me pick him up. "Can't be that long. He remembers me."

Juliet reaches up to fix the collar of Atlas's T-shirt. "You might be right. He doesn't let just anyone hold him."

As if to agree with his mother, Atlas curls his fist in the ends of my hair and yanks. "Strong grip, little buddy. We'll have you riding in no time."

"The hell you will," Juliet mutters.

I lift an eyebrow and she flashes an innocent smile. Hanging onto Atlas with one arm, I curl the other around Juliet's shoulders and squeeze her again.

"Daddy?" Atlas twists, seeking Vapor, and I hand him over.

"Well, come in," Juliet says, waving her hand toward the living room. "Don't stand there like you're going to bolt any minute. Let's have dinner."

I follow her into the kitchen, salivating at the scent of whatever she's cooking. Garlic. Lots of garlic.

"Smells good," I say.

"We'll see," she mutters, stirring a long, wooden spoon in a tall pot.

Vapor's busy setting what looks like a sectioned pet dish of bright blue plastic and chubby toddler utensils on the table.

"Why doesn't he get a normal dish?" I ask, lifting my chin toward the square plate.

"Please don't," Juliet warns. "He's fussy enough about trying new things. Don't insult his dinnerware."

"You can't be *that* fussy. Not when you're already getting so big," I mutter. I wink at Atlas and he burble-giggles at me.

A few minutes later, Juliet sets heaping bowls of bow-tie pasta and meatballs in a thick, rich red sauce on the table.

Vapor spoons a bit of everything into the separate sections of the toddler plate. Atlas shows interest in the pasta. And by interest, I mean squeezing it to mush in his chubby little fists. Vapor stabs a chunk of meatball and piece of pasta onto a fork and offers it to Atlas who takes an uncertain bite.

I reach over and run my finger over one of his hands. "The three of you really need to come up to the clubhouse on family day. He'd have a good time with the little guys."

Juliet and Vapor share a look.

"You've met some of the ol' ladies," I remind her. "Hope asks about you all the time. Her little girl's just a bit younger than Atlas. We've got a couple kids up there now. He'd have other kids to play with."

"He has friends at daycare," Juliet says.

"That's not the same. I'm talking about *family*."

"But your club isn't *our* family," she insists.

"They're your family, whether you think so or not," I say. "Now that you guys are living in New York again, I'd like to see you more often."

Vapor's wisely chosen to stay out of this conversation. I catch his eye. "And not just when I have a job for you."

"You still after Griff and Remy about a support club?" Vapor asks.

"Yeah, but it's gonna need to be more than the two of them." *Hint, hint, you big pain in my ass.*

Juliet chuckles. "Molly's been a sweetheart. She's watched Atlas for us a couple of times. It's adorable how she's always complaining about Remy being too overprotective."

That sounds about right. "That's what big brothers do."

"I wouldn't know," she murmurs.

Oof, there's that stab of guilt again. I'd been so lost in my grief after

Debbie died that I didn't pay enough attention to what was going on in Juliet's life. I thought she was safe living with her biological aunt and uncle. Only much later did I learn that wasn't the case. Regret that I didn't do better for her still haunts me.

"We moved the party clubhouse to Empire," I say, shaking off the bitter memories. "When I say *family day* up at the compound, I mean it."

"Oh." Juliet stares at her plate and cuts one of her meatballs into twenty little pieces with the side of her fork. "You sure it'd be okay?"

"Yes." I flick my gaze to Vapor.

"We'll check it out. Just say when," he promises.

Well, that's more than I expected, so I won't push. "Murphy and Z built this ridiculous jungle-gym-playhouse thing for the kids. It's bigger than what some parks have."

Juliet's eyes glint with interest. "Really?"

Guess I should've led with that. "Yeah. Couple other things for the kids there. Atlas might be too young for some of it, but he'll have fun. When he's older he can ride four-wheelers through the woods with the other kids."

"Okay," Juliet says with more enthusiasm this time.

After dinner, Vapor and Juliet apparently have a whole nighttime routine with Atlas. I help clean up the kitchen, then park my ass on their couch, listening to their happy family noises in the other room.

How'd they even figure out all this shit? Would I have been as involved as Vapor seems to be? Christ, I was a fucking kid, scared shitless when Debbie found out she was pregnant. Would I have helped her do all the tedious baby stuff? Or would I have been too busy trying to earn whatever money I could to keep a roof over our heads?

Emptiness settles in my chest. I never had the chance to find out. Thinking about this shit usually has me itching to hit the road. Tonight, for some reason, I'm able to look back at the painful memories without feeling like I'm suffocating. Must be from having Juliet living in the same area code again. She's my last connection to Debbie and I feel better knowing she's close enough to check up on and help out when she needs it. She's an adult with her own family now, but she'll always be my little peanut.

"Ready to go?" Vapor asks, returning to the living room dressed all in black. In his hands, he carries a black knit cap and a pair of black leather gloves. *Ah, I've taught him well.*

"Yeah." I peer into the darkened hallway. "Juliet?"

132

"Don't go yet!" She hurries into the living room and hurls herself at me, wrapping her arms around my neck and hugging tight. I embrace her with the same intensity, lifting her off her feet.

"Thanks for dinner, peanut," I say against her hair.

"Anytime." She releases me and I set her down. "Please be careful."

"Always." I step outside but Vapor doesn't follow.

I stand there listening to the two of them murmuring back and forth for a bit before he finally joins me, closing the door behind him.

Should I really involve him in my shit? It's MC business. I could've just waited for Z to go with me. "You don't have to do this if you don't want to," I say.

He stares at me, a slight frown forming on his face. "I could use the extra cash."

"If you need money—"

He holds up his hand to stop me from getting out the full thought. Vapor won't accept charity. I get that. Respect it, even. "Who's gonna have your back if I don't go with you?" he asks.

"I'll be fine."

"What if they've got a dog who takes a chunk out of your ass?"

I roll my eyes. "There's no dog."

"What if they've got a knife or pull a gun on you?"

"Wouldn't be the first time."

"You're a crazy motherfucker, you know that?" He shakes his head and starts walking to the driveway.

"Let's get going," I grumble.

He sweeps his hand toward my bike. "Lead the way."

About an hour later, we roll into Ironworks. We weave through traffic until we find our way to a seedy but quiet, narrow, one-way street. I stop at the corner and park at the curb. Vapor pulls in behind me.

He sets his helmet on his bike and makes his way over. "Feels like old times," he says, slipping on his gloves. "You remember that night you whisked me away from my *actual* job to pay some poor bastard a visit? I barely knew your psycho ass. Probably should've thought twice about gettin' in your vehicle."

I snort at the memory. As a teenager, Vapor was as fearless as he was distrustful. "Had to see what you were made of, kid."

He smirks at *kid*. "Nah, be honest. You just wanted to give a visual demonstration of what would happen to *me* if I ever hurt Juliet."

He's got me there. "Damn right." Why bother lying about my motivations?

"Now that we're family and all, you know you can trust me," he says with a dry laugh. "You plannin' to tell me what *this* guy did to earn a visit from your grim reaper ass?"

"Roughed up one of our girls."

He grunts. "Sometimes I think you only run that strip club to find abusers to take out your frustrations."

"Interesting theory. I'll run it by my therapist." I wave my hand impatiently. "Can we get on with it now, Doctor Hawkins. Or would you like to head shrink me some more?"

"Please." Vapor risks death by tapping a finger against my temple. "That's the last place I want to crawl inside. Fuck only knows what sort of demons lurk in your head."

He has no idea.

"Well, what's your plan?" he asks.

If it was someone who owed the club money, I'd use a weapon—lead pipe, hammer, or whatever's handy. But with these fuckers, I prefer to get my knuckles bloody.

I flex my fingers. "Keep watch. Let me know if we're drawing attention or if someone's calling the cops. Although, in Ironworks, it could be hours before anyone bothers to show up."

"Good to know." He pulls his knit hat over his ears and shoves his hands in his pockets.

Together we navigate the uneven sidewalk. Christ, Ironworks is a dump. At least this part of the city is.

We stop in the shadows of one of the nicer brownstones on the street. The double front doors are painted a red that compliments the brick building. I take a quick look up and down the street, then jog up the wide stone steps.

To the right, three buttons and mailboxes announce the names of the tenants. No reason to bother poking at any of them to see if someone lets us in, though.

The double doors have two wide panes of glass, allowing a view of another set of double doors and the entire first floor hallway. Large, curved staircase to the left. Our target's door on the right—only a few short steps away once I get through the front entrance.

I reach for the metal knob on the door, slowly twisting. It turns easily and the door swings open with a metallic creak. Black-and-white tile that was probably once a pattern of some sort but now is too dirty to tell, covers the narrow entryway leading to the next set of doors. Too small for both of us to comfortably fit inside. Vapor remains at my back. I don't have to turn around to know he's scanning the street, searching for anyone who might see us and have questions.

"What's even the point?" he mutters.

"Double doors? Probably to keep the heat in and the drafts out during the winters."

He grunts in acknowledgment. "Thanks for the science lesson."

I roll my eyes and reach out to touch the next doorknob. This one doesn't budge. No deadbolt, though. Just a simple, almost antique-looking lock. I brought a lockpick kit but this will be simple. Instead of my tools, I pull out an old gift card, bending one corner just a bit before sliding it between the door and frame, careful not to snap the thin plastic in half. I push and jiggle the card until it catches the latch, then apply pressure while turning the knob.

The door opens with a rusty sigh. I shove the card back into my pocket and cross the threshold with Vapor right behind me. He quietly pushes the door closed.

"Christ, it's bright in here." He squints at the light fixtures about twelve feet above our heads.

"Not planning to stand out here for long."

Canned noise from a television at peak volume drifts down the stairs. At least we shouldn't have to worry about the neighbors overhearing our visit.

I hit my fist against the door, then slap my palm over the peephole and turn my body slightly to the side. Vapor leans against the wall, out of sight from the apartment door.

"You stupid bitch!" someone shouts from inside. "Forget your keys again?"

I'm going to enjoy this one.

Vapor shakes his head and smacks his fist into his open palm.

"What the fuck? Who is it?" the man grumbles from the other side of the door.

Open and find out, motherfucker.

Curiosity outweighs his sense of safety and a few seconds later metal scratches against metal as he unlocks what sounds like several different latches and slowly swings the door open.

The man stands in the doorway wearing gym shorts, a crusty T-shirt, and holey socks. "Who the fuck are you?" He scowls at me.

"Stan?" I ask. "Stan Elliot?"

"Who wants to know?" His gaze drops to my Lost Kings MC patches. Recognition flares in his eyes. His body jerks forward in an attempt to slam the door in my face. It bounces off my boot and I push my way inside. Vapor slides in behind me and shuts the door.

"Kyla live here?" I ask.

"Why?" He snorts and steps away. His gaze darts around the room and his jerky movements keep me on alert. "You fuckin' her too?"

"No." I slam my fist into his jaw. "And you've put your hands on her for the last time."

"Fuck you." He cradles his jaw with his hands. "It's none of your business."

"The fuck it's not." I hit him in the stomach. He wheezes and staggers backward, clutching his gut.

I must be losing my edge. He recovers fast, lunging for a side table and scooping up a knife. He flicks it open and waves it at me.

Slightly bigger than a simple pocketknife, it'll hurt if it slices through my skin. Possibly kill me if he gets lucky and aims right.

"Put that oversized butter knife away, jackass," I warn.

"Jesus," Vapor mutters, coming up next to me.

Like his name implies, Vapor moves with deadly silence. Stan's eyes widen when he realizes I'm not alone. Not one, but two living nightmares have come to deliver his punishment.

He waves the knife at Vapor. "Stay back. You broke in. I can stab you."

"You stab me, you better pray you kill me," I sneer and take a step closer, drawing his attention to me instead of Vapor.

Stan backs away. Fuck knows what other weapons he has in the apartment. I don't want him retreating to another room or worse, escaping through the back door.

By unspoken agreement, Vapor starts to circle Stan on the right and I move to the left. He can't stab both of us at the same time.

Stan hesitates and that's when I strike. I bring my hand down on his wrist like a hammer, knocking the knife out of his grasp.

"Shit!" he cries. "Help! Help!" he yells toward the ceiling.

"Yeah?" I grab him around the throat. "Kyla yell for help too? Your neighbors come running to check on her?"

His eyes bug and he shakes his head.

"No one helps? Or she's a stronger person than you and doesn't call for help?" I ask, punctuating the question with another punch to his face.

"I got money," he gasps as he slides to the floor.

"And you're living *here*?" Vapor asks with a snarky headshake.

"I don't give a fuck about your money." *Punch. Punch.* "I want you to understand how it feels when someone bigger and stronger kicks the shit out of you." I slam my boot into his ribs, then pick him up and punch him a few more times.

Stan's face is a broken mess of blood, spit, tears, and snot. Barely out of breath, I drop him to the floor and step back. "You gonna go near that girl again?" I ask.

"Nuh-nooo," he moans.

I squat next to him and pat the top of his head. "Good boy. You learn quick."

The metallic scent of blood and something more foul taints the air. I deliver a final kick to his other side, and he rolls himself into a ball.

"Don't make me come back," I warn. "I won't be as friendly."

I don't bother telling him not to call the cops. I really don't give a fuck if he does. My club will back me up.

I glance around, looking for something to wipe the blood off my gloves.

"Not bad." Vapor hands me a greasy looking kitchen towel. I wipe the gloves down and drop the towel next to Stan.

"Didn't even let me get a hit in," Vapor says, staring down at the guy.

"Knock yourself out." I wave my hand over Stan's wheezing body.

"Well, now it's no fun." He prods Stan with the toe of his boot and the guy moans in misery.

"Sorry," I say with absolutely no apology in my tone.

"He'll live." Vapor shrugs. "Maybe."

"Too bad. World would be better off without him," I grumble, turning toward the door.

"Got that right." Vapor follows me outside.

Neither of us say a word as we walk back to our bikes. Once we reach them, I pull a folded-over envelope out of my pocket and hand it to Vapor.

He accepts it without checking inside. "Don't feel like I did all that much."

"You had my back," I assure him. "That's all I needed."

He gives a thoughtful glance toward the brownstone. "He's gonna be pissed when she gets home. What if he takes it out on her?"

"She's staying at Willow's apartment for now. Took most of her important shit with her yesterday."

"All right." He nods. "Sounds good."

I hold out my hand and he slaps his palm against mine. Before he can get away, I yank him closer and slap his back. "Thanks, brother."

"Any time."

We say goodbye and ride out of Ironworks together. Once we reach the highway, we go our separate ways.

My fingers ache. Not enough to interfere with handling my bike but a throbbing reminder of the violence committed tonight. Sometimes fists and raw violence are the only means of communication a bully understands. It was necessary. Some people need protection from the bullies of the world. And I'm fine with being that protector.

But no matter how many times I've had a night like this, it doesn't make up for the times I've failed my loved ones.

And it never completely chases away my demons.

Emily

Horrors from my past hold me hostage. Dread and panic rip out my throat, stealing my voice.

I can't do anything for them now.

Gruesome. Blood. So much. Everywhere. The stench of death.

Don't look.

Find Libby.

"Libby! Libby!" I keep trying to scream until my throat's raw, but no sound comes out of my mouth.

Blind, I search the home where I grew up. Every room. Every closet. No Libby.

Then it turns into my aunt's home. I shove my way into Libby's room. A pool of something dark leaks from under her closet door.

"No, no. Libby. Please, Libby. No..."

"Emily! Wake up!"

Bright light snaps me awake. My sister's firm grip on my shoulders sears the last remnants of my nightmare away.

"Libby. Are you okay?" I throw my arms around her, hugging her tight.

My wild heart thunders as the last bits of the nightmare recede into the haunted corners of my mind.

I press my palms to her cheeks. No flecks of blood. Her eyes are full of concern, not horror. Brutality hasn't stolen her voice. The older Libby of the here and now replaces the memories I've tried so hard to bury.

"You're okay," I whisper, more to reassure myself than anything.

"I'm fine." Libby wiggles out of my hold. "You were screaming and sobbing." Sadness haunts her eyes. "You haven't had a nightmare like that in years."

The damn letter. As much as I tried to ignore it and pretend it didn't bother me, obviously it burrowed into my subconscious.

"I'm sorry." Guilt bites into my soul. Libby's endured enough in her short life. "I didn't mean to scare you."

She squeezes my hand. "You didn't *scare* me. I was *worried* about you. That's all."

"I'm okay," I try to assure her. How embarrassing for my little sister to have to comfort me like I'm a child. I'm supposed to be the parental unit, not her.

"You tried to deny it, but I *knew* you were scared of Chucky," she says, but there's no smile to go with the joke.

"Yeah, that must've been it," I murmur.

"Was it about Mom and Dad?" she asks in a small voice.

Little sister or not, she knows me too well. "Sort of. Not exactly."

How can I say the dream was about *her*? Instead, I pull her into my arms and hug her.

"Thanks for coming to check on me," I whisper against her hair.

"Always." She returns the hug then pulls away. "I don't have to go on my trip to the city this weekend," she says, her eyes focused on the comforter.

"No way." I reach down and squeeze her hand. "You've been looking forward to this trip since September."

"True." She shrugs. "But I don't want to leave you all alone."

"I won't be *all alone*. Geez. I'll be fine."

"Oh, realllly." She drags out the word, teasing me. "Is Dex gonna come over?" she sings.

"Maybe. We'll see. That's none of your business, young lady."

She giggles. "Oh, he's *so* coming over to keep you company."

"Ugh." I flop back against the pillows.

She stands. "You need more sleep."

"So do you."

She searches my room. "Do you want me to leave a light on?"

"No, it's okay." I yawn.

"All right. Night, Em." She shuts off the light and quietly closes the door.

I turn over and close my eyes.

The horrible images return immediately. The dread, the horror. All of it.

This is what I hate about nightmares the most. Sometimes, they never let go of you.

CHAPTER EIGHTEEN

Emily

THE DRIVE HOME Friday night is a blur. A rush to get home. As I pull into my driveway, I spot something colorful on the front steps. I park and hurry to the front door.

A short but full bouquet of flowers sits in a square, orange glass vase. Protective see-through wrapping is pulled up over the arrangement, but inside, I make out hot-pink roses, orange Gerbera daisies, and other bright, happy blossoms I don't know the names of. I pick up the flowers and bring them inside, setting them on the entry table.

Carefully, I peel off a small card taped to the wrapping.

Emily.

Looking forward to seeing you tonight.

Dex.

The words are printed in black ink. Something he probably typed online when he ordered the flowers. I clutch the note to my chest and smile. How sweet.

I invited Dex over for dinner and to watch another movie. But it's a cover story. After last weekend, and now the flowers before he even gets here—my need to jump this man is sharper than any desire I've ever felt before.

Still, I plan to make dinner. I'm not a complete hussy. Something quick and light.

I rush into the kitchen and peel the wrapping off the flowers and place them in the middle of the table. Nah, I'd rather have them in my bedroom so I can see them first thing in the morning. I poke my head in the fridge to make sure I have everything I need, then carry the flowers upstairs. In my bedroom, I set the vase on my desk, then hurry to shower and change.

Twenty minutes later, I'm searching my underwear drawer for something sexy and flattering. My hand brushes over a hot-pink satin bra. It's a bit snug. I only break it out for special occasions. It makes my boobs look amazing. There's a matching pair of panties here somewhere. I rummage through my drawer until I find them tucked into the bottom corner.

Once I've settled on the underwear, I search for an outfit. Why didn't I plan this earlier in the week?

I yank open a dresser drawer, searching through stacks of sweaters. My hand brushes over a soft emerald green one. I look good in green. It'll clash with my underwear though.

Dammit.

I race to my closet, sliding the door open so fast it bangs and springs forward a few inches.

Jesus, Em, calm down.

Why do I have so many clothes and nothing to wear? My fingers skitter over something thin and soft. Black lace. *Aha!* I yank the blouse off its hanger and study it. Soft, clingy jersey fabric. Plunging neckline—which is why I've never worn it to work. But the lace edging along the deep "V" keeps it semi-classy. I hope the hot-pink bra doesn't show through.

Actually, I hope it does.

Skirt or pants? I stare at rows of neatly hung clothing. This is why I prefer to wear dresses. No mixing and matching required. Black-and-white houndstooth pants? Too formal. Houndstooth skirt? Why do I own so many black-and-white bottoms?

Jeans. Can't go wrong with jeans. I find a pair of gray skinny jeans and wriggle into them. The last time I wore these, Libby laughed and said no one wears skinny jeans anymore. But I don't give a damn. The teenage fashion critics of the world will have to pry my skinny jeans from my cold, dead hands.

I prefer heels but hate the idea of clacking around the house in them. Instead, I slip into a pair of black, pointy-toed flats with little silver studs decorating the tips. They look kinda biker-chick. *Perfect.*

A distant rumble draws my attention.

He's early.

Shit, shit, shit!

I race around my room, stuffing underwear, panties, and sweaters back into their proper drawers. Thank God I made my bed this morning. I click the remote to turn on my set of white flameless candles, checking that the batteries still work. They flicker to life, casting a soft glow. They'd be better off on the nightstand, right? I pick up all three and set them on the nightstand next to the bed.

Is that romantic? Or too eager?

The thundering of his bike increases, then cuts off. My heart thumps. *He's here.*

I run down the stairs, skidding to a stop in the entryway. Dammit. I never put on makeup. I turn and stare in the small, round mirror over the entry table. Pale as a frickin' ghost. I grab my purse and dig through it for a lip gloss or something. *Aha.* I pluck a deep-berry lip stain from the depths of my bag and quickly pat it on, leaning in close to the mirror to make sure it's perfect.

For fuck's sake, Emily, calm down.

I shouldn't be this eager, but I throw open the door before Dex has a chance to knock. No sign of him. I step outside and there he is. Dear Lord, it should be illegal for a man to look that good just *walking.* Swaggering like he owns my whole damn yard.

He's so serious. Almost scowling. But then his gaze lands on me and his expression shifts. His lips curve, the smile reaching his eyes where they crinkle at the corners.

"Emily."

That's it. My name in his low, rumbly voice sends tingles racing over my skin.

"Hi," I answer.

Then, he's standing in front of me. He rests his hand on my hip, holding me in place. "What're you doing out here?"

"I…heard your bike and I…" Words won't come when he's standing so close. Staring like he wants to devour me.

"I've missed you," he says. Blunt, sincere, and to the point.

"I missed you too," I admit.

His hand moves lower, tapping my behind. "Let's go inside."

"Oh. Sure."

"How's Libby's trip going?" he asks.

Is that his way of asking if we're alone or is he genuinely concerned about my sister?

"So far, so good. She sent a few selfies throughout the day." I pull out my phone and find one of the photos, turning the screen his way.

He takes my phone and thumbs through the pictures, genuine interest in his expression. "Looks like she's having fun."

"I hope so." I slip my phone back into my pocket.

He slides his leather vest off his shoulders, then unzips the sweatshirt underneath. I hold out my hand for both, then hang them in the closet.

Amusement chases the remaining storminess from his eyes.

"What?" I ask, closing the closet door.

"Nothing." He taps a hook on the rack outside of the closet. "Normally, I drop it here. This feels like you want me to stick around."

He's teasing but I don't laugh. "I always want you to stay. It's just—"

"I get it."

My gaze drops to his tight, black T-shirt. It's plain but highlights his hard muscles and inked arms to mouth-watering perfection.

"You wear that T-shirt really well." I mean it as a sexy compliment but the words leave my mouth in an awkward jumble.

"Yeah?" Dex lifts an eyebrow.

I clutch his bicep. Damn, does the man spend his days chopping wood or something?

"Are you hungry?" I ask.

"Ravenous."

Again, I don't think we're discussing food.

I shake off my nervous energy and head for the kitchen. "Well, follow me."

In the kitchen, a stray rose petal on the table catches my attention. "Thank you for the flowers."

I turn and collide with his hard, warm body.

"Oh," I breathe out.

He gently tugs on the ends of my hair. "They reminded me of you."

"They're beautiful. So vibrant," I babble.

"Mmhm," he hums in agreement.

I point to the ceiling and realize my hands are shaking. "They're upstairs. In my bedroom. So I could see them first thing in the morning."

"Good." He studies me and presses so close, I have no choice but to back up against the counter.

"Are you...okay?" I stammer, my voice rising with each word. "I really loved the arrangement. I was going to leave them down here..."

Why am I still rambling on about flowers?

"I'm more than okay. I'm with you." His voice drops to a low rumble that vibrates through my body. "And all I've been thinking about this week is how I want to rip off your clothes, kiss every inch of your body, and make you scream my name."

Yes, yes, yes.

I blink and open my mouth like a goldfish gasping for air until an answer pops out. "I'm not a screamer."

One corner of his mouth slides up. "You will be."

CHAPTER NINETEEN

Dex

EMILY COULDN'T HAVE CHOSEN A BETTER outfit to drive me out of my mind. The deep, sexy "V" of her blouse edged with black lace allows a glimpse of her skin if she turns just the right way. A flash of bright pink under the black lace also teases the hell out of me.

She's still speechless. Too bad she doesn't realize what she's gotten herself into. Fucking her until she screams my name is only the tip of the iceberg of filthy ideas in my head.

I back up and give her some room, moving to the sink to wash my hands. Riding gloves always leave me feeling grimy and I'm dying to put my hands all over every inch of Emily's soft, perfect skin.

She stands so close our elbows bump together. When I shut off the water, she hands me a paper towel.

"That's better." I toss the towel in the trash and reach for her again. "Come here."

The corners of her mouth twitch and she backs up a few steps. "Come where?"

On my face, dick, fingers, I really don't care.

I pull her close again, lightly gripping her chin and tilting her head back. She stares up at me, breathing hard. I lean down, fusing my mouth to hers, stealing kisses like a starving man.

Like a match set to dynamite, she blazes to life, curling her arms around my neck. Sliding both hands from her waist to her ass, I lift her in my arms. She hugs me tighter, kisses harder.

"That's my girl," I whisper against her lips. "Wrap your legs around me."

My cock's painfully trapped behind my fly and Emily rubbing herself up against me only increases the agony. The walk out of the kitchen is painful and clumsy as she keeps kissing me and I try not to bang us into walls or furniture.

"Where's your bedroom?" I rasp, dragging my mouth away from hers.

"Upstairs."

Of course it is.

I *could* carry her up the stairs but I don't want to risk dropping her. No delays. And I couldn't stand it if I hurt her. I set her on the bottom step and with my hands at her waist, turn her around.

"Show me the way."

She reaches for my hand, closing her soft fingers around mine, then turns and heads up the stairs. Yeah, this view was definitely worth letting go of her. I want to sink my teeth into her ass.

"I like these jeans on you," I say.

"Libby says they're out of style."

I snort with laughter. "I like your style." Hell, I like every last thing about her.

She leads me into a room near the top of the stairs. It's too dark to make out many details. And I'm not exactly concerned about the decor at the moment.

She picks up a little rectangle, presses a button, and three candles flare to life. Enough light to see where I'm going.

With quick, eager steps she crosses the room to curtains covering a large window. Orienting myself, I figure it must look out at the side yard. But she doesn't open the curtains for the view. She bends over and flicks a switch. A shower of tiny white lights twinkles against a backdrop of silvery fabric.

"Serena got me into all these little lights and stuff," Emily says, shrugging and wringing her hands. As if she expects me to criticize her lighting choices.

"I like it." I reach behind me and nudge the bedroom door closed. Her whole bed somehow stands between us. "What are you doing all the way over there?" I ask.

She leans over and touches something on a small desk near the window. "I wanted to show you the flowers."

My gaze lands on the bouquet. She really did leave them in a spot where they'd be directly in her line of sight. Now I'm even happier I remembered to send them.

I move closer to her and study the arrangement for a few seconds. I wanted to give her something pretty, and unique—like her. "They reminded me of you."

"You said that." She presses closer to my side, brushing her arm against mine.

I turn to face her and lean in, inhaling her fresh, clean scent. With one hand, I sweep her hair over her shoulder and brush my lips against her neck, over her pulse.

"Oh." She gasps in surprise and angles her head to give me room.

I clamp one hand on her hip and pull her against me. The sweetest moan passes her lips. Her fingers dig into my shoulder, bracing herself. I find my way to her lips again and she opens for me immediately. Her fingers slide from my shoulder into my hair, tugging with an eagerness that makes me groan.

Somehow, I work my hands between us, tugging at the tiny hidden buttons of her blouse. Jesus, my big hands were *not* made for buttons this damn small. It takes some finessing but I work the first few loose.

Emily lets out a throaty laugh and pulls back, quickly unbuttoning it the rest of the way and letting the material slip from her shoulders. She tosses the blouse on the desk.

Fuck me. I step back and take in the bright-pink bra barely containing her breasts and run my hand over my chin.

She brings her hands to the button of her jeans and plays with it for a second. "Should I continue?"

"Definitely."

Laughing at my not-fucking-around response, she slowly slides them over her hips. Matching pink panties come into view. Damn, that's cute.

"You match the roses," I say. At least I think so. I can't take my eyes off her long enough to verify.

The corners of her mouth quirk. "Happy accident."

"Indeed." I wave my hand between us. "Continue."

"This seems unfair," she says, curling her fingers around the hem of my T-shirt.

"What?"

"Take this off. I want to see more of you."

"This?" I pinch and pull the fabric away from my chest. "I thought you liked this shirt on me. Now you want me to take it off?" I frown with fake confusion.

Her mouth slides into a sly smile. "I *do* like it on you. But I think it'll look even better over there." She jerks her thumb over her shoulder toward her desk.

"All right." I strip it off and toss it next to her blouse.

She sucks in a quick breath. "Holy fuck, you're hot." Awkward laughter follows and she slaps her hand over her mouth. "Sorry."

I curl my fingers around her wrist and drag her hand away from her lips. "Why? I want you to like what you see."

"Oh, I like. Very much." She steps closer and lightly runs her fingertips over my shoulders, leaving a shivery sensation behind. My dick's painfully close to punching a hole through my jeans.

Then, she leans in and presses a kiss over my heart.

For a second, I'm too stunned by the sweet gesture to respond. She lifts her gaze to mine. Even with the wicked smile playing over her lips, there's something vulnerable shining in her eyes.

"Come here." I grip her chin and tilt her head, then fuse my lips to hers. She mashes up tight against me. The silky fabric of her bra sliding over my skin. Her hands tickle along my spine, then sneak under the waistband of my jeans.

Together, we shuffle and nudge each other toward the bed. She hits it first and drops onto the mattress, breaking our kiss.

Quick and eager, she kneels in front of me and tugs at my belt. She has the lightest wash of freckles over her chest and shoulders. How did I miss those before?

"Easy." I close my hand over hers. "There's no rush."

Her forehead crinkles and she pushes her lips into a playful pout. "But this looks painful." She cups me through my jeans and rubs hard enough to make me groan.

Why am I trying to slow things down?

Because she's not a quick fuck.

"I want to see you, first." And I enjoy playing with her way too much.

She hooks her thumb under her bra strap, teasing it on and off her shoulder. "I'm right here."

My gaze darts to her nightstand. How much can my playful girl handle? "Do you have any toys?"

"Toys?" She sits back on her heels and frowns. "Like Legos? Or sex toys?"

I choke on a laugh and shake my head. "Like a vibrator."

Another frown and a twist of her lips to the side. "We already know you don't need any assistance getting me *there*."

Fuck, yes. I haven't stopped thinking about the way she catches fire since that night on her couch. "True. But I still want to know if you have any."

"Will you judge me if I say yes?"

"I'm the one who asked." I step away and clasp my hands behind my back, like the good boy I'll pretend to be for at least a few minutes. "Show me."

She arches an eyebrow. "Come again?"

"No, that's what *you'll* be doing. Again and again tonight." I locate a short stool in front of her dresser and roll it over to the end of her bed. I drop onto it carefully, praying the delicate thing can hold my weight.

"What are you doing?" she asks.

I guess it's time to use plainer words. "I want to watch you get yourself off."

She reels back and shifts to the middle of the bed. "No way."

"Why not?"

"Because." She sputters and looks around, like the answer can be found tangled in the blankets. "That's *personal*." She whispers the last word.

I stare her dead in the eyes. "I've had my tongue buried in your pussy. It doesn't get more personal than that."

The prettiest shade of pink spreads over her chest up to her cheeks. But she lifts her chin. "You've got a point," she says with a boldness that seems to override her embarrassment. Her gaze drops to my belt. "Take your pants off and I'll consider allowing you to meet Little Roger."

Now I lift *my* eyebrows. "You named it *Little Roger?*"

She shrugs but blushes an even deeper shade of pink. "Like Roger Rabbit. Never mind." Her nose wrinkles. "You're not going to get jealous and try to throw him out, are you? I had a guy throw a tantrum once and I have to tell you, it was a very unmanly scene. Left my vagina drier than a pinecone."

I choke on another laugh. Jesus Christ, the stuff that comes out of her mouth. Then I frown as I picture her *here* in this bed with another man.

"Real men aren't intimidated by toys." I flash a wicked smile. "And they like to know every possible way to get their partner off."

"Every possible way." She touches her fingertips to her chest. "Oh, my."

She leans toward the nightstand, stretching and arching her back in a way that's tempting as fuck. My heart rate revs as she digs around in the drawer for a few seconds. Finally, she pulls out a little white-and-purple wand with what looks like two pointy purple bunny ears.

"That's it?" I ask.

She slants a warning look my way. "You said you wouldn't judge."

"No judging." I hold up my hands.

She flicks a button and the little thing buzzes to life, ears vibrating like crazy. Stronger motor than I expected. She clicks it off and stares at me.

"Well?" I prompt.

"Your pants are still on."

Biting my lip to hold in my laughter, I unbuckle my belt. She slicks her tongue over her bottom lip, eyes shining with anticipation. The way she looks at me could easily turn into my new favorite addiction.

Before taking off my jeans, I pull a few condoms from my pocket and toss them on the floor next to my foot.

Emily crawls to the edge of the bed and slips her fingers under the band of my boxer briefs.

"No." I wrap my fingers around her wrist. "You only said *pants* off. Be a good girl and honor your end of the deal."

My voice remains firm and steady, but fuck me, if her hand slides any lower, this game is *over*.

"Fair," she concedes, nodding and moving back into the center of the bed.

"No." I ease onto the stool, dragging it as close as possible. "Down here." I pat the foot of the bed.

The first hint of real unease flickers over her expression. "That's, um, really front and center."

"I don't want to miss anything."

She bites her lip.

"What are you worried about?"

"Dimples on my thighs? Stray hairs?" She shrugs. "I don't know."

I bark out a harsh laugh. "I assure you I'll be one hundred percent focused on where that rabbit is."

She lets out an annoyed huff. "Fine." Quickly, she scooches toward me.

When she stops, she's still too far away. I wrap my hands around her ankles and drag her all the way to the edge.

"I don't know if I'll be able to do it with you watching so damn close," she mutters.

"Yes, you can." I tease my fingers over the straps of her underwear. "Need help?"

"No." She tilts her head. "Do you want to watch how *I* do it, or is this purely for your viewing pleasure?"

Interesting way to put it. And I understand the difference better than she realizes. Women writhe, moan, and roll around touching themselves in the hopes of capturing my attention all the time. That's not what I need or want from Emily, though.

"I don't want a performance, Emily," I answer honestly. "I want the real you. All of you. Pretend I'm not here."

"That's kind of hard to do when you're right up in my business." She waves her hand between us.

I sit back, crossing my arms over my chest. "I'll behave."

"Okay." She's still hesitant but she brings her legs up, placing her feet on the bed and leaning back on her elbows.

I open my mouth, then swallow down my filthy words. I promised to be a silent viewer. And I'm dying to see exactly what she likes.

"God, I can't believe I'm doing this," she mutters so low I almost don't catch the words.

Then she clicks on the vibrator and I fight the urge to tell her to open her legs.

She's slow at first. Tentative. Because I'm here or that's how she normally starts, I'm not sure. I uncross my arms and lean forward.

"Are you watching?" she whispers.

I'm close enough to brush my lips against her shin and kiss the inside of her knee, silently answering her question.

"Oh." She lets out a shivery little laugh and parts her legs.

Much better.

Nervous or not, the fabric between her legs is slightly darker than the rest of the material. Evidence this is turning her on. She drags the little rabbit over her underwear, lazily tracing a path along the seam of her lips. Each time she passes over her clit her body jumps the tiniest bit. After a few minutes of gentle teasing, she lifts her hips and hooks her free hand in her underwear.

"Off?" I ask, my hands already gripping the fabric.

She whimpers and nods.

I ease them down her legs, dropping them on the floor.

"Good girl." I curl my hand around one of her ankles and kiss her calf. "Keep going. Please."

She presses the rabbit tightly against her body and lifts her hips, chasing release. After a few maddening circles, a frustrated sound tears from her throat.

"Shh. Relax." I kiss her other leg. "You're so beautiful. Slow down. There's no rush."

I don't know what she was so worried about. She's perfection. Pink and glistening. Every movement of her body is honest. Every sound raw. Not loud, fake, or forced.

I'm not going to make it much longer.

Emily

Am I really doing this? Masturbating in front of Dex? It's kind of hot but I can't...shut off my brain. Even though I balked at first, having him so focused on me is an intense rush. Whether he realizes it or not, he keeps making this hungry growl of approval that bolsters my confidence.

Dammit. Little Roger never lets me down. I punch the button to turn it up to the highest setting. That usually does the trick in minutes. But I'm still obsessing over why he wanted this and how I must look to him. All the noise in my head won't let me *finish*.

A soft brush of Dex's mouth against my calf sends a thrill through me. Who knew a gentle kiss on my *leg* could be so hot? It helps me focus, work the little vibrator harder against my clit, pushing my body toward the edge of a cliff.

Sweet, sweet relief.

I moan through the orgasm, my body thrashing and twisting in the blankets. I'm riding the final waves of pleasure when the bed dips. Dex's big hands press my thighs wider apart and he licks and kisses me.

Little Roger, your services are no longer required.

I toss the vibrator on the floor with a clunk. It continues buzzing loudly against the hardwood.

"Oh my... oh shit." I twine my fingers in his hair and force my hips up. He growls noises of encouragement, not at all put off that I'm grinding myself against his face. But, oh God, *that feels amazing.* He slides two fingers inside me, slowly working them in and out.

Another orgasm hits, slamming into me harder than the first.

"That's it," Dex encourages. "God you're beautiful." He kisses the crease of my thigh, scrapes his teeth against my hip, kisses my stomach, over my ribs. At the edge of my bra, he stops.

"This needs to go. Now," he says.

"Help me." I lift off the bed, wrapping my arms around his neck to hold myself up. We're totally in sync. His hands work my bra clasp loose in seconds and I quickly strip it off the rest of the way.

"Better?" I ask, falling back against the bed.

"Much." He presses one palm against the mattress, next to my face, dipping down to kiss me. "Thank you."

"Thank *you*," I whisper, lifting one leg and rubbing it against his side and hip.

He palms my breast and strokes his thumb over my nipple. Sparks shoot straight to my core. He ducks his head, closing his lips around my nipple and sucking hard.

I groan and shove my hands through his hair, then clutch his broad shoulders.

He lifts his head and stares into my eyes. His cock nudges my entrance.

"Yes, yes." Then my body freezes. "Condom?"

"Way ahead of you." He pushes forward again and I lift my other leg, hugging them to his sides.

"Then please fuck me."

His lips twist into a sadistic smile. "Patience, my little firecracker."

I curl my fingers in his hair and drag his face closer, kissing him hard. He groans into my mouth and loses the last threads of control.

"Finally, finally, finally," I sigh against Dex's lips as he enters me.

"Easy, we're just getting started," he says.

I squirm and try to open for him, adjusting to his size. "Jesus," I breathe out. "Is that why you wanted me to play first? To make sure I'd be prepared to handle your massive cock?"

He rumbles with laughter and leans in to kiss my forehead. "You figured me out."

I clench my legs around him tighter. He kisses me again and I lose myself to sensation, opening as he deepens our kiss, sucking my tongue into his mouth. Everything about his movements and his delicious kisses sends me spiraling higher. He moves faster, pumping into me harder with every single thrust. I can't get enough. I lift my leg higher and he hooks his arm around it, then the other one, spreading me impossibly wide.

"Oh my God," I gasp.

"Think you can come for me again?" he rasps.

"God, yes. If you keep…doing…exactly that."

He growls rough and sexy, but maintains his pace, just as I asked.

"Oh, that's good. That's so good. Right there." Jesus, we fit together like puzzle pieces. The man's designed to hit every single one of my pleasure spots. "Right there."

Another toe-curling orgasm seizes my body, leaving me shuddering and breathless. My release seems to flip a switch in him. He groans and squeezes his eyes shut.

"Fuck, Emily," he rasps. The intensity in his voice and the tension in his body are beautiful things. His body jerks, and he curses as he comes.

Sweaty and breathing hard, he smiles down at me, then collapses on the bed. Gathering me in his arms, he slides closer, until our slick skin fuses. He kisses my cheek. "I wanted that to be *much* longer." His hand slides over my ribs, stops to clutch my hip, then roams to my butt. He can't seem to stop touching and exploring my body and I'm definitely not complaining.

"Watching you with that little rabbit when I've been thinking of you nonstop all week was probably a bad idea."

My heart stutters. He's really been thinking of me all week?

"You've been on my mind a lot too. You're lucky I didn't pounce on you in the driveway." I touch my finger to his bottom lip. "And I think you did just fine." I give him a playful squint. "You're quite loud. It's really hot."

He rumbles with laughter. "Glad you think so."

"So, is that your thing?" I slide my finger to his chin, then trace his jawline. "You get off on *watching*?"

"No," he answers without hesitating. He frowns as if searching his memory. "You're the first person I've ever asked."

"Really?" I wrinkle my nose. "From what I've read, motorcycle clubs have tons of young women hanging around, waiting to do any raunchy thing a biker's heart desires."

I'm joking, or at least it started as a joke. But it seems to touch a nerve. He lets out a dismissive grunt, pulls his arm out from under me, and rolls to the edge of the bed. For a moment, he just sits there staring at the door.

"Dex?"

"Where's your bathroom?" he asks over his shoulder.

The abrupt shift in his mood rattles me. "I didn't mean anything—"

"Just give me a second to clean up."

Damn, why'd I have to open my big mouth? "Sure. Middle of the hallway on the left."

Awkwardness crawls over my skin but it doesn't stop me from staring at his perfect buns as he slips out of my bedroom.

"Fuck," I mutter, swinging my legs over the side of the bed.

Poor Little Roger's still buzzing somewhere under the bed. I reach down and grab it. I pull a T-shirt out of one of my dresser drawers and slip it on, then head downstairs to use the other bathroom. He may have watched me get off and then fucked me silly, but I refuse to pee in front of him.

After the bathroom, I stop in the kitchen for a glass of water. As I'm headed back upstairs, the pipes clank and rattle. Is he showering? What's next, leaving?

The man watched my makeout session with Little Roger, so I feel justified barging into the bathroom. "Are you planning to leave?"

"What?" he calls out over the sound of the pounding water and overhead fan.

For some reason, I'm still carrying my little vibrator in my hand. I toss it in the sink and set my glass of water on the counter.

Dex pulls back the shower curtain and pokes his head out.

Dear God, absolutely no one should look that good with wet hair plastered to their face.

He flashes a grin and holds out his hand. "Join me?"

"Oh." I stare at him like an idiot.

He raises his eyebrows and wiggles his fingers. "Hurry."

I quickly strip off my shirt. "The hot water doesn't last long."

"I figured. Come on."

I take his hand and step into the tub. The lighting is terrible, and we don't have a ton of room to move around, so I end up sliding my body against his. Not that I'm complaining. God, he's a solid man.

"Are we okay?" I ask.

He's blocking the spray so the narrow stream of water has barely wet my skin.

He stares at me for a moment. "We're fine. Why?"

My gaze latches onto tiny water droplets clinging to his lashes. I already like him so much more than I should. "What I said." I tilt my head to the side. "I was joking." *Sort of.*

"There's always an element of truth to every joke, though, right?" he says.

Before I can open my mouth and respond, he continues.

"You're not wrong. MCs have that reputation for a reason. That's the attraction for some guys to join." He shrugs. "I've *seen* plenty of shit. I didn't *ask* for it, though."

I'm not quite sure how to interpret his explanation. It's not like he's being held down and women are flashing their vaginas at him against his will, right?

Don't say *that*.

"You said that's why some guys join. Why'd *you* join?" There, that seems like a safer question.

He frowns and picks up a bottle of bodywash. "Sleep blend?"

"Yes." I grab the bottle from his hands. "It smells good. I use this and the matching lotion. It's part of my night-night routine."

The corners of his mouth quirk. "Your *night-night* routine?" he repeats.

Do I feel like explaining all the demons that chase me in my sleep? Not really. "I don't sleep well. So I use whatever I can to help."

His expression shifts from amused to concerned. "Why can't you sleep?"

I shrug. "Nothing I feel like talking about." Especially when he not-so-subtly dodged my question about why he joined his MC. "Not when I have a hot, wet, naked man in my shower."

He stares at me for a few beats then nods. I doubt it'll be the last time he asks. Eventually I'll have to tell him.

And maybe he'll trust me enough to answer *my* questions.

CHAPTER TWENTY

Dex

I HATE like hell rolling out of Emily's bed the next morning. It took a while to get here. Leaving seems like spitting in the face of destiny or some shit. But I can't miss church. Other than being out on the road or stuck at Crystal Ball with some emergency, I never miss church.

I stare at Wrath's text.

Church. Noon.

Wrath's not one to waste words.

I need to leave soon if I'm going to be on time. Showing up late will only get me fined and ridiculed by my brothers.

"Do you have to go?" Emily whispers, sitting up next to me.

Christ, she's making this harder—all rumpled and sleepy. Still modest, though. Pressing the sheet to her chest like a football team's about to burst through her bedroom door.

"Got church," I answer. "Have to be there."

Her forehead wrinkles. "Don't take this the wrong way, but I didn't think you were the religious type."

I can't quite tell if she's serious or not. Turning my head, I study her face. Last night I took her comment the wrong way—proof I really have no business getting into a relationship with her or anyone else.

But she's too damn tempting. I roll to my knees and rip the sheet off her, pushing her flat to the mattress. "I'm not." I drop kisses on her forehead and cheeks. "Only place I want to worship is here." I press a kiss to her lips, then slide lower. I curl my hands around her breasts and pause to suck at each nipple. "Here."

"Oh." She laughs softly and runs her fingers through my hair.

"I'm not done." I keep kissing my way down her body.

"I get it! I get it!" She giggles and squirms to sit up again. "My temple is closed this morning."

I rest my forehead on her knee and shake with laughter. "You catch on quick."

She reaches down and runs her fingers through my hair. "Tell me more about church?"

That question stops me from burying my face in her pussy. I lift my head and meet her inquiring eyes. "What do you want to know?" I ask carefully.

"Do you all get together to worship at the altar of Harley-Davidson?" She wiggles her eyebrows. "Confess your sins of the week?"

"None of my brothers are equipped to handle that." I snort with laughter. "We're our brothers' keepers, not their priests."

"Brother's keeper, huh." She tilts her head, staring toward the window. "That's nice."

"Nice? None of us are nice, sweetheart."

"That's not true. Grayson's nice."

I let out a short laugh. "To you and Serena maybe. To us, he's a grumpy fucker."

She pokes her big toe against my stomach. "That's mean."

"The truth is often unkind." I wrap my fingers around her foot and tug. "Are we done with twenty questions?"

"Twenty? I only asked one and you never answered it."

"Do we worship at the altar of Harley-Davidson didn't seem like a genuine question."

"What is *church* and why is it such a big deal to be there?"

How can I put it so that her civilian mindset understands? "It's a club meeting. We discuss club business and whatever else is going on." There. True but vague.

She nods slowly. "Club business is stuff you can't talk about with people not part of the club." It's a statement, not really a question.

"Right."

Thankfully my answer seems to satisfy her.

"Come here," she says, patting the bed next to her.

"I wanted to help you come up with a new morning-morning routine." I crawl up her body and flop into the warm divot next to her.

She smacks her hand over her face. "I can't believe I told you that."

"Why?" Except for the part where she has insomnia, I thought it was fucking adorable. I didn't want to call a grown-ass woman "cute" but she was.

I pull her hand away from her face. "How'd you sleep last night?"

She shifts, craning her neck so she can look me in the eye. "Good." Her forehead wrinkles. "Too good."

I cup her face, running my thumb over her cheek. "Why do you make it sound like a bad thing?"

Her shoulders jerk and she pulls away, dragging the covers with her. "I don't want to treat you like a big, warm, emotional support blanket. You can't stay here every night."

I open my mouth to say, "why the fuck not," then reconsider. Why make promises I probably can't keep?

Emily

I don't quite understand Dex's need to rush to this club meeting. I mean, it's a club, a fun thing, a hobby, not life or death. But it seems important. And I'm trying not to be clingy just because we had sex.

While he hops in the shower, I run downstairs to boil water for tea and start the coffee maker. When I return to the bathroom, he's standing in front of the mirror with a towel wrapped around his waist.

God, he looks amazing.

I lean against the doorframe, staring at the Lost Kings MC tattoo taking up most of his back. The club's literally plastered all over his body. Embedded in his skin. Thinking it's just a hobby was a seriously stupid miscalculation on my part.

"Here, let me grab you a toothbrush." Duh, why didn't I do that for him sooner?

I open the tiny medicine cabinet over the sink. Two tiny square packets of birth control pills tumble out, clattering into the sink.

My morning reminder to take mine. *What perfect timing.*

Dex frowns at the labels on the backs of the packets.

"Oh, shit." I set mine on the counter and grab Libby's, shoving them in the medicine cabinet. I pluck a toothbrush off of a different shelf, then slam the door shut. "Don't judge."

"No judging." Dex holds his hands in the air. "But shouldn't she have them *with* her?"

"It's not...my sister's not...yes."

"Relax. It's none of my business."

"They're not for *that*. For her, I mean. We both have..." I blow out a frustrated breath. Eh, fuck it, if talking about this stuff scares him away, he's not worth the energy. "Basically, one week out of the month and honestly, a few days before, this house is a hellscape. You're best avoiding it at all costs."

He chuckles softly. "Or, I could always leave a bag of steaks and chocolate on the porch and run."

Wise man. "Steaks?"

"Iron?" He shrugs.

It's such a sweet thought, I won't contradict him by explaining the prostaglandins in red meat can actually make cramps worse. "Anyway, please don't tell her I told you any—"

"Emily." He frowns as if searching for the right words. "I can't think of *any* reason why that would come up in conversation with your little sister."

"She embarrasses easily, that's all."

His gaze strays to the cabinet door. Pain creases his forehead, and he seems to be struggling with his next words. "Don't take this the wrong way," he says carefully, "but my wife's parents didn't think they had to worry about anything either."

He's clearly uncomfortable with the topic, so I hang onto my protective big sister retort. I kept a *lot* of things from my parents when I was a teenager. Some far more dangerous than skipping a pill. I like to think Libby and I have a more open relationship but I also try to give her space and independence where I can.

Then, his words hit me full force. Does he have a kid? He said his wife died. Did she...I open my mouth to ask, then snap it shut. If he wants to tell me, he will.

"I'll talk to her when she gets home," I finally say.

"I'm sure that'll be fun." The corners of his mouth tip up.

"Maybe I'll have Serena talk to her, she seems to open up to her easier," I say.

"Serena's been through a lot. I'm sure she's a good listener."

"She is."

Now that this completely bizarre and embarrassing conversation is over, I pop my own pill, chase it with a sip of water, and leave Dex to finish up in here.

If our time this morning is limited. I don't want to waste a minute.

CHAPTER TWENTY-ONE

Dex

NOTHING EXCITING HAPPENS IN CHURCH, which is a good thing for change. Grinder seems grumpier than usual but I really want to ask him about his old apartment, so I'm willing to risk his surly attitude.

I don't want to discuss this while most of the club still lingers in the war room to overhear my business, but Grinder looks like he's ready to bolt so I better ask now.

"Hey, before you leave." I reach over and rest my hand on Grinder's arm. "What'd you do with the lease on your apartment?"

"Didn't have one." His gaze shoots across the table to Teller.

Teller narrows his eyes and lifts his chin. "Why are you asking?"

Great, now Teller's gonna be in my business. "If it's still available, I want to rent it."

"Why the fuck you want to be way out there?" Wrath bellows from somewhere behind me. "It's like an hour from CB. Forty-five minutes from here." He pulls out his chair and drops into it again.

"I'm aware of where it's located." Goddammit. Can't anyone have a private conversation around here?

"You want to be closer to Emily?" Grinder asks. Bet he's smirking under that bushy fucking beard.

"Yeah." Why bother lying?

"Puts you closer to our wee support club, too," Murphy adds.

"Saying *wee* doesn't make me not want to call you a leprechaun, you know," Wrath says.

"You can have the place," Teller says. "Rent free."

My gaze swings between Teller and Grinder.

Teller sighs and sits forward, resting his elbows on the table. "I own the building."

"My, my, look at you." Wrath clucks his tongue. "Our little prince is a real estate mogul."

"Look who's talking," Teller says. "Aren't you and Trinity about to close on your retreat up north?" Teller focuses on me again. "Top apartment is available to any brother in need. Still furnished. Nothing fancy. But it's yours if you want it."

Well, shit. That was simple. And I don't even have to deal with Grinder's grumpy ass. Just Teller's. "Thanks, brother."

Wrath pushes his chair away from the table, stands, and pats my shoulder. He doesn't offer any more thoughtful commentary, thank fuck.

"I gave my keys back to the little prince," Grinder says, lifting his chin in Teller's direction.

Teller rolls his eyes. "We can stop with the *little prince* bullshit any time now."

"I'll catch you later," Grinder says.

"Everything all right?" I ask.

"Serena wasn't feeling too hot this morning. I want to get back to her."

Aw, shit. "She's close to her due date, right?"

"Yeah," he says in that slow, irritable way of his, "that's why I wanna stop gabbing and get back to her."

"Go, go." I thump his back. "Call me if you need something."

"Keep us in the loop," Rock says as Grinder hurries out the door.

"Not that it's a contest, but I want to check on Charlotte," Teller says, pushing his chair in. "Stop by my place when you get a chance and I'll give you the keys."

"Shouldn't you put like a keypad or something on the place?" Murphy asks.

Teller scowls. "I guess I could. Then I'd have to run out there and change the code every time one of my deviant brothers spent the night there." He glances my way. "Not you, Dex."

"Didn't think you were talking about me."

Rock catches my eye. "Stick around for a minute."

What now? "Sure, boss."

Murphy and Teller leave, tossing insults and jokes at each other the whole way out.

Rock shakes his head as he watches them.

"Things are getting back to normal," I say. None of us brought it up but we'd all felt the tension between Rock, Teller, and Murphy right before Rock and Teller announced their familial relationship to the rest of the club.

"Feels like it." The corners of his mouth turn up. "I think Bit-bit's arrival helped."

"Hard to be mad at your best friend when he's your kid's uncle, I guess."

He snorts. "Yeah, something like that." He slaps his palm against the table and sits forward. "Enough about those knuckleheads, you doing okay?"

The answer rolls out of my mouth with ease. "Everything's good."

"Moving out to Johnsonville?"

"I don't know about *moving* out there. Just looking for a place to crash when I need it."

"So, you're good?" he asks again. "Need extra help at Crystal Ball?" He runs his hand over the back of his neck and shifts his gaze toward the door. "Any time off?"

"Nah, things are finally picking up. I hate saying this since he's pissed me off a few times lately, but Rav's able to lock his bullshit down and actually be helpful at the club."

He snorts. "Must be why he's been extra obnoxious when he's *here*."

"Ahh." I rub my chin like a great truth has been revealed. "It all makes sense now. I guess I'll forgive him for giving me shit about Emily."

His lips quirk for a moment, then he turns serious again. "Besides Crystal Ball, things are going well?" he asks carefully.

What's with the hesitation? Rock's usually direct and to the point. And why does he keep asking me the same question in different ways?

"Life is good. No complaints."

"Think you'll bring Emily around here soon?" he asks. "I spoke to her at Marcel and Charlotte's wedding. She's a lively one." His lips curve in a fond way.

"Uh, it's a little soon to make that call, Rock." I run my hands through my hair. "I'm not quite sure how she feels about the club."

"Serena must have mentioned—"

"Yeah, about her time with Shadow."

"I'd love to dig that asshole up, just to slit his throat again myself." His gaze shifts to the door behind me. "Emily was at Serena's baby shower. Got to spend time with all the women. Seeing Serena with Grinder hasn't eased her concerns?"

"She hasn't really voiced any *concerns*." The last thing I need is Rock thinking Emily will cause the club trouble. "But she's the guardian for her sister, and protective of her."

"Libby, right? I met her too. Nice girl."

"She is."

"When you're ready to invite them up, let Hope know, so she can be here." He waves one hand toward the rest of the clubhouse. "She can help you ease them in slowly."

My throat tightens. *This* is why the club's always been my family. Our former president didn't give a fuck about what was going on in our personal lives. And he enjoyed pushing buttons to get the ol' ladies and any other women associated with the club to fight each other. Never would've occurred to him to have the ol' ladies look after each other and form their own sisterhood, which in turn benefits the whole club.

"Appreciate that, Rock. I'll check in with Hope when I'm ready. Pretty sure Wrath dug around in her background when Serena was staying at Emily's."

"Sounds about right. Plus, we all know Grinder thinks highly of her."

"Yeah." I jerk my thumb over my shoulder toward Grinder's now vacant chair. "He's been lecturing me on how he'll break my bones if I break Emily's heart."

I was trying to make Rock laugh, but more grief seems to weigh him down.

"It's all good, Prez. We worked it out," I assure him.

"All right." He pauses. "If you do need something—anything. You can always call me."

"I know."

We both stand and push in our chairs. He comes closer and rests his hand on my shoulder, steering me toward the door. "Are you sticking around?"

"Not today. I have a lot of work to do."

"Inventory?"

"Yup. Willow's helping, so it should go quick."

"No...other plans?" He snaps his mouth shut and nods. "That's good. If you run into any issues, reach out to Z."

"I have. He stopped by and helped me with a few things not that long ago."

"Good."

Outside the war room, Hope's waiting for Rock in her usual spot on the corner couch. Grace is on the floor at her mom's feet, busy playing with some sort of board with little animals attached by Velcro. By her big grin and happy squeals, ripping the toys off the board is the best part of the game.

"Where's your partner in crime, Gracie?" I ask.

She whips her head around and grins up at me. Then her eyes land on Rock and she forgets all about me.

"Daddy!" She lifts her arms in the air and Rock bends over to grab her.

"Uncle Wrath was telling her how tasty the deer are." Hope flicks the tiny stuffed deer on Grace's toy board and rolls her eyes.

Rock chuckles.

Hope stands and leans up to kiss Rock. She fusses with the bow in Grace's little red-gold ringlets before settling her inquisitive eyes on me.

"How are you, Dex?"

"Not too bad." I nod at Grace. "She's getting bigger every time I see her."

She shines a soft smile on her daughter and husband. "Don't I know it."

"Gracie! Come on!" a little boy's voice shouts.

The three of us turn to see Z's son peeking around the end of the hallway, frantically waving his hand.

"Pancakes!" he yells.

Grace squirms and wiggles until Rock sets her down.

"Easy," Hope warns.

Even in his excitement, Chance is gentle with Grace. He takes her hand and hurries her down the hallway toward the kitchen. We follow them part of the way. Rock watches them like a hawk until he spots Lilly waiting for them outside of the dining room.

"It's good they all have each other to play with," I say to Hope.

"It is," she agrees. "Although, Ravage keeps insisting Chance needs another little boy to play with so he doesn't turn out *too girly*." She rolls her eyes.

"I've been trying to talk Juliet into bringing Atlas up here so he can hang out with the kids."

"Oh?" She lifts her eyebrows. "That would be nice. Why do I sense an issue?"

"Vapor's fine with it." I shrug. "The club concerns her, though."

"She's a young mom. I'm sure she's cautious. Does she have any other mom friends?"

"I honestly don't know."

"Maybe Heidi and I could meet her somewhere away from the club?" she suggests. "Then the little guys could hang out, but it won't feel too club-related?"

There's that tightening in my throat again. It's a sweet offer. Fuck knows Hope has enough to keep her busy without acting as our Lost Kings MC outreach counselor. And this isn't even about trying to bring Vapor into the club so he'll patch-in. It's about bringing family into the fold.

"Thanks, Hope. I'll keep that in mind."

One of the dining room doors slams open. "Daddy!" Grace shrieks.

The swinging door is on its way back when Z slams his palm against it, stopping it from hitting Grace on the nose.

Rock slaps my shoulder. "You need anything—time off or whatever, reach out to me."

I thought we already covered that, Prez?

"I'm good," I assure him.

It's not until I'm back on the road heading to work that the reason *why* Rock kept asking me how I was doing worms its way into my brain. And why parts of our conversation felt so stilted. His hesitation.

This is the first year since Debbie died that I *haven't* gone on my solo road trip. Usually my grief and guilt overwhelm me until I have no choice but to escape to the peace of the open road. I was planning this year's trip the day I ran into Emily in the cemetery.

Then I somehow just forgot all about it? How?

No, I didn't forget. The urge to run seemed to *disappear*.

Because I've been focused on getting to know Emily better.

And I don't know how to feel about that.

CHAPTER TWENTY-TWO

Emily

AFTER DEX LEAVES, I pick up my phone and call Serena.

"Ah, I was wondering if I'd hear from you this morning," she answers. "I thought you might call as soon as Dex left for church."

"How'd you know he—oh right. Is Gray at the same meeting now?"

"Yup. Tell me about your date. Did he stay over?"

"He may have."

She laughs softly.

I can't hold this in any longer. "Serena, you don't understand. I've never been with someone who's so...*attentive* to my needs."

"You mean focused on giving you lots of orgasms?"

"Okay, I was trying to be polite. But yeah."

"What's wrong with that?"

"Nothing. Absolutely nothing at all. He's so patient, too." I grin at the wall like an idiot.

"Mmm, nice combo."

"Enough about me," I say. "How are *you* feeling?"

"Honestly? Kind of shitty. I want this little goblin out of me. But I'm scared of labor. And terrified about actually taking care of him when we bring him home."

My heart twists. Serena has major life changes ahead of her and here I am giving her my orgasm stats.

"Aw, honey, you're going to be such a good mom," I assure her. "I know you are. Gray seems like he's looking forward to being a dad."

"He really is. You want to talk about patient? He's been…God, Emily. The more mommy blogs I've been checking out, the more I realize not all fathers-to-be are this supportive."

Tears warm my eyes and I close them briefly. "That's wonderful, Serena." I sniffle, then laugh. "And, ew, what are *mommy blogs?*"

"Ugh, you don't even want to know."

Facts.

"Hey, you know I'll do whatever I can to help you out too. Libby keeps asking about you, so she might even babysit once or twice." I try to end with a joke, but I don't think it lands right.

"Thanks." She sniffles. "Lilly's been such a big help. I think she's happy she'll have another boy mom around."

Jealousy stabs through me, followed by shame. I don't want to share my bestie with anyone else, even Lilly who I actually like. Also, *boy mom?* There's going to be a lot more of this mom-speak stuff in Serena's future, isn't there?

"Well, I can't wait to meet baby Lincoln." *And promptly hand him back to you.* Nothing. Absolutely nothing she's shared about her pregnancy has made me want to experience it for myself.

"So, when are you seeing him again?" Serena asks in a lighter singsong voice that reminds me of Libby's teasing.

"Tonight, I think. Libby doesn't get home until late tomorrow."

"Well, I'll expect a full report." She laughs then yawns. "I'm about to take my second nap of the day."

"Nap while you can."

"That's what I hear."

We say our goodbyes. While I still have my phone in my hands, I send Libby a text asking about her trip. Not that I expect her to be staring at her phone at all times, but when she doesn't answer right away, worry taps a frantic beat in my chest.

I never should've let her go on this trip.

Ping.

Libby: Having a blast. Miss you.

She follows up with several kissy face emojis.

Me: Be safe.

Not wanting to wait for the inevitable eyeroll emoji, I set down my phone and pick up my laptop.

What the hell did Dex say the name of his nightclub was? He calls it CB...Crystal Ball! That's it.

I type it into Google. Dozens of pictures and entries come up. Some for actual crystal balls and fortune tellers. Who knew there was a psychic right on Central Ave.?

I try again. *"Crystal Ball" + "Nightclub" + Empire, NY.*

Several colorful images appear.

"Oh my God." I sit and stare at the screen.

Young, pretty women, in revealing outfits in seductive poses. A stage with poles. Cozy looking "VIP" rooms.

Crystal Ball isn't a *nightclub*. It's a "gentleman's" club. A strip joint. A fully nude strip club that doesn't serve alcohol and has huge, menacing bouncers at the front door, according to hundreds of Yelp reviews.

Why did Dex lie?

No, I guess technically he didn't lie. Crystal Ball operates from early afternoon until late in the night. And it's a club.

Son of a box of biscuits.

Anger burns through me, followed by a heavy sadness. I thought Dex was better than this. But it turns out he's just another man making money off of selling women's bodies?

Why didn't he tell me from the start?

Probably because he knew I'd react like *this*. What woman wants to think of her boyfriend watching young, pretty, naked women all night long?

Even worse, all the tawdry stories I've heard about how strip clubs operate stand front and center in my mind. VIP rooms used as a cover for prostitution. Club owners who extract sexual favors from the dancers. Dancers not being paid a fair wage or managers taking most of their earnings. Ugly fragments of things I've heard over the years scroll in an endless loop—like a twenty-four-hour news network offering bits and pieces of sensationalized headlines—inside my head and I can't shut it off.

Oh my God. Is that why he wanted to watch me masturbate last night? He's used to women putting on a show for him? Hot shame turns my cheeks red. I probably looked *so* stupid. He's used to professional dancers who know to look sexy and enticing from every angle.

"I don't want a performance, Emily." His words echo in my head. Doubt slows my freakout spiral. Was he sincere?

This is why I had a *don't sleep with a guy until you've dated him for at least six months* rule.

I don't know a lot about Dixon Watts. The things I've learned are superficial—what toppings he likes on his pizza, motorcycles are more than a hobby, he's a widower—okay, that one isn't superficial.

But I thought I *knew* him. He's a good man. Thoughtful, kind, amazing in bed. My intuition—not my lady bits—thinks he's a good man, right? But doesn't this change everything I thought I knew?

Let your intuition guide you, not your past trauma.

Desperately, I type in another search. And another. Maybe there *is* an actual nightclub with the same name?

Crystal Ball + Slater County.

Dance club + Crystal Ball.

Crystal Ball nightclub + Ironworks

Crystal Ball + New York.

Crystal Ball + Dance club.

No other clubs by that name.

Minutes from a zoning board meeting dated a few years ago pop up. Crystal Ball expanded and renovated the interior. Dex's name isn't listed anywhere. Just a law firm. The Lost Kings Motorcycle Club is briefly mentioned in the transcript as an "unsavory element" associated with Crystal Ball. But the board member who brought it up is shut down. By the end of the meeting, he votes to approve the renovations.

I'd looked up the MC when Serena was staying with me and don't remember finding anything about a strip club. Then again, my only concern was that Grayson might send someone to hurt Serena. A concern that turned out to be silly. The man treats her as gently and reverently as finely spun glass.

At Serena's baby shower, I'd gotten to know some of the other wives and girlfriends. Charlotte had even invited me to her wedding. None of them ever mentioned Crystal Ball, strippers, or anything else unsavory. They only had sweet and affectionate stories to share about their husbands.

This isn't accomplishing a damn thing. I shut my laptop down and set it on the end table. I need to take a breath, then go talk to Dex like an adult, instead of making assumptions. That's the rational thing to do. At least my brain says so.

My heart's ragged and torn in two.

CRYSTAL BALL WAS easy enough to find. It's actually not far from my office. It's in a part of Empire I rarely venture into. After work, I usually race to beat rush-hour traffic out of the city. Wandering around and checking out strip clubs is low on my priority list. I don't have any friends or men in my life that visit such establishments, either.

Or at least I thought I didn't.

Parking right in front of the building seems too obvious. Besides, what if someone recognizes my car and thinks this is my part-time job?

I circle around to the back parking lot. Several cars are parked in the last row and that's where I tuck my car. It gives me a prime view of the back door. I scan the row of motorcycles lined up along the cinder block wall of the building. My search stops on Dex's Harley. I let out a sigh. Part of me hoped I'd made a mistake.

Nothing about the plain building suggests tawdry things are happening inside.

It's a strip club, Emily. Hundreds and hundreds of Yelp reviews confirmed it.

Keeping a watch on the door, I recline my seat. What's my plan? Jump out and start firing off questions as soon as I see him? *If* I see him at all.

What if he's with another woman?

Is this the kind of relationship I want to be in? One where I can't trust the guy to go to his job?

"This is stupid," I grumble.

But a few minutes later, I'm rewarded for my stalking efforts when Dex steps outside. Alone.

My stupid heart jumps at the sight of his large frame and serious expression.

Like I tumbled into a bad Lifetime movie, where the girl flips out and stalks the boyfriend who rejected her, I stare.

Why does his scowl make him even hotter? Maybe because around me he's all relaxed smiles and sexy determination. Even from here, I notice the tension in his shoulders and jaw. The silly, smitten part of me wants to rub his back or do something to take the tension away.

My phone buzzes, scaring me out of my trance. I jump, banging my elbow into the door.

"Ow. Dammit." I grab my phone and stare at the screen.

Dex: *Thinking of you.*

A sliver of the icy doubt around my heart melts. He stepped out of a club full of naked women to send *me* a text? Why is he thinking of me when he's in the middle of a shift at every man's dream job?

I need to talk to him. Not sit here and watch like a lovesick teenager. I'm too old to behave this way.

I wrap my fingers around the door handle and push it open.

"Dex!" a woman's voice calls out.

Keep my man's name out of your mouth, bitch.

Chill, it's probably someone who works here.

Quietly, I slink back into my seat, leaving the door slightly open so I don't make a sound and draw their attention.

They're too far away for me to hear their conversation but they definitely know each other. She's tall, skinny, and blonde. An ex-girlfriend?

I wish I'd never come here. Why did I have to let my curiosity get the best of me?

When she steps closer and touches him, I die a little inside.

CHAPTER TWENTY-THREE

Dex

It's mid-afternoon when I step outside and squint into the sunsh... Crystal Ball's heavy back door clanks shut behind me.

Fifteen minutes to myself. That's all I want. A few moments of quiet with none of the girls following me outside to bitch about hours, locker assignments, or whatever else has them in a tizzy.

The relentless throb of the music inside chases me away from the door. The parking lot isn't packed at this time of day. We're not fully staffed yet. Most of the dancers and employees usually park back here. Customers do too, sometimes. They're the reason I make sure someone walks all the girls to their cars at the end of the night.

Someone parked a dark red SUV I don't recognize directly across from my bike. I frown at it for a second. Hell, I can't keep up with all the different vehicles these girls drive.

I walk over to my bike, contemplating getting on it and riding away. No, not *away*. To Emily's house. I can't stop thinking about her. Seeing her every time I close my eyes.

I pull out my phone and send her a text.

Thinking of you.

I stare at the screen for a few seconds, waiting for a reply.

A car door clunks shut somewhere behind me.

"Dex?" a woman's voice calls.

Bitter unease slides down my spine.

That better not be who I think it is.

I glance up. A tall, slim figure skirts around the front of the dark red SUV. Shoulder-length blonde hair frizzes around her face. Skinnier than I remember. Large sunglasses hide most of her face, but I recognize her anyway.

Inga.

Fury seizes me. I jam my phone in my pocket and stomp closer. She better be a goddamn hallucination.

"What the hell are you doing here?" I roar, not giving a fuck who hears me.

Inga recoils, placing her hand against her chest.

Did she really expect me to be thrilled to see her? After the shit she pulled with my club?

Her initial shock seems to wear off. She pushes her sunglasses to the top of her head and continues to approach. Hips swaying, head tilted—all the subtle signals she's always used to get her way. I take in her gaunt face and the circles under her eyes. Her heeled boots scrape against the pavement, further grating my nerves.

"Dex," she says in a let's-be-reasonable tone, resting her hand on my shoulder.

I shrug it off. "Touch me again and I'll break your fucking hand," I warn. I've never intentionally hurt a woman but Inga's begging to be the first by even showing her face here.

Shock widens her eyes and she holds up both hands in surrender. She clearly thought I was the easygoing brother who might let her traitorous deeds slide.

Wrong.

"Why the fuck are you here?" I ask.

She shrugs. "Seemed like the best place to find you."

No, it probably seemed like the *safest* place to find me. "That's not what I meant and you know it."

"Why are you so hostile?" she asks in an offended tone. I'd laugh if I wasn't so fucking pissed.

"Why?" My voice drips with disbelief. "You're kidding, right?"

Her nose wrinkles as if she's searching her memory banks for all her possible misdeeds. What a deep, dark well of memories *that* must be.

"What's wrong?" I ask. "Did all that coke you snorted rot a hole in your brain?"

"I'm clean now," she snaps.

I scan her bony frame and chalky complexion. *Doubtful.*

"You sued eight of my brothers *and* me for paternity." I speak each word slow enough for her selfish little brain to process. "Ring a bell?"

"*That's* what you're so mad about?" Her skeletal face screws into a scowl. "I didn't really have a choice. You think that was fun for *me*? It was humiliating."

Me, me, me. Inga's favorite song. She's looking in the wrong place for sympathy.

"You didn't have to send the papers to Rock's wife," I remind her. *That* had been the most fucked-up part of the whole situation. My brothers and I fucked around and found out. We owned that. And if any of us had been the father of her kid, we would've stepped up. Hope was innocent in the whole situation. She shouldn't have been included in Inga's vendetta against the club. "There was no reason to send Rock's wife the lawsuit other than you being a spiteful bitch and you know it."

A slight smirk curls the corners of her mouth, betraying her innocent excuses. "Well, she did legal work for you guys. How should I know?" she says as smoothly as a kid lying about not eating any cookies before dinner. "Are they even still together?"

As if I'd ever divulge information about my president or his wife to this little snake. Ignoring the question, I continue, "You knew damn well Glassman handled Crystal Ball's legal matters. You had no problem sending your other lawsuit there." I rub my fingers against my temple. "You know what? It doesn't matter. Get the fuck out of here and forget this place exists."

"Dex, I just want to schedule a few shows." She swipes a finger under her nose. "Please? I'm desperate here."

No kidding. Desperation's rolling off her in waves. "That's not my problem."

If she's not on coke, it's gotta be something else. She just doesn't look *well.* A couple of years ago, I would've tried to figure out what was wrong and help her. Now, all I feel is icy indifference. Besides, her looks aren't the point. She could look like the hot twenty-two-year-old who auditioned here years ago, and the answer would still be *fuck no.*

"Where's your kid?" My gaze shifts to her vehicle. Probably a rental. No one else seems to be inside. "Does he even exist or did you make him up as part of your scheme to cause us trouble?"

"No, I didn't invent a son," she snaps. "He's at my mother's."

"You hate your mother." I can't count how many times Inga ranted about her mother's unwillingness to accept what she did for a living.

She rolls her eyes. "We worked out some of our issues while I was in rehab. And she's so happy about her first grandbaby, she's willing to overlook my...career choices."

"You ever figure out who the father is?"

"Yes." She glares at me. "It's none of your business."

"The fuck it's not. You made it my business when you sued me and forced me to go in for a DNA test."

"Dex," she whines. "Come on. It's not like you to be so petty."

Says the empress of petty.

"Aren't you a little old for this anyway?" I sweep my hand toward the club. "You always told me you had a plan to get out of porn and dancing."

"Yeah, well, life wrecked all my plans," she grumbles.

"Life or karma?" I sneer.

She steps closer and rests her hands on my shoulders, tipping her head back. "Come on. Let's go inside and I can give you the *highlights* of my resume. Refresh your memory."

I shrug her off. "Hard pass."

Her gaze shifts to the club's back door again.

"Don't even think about it," I warn. "You have no friends left in there. In fact," I pull out my cell phone and take a quick picture of her. "I'll text this to everyone and tack a pic of your face on the wall, so the bouncers all know to throw you out on your bony ass."

"Dammit, Dex!" she screeches, jumping for my phone.

I'm forced into the childish position of holding it high in the air where her graspy hands can't reach. With my free hand, I push her away. "Settle the fuck down. You're embarrassing yourself."

She quits her mad frog hopping and crosses her arms over her chest. "You're really not going to let me have a shift?" she pouts.

"Nope."

Her gaze slips to the side. "They turned me down at the Royal Dolls in Deadbranch, too. What'd you do, blackball me at every strip club the Lost Kings own?"

My lips curve into a smug smile, pleased Digger, the old president of the Deadbranch charter, had listened to my warning about Inga. "I guess word gets around."

"Asshole," she spits.

"You cross one brother, you cross *all* of us." I nail her with a hard stare. "You know that."

"Fine," she huffs, and hitches her giant purse higher on her shoulder. "I always thought you were better than this, Dex."

"Guilt ain't gonna work, darlin'," I sneer in my most disinterested tone. Tension knots my shoulders. This has already gone on for way too long. "You need to leave. If another brother catches you here, they're not going to entertain your bullshit. I can't guarantee they'll be as nice as me."

Fuck, Wrath might snap her in two for including him in the lawsuit when he'd never even touched her. Trinity would probably happily help her husband dispose of Inga's body.

"What are they going to do?" She rests her hands on her hips. "Kill me?"

I glare at her, wanting her to understand the stakes. "It's always a possibility."

Her skin pales even further and tears glisten in her eyes. "I really thought you'd help me, Dex."

"You thought wrong." I jerk my chin toward her car. "You burned all your bridges here. Take your ass on back to California and stay there."

Her shoulders slump and she finally shuffles to her SUV.

She climbs in and stares at me through the windshield while she starts the vehicle. If she's contemplating running me over, she better do a good job.

I plant my feet wide and hold her stare, practically daring her to try it.

Finally, she puts it in drive and rolls out of her parking spot toward the exit. I take my phone out again and snap a picture of her license plate.

After Inga's gone, I check to see if Emily returned my text. I'd give anything to see her face after that nightmare from the past.

When the fuck did I turn into such a needy asshole?

Nothing from Emily.

Fuck it. I need to go inside and warn Malik to be on the lookout for a walking skeleton with blonde hair and an attitude of entitlement.

"Dex?"

Jesus Christ, what now?

I turn and like a prayer answered, Emily's striding toward me. With the sun behind her, lighting up her reddish hair like a fiery halo, she looks like the firecracker that I like to call her.

My gaze drops to her pinched expression.

A firecracker about to explode.

189

Now what could I have done to put that fury in her eyes?

By now, she's probably figured out Crystal Ball isn't just a nightclub.

"Who was that woman?" Emily asks.

Great. She saw me talking to Inga. Depending on what she witnessed, the intensity of our conversation could've looked like a lover's spat.

Of all the fucking days for Emily to find out where I work and pay me a visit. It *had* to be the day Inga returns to ambush me in the parking lot? I tip my head back, squinting at the sky.

I only do bad things to bad people, so why do you hate me so much, universe?

"Dex?" Emily prompts. "Who was that woman?" she asks in a softer voice. Hurt ripples underneath the question.

"Someone who used to work here." I hold out my hands to the sides. "Is that really the question you want to ask?"

She steps closer. So close, a hint of her citrus and vanilla scent tempts me to pull her into my arms.

But I don't.

Anger still crackles in the air around her. She might not be yelling, but she's far from pleased with me. Can't blame her, really.

Her mouth twists into a wry smile and she gestures toward the building. "Nightclub, huh?"

I shrug. "We're open at night."

"I don't like liars."

A smooth line about how technically it wasn't a lie won't work with Emily. And she's too important to me to even try it. "It didn't seem like good first date conversation. Then it didn't come up again. And honestly, I don't like to think about this place when I'm not here." *When I'm with you, I forget everything else.*

"I...I don't like it."

"I figured you wouldn't. The MC owns the place. My president used to run it, then our VP, and when he moved, I inherited the manager's job." I gesture to the empty space where Inga's car had been parked. "And now I get to deal with bullshit like *that.*"

I'm not looking for sympathy, but I want her to understand it's just a job.

Emily glances in the direction of the road where Inga's car disappeared. "She seemed pretty pissed."

"She was." *Don't worry, she's just a chick half my club fucked.* Then sued us all for paternity. Guilt crawls up my throat. No way is that a story I want to tell Emily. Maybe one day. But not now.

Shit, I need to get inside and warn Malik and Blue that Inga's in town.

"Can we talk about this later?" I ask. "I can be at your place around ten."

Her jaw sets in a firm line, like she's about to tell me to fuck off. Or maybe something more creative only Emily could come up with.

"Okay," she finally says.

Her words don't sound like a warm invitation, but I'll take what I can get.

"We can *talk*." She emphasizes the word *talk* in a way that sounds like a warning that there will be no *fucking*.

Understandable.

I step closer and take her hands in mine. "I'd rather talk this out with you *now*." I tilt my head toward the building. "But I don't have anyone to cover my shift."

"I can't even be mad." She smiles but shakes her head. "I respect that about you."

"Thank you." That means more to me than she knows. "Let me walk you to your car."

"You really want to make sure I leave, don't you?" she says in a teasing way, but something uncertain lingers under the question.

"I don't want you to leave at all." I tilt my head, challenging her. "I'll take you inside right now and introduce you around."

Her lips part but she shakes her head and doesn't say anything.

"Not ready for that?" I ask.

"No."

"Next time." I take her hand without another word, walk her toward the back row. "You really hid your car, huh?"

"I wasn't trying to spy on you. At first, I wanted to surprise you with lunch or something. Then, I looked up the place, realized what it was and…" Her voice trails off, almost into sadness.

"It's just a job, Emily."

The corners of her mouth twitch into a sad version of a smile. As if she's already saying goodbye to me in her head.

I can't have *this* be what ends *us*. And part of me recognizes with a woman like Emily, it's a real possibility.

CHAPTER TWENTY-FOUR

Dex

STEPPING inside Crystal Ball after Emily leaves has me questioning everything.

Why the fuck am I inside this dank, loud hellhole instead of following Emily home and showing her that she means more to me than a job?

The answer is simple.

This isn't just a job. It's a business my MC owns.

And MC business always comes first. That's how I've lived for the last sixteen years of my life. Club first. Everything else after.

Tonight it looks like business consists of two of my dancers about to throw down in the hallway outside of the dressing room.

I flick my gaze to the ceiling. *You've got jokes tonight, huh, universe?*

"Bitch, you ain't gettin' up on my pole tonight," one of the girls threatens in a loud screech.

I touch the girl who issued the threat on the shoulder and lean down. "Whose pole, Stacia?" I ask in a low, menacing tone.

She jumps and turns. Guilt and shock widen her eyes. "Dex! Where'd you come from?"

The girl she'd been yelling at, Desna, rolls her eyes and crosses her arms over her gold glitter-coated chest.

"You about to get yours, bitch," Desna taunts.

"Don't get too excited, Desna," I warn. "You." I point at Stacia, then the dressing room. "Go have a time-out and rethink that attitude. And I'll decide if you're fit to grace *my* stage tonight."

"But..." The protest dies on her lips as she takes in my face. "Okay. I'm sorry," she says, without looking at Desna again.

Stacia ducks her head and scurries into the safety of the dressing room.

Desna watches her leave with a smirk stretched across her face.

"And you," I say in a louder voice to capture her attention. "You're here as a favor to Loco. I find out you're starting shit, you're out. Got it?"

Her wide red lips part and challenge glitters in her dark eyes. Then she closes her mouth and nods. "I like working here, Dex. I wasn't tryin' to provoke anyone. I don't even know why she went off on me."

Unlike Stacia, Desna hasn't given me any reason to question her. A twinge of guilt prickles over me for snapping at her. "She's been here longer, so I guess she thinks she owns the place," I offer. "You're doing good, though, hon, so don't sweat it."

She glances down at her six-inch, clear heels, and wiggles her toes. "You'll tell Loco that, right?"

"What? That you're fitting in well?"

She lifts one shoulder. "Yeah."

"Why? He giving you a hard time?" Loco's an important business associate of the club. He's also a massive pain in our collective asses.

"No. But he'd be okay with me goin' back to escortin' too," she says quietly.

"Do *you* want to go back to it?" I ask.

"Not at all."

"You still livin' at his place?"

"For now." She glances down the hallway toward the stage. "I'm saving for my own apartment."

Normally, I only schedule the girls for a few shifts a week. Customers get bored if they see the same faces night after night. Desna's one of a handful of Black dancers on our roster. She's developed a devoted fan base. So far, I've been trying to spread out her shifts to keep her popularity high. But if she needs cash to get into a better situation maybe I need to readjust the schedule.

"You need more shifts?" I ask.

"Maybe one more night?" She lifts her eyebrows. "I can't do much more than that. I got school."

"Think on it and let me know what works with your schedule, all right?"

She nods quickly, relief lifting the corners of her mouth. "Thanks."

After she leaves, I wait outside of the dressing room, listening for sounds of fighting. But only the normal excited chatter filters through, so I continue down the hallway into the main part of the club. A quick glance to my left shows Lisa's on stage, high up on the pole, hanging upside down by her thighs while her long blonde hair flutters below her. I've watched her do this trick dozens of times and a knot of concern still squeezes my lungs for a second. But she's got it.

Sweaty, dazed men in a range of ages take up all the seats near the stage, offering their appreciation of Lisa's skills with dollars they toss on the stage.

Thank fuck Emily didn't take me up on the offer to come inside. Through my jaded eyes, all of this has become mundane. To Emily, it would be a shock. Crass and seedy.

"She's good, right?" a soft voice says next to me.

I don't have to look down to know it's Swan. "Hey, when'd you get here?" I ask.

"Just now." She lifts her chin toward the stage. "I taught her that move."

"Customers seem to appreciate it."

"Hmm." She tips her head back. "I think she's better at it than I am now."

"No one's better than you," I assure her. "Why else would I keep reeling you back in here?"

Swan's been trying to quit for ages. But her ties to the MC make it almost impossible. One of these days, she'll probably vanish, just to get away from us.

I continue weaving through the crowd, nodding at Willow behind the bar and continue to the front door. One of our bouncers—Blue—has his heavy frame draped over a tall wooden stool in the short, narrow entryway.

"Busy tonight?" I ask.

He nods. Blue rarely wastes words.

"Inga flew by on her broomstick to fuck up my afternoon," I say.

He lifts an eyebrow. "Porn star Inga?"

"Do we know any others?"

His mouth twitches with interest. "How's she lookin?"

"Rough." I roll my eyes. "That's not the point. She's not allowed in here for any reason. You see her, call a brother to toss her out."

"You got it. Too many fine females in the world to mess with that snake."

Got that right. "Malik outside?" I ask.

He nods once.

"Follow me." I jerk my head toward the door. Although Blue's worked for Crystal Ball longer, Malik's a prospect and I trust him more.

Outside, a line of men wait to be let inside. Been a while since we've been this busy. Malik's carefully eyeballing each of our would-be customers. Checking to make sure no one's drunk, carrying weapons, or on our "no entry" list.

I tap Malik's arm and jerk my head toward the club. Without a word, he hands the I.D. he's holding to Blue and follows me inside.

"What's on your mind, Dexter?" he asks in his low, deadly rumble.

I shake my head. "Dex is fine."

"Yeah, but everyone says you got your road name after that serial killer dude."

While that's partially true, it sounds stupid as fuck. Ignoring it, I pull out my phone and find the picture of Inga. "I need you to be on the lookout for someone. She's before your time, but back in town—probably to cause trouble. Under no circumstances is she allowed inside this club."

He takes my phone and studies the photo. "What's wrong with her?"

I can't tell if he's asking *why* she's banned from the club or commenting on her appearance. "Other than being a she-devil, she's addicted to causing trouble."

"Got it." He hands my phone back. "Send me that?"

"Everything all right out there?" I ask, tapping my phone to send the photo.

"Gonna be a busy night."

"Good." I glance around the club, noting who else is working tonight. "I'm gonna have Blue take over door duty and put you on the VIP rooms."

We go over a few details, then I send him on his way. Next stop is Willow to remind her not to talk to Inga if she calls or stops by. Willow's cheeks flush red. She'd been partially responsible for Inga sending the lawsuit to Hope, and even though I don't bring it up, she obviously still feels bad about it.

Nonstop fucking drama in this place.

The longer I'm in charge of Crystal Ball, the more I understand *why* Rock wanted to get the fuck away from here.

A few hours later, we're packed. Numbers are close to where we'll need to turn people away at the door soon.

In the back of my head, the impending conversation with Emily looms like a storm cloud.

From the hallway that leads to the VIP rooms, I catch Malik waving a hand to signal me.

"What now?" I mutter, pushing my way through the crowd. I almost knock one of the waitresses over in my hurry. She squeals and fixes the kitty ears on her head as I pass. Fucking *cat ears*. Maybe we need a uniform for the waitresses. One that doesn't include goddamn cat ears.

"What's wrong?" I ask Malik.

"Got two bros who don't understand the 'no touching' policy."

An evil smile curls my lips. *This* is what I need tonight.

"I already gave them one warning and they said they'd behave but I don't—"

Malik's cut off by a short scream from the room to our left. We bolt into action. Adrenaline thunders through my veins as I turn and push the door open.

I rein in my urge to murder while my eyes absorb the scene faster than my brain can process it.

Topless girl. In a customer's lap. Pushing and struggling to extract herself from his grip. His buddy's short, chubby fingers working to untie the strings holding her shorts together.

"Let her go. Now." My voice thunders over the music. The two customers turn toward us wide-eyed. The distraction gives the girl—Minnie, I now recognize—enough slack to scramble away from them. She trips over her high-heeled black boots, and I catch her before she hits the carpet.

"What's going on?" I ask Minnie, releasing her once she's steady.

She fixes the tiny straps of her red-and-white polka dot top into place with shaky hands but her voice is firm. "This dude is insane in the brain." She flings her hand toward the guy who'd been holding her. "Offering me more money if I suck his dick." She huffs. "I'm done with that shit," she adds so low I almost miss it.

"I got this, sweetheart." I tilt my head toward the club. "Go work the floor or take a break."

"Thank you, Dex." She leans up, like she's going to kiss my cheek, but I block her with my shoulder and pull away.

"Go on," I urge in a gruffer tone.

Behind me, Malik exchanges a few words with her before her heels click away. He cracks his knuckles while I study the two clowns in front of me.

I've been working at Crystal Ball and rolling around with the filthiest fuckers long enough to recognize the stench of trouble. It rolls off these entitled assholes in waves.

I'm going to enjoy this.

Am I worked up more than this situation calls for because of my earlier encounter with Inga? Maybe. But who gives a fuck? Purging this violent energy now will calm me for the conversation Emily and I need to have later.

Whatever the reason, I'm about to deliver a painful lesson.

Ever since we voted Rock in as our president, the MC has forbidden any exchange of sex for money inside Crystal Ball. Girls get caught offering anything more than a dance, they're fired on the spot. If customers try to solicit our dancers, they're kicked out. This is one reason I hadn't been thrilled about hiring some of Loco's girls. Even if *they* wanted to transition to dancing instead of prostitution, the customers didn't know that. Crystal Ball isn't located far from Loco's brothel. That our customers might overlap isn't a surprise.

We need to stay *off* of law enforcement's radar. Being known as the place strippers will blow you in the back room for a couple extra dollars is a surefire way to have cops in here on the regular. Eventually, that would invite questions about some of the MC's *other* activities.

The VIP rooms aren't big. Z redecorated each one with a different theme in mind. This one must've been his version of "sleazy hotel lobby." At least that's what I've called it since the first time he showed it to me. A curved leather-like couch lines one wall. A low, round table that the girls use as a mini-stage rests in the middle of the small room. The walls are covered in some kind of black-and-white velvet wallpaper. Two cameras in the corners are focused on the couch and table.

Malik's blocking the door behind me. He'll make sure no one escapes without punishment.

I stalk around the table, wishing for the thousandth time it wasn't nailed to the fucking floor so I could kick it out of my way. Shaking out my arms and flexing my fingers, I keep my eyes on the one who'd been holding the girl.

"What part of 'no touching' and 'hands to yourself' confused you?" I point to the large, red sign on the wall that has those words spelled out in white capital letters.

"It's a fucking strip club, my dude," he says in this overly goofy, boys bonding sort of way that irritates the ever-loving shit out of me.

"That means they dance, you watch," Malik rumbles. "Not *touch.*"

"Or help them off with their clothes," I add, slanting a look at the other clown. He grins at me like he's proud of himself.

You're gettin' punched first, smart-ass.

They take in the grave expression on my face and seem to realize I'm not here to congratulate them. The first one shoves his buddy and tries to work his way around the table.

I reverse direction, blocking his escape.

He tries to run the other way.

Not interested in a game of merry-go-round, I end the dance by jumping up on the table and bringing my fist down on the groper's cheek.

Pain ripples over my knuckles but I ignore it.

The guy falls back on the couch, clutching his face.

Behind me, Malik snickers. "You two fucked around with the wrong dude and now you gonna find out."

Ignoring him, I grab the other one by the collar, yanking him forward. This one has some fight in him. He throws a wild punch.

Crack.

His knuckles actually catch my chin. My head snaps to the side.

I let out an annoyed grunt as I absorb the blow. Standing on the table is no longer giving me an advantage. I throw the guy who hit me Malik's way and concentrate on the other one. He rolls off the couch, landing on his feet and springs up with his fists curled, prepared to block any punches.

Good for you, buddy.

He throws a punch and I easily dodge it, shifting my upper body to the side and laughing. "That's all you got?" I taunt.

He tries again and I weave the other way, avoiding the hit.

Throwing my fists up, I step closer, drop my shoulder and jab at him. *Once. Twice.* Jaw. Chest. I only throw a fraction of the force I'm capable of behind the punches. I want to teach him a lesson, not kill him.

He stumbles against the wall, then pushes away from it, launching himself at my midsection.

I only have a second to brace for the impact that drives me across the room into the other wall. This time, I fire off a left hook with more power behind it. His head snaps back. I let loose with another shot to his ribs. He stumbles to the side but stays on his feet.

"You had enough?" I ask, preparing to crack him again.

"I'm gonna sue you," he mutters.

I roll my eyes. "I'm shaken to my core."

"Your buddy's waitin' for you outside," Malik says. I turn and he grins at me. "Gave up quick, that one."

I wiggle my jaw, feeling something crack into place. "Great. Glad I got the feisty motherfucker."

From his position on the floor, the guy stares at my knees, like he's planning to tackle me.

"I wouldn't if I were you," I warn. "I've gone easy on you so far."

"I got this." Malik pats my shoulder and pushes past me, yanking the guy up by his collar and dragging him out the door.

"You'll hear from my lawyer!" he yells as he passes by.

In the hallway, a bunch of dancers crowd around me, cooing like I'm an injured toddler. Several of them offer to fix my injuries "in private."

"I'm fine." I brush them off. "Go back to work."

Ravage appears at the end of the hallway, thumbs hooked in his pockets, grinning like a fool. "Looks like I missed a good time, bro."

I meet him and start walking toward my office. Pushing back my sleeve, I glance at my watch. "You're early."

"You sounded stressed earlier. So I thought I'd give you a break." He jerks his head toward the front of the club. Stash waves at me from a barstool. "I brought reinforcements."

"Reinforcement or distraction for Willow?" I ask.

"Good point." Rav chuckles. He cocks his head as if he's listening to the music, then wrinkles his nose. "What's with all the pussy-licking music? You trying to give these guys ideas to take home to their wives?"

Since I hate everything that seems to be "bumpin'" right now, my opinion on the playlist is irrelevant. The girls and the DJ pick out their music. As long as they're making bank, I don't give a fuck what comes out of the speakers. "The girls know what music works for them. If they start pulling in less cash, they'll switch it up."

I point at one of the speakers overhead. "What's the matter, that line about *small dick energy* rubbing you the wrong way?"

He snorts with laughter. "Speaking of rubbing dicks—"

I hold up one hand and squeeze my eyes shut. "Can we *not*. I have more important things to talk about."

I fill him in on the Inga situation and a few other things, then take off.

Hoping like hell Emily's willing to give us a chance.

CHAPTER TWENTY-FIVE

Dex

SINCE WE BUILT the new clubhouse next to Crystal Ball, I've been spending a lot of nights there after work. It's just easier to walk a few feet and crash than it is to ride the half hour out to the outskirts of Empire County to the compound where our main clubhouse is nestled.

Tonight, as I straddle my bike and steer toward the highway that will take me to Emily's house, a rush of excitement washes over me. Night riding, when the roads are less crowded and the darkness surrounds me, has always been my favorite. The possibility of a deer jumping out of nowhere and splattering my body along the highway keeps the ride interesting.

I pull into her driveway and shut down the engine, sitting in the sudden silence for a moment. After the long ride, the ache in my jaw and knuckles is a relentless, annoying throb.

I pull out my phone and check to make sure there haven't been any more problems at work, then shut the damn thing off.

Emily will have my full attention.

I'm keenly aware she could decide she wants to end things. Having your man work in a strip club isn't something she'll be proud to tell her friends. Or her little sister.

Don't go worst-case scenario.

My boots seem to thunder over the concrete as I step onto the porch and knock on the door.

Emily

My stomach flutters as I approach the front door. Not the merry butterflies that usually swoon and dip every time I'm near Dex. No, this feels more like a swarm of carpenter bees drilling holes in the foundation of our budding relationship.

I've thought about him inside that club all night. The images I conjured up are probably worse than the reality. Sadness replaces my irrational jealousy. As if we've already said goodbye.

I peer through the glass to make sure it's Dex before opening the door. "Hey, you're early," I say.

"Couldn't wait to see you." He steps forward and lifts his hand, touching my cheek.

Fire sizzles through me.

Nope. I can't let myself get lost in him. Not now. We have too much to talk about.

I shouldn't even bother. I should just cut my losses and move on now. Before I get hurt.

He leans down and kisses my forehead. Cold air and the dry scent of woods and leather cling to him, circling around us.

My gaze narrows on a split in his bottom lip and a trickle of dried blood. "What happened to you?" I frown and pull away.

He touches his mouth and winces. That's when I notice his reddened knuckles.

"Were you in a fight?" I ask.

"Sort of."

I step back, allowing him all the way into the house. He closes the door behind him and shrugs off his cut, draping it on a hook.

Why do I like the way he seems to make himself at home here? How comfortable he seems to feel in my space.

"What exactly does *sort of* mean?" I ask.

He finishes unlacing his boots and setting them by the closet, then stands and faces me.

"It means, sometimes we have customers who don't respect the 'no touching' rule and need to be taught a lesson."

"So, you solve the touching problem by...*touching?*"

He snorts at my attempted joke but doesn't seem all that amused. "The girls there put up with enough shit. We have a zero-tolerance policy for touching in the VIP rooms."

Oh, so we're just diving right into this conversation, huh?

I open my mouth, then stop myself. Setting aside the strip club thing, if he were the kind of man who stood by and did nothing when another woman was being hurt, I wouldn't *want* to be with him. Then this whole prickly conversation we're about to engage in would be pointless.

"Let me get ice for that." I nod to the couch. "Take a seat."

"I'm fine, Emily. Really."

I stare at him until he walks over to the couch and sits.

"Do you want something to drink?" I ask.

"Water's fine."

"I'll be right back." I hurry into the kitchen. I grab a bag of frozen peas from the freezer and a dishtowel off the counter. I pour a glass of water from the pitcher in the fridge and return to the living room.

As soon as I step out of the kitchen, I have Dex's full attention. I hand him the glass of water, then sit on the couch next to him. I wrap the dishtowel around the peas and press it to the knuckles of his injured hand.

His jaw twitches but he doesn't make a sound.

"How'd you ride with your hand all banged up?" I ask quietly.

"Didn't feel it until I stopped."

I study his lip closer. "Let me get something to clean that."

"Emily—"

"Hold this." I tap the bag of peas and he closes his other hand around it, then picks it up and presses it to his face.

A knife of concern twists in my chest. I hate seeing him hurt. Even such a small injury. Shaking it off, I hurry to the downstairs bathroom, grab what I need, and return.

He allows me to clean him up without too much of a fuss. Once I've done everything possible to care for him and prolong what I really want to talk about, I sit back against the couch next to him. He curls his arm around my shoulders, pulling me closer.

"Thank you." He leans in, kissing the top of my head.

I sigh and snuggle closer. "I don't like seeing you hurt."

"I swear it's not a regular occurrence." He kisses my head again, then lingers, as if he's inhaling my very essence. "This makes it worth it, though."

Butterflies return to my stomach. Whatever problems I thought we needed to discuss evaporate.

Nope, nope, nope. Focus.

All afternoon and evening, I thought about what I want to say and how to express it without sounding like a judgmental prude. I mean, obviously I'm not a prude. The man's been in my panties more than any other man this decade. But now, after that admission from him, I don't want to say any of it.

"Tell me what you're thinking, Emily."

I take a deep breath and sit up to face him. "It bothers me that you earn a living off of women selling their bodies," I finally say.

He nods slowly. "So it's not just being around other women?"

"I'm not thrilled about that either."

"Okay," he says slowly. "First, they're not selling their *bodies*. We don't allow *that*." He must have decided to tackle one issue at a time. "That's why I'm so vigilant about enforcing the 'no touching' policy. The women are selling an *experience*. A fantasy."

"It's still..." Why can't I find the right words? I was full of them earlier. "I don't buy the argument that taking off all your clothes is somehow empowering. Even if it's supposedly your choice. If that's the only option a woman has, then it's not a choice, you know?"

He blinks a few times, as if he's entered into a different argument than he expected. "I get what you're saying," he says. "I do. I'm not trying to be a dick and play semantics with you. You're not wrong." He stops and takes a deep breath, letting it out slowly. "It *can* be a seedy business. No doubt about it. We try to keep everything clean and safe for the girls." He lets out a cynical laugh. "A lot of MCs run strip clubs. Sort of comes with the territory."

I didn't realize a "club" had the need to operate a business. "Why?"

"Cash business." He shrugs, indicating I can infer whatever I want from that. "I think I understand your point about choice. But a lot of the girls *are* dancing to pay for college. Others are stacking paper to reach a goal—to buy a house, a car. We have one girl saving to open her own nail salon. Some have kids to support..." His voice trails off, like he's frustrated he has to explain this to anyone. "It's not ideal. But it *is* a way for them to climb out of a bad situation."

I open my mouth, a snarky quip dancing on the edge of my tongue.

But...I'm stuck on what he said about having kids to support. What would *I* have done when our parents died if Libby and I didn't have Aunt Kim to take us into her home?

We had money that our parents left us. Later, we had the house and money from our aunt. But what if we *didn't* have those safety nets? I still wouldn't have placed Libby in foster care.

How would I have finished school *and* supported us?

Would I have had the courage to get up on a stage and bare every inch of my skin to strangers? Night after night? And then go to school the next day like everything was totally normal?

I shudder violently at the thought.

No. No, I wouldn't.

Even though life was difficult, painful, even, after so many losses, I was privileged to not have to even entertain *that* choice. My options never came down to dance naked or be homeless. Strip off my clothes or put my sister in foster care.

"I'm sorry," I whisper.

"You don't have to be sorry," Dex says gently. "I understand your concerns." He lets out a soft snort of laughter. "I think I'd be curious if it *didn't* bother you. But I don't take pleasure in upsetting you."

"I'm not upset. Just...surprised, I guess."

"You mean, you didn't Google everything about me right away?"

"No, I like to get my gossip the old-fashioned way. Besides, the last time I looked up info about the Lost Kings, it was terrifying."

He shakes with laughter. "Really? Our PR must be suffering since Z moved downstate."

"I don't know what that means."

He frowns as if he wants to explain in the right way. "We don't necessarily care what civilians think of us, but we prefer to present a friendly image to the public so people leave us alone."

"Huh." I pull at a chunk of my hair, twirling it around my finger while I consider his words. The blonde he argued with earlier returns to my mind. "So who was the woman in the parking lot today?" I side-eye him. "Just so we're clear, I'm not cool with you putting your penis in other women any time you get the urge. Even if you're surrounded by pretty, naked women all night long."

Dex snorts and glances toward the front door. "Is that what you think? I'm a sleaze who sleeps with his employees?"

"No, but come on. You're eyeballs deep in lady gardens all night long—"

He chokes on a laugh. "Lady gardens?"

I ignore the question and continue my thought. "I can't be the only woman you've ever dated who had...*concerns* about your job?"

Something in the air between us changes. He blinks and stares. No words. What in the hell? This big, strong man who doesn't ever seem rattled by anything suddenly looks like a deer caught in the headlights.

"You *have* dated other women since your wife died, right?" I ask slowly.

"Not really." His steady blue gaze drills into me as if daring me to doubt him.

"I'm the…"

"First one who made me forget—" He winces. "And reminded me that *I'm* still alive."

CHAPTER TWENTY-SIX

Dex

"Oh," Emily breathes out. "Oh wow."

Fuck, why'd I have to get so raw with her? This woman has a skill for making me admit things I'd rather not think about, let alone say out loud.

But the words are out now. They're true. And I'm not taking them back. No matter how much guilt wraps around my throat.

"Does that bother you?" I ask in a tight voice.

"No. Not at all." She leans forward and touches my cheek. Her thumb grazes my chin, but she's careful not to touch my split lip. "I haven't seriously *dated* anyone since...well, it doesn't matter. I made a commitment to raising Libby and sending her off to college. Figured I'd worry about a serious relationship after that."

Respect for what a strong woman she is grips me, followed by the fear of losing her. "So, I'm two years early, is what you're saying?"

"Are we...serious?" Her voice trembles ever so slightly. And it's not lost on me that she didn't answer the question. "This is more than a fling?"

The word *fling* slaps me in the face.

I curl my hand around hers, rubbing my thumb over her knuckles. So soft. "Emily, after the night I had, there's no one else I'd go forty-five minutes out of my way to see."

"I'm sorry."

"Don't say you're sorry. I'm trying to tell you—this isn't a *fling*. I *want* to be with you every second. I hated watching you leave. Wanted to chase after you." I've never admitted something like that to anyone before. Hell, I've never felt that way before.

"You did?"

"Yes." I refuse to play games or hide how I feel about her. "The woman you saw me talking to caused a lot of trouble for my club a couple years ago. For some reason, she assumed I had amnesia and would welcome her back with open arms." I shake my head. If only I could shake off that conversation. "I had to warn the other guys not to let her in. And then, work my shift."

"To enforce the *no touching* policy?" she asks with a wry twist of her lips.

"Yeah. I take it seriously, Emily."

"I wasn't trying to make light of it." She studies me carefully for a few seconds. "How...um, *grateful* are the girls?"

"Are you asking if they offer to thank me in pussy and blow jobs?"

She scowls at my crude question. "I guess if that's how you want to phrase it."

"Sometimes, yes."

Her fingers twist the loose flannel of her pants, balling it into her fist. "And what's your answer?"

"I don't...that's not how I run things."

"You've never dated...slept with one of the girls?"

Fuck. She's got me there. Frustrated, I run my hand over my hair. But I don't look away or try to deflect. "I have. But I knew them outside of work too. One was a huge fucking mistake." *That's an understatement.*

One corner of her mouth twists. "I'm assuming that's the one who showed up today?"

"Yeah," I grumble. *What are the fucking odds?* Inga must have fucking radar for when one of us is finally at peace in a relationship and her inner witch decides to swoop in and throw a wrench in things.

"So, she's an ex-girlfriend. I thought your conversation looked more personal than professional."

"Not an ex-girlfriend," I insist. As much as I want to be honest, I don't want to share more details. The story of Inga and her relationship to the club is seedy as fuck when I already feel like I'm walking a tightrope. Thankfully, Emily doesn't probe for more information.

Wanting to steer her away from talking about Inga, I shift back to the club itself. "It's not a den of sin where we throw an orgy after the doors close." I say it as a joke but given everything we've discussed, it lands awkwardly. "As much as a few of my brothers wish that was the case, it's not."

She snorts. "I can imagine guys applying for the job, thinking they'll get to bang a bunch of hot dancers—"

"Yeah, we don't hire those guys."

"I bet." She cocks her head, a teasing smile playing over her lips. "If you hire guys who just stare at the naked girls on stage instead of watching for trouble, your whole operation will crumble."

I rumble with laughter which feels damn good after this talk. Plus, she nailed it.

"Exactly." More seriously, I add, "It's more than that, though. If they look down on the girls for what they do, or refuse to walk them to their cars at night, they're not fit to work there. A lot of the customers are jackasses. We don't need employees making it worse."

"Wow, no one walks me to my car at my job," she jokes.

"It's necessary. We get creeps who think because the dancers pay attention to them inside the club, they must want to *date* them outside the club. They'll wait outside with flowers and badger them for a date."

"Yuck. I bet that's the *last* thing on their minds when they leave for the night."

More laughter pours out of me. "True." The smile slides off my face. "You can visit me any time you want. Come inside and see the place. You pick the night and surprise me."

"Me at a *strip* club?" She blinks, her cheeks turning bright pink. "I don't think so. I used to love to go out normal dancing. You know, with friends. But I've never…no."

It's cute seeing her so flustered. "We get women customers all the time. Some come in with their boyfriends or husbands." I frown, unsure I should add this. "Although, sometimes those couples are trouble too. They're looking for someone to live out their three-way fantasy."

"Eww." She wrinkles her nose. "Not the three-way thing. No judgment there. But assuming someone's job indicates they want to be any random couple's third-wheel fuck toy is super gross."

Dear God, the way this woman's mind works is incredible. The things that come out of her mouth…

"Let me be clear." Her voice sharpens and she drills me with those intense hazel eyes. "*I'm* not interested in three-ways. I don't share." Her gaze softens. "You're already a lot to handle. I couldn't stand any distractions."

I'm a guy, so I can't help my mind wandering *there*. But the reality of it holds no appeal. I sift my fingers through her silky hair. "Glad to hear it," I finally say.

"We get others coming in to party with their friends," I continue. "Even had a whole bachelorette party a few weeks ago." None of that changes the stubborn set of her mouth. "But I don't want to talk you into visiting me there if you're not comfortable."

"Huh." A crease forms between her eyes, like she's considering my offer. "You really wouldn't mind?"

"No. You can hang with Willow at the bar if I'm needed somewhere. You'll like her. She's worked for us forever."

"Okay. Maybe after work one night when Libby's busy with rehearsal, I'll stop by."

"Good." I want her to understand I have nothing to hide. She can show up unannounced and she's never going to find me fucking around behind her back. It just wouldn't happen. That's not who I am.

"I'd say you could visit *me* at work," she laughs, "but you'd be bored to tears watching me test water samples all day long."

"I wouldn't mind picking you up sometimes." *All the time. Every damn day.*

No. Don't want to overwhelm her.

She ducks her head, but I catch a smile playing over her lips. "But then you'd have to get up early to drop me off."

"I'd like that." It'd be even easier if I was waking up next to her every day.

Do not *say that. It's way too soon.*

"I don't know. Some days, I might tap you on the shoulder and tell you to keep riding into the sunset."

I lean in closer. "I'd like that too. Any time you want to escape, I'm your man."

Emily

I'm your man.

The way Dex says it sounds like so much more than offering a getaway ride.

Am I stupid for believing everything he said about his job? He did admit to having...*relationships*. He could've easily lied. It's not like I'm going to run around questioning everyone in his life to get an accurate count of how many women he's slept with.

"How did you end up as the protector of strippers?" I ask.

He frowns for a second. As if he thought we were done and moving on from this conversation. "I told you the short version. You want the long one?"

"You inherited the job from your former vice president. And lots of motorcycle clubs own strip clubs. That's the short version?"

"Yeah," he says slowly.

There's something honorable about the way he talks about his job. There has to be more to it. "What's the longer version?"

His jaw shifts to the side and he stares straight ahead for a few seconds. Did I go one question too far?

"My mom danced when I was a kid."

Horror washes over me. "Not at *your* club?"

"No. Fuck no." He turns and scowls at me. "I didn't move to this area until I was older. She had me young. Father split. Her parents threw her out." He shrugs. "She supported us that way for a while. Dancing at night gave her the days free to take me to school or whatever. The nights she couldn't find someone to watch me, she'd take me with her."

I try to keep the shock off my face and out of my voice. "Didn't her coworkers mind?"

"Nah. I was a quiet kid. Give me a few toy cars or whatever and I'd keep myself entertained for hours."

He says it fondly but an air of sadness creeps into the story. Picturing him as a child sitting on the floor of some dirty strip club rolling a few Hot Wheels around leaves an ache in my chest.

"Your love of vehicles started young," I say, trying to coax a smile from him.

The corners of his mouth curve slightly. "You could say that."

"So it wasn't a bad experience?"

He shrugs. "Looking back at it as an adult, it was a shitty place." He stares me straight in the eyes. "I can't say she was wrong for taking me there, though. Not when her only other option was to leave me home alone."

I nod quickly. Got it. I won't be passing judgment on his mother.

"The owners were creeps," he continues. "Customers were pigs. The girls all stuck together, though. There was no competitive bullshit. In a way, they were family. So when Mom was on stage, whoever was in the dressing room looked out for me."

"That was nice of them." Wow, that sounds lame, but I'm not sure what else to say. I can't imagine thinking it's okay to let a child hang out backstage at a strip club. But I don't want to insult Dex's mother when he already explained she had no other options.

"It wasn't ideal," he says as if he read my mind. "We run Crystal Ball as clean as possible and I still wouldn't be okay with our girls bringing in their kids. But we also pay them fairly so they can afford sitters or whatever."

"Where is your mom now?" *Please don't say she still dances.*

He glances down and briefly closes his eyes. "She died when I was in high school. She worked *so* hard to get herself out of the life, then couldn't even enjoy her success."

"I'm so sorry." God, we have more in common than I realized. I reach out and rest my hand over his. He closes his fingers around mine. "What happened to you then?"

"My grandparents took me in." He shakes his head. "But I already hated them for forcing my mom to struggle for so many years. So, I was a bit of an asshole, you know?"

"You'd also just lost your mother," I say gently. I understand all too well that desire to lash out at the world after losing people close to you.

His jaw sets in a firm, unforgiving line. "I met Grinder and Rock. They brought me into the club. My brothers were there for me…" he clears his throat, "when I needed them. The MC became my family."

"Chosen family can be more powerful than blood," I murmur.

His eyes widen and he nods slowly. "Few people understand that on a deep level."

"I…I don't have a lot of either—blood or chosen family. Libby's all I have left. And a few friends who've been there for me."

"You learn fast who your real friends are when life goes sideways."

"True," I whisper. "Friends of my parents said they'd always 'be there' for us but after the funeral, we rarely heard from them again."

"That's rough." He hesitates as if he has a question.

My stomach clenches in anticipation. I can't handle talking about my parents' deaths. Not tonight.

DEX

"Was that too much?" Emily asks quickly. "Did I ask too many questions?"

I cup her cheek, staring into her anxious eyes. Is she trying to deflect attention away from talking about *her* parents? I wouldn't force her to tell me something she's not ready to talk about. Besides, I'm too fucking happy she seems to be accepting everything I've shared with her tonight.

"No. Not at all," I answer. "It means a lot to me that you want to know. That you want to make things work."

She bites her lip.

"You can always ask me anything, Emily." I brush my thumb over her cheek.

"Is it your...I'm not sure how to put this..." She glances away.

"You're not going to offend me, I promise," I encourage.

"Is this what you plan to do with the rest of your life? Manage a... manage Crystal Ball?"

Interesting question. I haven't given it a lot of thought. "If that's what my club needs me to do."

Do I see myself doing this for the next however many years? The truth, painful as it may be, is that I haven't given a fuck about my future since my wife died. *Earn money for the club. Ride the wind. Do whatever my club needs.* Those are goals I've had for years now.

With Emily, I visualize something beyond tomorrow.

"I like what I do," I finally answer. "And I'm good at it. It brings money into the MC." More like we launder money *through* Crystal Ball but that's not a sentence I'd utter outside of the war room.

She tilts her head slightly and nods. Is that a hint of disappointment turning the corners of her mouth down or am I reading too much into it?

Would having her see what I actually do on a nightly basis help or hurt us? "I meant what I said. You can visit me there. Whenever you want."

A hint of playfulness returns to her face. Amusement in her eyes. A sly tilt to her lips. "What does a woman wear to visit her boyfriend at a strip club?"

"My woman?" I sweep my gaze over her. "Clothes. Lots of clothes." I curl my hand behind her neck and drag my thumb over her throat. "Turtleneck."

Whatever remaining doubts she had seem to melt. "Just a turtleneck? No pants?"

"Come here." I slip my hand from her neck to her waist and tug her into my lap. "One leg here." I pat the outside of my thigh. She gets the hint quickly, straddling my lap and resting her butt on my knees.

"You like me like this, huh?" She settles her hands on my shoulders.

"I like to see your face." I run my hands over her thighs up to her hips. "I like the weight of you against me. The best part of my day was starting it with you."

Holy shit. Now that she's unlocked these feelings, I can't seem to stop them from pouring out of my mouth.

Thankfully, she doesn't seem to mind. "I think we can end the day even better."

"I'd like that."

"Will you stay again tonight?"

She'd need a shotgun to pry me out of the house.

CHAPTER TWENTY-SEVEN

Emily

DEX's heavy-lidded stare washes over me like a spotlight, illuminating parts of me I'd rather keep hidden.

"Lift your arms," he whispers, tugging at the bottom of my shirt.

As if he's about to steal something more valuable than my wallet, I slowly raise my hands in the air. He neatly peels off my shirt, skimming his thumbs over my ribs, tickling my skin. Instead of laughing, I shiver. He tosses my shirt over the arm of the couch.

My gaze bounces around the long living room. The heavy drapes and shades cover the windows, but I can't help feeling exposed.

"Eyes on me." Dex taps the tip of my nose to recapture my attention. "No one can see us." Even so, he shifts his body to the right, reaching for the lamp and clicks it off.

Most of the outlets in the house have a small built-in night-light that provides a soft glow. Enough to see each other and the shapes of everything around us. Except for the bedrooms, the house is never truly dark.

I can't stand complete darkness.

"Emily." His low, serious tone pulls me out of my morbid thoughts. "Where are you?"

I snuggle closer, sliding my arms around him until they're caught between his warm, hard back and the soft fabric of the couch cushions. "Right here." I rest my head on his shoulder.

He slides his hands up and down my back in a slow, soothing motion.

Awareness tingles over my skin. Pressed together so tight, it's impossible not to feel his interest. I burrow into the crook of his neck and brush my lips against his pulse. He lets out a dreamy humming sort of sound that I answer with my own needy noise. I suck at the sensitive spot and he groans.

"Emily." His hands stop at my bra clasp and he quickly works it loose. I sit up so I can let the bra slide down my arms and toss it aside.

He cups my breasts, lifting, bringing me closer to his mouth. He captures one nipple between his lips, licking, nibbling, and sucking hard.

I throw my head back but keep one hand wrapped around his bicep to anchor myself.

He sucks my other nipple into his mouth, teasing until I'm shaking and whimpering. My pulse pounds between my thighs and I spread my legs wider, rubbing myself against him. He groans and tightens his arm around my waist.

"Em." His voice is a low growl. "Let's move this upstairs."

"I don't think I can wait that long." I roll my hips against him and he curses. The drawstring at my waist tightens as he tries to tug it loose.

I lean into him, rubbing my sensitive breasts against the soft material of his shirt, and fuse my lips to his. I lift myself enough for him to work my pants over my hips. His rough hand skims over my backside and gently squeezes.

"Emily." He tears his mouth from mine. "I wanted to take my time. Worship you nice and slow."

"We can do that later." I wriggle out of his lap and shimmy my pants off the rest of the way. "I need to ride your cock."

His gaze slides over my skin, hungry and hot. "Take those off," he growls, hooking his fingers in my underwear.

I slip them down my legs while he slides down on the couch enough to work his jeans open. He yanks his wallet out of his pocket and finds a condom, quickly squeezing his hard length into it.

"Come here." He clamps his hand over my hip, roughly guiding me to him. I don't gracefully drape my leg over him. It's more like I fall into his lap. I press one hand to his shoulder and lift myself, hovering over the tip of his cock.

"Emily?" He flicks his tortured gaze to mine.

I twitch my hips, teasing him again. This time he captures me with his hands at my waist. There's no point to a battle. He's stronger. He'll easily win. But he holds me still, staring straight into my eyes.

"Are you fucking or teasing?" he asks.

"A little of both?" I raise my eyebrows.

He groans and slowly lifts his hips, while his hands dig into my sides, pulling me down.

"Oh God." I squeeze my eyes shut. He feels *so* good. Such sweet agony as I slowly slide down his length.

Almost too much. I lift myself slightly and his body stills.

"Don't be shy. You can take it." He gives me a crooked smile. "I know you can."

"Why am I naked and you're still dressed?" I tug on his shirt.

"You're the one who couldn't wait." He leans forward slightly and I help him out of his shirt.

I wrap my arms around his neck, grabbing onto the back of the couch. "Don't be so irresistible then."

He chuckles, kisses my chin, and then my cheek. "You were desperate to ride my cock, so get to it, woman."

He squeezes my hip with one hand and cups my breast with the other. Like he wants to touch me everywhere all at once. I run my hand over his chest, admiring his strength. "I'm the one who should be worshiping you," I murmur.

"We can do that later." He teases me with my earlier words.

I stop torturing us both and work my hips in slow circles, adjusting to the feel and fullness of him.

"Faster," he mutters, closing his eyes.

"Watch me." I squeeze his chin.

He opens his eyes and flashes a wicked smile. "Your fucking cunt is magic," he says in a low growl.

That's never been my favorite word, but somehow having Dex say it when he's inside me turns it into poetry. I move up and down, riding him with agonizingly slow strokes. Enjoying the feel of every inch. All my nerve endings focus on the slow slide of our skin.

"Give me your hands," he says.

I hold them palms up between us. He carefully pulls them behind my back and uses one of his hands to pin mine in place. I have to arch my back. Without the ability to hold on, the fear that I'll fall digs into me.

"I've got you," Dex promises, resting his hand on my thigh. "Keep fucking me."

He's right. I'm worrying so much, I've stopped moving. I rock my hips forward and try to tug my hands free. But he tightens his grip.

"No." He cups one of my breasts. "I like you like this."

Heat pools inside me. I move faster. Without anything to hold onto, I focus on where we're connected instead, shamelessly grinding myself against him.

"That's it," he encourages.

He presses his palm flat against my lower stomach. The extra pressure sends a sharp ribbon of euphoria spiraling through me.

"Oh!" My eyes fly open, focusing on his determined face.

"Let go," he rasps. "Give it to me."

All the tension inside me explodes, rippling and spreading to every nerve ending.

"Good girl." He releases my hands and grabs my hips, driving himself up into me. Brutal thrusts that draw out my own pleasure. He curses and thrusts again, once, twice. His body goes completely still. He groans as he releases inside me. I rest my hands on his shoulders and slowly circle my hips until he groans again.

I'll hear those sexy sounds he makes in my sleep tonight.

After a few breaths, his eyes blink open. He reaches for my hands, staring at my wrists. When he seems satisfied he didn't leave a mark, he presses his lips to my pulse points.

Gentle. He's such a big man, but oh, so gentle with me.

"I'm fine." I lean closer, pressing my lips to his bristly cheek. He curls his arms around me, holding me tight for a few seconds. "Better than fine."

I carefully extract myself from his lap and lean over to grab my pants. He curls his fist in them and pulls.

"You don't need 'em."

"You want me to walk around my house naked?"

His gaze sweeps over me and he nods.

Laughing, I run my fingers through his hair for a second. "There's a bathroom down that hallway. And you know where the other one is." I nod toward the stairs. "I'm going to get some water."

He narrows his eyes but doesn't say anything. I snag my T-shirt and run for the kitchen, slipping it over my head before I push open the door. Smiling to myself, I grab two large, acrylic tumblers and fill them with ice water.

Above my head, water gurgles through the pipes. I guess Dex chose the upstairs bathroom. Why does it make me so damn happy he's that comfortable here?

Carrying the glasses of water, I push through the kitchen door and head upstairs. I pass a mirror on the wall and stop. I'm a mess. My cheeks and chest glow red. My hair's fuzzy, some of it sticking up in weird places.

Am I so hypnotized by the best sex of my life that I'm really going to overlook the fact that Dex runs a strip club?

I stare at myself for a few more seconds, then shrug. He didn't go home with any of them. No, he rode straight to *my* house.

Feeling lighter, I trot upstairs.

Light spills from my bedroom doorway. My lips twist. Did he find his way to my bedroom already? I step inside and almost drop the water glasses. He's already turned on the fairy lights and lit the candles by my bed. A simple thing but it seems really sweet.

Barefoot and bare-chested, he crosses the room, taking one of the glasses out of my hands. He brings it to his mouth and takes a deep swallow. He curls his other arm around me, pulling me closer, and shuts my bedroom door.

Ding!

I blink and stare at my phone, then the clock.

1:07 a.m.

What the hell? Sleepy and confused, I grab my phone and flick the screen on.

Serena: It's go time!

"Oh my God!" I squeal.

Behind me, Dex stirs.

Me: Are you okay? Should I come to the hospital?

Serena: Hurts. Gray will text when it's okay to visit.

Me: You've got this. Love you!

She sends back a row of heart emojis.

"Oh, wow." I fall back against the pillow, smiling to myself. Serena's going to be a mother.

Worry wraps itself around my happiness for my friend.

"Is Libby okay?" Dex asks in a sleepy rumble.

My chest squeezes. He's half asleep but still worried about my sister. Not wanting to startle him awake, I lightly rest my hand on his arm. "It was Serena. She's on her way to the hospital."

"What?" He sits up, rubbing his eyes. "She okay?"

How does he do it? Worrying so much about everyone around him? Who worries about him?

I rub my hand over his back. "She's about to push a tiny human out of her vagina, so no, I wouldn't say she's *okay*. She's in labor."

He glances over at me with *what the fuck* clearly written all over his sleepy face. "I didn't need *that* image of my brother's ol' lady in my head."

"Sorry."

He reaches over and checks his phone. Curious, I peer over to see what he's responding to.

Dex: Call me if you need anything.

He sets his phone down on the nightstand. "Group text came from Z."

"Aw, the whole family got a middle-of-the night baby-on-the-way announcement?" For a club of big, rowdy bikers, that seems really sweet.

He huffs a laugh and reclines against the pillows. "Yeah." Stretching one arm over to my side of the bed, he tilts his head. "Come here."

I set my phone down and curl up next to him, dragging the covers up over us.

He lets out a contented, sleepy sigh and kisses the top of my head.

In his arms, with his warm, solid body between the world and me, this is the safest I've ever felt.

I'm scared to get used to it.

CHAPTER TWENTY-EIGHT

Dex

NUMBNESS CRAWLS UP MY ARM, pulling me from sleep.

Emily. Snuggled up next to me. One of her legs entwined with mine and most of her upper body on my trapped arm.

The darkness of night still surrounds us. Careful not to wake her, I slide free.

She sighs and turns over. I roll to my side, curling myself around her and rest my hand on her hip, drifting back to sleep.

A few minutes—or hours—later, a different pain wakes me. My rock-hard dick nestled against Emily's ass.

No, it's not the erection that woke me. It's Emily's hips, slowly rocking in her sleep. The dreams running through her head must be filthy as fuck. She moans.

I better be the only other person in that dream.

She shifts again and I'm consumed with the need to touch her. I slide my hand to her hip, finding soft, bare skin. All she wore to bed was a skimpy tank top and now it's tangled up around her waist.

I bury my face in the crook of her neck and taste the salt from her skin.

"Mmm," she sighs, and grinds her ass against me again.

My skin burns in all the places we're touching. Almost feels too tight for my body. I slide my hand along her hip to the crease of her thigh. Her skin's so silky right here. I think this is my favorite spot.

Her legs shift again. I wedge my hand between her thighs and hiss as my fingers slip against her hot, wet skin.

She gasps, coming fully awake.

"Stay just like this." I kiss her neck. "I'm going to stroke your clit."

Her breath hitches and she parts her legs to give me room.

"Good girl," I whisper, dragging my wet fingers to trace slow circles around her clit. "Keep your eyes closed."

She whimpers and nods.

For a while, I take my time, just slowly stroking and touching, discovering where she likes my fingers the most. The way she shudders and stretches against me is its own reward.

She lifts one arm and hooks it around my neck, lifting her shirt to uncover more skin.

"That's it." I drag my thumb over her clit. "Feel good?"

"Y…yes," she stutters and gasps, rolling her hips, rubbing herself against my fingers.

"Do you want my fingers in your pussy?"

"God, yes," she whispers. "Please."

"Show me how much you want them."

She twists her lower body and places her hand over mine, dragging it down and pressing hard.

I catch her earlobe between my teeth. "You're such a good girl," I whisper in her ear.

She whimpers and nods.

I press my palm hard against her and slip two fingers inside, groaning at how hot and tight she is around me. She grinds herself wildly against my hand.

"Dex," she gasps.

"Don't hold back." I bury my nose against her neck and lightly scrape my teeth over her skin. "Give it to me."

Those words seem to be the key that unlocks her. High-pitched whimpers and quick breaths pass her lips. Wave after wave of pleasure seems to toss her around until she's a hot, needy, squirming beauty in my arms.

"Oh God." Her back arches and her face screws up as if the orgasm that rocks her body hurts. "Don't stop," she pleads.

Her body twists until she's almost on her back. I bite the fabric of her shirt and drag it up over her breasts, sucking one nipple into my mouth.

"Oh my...*fuck!*" Her ragged breathing quickens. "Dex." She flails her arm in the air, dislodging me from her breast. I growl in frustration.

She points again to something behind us. "Condoms," she gasps. "I...I dumped a whole box of them the other day. In...drawer."

I'm torn. I want to fuck her like I want my next lungful of oxygen but I don't want to take my hand away.

"Don't move." I drag my hand over her hip, stopping to squeeze her flesh to emphasize how much I want her to stay put. Stretching my hand over my head, I aim for the knob and yank the top drawer of her nightstand open, praying like fuck it's the right one. Twisting and stretching, my fingers finally encounter what feels like a sea of little foil squares. Jesus Christ, how many are there? My lips curl, pleased she's planning for a *lot* of fucking in our future. Finally, I capture one of the slippery little fuckers between my fingers. I rip it open with my teeth and roll slightly away from her to smooth it on. She lifts herself on one elbow.

"What did I say?" I press her to the mattress, positioning her the way I want.

She laughs and wriggles away to untangle herself from her shirt.

"Okay, that I'll allow." I slide my hand between her thighs, slightly lifting her leg. "Shift your ass toward me. The way you were when you woke me up."

"I didn't wake you up." Her voice indignant while she shifts her butt into place.

"Oh yes you did." I guide my cock to her entrance, sliding it along the seam of her lips first, nudging her sensitive clit until she gasps. "Your hot little ass was rubbing up against my dick."

She answers by raising her leg higher, draping it over my hip. I gather her in my arms, pressing her tight against me and push my hips forward. She squeaks as I slide into her. I nip her earlobe and suck at her neck. One of my arms tightens over her chest and I use my free hand to cup her breast, teasing her nipple between my fingers.

"That feels so good," she repeats over and over in this desperate, breathy whisper.

I can't quite get as deep as I want at this angle, but I love her open and exposed so I can touch her everywhere. In the darkness, I use my hands to map her body, sliding from her breasts, down her ribcage, over her belly, and then reverse direction, stopping to tease her nipples.

She turns her head, catching my mouth for a kiss. Nose to nose, she stares at me in wonder while our lips slide together.

"Your cock feels *so* good," she whispers between kisses.

I slide my fingers into my mouth, wetting them and tasting her on my skin from earlier, then reach down to play with her clit.

She moans and closes her eyes, writhing against me.

"That's it," I encourage. "You're so beautiful." I kiss her temple and rub her clit even faster.

A louder moan tears from her throat. "Please." Her nails graze my cheek as she tries to pull my face closer for another kiss.

Our lips fuse. Pleasure rises in steady waves. She feels so fucking good around me. Hot, slick, squeezing down so hard.

"Go off for me, little firecracker." I suck at her neck, squeezing my arms around her even tighter.

A long, guttural moan tears from her throat.

My control finally snaps. I grip her thigh, pulling her almost sideways and drive into her as I follow her over the edge. She keeps rolling her hips, drawing it out for both of us.

Spent, we lay there in a pile of shaking, sweaty limbs. She carefully pulls away and flips over, facing me.

"That's the hottest way I've ever been woken up in the middle of the night." Her voice is hoarse, a low, sexy rasp.

"Same," I answer automatically.

I've never woken up next to someone, with such a *desperate to have them or I'll die* feeling. I reach over and brush her hair off her cheek. "I mean that."

Why did I feel the need to take that thought further?

She doesn't seem to mind, though. She smiles softly. "Me too."

The unpleasant, soggy condom on my softening dick registers and I groan. "Give me a second."

"I'm going to run downstairs real quick." She presses a kiss to my lips and scoots out of the bed, scooping up her shirt and slipping it over her head.

"I wanted you right here when I get back." I pat the mattress.

"Well, I need to pee." She leans in and kisses my cheek. "And I'd rather not do it in the bed."

Rumbling with laughter I stand and shake my head. "How are you so sassy in the dead of night?"

She gives me a quick shrug. "Probably from the multiple orgasms."

I MIGHT HAVE A PROBLEM. I can't seem to sleep more than a couple of hours without pawing Emily.

At least there's sunlight spilling into the room this time. She's still out cold, allowing me to enjoy the sight of her breasts spilling out around the edges of her tank top.

A faint red line along the side of her right breast catches my attention. Frowning, I lean in closer, careful not to wake her. It's thin, pinkish red with whiteish jagged edges, like someone didn't stitch it properly. I've had my hands and mouth all over her body. How'd I miss that scar?

Because you're always busy shoving your face between her legs.

It's not an implant scar. Fuck knows I've seen enough fake tits to know the scar would be somewhere less noticeable. And I've spent plenty of time with my hands and mouth on Emily's breasts. They're a hundred percent real.

It's not a self-harm scar, either. It's too difficult a spot for her to reach and it's only the one line. I'm not an expert, but the cutters I've known go for easy-to-reach and hidden places—arms and upper thighs are what I've seen the most. I want to turn her over and check her other side, but don't want to risk waking her.

She rolls her head to the side and her hair fans away from her face. Another fine red line runs along her neck, under her jaw.

Like someone once held a knife to her throat.

Fury races down my spine at the thought of anyone hurting her.

"Why are you staring at me?" she mumbles.

I lift my hand and trace my finger over the scar on her breast, then her neck. "What happened, baby?"

She sucks in a deep breath, coming fully awake. "What?"

I inch closer, pressing my lips against the line along her breast, then move up closer to kiss the one on her neck. "Did someone hurt you?"

She turns over and blinks up at me, sleep rapidly being replaced by anxiety in her eyes. "I suppose you're too smart to buy the underwire from my bra stabbed me?"

I tilt my head. She can't be serious. "It get your neck too?"

"Damn it." She sits up and fixes her tank top to cover herself and pulls her hair over her shoulder, fluffing it around her neck. "I don't want to talk about that."

I open my mouth to argue with her, then close it. As much as it's killing me, I'll wait until she's ready to tell me.

She glances at me over her shoulder. "You're not going to keep badgering me with questions?"

"Do you want me to?"

"No." She shifts to the edge of the bed. "I'll be right back."

I wrap my hand around her arm, stopping her. "Where are you going?"

"I don't know," she whispers, misery and defeat clinging to her voice.

I inch closer and wrap my arms around her waist, dragging her into the middle of the bed. "Then stay here and let me hold you." I kiss her cheek, furious with myself for starting this. "I think every inch of you is beautiful, Emily."

That apparently wasn't the reassurance she was looking for. She tries to pull away but I hold on tight.

Her jaw clenches. "I don't care about the scars. I barely notice them anymore. They're just there." She rubs her fingertips over her chest. "Like freckles or something."

"They're not that noticeable."

She scowls even harder. I really should shut the fuck up.

"They remind me of what a dumbass I was when I was younger," she says with the heat of self-loathing.

I choke on the weight of her words. "I'm familiar with that feeling," I say, releasing her.

She turns, tucking her leg underneath her so she can face me.

"Do you really want to hear this?"

Her volatile response has me prepared for the worst. "If you want to tell me."

"I think I've told you my parents were kind of strict with me. Having me so young didn't inspire them to give me much of a sex education. They only told me, 'don't.'"

I snort at the absurdity. "Not an effective plan for curious teenagers."

"Nope," she agrees with a bitter edge. "So I was trying to discover my sexuality and craved male attention more than I should have." She drops her gaze to her lap. "I can't believe I'm telling you this."

"I want to know you," I say.

She blows out an irritated breath. "I'm *not* that girl anymore."

"Believe me, I understand." I'm not the shy, gullible teenager I once was, either.

"So, I thought I was so *adventurous* and liberated." She curls her fingers into air quotes to go along with the sarcastic tone. "Game for anything and everything, because that's what boys like, right?"

She's not really asking for an answer, so I wisely keep my mouth shut.

"All I did was attract a weirdo who wanted to hurt me so he could get off."

I blink and stare at her. "What?"

"Sick asshole. He called knife play his *kink*. I thought that was so cool and edgy." She curls her lip in disgust. "He swore the endorphins would be the *best orgasm ever*. It was *not*."

"How old were you?"

"Eighteen."

I have a feeling I won't like the answer to my next question. "How old was *he*?"

She glances away. "Twenty-eight. But we met when I was seventeen. I didn't realize...Well, it doesn't matter now."

Fury bubbles through my blood. "Tell me the rest."

"He gave me a 'safeword,' then got pissed when I used it." She touches her neck. "Threatened to kill me if I didn't stop screaming."

This is so much worse than I expected. "How'd you get away from him?"

Her lips twist into a mixture of sadness and maniacal glee. "Do you really want to know?" she asks in a low, conspiratorial tone.

"I wouldn't have asked if I didn't."

"I had this lamp on my bedside table. Someone gave it to me when I was a kid." She holds out her hand, curling it like she's about to pitch a softball. "This pretty, stained glass turtle sitting on a heavy brass base shaped like a log or flowers or something." Fear seems to freeze her in place for a few seconds.

I wait for her to continue.

"He had the knife at my neck. I reached over, desperate for anything to get him off of me." She blows out a sharp breath as if shaking off lingering wisps of the past.

"My fingers encountered the lamp first." She swings her arm in a wild arc. "*Bam!* Nailed him right in the side of the head."

I release the breath I'd been holding since she mentioned the lamp. "Good job. That could've gone badly. Enraged him even more."

"It was instinct. I was afraid he'd kill me."

I squeeze her tight and kiss her cheek. "You're incredibly brave."

"Incredibly *dumb*," she corrects.

"You were *young* and open to being influenced by someone older maybe, but *not* dumb." The heat of conviction flows through my words, and I hope she takes them to heart.

"Dex?" She tilts her head back so she can see my face. "I haven't told someone I'm seeing that story in a very long time."

Why does that hot spike of jealousy poke me in the ribs every time she alludes to anyone else ever being in her life?

What she said sinks in. "Why?"

"Because the last guy I told—someone I was talking to online—I wanted him to understand why I was a little hesitant to meet up in person. And he was *way* too interested in poking at my trauma. It was disturbing how excited the story made him. Then he told me it was my own fault."

What the fuck? "I hope you told him to fuck off."

"Even better. I blocked him. Deleted myself from all the dating apps. Locked down my social media. Done. All those little red flags that had jumped out at me before, I finally learned to recognize. I listened to that inner voice screaming *danger*. And instead of doing the whole, *maybe you misunderstood, give him a chance* bullshit, I ghosted his creepy ass. *Poof.*" She flicks her fingers in the air like she's tossing a pinch of glitter.

"Good. He didn't deserve an explanation." *A bullet to the kneecaps, maybe, but not an explanation.*

"By then I realized I had no business trying to date. Then my parents died..." Her voice trails off into sadness.

After a few seconds of silence, she taps her forehead. "I wanted to get right in the head. Be smarter. Before I let anyone in here." She taps her chest.

Our pasts might be different, but the results share things in common. "You're incredibly brave and smart." I kiss her temple. "A lot of people keep repeating the same pattern over and over, expecting a different outcome."

"Aunt Kimmy helped." Her mouth curves into a fond smile. "She was a badass who didn't take shit from anyone."

"You definitely take after her."

"I hope so. Before Libby came along, I used to spend my summers with Aunt Kimmy. I loved being around her so much." She lets out a fond sigh. "She had men swarming around her like bees, begging her to marry them. But she always said it wasn't worth ruining her peace." She tilts her head as if remembering another important detail. "Funny, how all those men disappeared once she got sick."

"What made you tell me now?" I ask.

Her eyes search my face. "I trust you." She drops her gaze to the comforter, picking at a loose thread. "Do you remember the first time we met?"

"Yeah." Couldn't forget it if I wanted to. At Grinder's request I'd already been watching Emily for a while. But the first time we *officially* met was when I knocked on her door, looking for Serena. "I knew you were lying through your teeth about Serena staying here. But I admired how fiercely protective you were of your friend."

"Really? Huh." She nods. "Well, besides being dumbstruck at what a perfect specimen of masculinity you are, I liked how restrained and respectful you behaved."

This isn't the time to preen about that *specimen* comment. "How so?"

"I told you no when you asked to come in the house and you accepted it." She runs her gaze over me. "You could've easily ripped the door off its hinges, if you wanted to."

"Grinder asked me to search for Serena, not terrorize you."

"Well, I could tell you were frustrated but you didn't keep asking or try to force your way in."

I shake with laughter. "*Frustrated* isn't quite how I'd put it. I had a grudging respect for your tenacity."

"Hmm. I like that. Thanks."

"Emily?" Damn, I really don't want to go back to this but I have to know. "The guy who got the lamp to the head, what happened to him?"

She shifts her body, putting distance between us. "I don't know."

"You don't know?" I repeat. "What do you mean?"

She picks at a loose thread on the comforter. "I think...I think my dad might have killed him."

Emily

How'd I walk myself into this corner? No one I've told that story to—my therapist, Aunt Kim, Serena—none of them ever asked what happened to the guy. They asked if I pressed charges and I said no, which was the truth. I think they assumed I was too scared or embarrassed to go to the police.

I've never, ever told anyone what I suspect happened.

Dex stares at me with the strangest expression. "Why do you think your father killed him?"

"I knocked the guy unconscious. I wasn't sure what to do next. While I was freaking out, my parents and Libby came home." It feels like a lifetime ago. Something I never intended to talk about again after finishing therapy.

"My dad saw I was bleeding. When I told him what happened..."

The disappointment and rage in my father's eyes haunted me until he died. And then those memories were replaced with other horrors.

"He called his friend to help him," I continue. "They said they dumped him at an ER a couple hundred miles away but," I shrug, "I never heard from him again."

"Your father probably warned him he'd be taking a dirt nap if he ever contacted you again."

I nod slowly. "That's pretty much what they told me."

That's enough of my history. Too bad that isn't the stupidest thing I've ever done.

"Thank you for trusting me." Dex curls his hand around me and tugs me closer, then presses our joined hands against a tattoo on his side. It's a complicated design that I've admired but never studied. I'm usually too eager to lavish attention on *other* parts of his anatomy.

My fingertips brush against his skin, feeling a raised, smooth area the size of a quarter. As I stare at the ink, I recognize an old scar's embedded in the design.

"I did time when I was younger," he explains slowly, like maybe this is part of *his* past that he thought he'd buried. "Found out the hard way, those stories about getting shivved were *not* urban legends."

"Wait. Did time, where? In prison?" I finish on a whisper.

"Actually, county jail but I was there long enough to spar with a few enemies of the club."

"Enemies of the club," I whisper.

A menacing light enters his eyes. "Long gone now."

"And they stabbed you because of a beef on the *outside?*"

"More or less. Guys inside will stab you over a cup of Jell-O. Especially if they're looking at doing hard time."

"What were *you* accused of?"

"Accused of," he repeats. "Not, *what did I do*. An important distinction."

"Innocent until proven guilty is the bedrock of our legal system."

An invisible mask seems to slip over his features. As if Dex, the amazing orgasm giver, has left the room, and Dex, member of a motorcycle club, has entered the conversation. "I was accused of being involved in the disappearance of a very bad man."

"And?"

He lifts one shoulder. "They didn't have a case and had to let me go."

Not exactly a declaration of innocence.

"I told you, I was an angry shithead when I was a teenager." He rests his hand over mine. "But I've never hurt anyone I care about. People who've hurt *my* loved ones, though," he shrugs, "that's a different story. I'm not ashamed of that." He taps his finger against the scar. "But the reminder to be smarter about it remains."

A sane woman would have gotten up quietly and run away by now.

But I'm still here.

CHAPTER TWENTY-NINE

Emily

My father must be spinning in his grave.

Too bad. He didn't exist on a moral high ground himself.

Am I nuts? Nothing Dex said scared me. And no lingering embarrassment from sharing my story with him follows me into the kitchen either.

While Dex is in the shower, I put my teakettle on the stove and flick the burner on.

I haven't always had the best judgment about men. Is that what's happening here? Shouldn't the fact that he openly admits to hurting people who've wronged him be a giant red flag?

Somewhere around here I have a French press and a bag of coffee beans. On tiptoes, I reach for the shelf where I think I stashed the coffee.

"Now, *that* is the perfect morning view," Dex says from behind me.

I turn, realizing my T-shirt isn't covering my ass. "You're tall. Come here and grab this bag for me so I can make you coffee."

Regret flashes across his face. "I have to get going."

"What?" Disappointment spills into my voice. "Why?" Damn, that sounds so clingy and needy. Just because I have no life, doesn't mean he has nothing to do on the weekend.

"I probably should've done it yesterday." He hesitates. "But I need to talk to my president about some work stuff."

"What's the work stuff?" Why am I being so nosy? We've shared enough personal info for the day. His club stuff isn't my business. And yet, I plow ahead with the question. "Your ex-girlfriend? The stripper who came back from the dead?"

His eyes narrow. "She is *not* my ex." He snorts a humorless laugh. "But yeah, I need to warn him about that, and it needs to be in person."

I sense it's important that he came here to talk to me last night. Then he spent a very patient morning listening to me share some dark shit. I dial back my disappointment that he's leaving.

"Do you want to come up to the clubhouse with me?" he asks slowly, as if the question feels foreign on his tongue.

My heart jumps. I don't think it's an invitation he issues often. But I don't think I'm ready for that, yet, either. "I can't. I need to get my hair done." I twirl a piece of my hair around my finger. "And I have to be at the school to pick Libby up when her bus gets in later."

Disappointment flashes across his face, followed by what looks like relief? Maybe he's not ready for that step either. "All right."

I rest my hand on his arm. "Ask me again, though."

"I will."

"Come over for dinner later." I pause, then quickly add, "If you want."

"Don't you want to catch up with Libby?"

"I'm sure she'll be done filling me in by dinnertime."

"Okay." He leans down and kisses my cheek. "I'd like that."

Both of our phones ding. I turn mine over on the counter and flick the screen on. A photo of Serena holding a red-faced little bundle swaddled in blue blankets fills the screen. I sigh, smile, and get teary all at once.

"Baby Lincoln has arrived," I say. "He looks pretty pissed too."

Dex seems to be studying the photo more than I'd expect him to. Did he get a message with his?

"Aren't they sweet?" I try to coax an answer from him.

"Huh?" He clicks his phone off and forces a tight smile. "Yeah. I just hope they have good doctors looking after them."

I open my mouth, but I'm not quite sure how to respond to that. Obviously I hope so too, but that wouldn't be my *first* thought. "I'm sure she does. Empire Med is known for having a top-notch birthing center. That's why she said she didn't switch to someplace closer to their new house."

"Yeah," he mutters absently, his gaze now focused on the window behind me. "Hope and Heidi were there too and did okay."

For a single guy, he sure seems to know a lot of obstetrics info about his brothers' wives. It's sweet. But I can't help wondering if there's more to it than plain concern.

Dex

The long ride from Emily's to the clubhouse is turning into a blessing. It gives me plenty of time to clear my head and organize my thoughts.

I ride up our long driveway and pull into the garage. Rock's vehicles are here. That doesn't always mean he'll be easy to track down. Unlike Z, I'm not comfortable barging into Rock's house on the weekends...or any other time.

I'll check the clubhouse first and if he's not there, I'll text him.

Inside, a few people are hanging around the living room watching television. I nod to Sparky and Stash, who *surprise, surprise* seem to be high. Sparky waves, then stares at his hand.

The war room door stands open and the lights are on. No one called church but it's not unusual for brothers to use the room to chat about stuff they don't feel like sharing with the entire house. Rumor has it our president has used our table for "private time" with his wife, but that's none of my business.

I poke my head inside. Rock, Wrath, and Z are at the table. Rock and Wrath are in their usual places. Z's sitting in Teller's spot.

Z notices me first and flashes a big, dimpled grin. "Look who it is!"

Rock lifts his hand, motioning for me to come in.

I pull out the chair next to Wrath and take a seat. "Looks like we have another baby King."

Z grins. "He's a cute little shit, right?"

"I don't know about cute. He looks as grumpy as his father," Wrath adds with a hard laugh.

Rock shakes his head. "We were talking about what we can do to help Grinder out."

"I've already been trying to ease him into his position slow," Z says, all serious now. "Things are quiet down there anyway."

"Why'd you have to say that and jinx us?" Wrath snarls. "Now all hell will break loose."

Z rolls his eyes, then taps his knuckles against the hardwood table. "Better now?"

"When your clubhouse gets raided again, I'm going to remind you of this," Wrath warns.

Rock blows out a heavy, irritated sigh.

"What have you come up with so far?" I ask to move them along.

Rock chuckles. "Hope's bought enough clothes for ten baby boys."

"Is she trying to tell you she wants another baby?" Z asks.

Rock slices a cool look Z's way. "No."

Wrath snorts and rolls his eyes. "You've got babies on the brain more than any chick I've ever heard of."

"Whatever." Z flicks away the comment with a middle finger aimed at Wrath. "Lilly and Trinity cooked a bunch of meals for them and stocked their freezer. I hired someone to come over and clean that giant house for the next couple of months. Although, I have a feeling Grinder's going to fight me on that one."

"He doesn't like strangers in his space," Wrath agrees.

"I would've asked a couple club girls to do it, but I didn't think Serena would like them roaming through her house." Z scowls at Wrath. "This is a bonded, professional company. Not bums off the street."

Wrath holds up his hands in an unusual sign of surrender. "I'm with you, brother. Just sayin' be prepared for G to give you a hard time."

"Tough shit if he doesn't like it," Z says.

"He might bristle, but he'll appreciate the gesture," Rock assures Z.

"Sounds like you've covered everything," I say.

Rock holds up a finger to indicate he's not finished. "One last thing. Let's at least pretend to try to respect their privacy."

Z scratches the side of his head. "What's that?"

"Give them a call before showing up at their house." Rock slices a look at Z since that's who this warning is really for. "Stuff like that."

I bite my lip to stop myself from laughing.

"All right." Wrath slaps his palm on the table. "You know where I'll be if you need me."

He and Z leave but end up right outside the war room.

"Well, at least I tried." Rock shrugs. "If Grinder shoots Z for showing up unannounced, my conscience is clear."

I snort with laughter. "Doubt it'll come to that. While we're here, I need to talk to you."

"Is this a closed-door discussion?"

I glance at the open war room door. Wrath and Z are still talking to each other but not paying attention to us.

"No, we're fine."

Rock stands and braces his hands against the back of his chair. "What's on your mind?"

I take a long, slow breath, hating that I'm about to piss off my president and ruin his afternoon. "Inga stopped by CB yesterday."

Rock's entire body stills. He doesn't explode and start yelling. In all the years I've known him, though, his deadly silence has always somehow seemed more dangerous.

I wait and don't say another word, to see where he lands.

He closes his eyes and curls his fingers around the back of his chair until his knuckles turn white.

"And *what* did she want?" he spits out between clenched teeth.

"What else? To dance at the club again."

Laughter, harsh and menacing, explodes out of him. Jesus Christ, I don't want to be responsible for making Rock snap and go on a murder spree.

I cast a glance over my shoulder. Wrath's now watching us with narrowed eyes.

"That's priceless," Rock finally says. "Of course she does. Sure. Why not? I guess she forgot about suing all of us?"

"You could say that." I still can't believe this part. "She didn't seem to understand why the club was pissed at her."

"I'm sure she didn't," Rock sneers. "Well?"

He can't seriously think I'd let Inga step foot inside Crystal Ball after what she did? "I told her no fucking way in hell and that I didn't want to see her face again. None of us do."

"Good." He nods and releases the chair, standing straight. "Jesus Christ." He scrubs his hands over his face. "She's like a blood-sucking mosquito that keeps dodging the swatter."

I snort with laughter. "She kinda looks like a mosquito, to be honest. Even if she didn't have such bad history with the club, she wouldn't be hirable."

He tilts his head in an I-really-don't-give-a-fuck gesture. "I doubt she can still find her way up here. But keep me posted if she shows up at CB again."

"I will. I'm sorry, Rock. I guess she thought she could approach me, because…I don't know."

He dismisses my apology with a quick headshake. "Not your fault."

"I should've told you right away—"

He holds up one hand to stop me. "Fuck." He shakes his head. "You know what I hate the most? I can't even be as pissed at her as I should be. Without that stupid fucking lawsuit, I might never have found out about Teller and—"

"Yeah, it was the only silver lining of that clusterfuck." I cock my head in a questioning way. "I guess."

He snorts. "Silver lining. Life altering. Same difference, right?"

"Right." I run my hands through my hair. "I told everyone to be on the lookout for Inga if she shows up again. Malik's got her picture so he knows who to look for. Everyone else knows her and they've been warned not to allow her in the building for any reason. They're supposed to call me right away if she shows up again."

"Thanks, brother." He shakes his head. "Sorry you had to deal with that."

Should I even bother telling him this part? "It kinda caused my own problems. Emily saw me talking to her and assumed the worst."

He tips his head back and stares at the ceiling for a second. "That she-devil with her shit timing."

"Right?" I force out a laugh.

Remorse seems to cloud his eyes. "Think you'll work it out with her?"

"Yeah, we talked." My mouth twists with annoyance. "I should've been up front about *where* I worked in the first place."

He raises an eyebrow, quietly asking for more details.

"I said I managed a nightclub." I hold my hands up. "In my defense, it's technically true."

He chokes on a laugh. "Yeah, how'd that work out for you."

"Not that great." I didn't say this to Emily, but I'd thought about it a lot. "Still, I have a feeling if I'd gone the total disclosure route in the beginning, we wouldn't still be together."

"If I can give you one piece of advice," his gaze flicks over my shoulder, then back to me, "*certain* folks might claim honesty is the best approach if you want to bring a civilian into our world."

By "folks," I assume he means Wrath. Our SAA is full of opinions and not shy about sharing them. "But?"

"My advice is to disclose things on an as-needed basis."

I scratch the side of my head. "I seem to remember that not working out for you and Hope sometimes."

A sly smile creeps over his face. "I'd argue everything worked out fine."

He has a point. Hope's as loyal and ride-or-die as any of the brothers.

The stuff she's been through and the way she's always defended the club, maybe Rock's right. Once Emily understands we'd all die to protect each other *and* her, she'll accept the MC and all that comes with it with no problem.

Right?

CHAPTER THIRTY

Dex

WHILE I'M at the clubhouse, I decide to take advantage of one of our large garages. That's one thing we didn't add to the new clubhouse down in Empire—a big enough garage. Rav and the others had been too focused on making it a party spot than a functional MC clubhouse. It should've had enough room to service more than two or three bikes at a time. Instead, they'd been worried about having enough flat surfaces for fucking.

Murphy kept the garage neat and organized when he was road captain. I've taken it a bit further by adding more cabinets to store parts that we go through regularly. I'm counting how many air filters we have left when happy little chatter echoes from outside the garage. I glance toward the open doors. Hope's standing right outside, holding Alexa's hand. They both wave. Heidi's daughter's getting bigger. I swear she's shot up two inches since I last saw her.

I set the boxes in my hands on the shelf, close and lock the door, then meet them outside.

"What's up, First Lady?" I glance down at Alexa. "And little lady?"

"Hi!" Alexa wiggles her fingers at me.

"Heidi rope you into babysitting?" I ask Hope. "Where's *your* little one?"

She glances over her shoulder at the clubhouse. "Grace is with Rock."

She swings Alexa's hand back and forth. "*Someone* was restless and wanted to peek in the garage."

"You did?" I squat to Alexa's level. "You want to help me change some air filters?" I say in a chipper, kid-friendly tone.

Alexa giggles. "I can help."

"Why doesn't that surprise me?" Hope says.

"She might be a good road captain one day." I stand and ask Hope, "How are you?"

"Good. Waiting to hear when we can go see baby Lincoln."

An ice-cold trickle of painful memories rolls down my spine. I fucking *hate* hospitals. "I'm surprised the whole club isn't in a waiting room at Empire Med."

I'm hoping like fuck Grinder tells us not to come at all.

"I don't think they let you do that anymore." Her mouth scrunches into an amused pout or disgusted sneer—hard to tell. "I hear the club's favorite dancer is in town."

I lift my gaze to the sky. *Why the fuck would Rock tell her about Inga showing up?*

"He doesn't want me leaving the compound by myself," she explains, as if she heard my unspoken question.

Guilt prickles over my scalp. "I'll take you anywhere you need to go if Rock's not around."

"I highly doubt she'd bother stalking me." She flips her hand in the air, dismissing the issue.

Rage spikes the guilt out of my system. I'd fucking murder Inga myself if she ever approached Hope.

Hope glances up at the trees and inhales deeply. A peaceful expression settles over her face. "Don't worry about me. I'm perfectly content." A devious spark lights up her eyes. "Besides, I can always borrow one of the ATVs and escape to Charlotte's if I need some adventure."

"She okay?" I ask. "I haven't seen her the last few weekends."

"She's good." Hope tilts her head toward the clubhouse. "You haven't been around here much lately." She arches a brow. "Did you abandon us for the snazzy new clubhouse downtown?"

Heat crawls up my neck. Hope's noticed my absence?

"No. Not there." I run my hand over the back of my head. Why do I suddenly feel like I'm being grilled by my favorite big sister? "I, uh, I've been staying at Grinder's old apartment some nights. It's closer to Emily's place."

As if those were magic words, Hope's entire face lights up. "Really?"

"Why do you sound so shocked?" I ask, although it's not shock I sense in her words or expression. It's something more unnerving—relief and excitement. I can practically hear the wedding bells ringing in her ears.

"I didn't realize you two were that serious." She cocks her head. "Why haven't you brought her up here, yet?"

Wanting to end this before Hope gets carried away, I fake disinterest. "Who says it's serious?"

"You moved closer to *her* and farther away from everything else?" She shrugs. "Sounds serious to me."

"I'm not particular about where I lay my head at night." My mouth slides into a smirk. "Maybe I just want easier access to my hookup."

She snort-giggles, which makes Alexa laugh too.

"Easier access?" She turns, gesturing toward the clubhouse with her free hand. "What's easier than girls throwing themselves at you in your own living room?"

"You've got me there, I guess."

"What's wrong?"

Am I really going to burden her with this? I know some of my brothers—especially Murphy—like to think of Hope as a motherly sounding board for all their relationship issues. Or our own personal Wendy looking after all the lost boys here at the MC compound as Teller might put it. But I'm not a boy who needs dating advice. At least I don't think so.

"You're usually so..." She seems to be searching for a word that won't offend me. "Secretive. The fact that you mentioned her at all seems serious."

"I'm not secretive. I just don't like broadcasting all my business to everyone." I flick my hand toward the clubhouse. "I don't know if it's serious or not."

Who am I trying to lie to, here? Hope, or myself?

I tug the rag out of my pocket, absently twisting it around my fingers. "I...like Emily a lot. I haven't felt so...connected to anyone like this since..."

Why can't I force Debbie's name out of my mouth?

Hope rests her hand on my arm. Either to offer comfort or to let me know I don't have to continue. Whatever the reason, her touch gives me the nudge I need to finish the thought. "Since my wife died."

Her eyes widen in surprise. "Oh."

"Rock never told you?" I ask.

She drops her gaze to the ground. Rock must've given her a short version. "I didn't realize you'd been married until I met Juliet down in Florida and she mentioned it."

My lips curve at the mention of Juliet's name. "She was just a kid, but Debbie loved that girl something fierce." *And I did a shit job of looking out for her the way I should have.* "It's been so long." I press my fist against my chest. "But seeing someone else still feels almost disloyal...maybe that's not the right word."

"Can I ask what happened?"

"It's...complicated." I run my hand over the back of my head again and drop my gaze to Alexa, who's busy collecting little rocks and stacking them at our feet. "Shoot, you know the last person I talked about this with was Axel?"

Hope frowns at the mention of Heidi's dead first husband. "Axel? Why?"

"When Heidi got pregnant, he had a hard time...accepting it."

Her mouth sets into a grim line. Hope had liked Axel and I think it hurt when she learned he wasn't the nice guy everyone thought he was. "I remember," she says in a tight voice.

"Anyway. I'd been in his shoes. Knew how he felt. I thought I could help him through it. But man, all that fucker did was bitch about her..." My gaze drops to Alexa again. She's too little to understand what we're talking about, right? "Not having an—"

Hope holds up one hand. "I understand."

"The first time he said it, I kind of understood. I'd been there. But let's just say, I was younger than he was when it happened to me, and I still moved on to acceptance a lot sooner."

"Everyone processes things differently, Dex," she says as if she feels obligated to point that out.

"Yeah. I get that. But some of the shit he said rubbed me wrong. He *should've* been thankful he had a wife and healthy baby girl instead of acting like the world robbed him." Anger turns my tone harsher than I intended and I take a breath.

I twist the rag between my fingers again. "I was already iffy about him based on how he acted at Crystal Ball and the shit that went down when he didn't patch-in. But his attitude about his own kid sealed it for me."

Hope blinks, sadness clouding her green eyes. "I never knew that."

"I didn't want to start shit." I tilt my head toward the clubhouse. "He'd

252

left the club by then. Teller was already pissed about the whole situation. I didn't want to make things harder on Heidi. Or say anything that would hurt her, you know?"

Sympathy shines in her eyes. "Sure."

"I tried giving Murphy a heads-up but you know how that went." I glance down at Alexa again. "I'm just glad they both have Murphy taking care of them now."

She nods, then stops and takes a deep breath. "While this has been enlightening, I feel like you're deflecting from talking about your feelings for Emily."

God, she's a brave woman. Shrewd as fuck too. She knows how to probe and poke all the right spots. "You miss being a lawyer?" I ask.

She crosses her arms over her chest. "Not yet."

Her clipped answer almost sounds like a warning to stop fucking around.

"I don't know how to feel," I finally say. "It's been a long time since I could picture a future with another woman. Actually, it's the first time."

"You see a future with Emily?" she asks, her voice barely above a whisper.

"I really do." A goofy rush I haven't felt since I was a kid comes over me. "She's funny as hell. Fierce. Loyal. I feel at peace when I'm with her. *Happy.*" The last word comes out almost like a question.

She reaches out and rubs her hand over my bicep. "It's a nice feeling, huh?"

"Yeah."

"You deserve that, Dex."

"Do I?"

"*I* think so. You work so hard for the club. You're good to your brothers." The corners of her mouth tilt up. "To all of us. You deserve peace and happiness for yourself."

"I love my family."

"Does she know? About your...about Debbie?"

Hearing Hope say my wife's name pricks like a needle digging into my skin. I swallow hard. "I told her I married my high school sweetheart and that she died. But no more than that."

"Did she ask?"

"No, which was a relief, honestly." Emily seems to understand me in a way no one else ever has.

Hope nods. "Sorry, I didn't mean to pry."

"I don't mind talking to *you* about it. I started this conversation, remember?"

"Well, I interrupted you first." She gives me a faint smile. "Try not to let regrets about the past steal your future. I know it's hard. Believe me, I do."

Somehow, I always forget she was married before she met Rock. The way our club collects widows and orphans is uncanny.

"So many memories have just melted into the years," I whisper, shame choking off my voice.

"That's normal." She touches my elbow. "That's your mind helping you cope with the pain."

I never thought of it like that.

"Moving on doesn't mean you were a bad husband." Her lips quirk. "Or that you won't be a good husband in the future."

"Whoa." I tap my hands into a *time-out* position. "Slow your roll, First Lady."

She laughs. "You know what I mean."

"Rock wanted me to let you know when I'm planning to have Emily visit." I shrug as if it's no big deal.

"Yes, I'd love that. We can have you guys to dinner at our place if you're worried," she rolls her eyes toward the clubhouse, "*certain* brothers might scare her away for the first visit."

"I assume you're referring to Rav?"

She snorts. "I plead the fifth."

"Nah, if I'm ready to have her here, might as well give her the full experience." My smile fades. "If we're going to have a future, she has to accept the club too. Degenerates and all," I say. "But thank you."

"Maybe a Sunday family dinner when Downstate's visiting would be nice?" she suggests. Hope won't be happy until she has a firm commitment to bring Emily here. "Lilly and Emily planned Serena's shower together and Lilly adored her. Maybe more familiar faces would help Emily feel comfortable. And you'll have to invite Libby too, of course."

"Maybe," I agree to appease Hope. I wouldn't be a bit surprised if she's on the phone with Lilly the second we end our conversation.

If I'm not careful our two first ladies will have Emily and me walking down the aisle, their kids as our flower girl and ring bearer, and building us a house out in the woods.

And I'm definitely not ready for any of *that*.

CHAPTER THIRTY-ONE

Emily

IT's dark by the time I arrive to pick up Libby. It's a cool evening. I lean on my car in the circular parking lot with parents waiting for their kids.

Libby sent me a text about ten minutes ago saying the bus just got off the Thruway. How slow does that thing go?

The dad of one of Libby's friends slides up next to me. Evan? Ethan? Eric? Something with an E, I think. In my head, I've always referred to him as creepy-old-dude-who-stares-at-my-tits. I zip my jacket up to my chin.

"Sounds like they had a good time," he says.

While I hadn't gotten as many updates as I would've liked, the messages Libby *did* send seemed positive. "It does."

"Caroline's trying to convince me to take her again next month. You and Libby should join us."

Hell no. "Thank you, Eric—"

"Frank," he corrects.

I nod to acknowledge his name. "I'll ask my boyfriend if he can get off work."

Of course the excuse backfires on me.

"I didn't realize you had a boyfriend," he says, not bothering to hide his disappointment. "What does he do?"

Fuck. "He runs his own business." Dex said his MC owns Crystal Ball, he's an officer in the club. Therefore, that's close enough.

He opens his mouth as if he has follow-up questions but we're interrupted by another parent. She slides up to Frank and wraps her hands around his arm in a possessive hold.

He's all yours, lady.

"Emily, this is Melanie's mother." Frank shakes free of the woman and nods at me. "Melissa, have you met Libby's—"

"Oh my gawd!" Melissa shouts, raking her gaze over me. "You musta been a baby when you had that girl."

"Uh, I was a teenager when *my parents* had her," I correct.

"Oh, right, right." She waves a hand in my face. "Forgot."

Did this lady come to pick up her kid after guzzling a bottle of merlot?

I'm saved from any more of this conversation by the bus headlights sweeping over the parking lot. Some of the parents cheer the arrival. I use it as an opportunity to escape whatever weird thing Frank and Melissa have going on.

Libby's one of two dozen weary teenagers who stumble off the bus. Each one of them trying to appear cool and not all that eager to hug their parents in front of all their peers.

I finally spot Libby and raise my hand. She says something to one of her friends who turns and waves at me. A few seconds later, Libby makes her way over to me. I hold out my hand for one of her bags.

"Thanks," she huffs, and hitches her backpack on her shoulder.

I want to hug her and pepper her with a dozen questions. But I'm careful not to embarrass her in front of her friends. "Ready to head home?" I ask.

"God, yes. Get me outta here," she mumbles.

Chuckling to myself, I lead her to the car.

"So, how was the trip?" I ask.

"Good," she answers without much enthusiasm. "I'm beat though. We hardly slept."

As I pull out of the school's parking lot, she rummages through her purse. "Em? Oh, wait. Never mind. Phew. I thought I left my phone on the bus."

"Speaking of forgetting things, you left your pills at home."

"Aw, crap." She smacks her forehead. "I totally forgot. I wondered why I felt all crampy this morning."

"Eh, I've done it. It's only a problem if—"

"I...I didn't hook up with anyone," Libby says in a mortified rush of words.

Once we leave the lit-up area around the school, I flick on the high-beams.

"I wasn't saying you did," I assure her. "I wouldn't be upset if you had," I lie, smooth as butter. "You can always come to me with anything that's on your mind. Good or bad."

"Trust me, if I *had* hooked up on the trip, I'd be begging you to drive me straight to Walmart to buy me some Plan B." She sits forward and points at the windshield.

"And I'd be stepping on the gas," I answer.

She chuckles, then sighs. "Caroline kept trying to hook up with Troy. It was so cringey to watch."

"Is that the kid who's helping you with math?"

"Yeah. We were trying to hang out when everyone went ice skating but she kept butting in and flapping her long, fluffy, fake eyelashes at him." She huffs.

"That's not nice," I answer carefully. "If she knows you like him."

"I don't *like* him." She crosses her arms over her chest.

Suuuure you don't. "So, why'd it bother you that she was flirting with him?"

"Because it's *rude*," she says with the sweet outrage only a teenager can express. "He and I were chilling and having fun. And she kept making it weird by pushing her boobs in his face and talking in this fake baby voice."

I bite back my laughter. "That sucks." Sounds like Caroline takes after her dad. I keep that to myself, though. I don't like to talk trash about her friends' parents if I can help it. "Did you hang out with any of the other kids?"

She rattles more names than I can keep track of. At least it sounds like overall she had fun.

"Is Dex coming over?" Libby asks.

"Uh, maybe. He said he might swing by for dinner." Damn, I shouldn't keep making my sister hang out with my boyfriend. "Why? Is that okay with you?"

"Yeah. I have something I want to give him."

She what? I glance over. "You do?"

"Uh-huh." She twists in her seat. "It's in my backpack somewhere."

"That was nice." I'm not sure what else to say. A warm, fuzzy sensation slides through my chest.

"Can we *please* have pizza?" she pleads "Everyone told me New York

City is supposed to have the best pizza in the world. But the place they took us to was trash." From the corner of my eye I catch her exaggerated yuck face. "Too much sauce. Not enough cheese. And I'm pretty sure one of the olives on Caroline's slice was actually a roach."

"Ewww." I gag and laugh at the same time. "I've had amazing pizza there, so it's not all bad."

"If you say so."

"Besides the lackluster pizza and Caroline horning in on your friendship with Troy, did you have fun?"

"Yeah," she answers slowly. "But I wasn't all 'oh my gosh,'" She waves her hands in the air wildly. "'Greatest place in the world!' It was loud, smelly, dirty, and rats were just chillin' in the subway like no big deal. When have you *ever* seen a rat around here?"

"Uh, never. Mice, yes. But no rats."

"And people were just acting like rats are normal. I mean, has no one read about the bubonic plague?"

I sputter with laughter. "So you're telling me you want to stay a country girl?"

She slants a look my way. "We don't exactly live out in the *country*. Johnsonville is sucky, though. And Empire is kinda boring."

"You have plenty of time to figure things out, Libby." I'm happy but also almost jealous of all the opportunities ahead of her. I want to make sure she's able to go anywhere and do anything she wants.

Even though that was really never an option for me.

CHAPTER THIRTY-TWO

Dex

WHY DOES it always feel so good to park my bike in Emily's driveway?

An engine rumbles behind me. I get off the bike and take off my helmet. A tiny white sedan stops at the curb and a tall, gangly guy jumps out of the driver's side. A little triangle on top of the car advertises the local pizza place. I hurry over the lawn to meet him, hoping Emily didn't use a credit card when she ordered.

"Is that for Walker?" I ask.

He must not have heard me coming. The guy jumps, jostling the boxes in his hands.

"Jesus, dude. Warn a guy, would ya?"

He's just a kid. Can't be more than twenty-one, twenty-two. *Don't punch him.*

I lift my chin at the stack of boxes in his hand and shoot an impatient glare. "Walker?"

"Yeah, yeah. It's for Emily." He glances at the house, then takes a longer look at me. His gaze slides over my cut, then skips to my bike. He swallows hard, like a cartoon character. "Y-you live here? With Emily?"

Poor kid sounds heartbroken.

Ignoring his question, I take out my wallet. "What's the total?"

He glances at the tag stuck to the box on top of the stack. "Fifty-seven fifty."

I hand him enough to cover it, then add an extra twenty to cover the pants he probably just shit and take the boxes from him. "Thank you."

When I turn around, Emily's waiting on the porch with her arms folded over her chest and a smile teasing her lips.

She lifts one hand and waves. "Thanks, Sam!" she calls out.

I can't tell if he returns the gesture or not. The engine starts, though. A few seconds later, tires screech away from the curb.

"Did you *have* to scare our regular delivery boy?" she asks.

"Seems the delivery boy has a crush on you." I lean in and kiss her cheek. "Just wanted to warn him that the Walker sisters have someone looking out for them."

She lets out a low chuckle and leans up on her tiptoes to kiss my cheek. "You didn't have to pay for that. I invited you."

"Guess you'll have to time it better in the future." I kiss her cheek again. "Missed you," I whisper in her ear.

"I'm really glad you're here," she says.

She turns and opens the screen door for me. I head straight for the kitchen, bumping the door open with my hip, and setting everything on the counter.

"Where's the city girl?" I ask Emily.

"Ah, turns out she's not much of a city girl."

"She didn't have fun?"

"No, she did but she doesn't want to return any time soon."

"Does that mean you're happy she won't be flying far from the nest?"

Emily tilts her head, as she seems to contemplate her answer. "I want her to go as far as she wants. And be happy," she finishes on a whisper. "Safe and happy."

The air between us suddenly feels ten times heavier. I can't tell if it's the thought of her sister going away to college in a few years or if she's thinking of her parents.

"Come here." I pull her into my arms. "You're doing a good job of making sure she's both."

She nods against my chest and blows out a breath. Whatever cloud settled over her seems to evaporate. "How was *your* day?"

"Better now."

"Dex!" Libby bursts into the kitchen. "You're back!"

Not expecting Emily's sister to be so excited to see me, I take a second to respond. "*You're* back. How was your trip?" I ask, not letting on that Emily already gave me a summary.

"Excellent! My feet are killing me. We walked everywhere. But it was so much fun." She skates over the kitchen tile in her socks and skids to a stop in front of me with her hands behind her back. "I got you something."

Surprise ties my tongue in another knot.

"Just something small." She ducks her head and holds out her right hand. "So you can remember the Walker sisters wherever you are."

In the palm of her hand rests a Statue of Liberty key chain. I reach out and pick it up, letting it dangle for a moment. A smaller, yellow charm hangs from the split circle ring. A lemon.

"Lady Liberty for me." Libby grins and touches her left hand to her chest. "And a lemon for Emily." She frowns. "Because she loves lemons, not because she's sour," she hurries to add.

Behind her, Emily chuckles. "I'm definitely more salty than sour."

"Thank you, Libby." I accept the gift and pull my keys out of my pocket, slowly working the new addition into the set. "The Walker sisters are hard to forget, though."

She grins. "True statement."

And with that, she slides her way out of the kitchen.

Emily comes closer and rests her hand on my arm. "I'm glad you came over. She's been dying to give you that since she got home."

"I..." No words come to me. "She didn't have to get me anything. But I love it."

"Good."

I turn the miniature statue over in my hands. "Is Liberty really what Libby is short for?"

An affectionate smile curves her lips and she rolls her eyes slightly. "Liberty Isabelle, yep. My parents went from traditional to hippy dippy as they got older."

I snort with laughter. "I thought it was usually the other way around."

"Well, my middle name is *Clementine*, so maybe they always had a wild streak."

Do not *mention the dancer at Crystal Ball who goes by Clementine.* "I'm pretty sure Clementine is the subject of an old American folk song," I say.

"Yep. I remember that one. It's why I never, ever tell anyone my middle name."

Thank you, universe for Shelby's endless musical knowledge that has somehow rubbed off on me.

"You told me," I point out.

She wraps her arms around my waist and nuzzles her forehead against my chest. "Yeah, I did."

My heart's slamming so hard, she must be able to feel it.

"Liberty is a pretty name," I say, rubbing my hand over her back. "They could've gone with worse."

"True, and it fits her." Emily lets out a sweet laugh and pulls away. "I'm still glad they chose Emily for *my* first name."

"I like it." I rest my hand on her hip. "It rolls off the tongue nicely."

She reaches up and taps my bottom lip. "You definitely know how to roll that tongue around."

I lean down and whisper in her ear, "I'd like to use my tongue on you right *now*."

"Save that energy," she whispers back.

Libby bursts through the kitchen door, this time with what seems to be a tan crinkly bag of candy in her hands. "I went to the M&M store, and brought home a trophy, Em."

"Oh yeah?" Emily turns around. "Are you planning to share or hoarding them in your room?"

"I'll share." She hugs the bag to her chest. "Maybe."

"What is it?" I ask.

"Almond M&Ms," Libby whispers like someone's about to break in and steal them.

Emily frowns. "I'm pretty sure they still sell those at Walmart."

"But *these* are special."

"Almond, huh?" I ask.

Libby cocks her head. "They're the *best*," she says, like I'm dense for not knowing this universal fact. This kid cracks me up.

The smell of the pizza's killing me. "What'd you get?" I ask Emily, nodding to the boxes.

"Well, we were feeling fancy tonight," she announces. "We went with a white broccoli pizza, a meat lovers, and wings."

"Sounds good," I say.

Libby gathers plates, utensils, little dipping cups, and a large bottle of blue cheese dressing. "They never send enough dressing and it's always warm when it gets here," she explains with a shudder. "So gross."

"You've thought of everything."

The three of us sit at the larger table by the window. Libby shares the highlights of her trip with us—including her suspicion that a friend had been served a *roach* as a pizza topping.

I set my slice down.

"You'll notice the lack of olives on our pizzas tonight," Emily says with a wry laugh.

When we're finished, I help Emily clear the table while she wraps the leftovers and stores everything in the fridge.

Libby pulls three small bowls from one of the cabinets. M&Ms hit the glass with a crisp *ting, ting, ting* as she pours an equal amount for each of us.

"I feel so special," I whisper to Emily.

She presses one hand against my shoulder and leans up to kiss my cheek. "You are."

"I'm really beat," Libby says, popping an M&M in her mouth.

"Sounds like you had an exhausting weekend," I say.

"And you have school tomorrow," Emily reminds her.

"I know. You'd think they'd give us the day off or let us come in late or something."

"What an injustice," Emily scoffs.

I chuckle and pop a candy in my mouth. *Not my business.*

Libby huffs, grabs her bowl, and waves over her shoulder. "Night, Dex."

"Night, kiddo."

"Why *did* the school bring them back late when her classes start so early?" I ask Emily after Libby's gone.

She shrugs. "Timing, I guess. She'll be fine. She's up way later than this most nights."

I reach over and take her hand. "And what about you. How late are you usually up?"

"Probably not as late as you." She taps my chest. "Ugh, I'm so glad I didn't have to be at the school any longer. Her friend's dad was trying to invite me on a trip to—"

"I'm sorry, what?"

"No, not like that. He framed it as taking the girls back to the city for another weekend. It just felt...*odd*. But he's always weird with me."

"Weird, how?"

"Same thing most middle-aged guys do when they're sprinting toward a midlife crisis. Check out women half their age and stare inappropriately."

"Yeah, trust me, I make a living off those kinds of dudes. So what'd you tell him?"

She fists her hand in my shirt and pulls me closer. "I said I'd check with my boyfriend and see if he could take the time off work."

"Yeah, and did he ask you what your boyfriend does *for* work?"

Her gaze snaps to mine, like she can't believe I guessed how the conversation went. Or she doesn't want to tell me how she answered.

"I was only trying to work into the conversation that I had a boyfriend," she says.

I'm sure she was. "That doesn't answer my question."

She folds her arms over her chest. "How'd you know he asked me that?"

"Like I said, I make a living off those types. He was testing you. To see if you really had a boyfriend or if you were using it as an excuse. I've watched and listened to enough creeps to know how they operate."

"How'd you know he's a creep?"

"He's a forty-something dad hitting on his daughter's friend's sister?" I shrug. "And also, you basically said so."

"Well, I took care of it."

"I'm sure you did. I'll still go with you to the next school event." Like hell am I letting some dude make my girl uncomfortable. Not when my presence alone should be enough to scare him off.

She rolls her eyes. "You don't have to do that. I think he's seeing one of the other moms, anyway."

"And yet, he felt comfortable suggesting a weekend away. Together," I point out.

"With the girls."

"*Yeaaah*, okay."

"I didn't tell you so you'd be jealous and go all caveman."

"I'm not talking about showing up to beat on my chest and hump your leg in front of everyone." I thump my fists against my chest a few times. "Emily. Mine."

She giggles at my territorial Tarzan impression.

I curl an arm around her shoulders and pull her closer. "I just mean, you don't have to do everything alone."

"It's been that way for a long time."

I hold her for a few minutes thinking of how to put my thoughts into words, then decide the easiest answer is the simplest. "But it's not that way anymore."

CHAPTER THIRTY-THREE

Emily

A WARM, heavy presence surrounds me when I wake the next morning. Dex spent the night again. I blink my eyes open. It must still be early. A contented sigh slips out of my mouth. I shift and stretch my back. Hard steel presses against my butt and I inch backward.

A deep, sexy groan rumbles against my back. One of Dex's heavy hands clamps over my hip, stopping my movement. "I don't think you want to do that right now."

Is he kidding? "Why? As I remember, we fit together really well this way."

"Shhh." Dex's warm breath tickles over my neck and shoulder. "I think I heard your sister up and about."

Shit! How could I completely forget? "What? Really?"

"I meant to leave but ended up plastered to you all night." He trails his lips against my neck and teases my earlobe between his teeth.

As if on cue, Libby taps on my door. "I'm leaving for school, Em!" she shouts. "Since Dex's bike is still in the driveway, I assume he's in there with you. Morning, Dex!"

Dex rumbles with laughter, shaking the whole bed. "Morning, kid!"

"Oh, Jesus," I gasp. Louder I shout, "Have a good day, pudding!"

She mutters something I can't make out and stomps down the stairs.

"God, what am I doing?" I cover my face with my hands and slide under the sheet.

"What's wrong?" Dex asks, peeling the sheet back and prying one of my hands away from my face.

"Nothing. I just don't have guys sleep over. My sister's still a teenager. I want to set a good example. Not—"

"Hey." He pries my other hand off my face and cups my chin. "I'm not 'guys.' I'm not some rando one-night stand you brought home from a bar." Hurt twists his voice into a low rasp.

"I'm sorry. I didn't mean that *you* were. I trust you around her."

"Whoa." He pulls back, staring at me with a curious frown on his handsome face. "What does that mean?"

"She's a teenage girl. I don't just let any man around her." It's way too early to have to think this hard. "The last 'boyfriend' I actually dated was inappropriate around her."

"Inappropriate *how?*" he asks in a deadly tone.

"I can't quite explain." I press my hand against my stomach. "It was a feeling in my gut. He'd ask her about boys, and if she had a boyfriend. Tell her how pretty she was. He'd go out of his way to hug or touch her. She was like *eleven.*" I grind my teeth together as the old anger bubbles up again. "The last red flag was this fucking see-through shirt and miniskirt he bought her as a 'back-to-school' outfit."

"What the fuck?"

I'm so ashamed I let someone like that near my sister, I can't look him in the eye. "Libby, thankfully, thought it was ugly, so she gave it to me."

"And then what?"

I lift my gaze. "I kicked him to the curb."

"He go willingly?"

"More or less."

His jaw ticks. "Where is he now?"

I cock my head. He's seriously considering hunting down a guy I broke up with years ago, isn't he? "I don't know. Last I heard, he moved to Denver."

"Still not far enough way."

"I haven't heard from him since." I shrug. "I told him I'd call one of my dad's old cop buddies if I ever saw him again."

It had been a lie. None of them had reached out to me in years by that point.

Dex stares at me. "Forgot your dad was a cop. I can't believe none of them tried to help you after he died."

I glance away. That's not a topic I want to go near.

He snorts. "If *we* have a brother who dies, the club takes care of their family. We don't leave them to fend for themselves. But everyone calls *us* the criminals." He shakes his head in disgust.

The angry urge to defend my dad's friends comes on hot. But as fast as it bubbles up, it ebbs away. After the funeral and goodbyes, no one had cared about what happened to Libby and me. No one but our aunt.

"Even if they did something bad?" I ask. "You still take care of the family?"

"Bad, how? Against the club?"

"Uh, yeah. I guess."

His gaze shifts to the side as if he's searching for the right answer. "Yes," he finally says. "Depending on the circumstances and how close the family was to the MC, we still take care of them."

"That's loyalty beyond the grave."

"When I say the club is my family and I call someone 'brother,' I'm not just throwing those words around."

It's starting to sink in. If I'm going to be with Dex, that means I better start learning more about his club.

CHAPTER THIRTY-FOUR

Emily

AFTER WORK, I'm finally able to visit Serena in the hospital. Actually, duck out a few minutes early so I can skip the rush hour traffic around Empire Med. I suppose I could've waited until Serena gets discharged, which I thought she would've been by now, but she seemed to really want me to visit when I spoke to her this afternoon.

Even though I already threw her a baby shower months ago, and I have more stuff for her at my house, I hate the thought of showing up empty-handed. I duck into the drugstore next to the hospital and search the shelves for something useful she might have forgotten to bring.

My gaze lands on a jumbo-sized healing balm stick that claims to be good for chapped skin and safe for baby. Perfect. Serena's always preaching about the importance of moisturizing. This sounds like something she'd use. I grab that and a tiny blue gift bag and head to the register.

I make my way through the maze of long hallways to the birthing center at Empire Med. A nurse in pink scrubs narrows her eyes at me. I flash a quick smile. *I'm not here to kidnap any babies, promise!*

Ignoring her, I hitch my purse higher on my shoulder and keep walking.

Finally, 219. I slap the lever on the dispenser of hand sanitizer outside the door and slather it all over my hands.

A curtain's drawn, separating the two beds. "Serena?"

"Over here!" she calls out.

Gray steps out from behind the curtain and pushes it aside. "Hey, Emily." He smiles warmly at me and motions for me to come closer.

"Congratulations." I reach up and hug him.

For a second, he freezes. Then he returns the hug. "Thanks for coming. She's been looking forward to seeing you," he says against my ear.

Now I wish I'd left work earlier.

He releases me, and my gaze lands on Serena. She offers a weak smile and pushes herself upright. Somehow the hospital bed makes her seem smaller than I remember, like all the white sheets could swallow her whole.

"How are you feeling?" I ask, stepping closer.

"Exhausted," she says. A weak smile curves her lips. "Hopefully, they let me go home soon."

"You'll stay as long as they tell you to," Gray says, pulling a chair next to the bed and gesturing for me to sit next to Serena.

"He's right," I say, dropping into the chair and draping the strap of my purse over the back.

"Don't start," she says. Her gaze falls on the little blue bag I'm still holding.

I hold it out to her. "I wanted to bring you...something. I saw this and thought it looked neat."

She accepts the bag and pulls out the fat little stick. "Oh! This is perfect. Thank you. My skin feels like a paper bag in here." She scowls at the hospital room, then rips into the thin protective plastic around the balm. "Ahhh," she sighs as she smears it on her lips and cheeks. "Much better. Thank you."

Gray watches her with concern. "Why didn't you say something?"

"I didn't know I needed it until I saw it." Serena shrugs. "I could use some ice water, though."

"You got it." Gray glances at me and lifts an eyebrow.

"I'm good."

Serena watches him leave with hearts in her eyes. "He must be exhausted," she says. "He won't even go up to the clubhouse to sleep for a few hours."

Honestly, I'm relieved to hear it.

"So where's the baby?" I ask.

"The nurses have him for a bit." She shifts again. "Rock was here with

Gray for a while. And he's been itching to have some of the other brothers here, but I wanted you to meet Lincoln first."

"Really?" I ask.

"Duh, of course."

"What do you think, Serena?" the nurse in the pink scrubs I'd encountered earlier asks as she walks into the room carrying a little blue bundle. "Ready for him?"

Serena beams and holds out her arms. "Yes."

The nurse gently transfers the baby to Serena, watches them for a few minutes, checks machines I hadn't even noticed, then briskly walks out.

Gray steps in a second later, carrying a mauve pitcher and several plastic cups wrapped in plastic. He sets them on the rolling table next to Serena's bed and watches her with the baby.

"Everything okay?" he asks, with the gruff tone of a man who might burn down the hospital if Serena and Lincoln aren't perfectly content.

"We're good," Serena coos, staring at the baby. She looks at me. "Do you want to hold him?"

I lift my hands in the air. "I bathed in sanitizer before coming in the room."

She chuckles and tilts her head, motioning for me to come closer.

Little Lincoln is rosy-skinned and kinda wrinkly, but so freakin' cute as I take him in my arms. He blinks his eyes open and stares up at me with a serene expression. "Hi, baby," I whisper.

He closes his eyes and smacks his lips.

I hold him for a few more seconds, then hand him to Grayson.

"He's really precious," I say.

"So." Serena curls her hand around mine, tugging me so close, soon I'll have to crawl into the bed with her. "Grayson and I have something we want to ask you."

"What's that?" My gaze shifts between Serena's eager, hopeful expression, and Grayson's determined one.

"Will you be Lincoln's godmother?" she whispers.

I blink and process the question.

Joy bubbles up inside me. "Me? Are you sure?"

"I can't think of anyone I'd trust more, Emily," Serena says.

Grayson nods. "We'd be honored."

"Oh, wow." I step back, pressing my hand to my chest. Maybe to some people it's nothing more than an honorary title to toss around, but it means something to me. I'm deeply touched. "Yes, of course I will."

Knowing how entwined Grayson is with the MC and how close Serena has gotten with the other men's wives, I'm surprised but so happy she asked. "I promise to be the best godmother," I say.

Serena beams. "I know."

Lincoln fusses and Serena takes him again, carefully opening her gown to feed him. I'm uncomfortable but don't want to make it weird, so I stare straight ahead and keep talking to her like normal.

"How was Libby's trip?" Serena asks without taking her eyes off the baby.

"Good, I think. She's really excited to meet the baby." I give her an outline of what Libby had shared with me.

"Aww," Serena sighs. "Sounds like she doesn't want to fly too far from the nest?"

"Maybe. At least she seemed comfortable away from home. I barely heard from her." Dex had distracted me this weekend. I didn't check in on Libby as much as I normally would. I frown, unsure of what that says about me as a big sister.

"Well, that means she was having fun," Serena says.

"I hope so."

As if they have everything perfectly timed, Grayson pops a straw into one of the cups and puts it to Serena's lips.

"Thank you," she whispers at him when she's finished. She flicks her blue gaze my way. "I swear this kid's sucking every ounce of liquid from me. Not just milk."

"You already look like a pro," I encourage.

I stay a little longer but then it's clear Serena's worn out. I squeeze her hand, wave goodbye to Lincoln, and leave. Grayson walks me into the hallway.

"She's okay, right?" I whisper to him.

He nods quickly but his gaze strays to the room. "Yeah. Things were... rough for a while. Doctor just wants to keep her here a little longer. Make sure they're okay."

"How about you?" I touch his forearm. "Are you doing okay?"

He stares at me for a few seconds. "I'm good. I'll be better once I have them settled safely at home."

"Well, let me know if she needs anything. And as soon as you're ready to have people over, I'll be there. Libby and I can make you guys dinner or something. Give you a break." I tap his elbow. "You're taking good care of her, someone has to do something for *you*."

His hard expression melts and he actually smiles at me. "Appreciate that, Emily. I'll definitely let you know."

My phone buzzes, letting me know I need to leave if I want to pick Libby up from rehearsal on time. "I have to pick Libby up from school."

"Are you two doing all right?" Grayson asks. "Need anything?"

"No. We're good."

His eyes narrow slightly. "Dex treating you all right?"

Why does my skin flare from my ears to my toes? Grayson's not my dad but his question feels like a fatherly sort of inquiry. "Yes. He's…he's wonderful," I gush like an infatuated teenager.

"Good." He nods. "Good. I'm glad to hear that."

A wail splits the air.

"Sounds like you're needed." I gesture to the room, but didn't need to say anything. Grayson's already hurrying to Serena's side.

I hurry to the parking lot, texting Libby that I'm on my way.

CHAPTER THIRTY-FIVE

Dex

I SIT on my bike and stare at the rambling Empire Medical comp[...] Grinder asked me to visit and see the baby. After everything h[e...] sacrificed for the club, I can't deny his request, no matter how much my body is screaming for me to get the fuck away from here.

Life is a series of choices. The wrong ones can change the course of your life and everyone you love. Indecision can also have severe consequences. No one knows that better than I do.

Still sitting on my bike, I study the key chain Libby gave me. I turn Lady Liberty over and over in my fingers, then stare at the hospital again. Libby's about the same age my daughter would've been, isn't she? Maybe a little older. My heart can't do the math. Funny, in my mind I never picture Carrie as anything more than the tiny preemie sentenced to a short term in an incubator.

I slide my thumb over the shiny, bumpy surface of the small lemon charm. Like if I rub it the correct amount of time, some magical creature will appear and grant my wishes.

Finally, I come to a decision. Visiting hours are almost over. At least that will make this a quick trip.

I stalk through the parking lot with my hands in my pockets and my head down.

"Dex?"

My head snaps up, and like a wish granted, Emily's standing in front of me.

"What are you doing here?" My gravelly tone wipes the smile off Emily's face. *Shit.*

"I visited Serena." She slowly lifts her hand, pointing her thumb at the hospital behind her. "To see the baby… Are you okay?"

"Yeah, I'm fine. Just want to get in there before visiting hours are up." The unpleasant sensation that my past and present are somehow colliding rolls over me, sharp and painful.

"Oh. Right. Sorry." She tries to sidestep me.

I hold my arm out, stopping her. "I, uh, sorry. Just have stuff on my mind. I wasn't expecting to see you."

"So I gathered."

Feeling like an absolute asshole, I lean down and press a quick kiss to her forehead. "I'll talk to you later."

"Yeah. Okay." Her tart tone doesn't sound all that eager to hear from me.

But I can't do anything about it now.

She moves past me.

If I turn around and watch her leave, I'll probably follow her. And I need to get this over with.

Dread follows me as I navigate the corridors to Serena's room. Machines beeping, babies crying, nurses hurrying from room to room, all of it brings back memories I've worked hard to bury.

I stop outside Serena's room. The door stands half open. I tap my knuckles against it. Grinder appears from behind a white curtain. He smiles and nods for me to come in. The first bed seems to be empty. That's good. I hope it means Serena has some peace while she's here.

"Thanks for coming, brother." Grinder holds out his hand and I take it. He pulls me in for a quick hug.

"Congratulations," I manage to say. "How do you feel?"

"*I* feel fine," he answers in a wry tone. "I didn't do a damn thing. Except worry."

"That's not true," Serena rasps. She sits up and offers a weak smile. "Hi, Dex."

Serena's pale, tired face sends a bolt of fear straight through my gut. "You all right, sweetheart?" I ask.

"I'm fine." Serena lets out a soft laugh and leans over to peer in the small hospital bassinet next to her bed. "I mean, I just pushed a watermelon through a lemon, but other than that, I'm okay."

Dear God, didn't Emily say something similar? I blink as the mental image forms in my brain against my will. "Thanks for the visual." I mean it to be teasing but it sounds more like a scolding.

Serena's nose wrinkles and she touches her index finger and thumb together, forming a circle. "Maybe a grape? It did *not* feel big enough for what I endured."

"Okay, I got it," I say.

She wiggles her fingers at me. "Come meet Lincoln, Dex."

Steeling myself, I step closer and peek into the crib. All that's visible is the baby's face. Red, splotchy little cheeks, closed eyes, little blue cap on his head. He's bundled in a white blanket with blue stripes. His little lips move in his sleep as if he's safe and content. He almost seems too small and perfect for such a large and evil world.

My lungs constrict.

Grinder and Serena have both gone silent. I lift my gaze and find Grinder watching me with a frown. Something, anything to break the silence swims through my head. I open my mouth to crack a joke about how the baby's too tiny to possibly be Grinder's. Thank fuck, I stop myself. What a shitty, disrespectful thing to say.

What the fuck is wrong with me?

Grinder grunts and bumps me away from his ol' lady's bedside. "You need anything, buttercup?" he asks.

She peers up at him with hope and affection in her eyes. "More water?"

Grinder nudges me with his elbow. "Dex and I will be right back."

"You need help for getting some water, old man?" I ask. There. That's better. Familiar territory.

"Stop running your mouth and move your ass," he grumbles.

Serena's soft laughter follows us as we step out of the room. "He's a beautiful baby, Grinder. Congratulations."

"Thank you, Dex." He pats my shoulder. "Walk with me."

The last thing I feel like doing is walking through the maternity ward. I'm not intimately acquainted with how this hospital is structured but if he gets me anywhere near the neonatal unit, I'm out of here.

But he stops at a small lounge area with a kitchen and goes straight for a stack of plastic pitchers, picking one up and setting it on the counter.

"I wanted to give you a heads-up," he says.

"About?" I stuff my hands in my pockets and breathe through my mouth. The crisp, antiseptic smell permeating the hospital is starting to get to me.

"Serena and I would like you to be Lincoln's godfather," he announces.

I stare at him. I know what all those words mean but I don't understand why he's directing them at *me*.

He drills me with a hard stare. "Dex?"

"Why me?"

"Why *not* you?"

"I'm not married. Don't you usually want a married couple to be the godparents?"

"Gee, I'm not sure. I've never done this before," he answers with a heaping dose of sarcasm.

"Wouldn't you rather have Rock do it?"

Grinder glares at me. "I'm asking *you*."

"Or Z? Z's your president now."

"Thank you for educating me on the hierarchy of the club, Dixon. What the fuck does that have to do with anything?"

"I…I don't know anything about being a godfather."

"Perfect. I know fuck-all about being a father."

"That's not true," I mutter. "You're going to be a great father."

"This is important to Serena," he explains. "She's comfortable with you. She likes you."

Those words steal the rest of my protests. "Okay. Yeah."

"Good." He pats my shoulder. "Now act surprised when she asks you." He grabs the pitcher and walks over to an ice machine. For a few seconds the grind and clink of ice cubes drowns out every other sound. He tops it off with water and jerks his head toward the hallway.

Conflicted, I follow him back to Serena's room.

She's resting against the bed with her eyes closed but slowly opens them when Grinder sets the pitcher down on the nightstand. "I thought you got lost," she whispers.

I really shouldn't be here. She needs her rest. And why hasn't a fucking doctor checked on her once since I've been here?

"Nah, Dex walks slow," Grinder says.

She sips her water for a few seconds, then sets the cup down. "Did Grayson already ask you?"

My gaze darts between them. "Ask me what?"

She squints at him, then shakes her head. "We'd like you to be Lincoln's godfather."

Even though Grinder already warned me—and may very well murder me if I say something that hurts Serena's feelings—I stare at them for a few seconds.

"Yeah, I'd be honored." I cock my head. "You sure you don't have me confused with one of the other brothers?"

"Nope, you looked so good in your suit at Teller's wedding, I said, you have to be Link's godfather," she answers with an amused smile.

Huh?

"I'm kidding! Seriously, you're always handing out sage advice." Laughter sparkles in her eyes. "Just maybe give it to Lincoln with a few less F-words sprinkled in."

I laugh and stare at my boots for a few seconds. "I can do that, Serena."

Lincoln seems to sense he's the topic of discussion and lets out an angry cry. I glance at the door. Is no one coming to check on them?

"All right. Thank you for coming, Dex." Grinder nudges my shoulder and pushes me toward the hallway. "She needs a minute."

"Thank you, Dex," Serena calls out.

In the hallway, Grinder places his hand on my chest, nudging my back against the wall.

I stare down at his hand. "This is happening with annoying frequency, Grinder."

"You all right?" he asks, ignoring my comment.

"Me?" I use my arm to dislodge his hand from my chest. "Shouldn't you be more worried about your ol' lady?"

"You're fucking green around the gills." He points at my face. "So, I'll ask again. Are you okay?"

"I'm fine." I glance at Serena's room. Lincoln's quieted down already. But all my worries rush to the surface. "But she looks so...tired."

"She just had a baby," he says like I'm an idiot.

Ignoring his tone, I hurry with my thoughts. "Just...make sure you keep an eye on her. Don't let those doctors talk you into anything. If you think...if she's not feeling right, you get someone else to see her. Don't take no for an answer. Or let them—"

"Okay," he says gently. Too gentle for Grinder. Almost bordering on pity. I need to get a grip. "Labor was rough on her, but I spoke to the doc earlier. She said everything's looking normal."

"They all say that. But doctors don't always know. They don't pay enough attention. It's up to *you* to make sure they take her seriously." I glance at the room again and take a breath. I sound completely un-fucking-hinged. "She's got a woman doc? That's good. Maybe she'll listen better to what Serena's going through."

Grinder frowns but nods slightly. "Yeah, Serena likes this doctor a lot. She's been thorough."

"Good. Good." I blow out a breath and tilt my head back, resting it against the wall. *Get control of yourself, for fuck's sake.* "I should head out. Let Serena know I said goodbye." I smile until my skin feels like it'll crack from the effort.

He frowns. "Maybe I should've waited. I thought…" His voice trails off.

Christ, could I have handled this any worse? "I'm good. Thank you. I'm sorry I was weird about the godfather thing. I'm honored, Grinder, really."

"Okay," he says, still sounding uncertain.

"I'll catch you later." My boots squeak over the shiny tile floor as I march away from him.

I'm thrilled for my brother. At least, I want to be. But every second of this visit has ripped open an old wound. Memories that I've spent years forcing into the dark corners of my mind bubble to the surface every time I'm in a hospital. This time, it seems worse than ever.

Once I'm finally outside, free from the antiseptic stench and endless white walls, I can finally breathe again.

The out-of-control feeling pisses me off. This is the last fucking time I do this to myself.

I'm never setting foot inside a hospital again. Not for any reason. Not ever.

CHAPTER THIRTY-SIX

Emily

IT TOOK the entire drive to Johnsonville to shake off the weirdness from running into Dex at the hospital. His gruff demeanor stung like hell. I keep trying to reassure myself that it had nothing to do with me. Hospitals make lots of people uneasy. Whatever the reason, I'm not reaching out to him first.

Libby's waiting on the front steps of the school talking to a group of her friends when I pull up. She and another girl jog to the car. Libby yanks the passenger-side door open.

"Do you mind giving Linda a ride home?" she asks.

"Of course not." I hit the button to unlock the back door and Linda throws herself across the seat. "Thank you," she breathes out in a rush. "My mom got called into work."

"No problem." I turn around so I can see her face. "Do you want to come over to our place?"

"No, no. I'll be fine. My brother's home. He just doesn't drive."

"Okay." I glance at Libby who shrugs.

The girls chatter about the play and I half-listen while I try to remember where Linda lives and forget about Dex.

"It's up here on the right." Linda's hand appears in my peripheral vision. "The one on the corner. Be careful at this intersection. Someone took down the stop sign and people fly through here," she warns.

That's just great. Thankfully, it's dark in both directions, no oncoming headlights illuminate the dark road, so I step on the gas. "That's dangerous."

"Yeah, my mom keeps calling town hall."

I pull up to the curb and Linda throws the back door open. "Thank you, Emily! See you tomorrow, Libby!" She grabs her backpack and slams the door shut, waving wildly as she runs over the grass. I wait until she's inside, then pull away from the curb.

"Thanks," Libby says. "I know it's out of our way."

"Not a problem," I assure her. "I'll always give your friends a ride. You know that." I glance over. "What was she going to do if she couldn't find someone to drive her home?"

Libby shrugs. "Call a Lyft, I guess."

"That could take forever out here," I mutter.

"One of the other parents probably would've done it," Libby assures me. "Anyway, I have rehearsals every night this week, except tomorrow. Saturday I'll be there all day."

Were school activities this much of a time commitment when I was in high school? Actually, I wouldn't know. I never had the chance to participate in any, except for a season of field hockey my freshman year. "When will you have time for homework?"

"*Emileeeee*," she groans. "Have I ever *not* done my homework?"

'No, but I don't remember you putting this many hours into a play, either."

"Really? I feel like they always swallow up my time."

"Isn't that the truth. Oh, hey, I stopped by to see Serena and the baby on the way home."

"Aw, you went without me?"

I glance at the clock. "Visiting hours are over by now. But I told Gray we'd come by the house and help out when she gets home."

"Is he cute?"

"The baby?"

"Duh, yeah."

I shrug. "I guess. They all look like little wrinkled prunes when they're that tiny."

"Ewww." She shakes her head.

I pull into our driveway. "What do you want for dinner?"

"I ate at rehearsal. They got us pizza."

"Lord, you're going to turn into a pizza pretty soon."

She chuckles and hurries ahead of me to open the front door.

Inside, I set my stuff down and head to the kitchen. I peer into the fridge and grab a slice of broccoli pizza and slide it into the toaster oven.

Don't think about having dinner with Dex.

While I'm waiting for it to warm up, Libby joins me.

I wanted to have this conversation in the car but I got distracted with giving her friend a ride and forgot to bring it up. The way Dex acted earlier, this conversation might not even be necessary.

My phone buzzes.

Dex: Did you and Libby get home okay?

I blow out a breath and close my eyes.

A childish urge comes over me to ignore the text. Let him think I'm still mad about earlier.

But I'm not seventeen years old. I like Dex too much to play games.

Yup. We're sitting down for dinner now.

I set my phone down and focus on my sister. "Hey, can I talk to you for a second?"

Libby plucks an apple out of the basket on the counter and turns it in her hands, studying the skin. The kid bit into an apple with a worm in it *once* and it scarred her for life. "Yeah, sure," she mumbles, still studying the apple.

"I'm sorry about last night, early this morning." Embarrassed to be having this talk, I turn around and fill a glass with water, then set it on the table.

She frowns. "What are you sorry about?"

"Well, it's not...I shouldn't have guys over...expose you to..." How can my little sister get me so flustered with one tiny question?

Finally deciding the apple must be safe, she bites into it with a hard crunch, then still munching away, leans on the counter next to me. "It's not like you're exposing me to weird randos in and out of our house, Em. Have you even dated anyone since Aunt Kim died?"

I don't want to bring up the creep who gave the sexy outfit. If she doesn't remember him, there's no reason to remind her. "Just a few bad apples."

She waves her apple in the air. "Clever." She pushes away from the counter and sits at the table.

The timer on the toaster oven dings, and I pull my pizza out, dump it on a plate, and join her at the table.

"Em, can I say something?" She sets the fruit down and squinches her brows into a serious expression.

"When have you ever held your tongue?" I ask.

She doesn't laugh. "I'm leaving for college soon. At least, I hope so." She swallows hard and glances to the side. "I hate thinking of you here all by yourself."

"You make it sound like I'm a recluse."

She twirls the apple around by the stem. "Besides, I like Dex."

A smile tugs at the corners of my mouth. "I noticed."

She stares at the kitchen door with a dreamy expression. "I like the way he watches you when you're not even looking."

I set my pizza down. "He does?"

"Yup." She flicks her fingers toward the window and our backyard. "From that first time he showed up with Gray to do the lawn." She wrinkles her nose. "He's kinda serious, though."

"And I'm not?"

"You're fun but," she sighs and sets the apple down, "you had to be a parent way too young. Jeez, Em, I'll be nineteen in a few years and I can't imagine doing what you did. What you still do for me."

Emotion clogs my throat and I take a sip of water before answering her. "We had Aunt—"

"I loved Auntie Kimmy," she cuts me off, "but she was old and had health problems. You were more like *her* caretaker than she was ours."

She's right but it feels icky to speak ill of the woman who took us in after our parents died. Libby didn't spend summers with Aunt Kim when she was little the way I did, so she doesn't remember her the same way I do. "I guess."

She fixes her gaze on the table. "Don't hate me for saying this, but… you were always like a mom to me anyway, you know? When I was little. I have more memories of *you* being there and doing things with me than I do of Mom."

Something like guilt closes off my throat. *It's not my fault.*

"Even before…what happened to them," she continues. "You dropped me off at school in the mornings."

"The elementary school was right next to—"

"You're the one who took me to drama classes, singing lessons, and ballet," she cuts me off with more heat in her voice. "*You* did all that stuff. Not Mom."

"Their way of keeping me out of trouble, I guess," I say with a quick shrug. "Mom and Dad loved you, Libby."

"Sure. I know. They always came to dance recitals and my plays. But *you* were the one who was there for the day-to-day stuff." She stares at me for a long moment. "I'm really sorry they made you do all that."

"I didn't mind." *Not too much, anyway.* I reach over and pat her hand. "You were always the cutest ballerina in the class."

She rolls her eyes. "If by cute, you mean clumsiest, then yeah." Her eyes widen. "Oh my gosh, do you remember Miss Blanch? She was so damn mean."

I remember telling the elderly ballet instructor if she ever yelled at my sister again in front of the whole class I'd rip her bun out by the roots. But I probably shouldn't share that story with Libby. "She was very regimented," I say diplomatically.

"It's not like I wanted to be a prima ballerina." Libby rolls her eyes. "But geez, she took everything so seriously."

"Fun wasn't in her vocabulary," I agree.

"Anyway, what I was trying to tell you is, I like Dex. And I like him for you. It's about time you have someone who looks after you and worries about you the way you worry about everyone else."

"It's just you and me, pudding. And you're pretty self-sufficient these days."

She slants a don't-be-dense look at me. "I'm not a little kid. There's no reason you can't have Dex stay over if you want him to. Geez," she flicks her gaze to the ceiling, "I feel like Melanie tells me about finding a different boyfriend of her mom's in the kitchen every week. Her mom is on like, every dating site out there."

"Damn, I didn't know the Johnsonville dating pool was that large," I tease.

She wrinkles her nose. "Gross. One was Caroline's dad and Melanie went nuclear." She reaches over and slaps the table in front of me. "So *one* guy staying over isn't the big deal you're making out of it, Em. Really."

I squint at her. "I don't know if comparing me to your friend's inappropriate mom is much of a compliment."

"Ugh." She groans and stares at the ceiling. "You're impossible."

"No. I hear what you're saying. Thank you." I slide my hand across the table and curl it around hers. I press my lips together to stop them from trembling. "Damn, when did you turn into such a grown-up?"

She glances down at the apple and pierces the skin with her thumbnail. "I like when Dex is here. I feel comfortable around him. Safe," she says. "Not like that one creep you dated."

I swallow hard, embarrassed by the memory. "I'm sorry. I should've—"

She holds out one hand in a stop gesture. "I didn't say it to make you feel bad. You listened to me. And never had him here again. That's all that matters."

Still, I should've done better. It's a sobering reminder that I haven't always used the best judgment.

CHAPTER THIRTY-SEVEN

Emily

A FEW NIGHTS LATER, Libby's busy with rehearsal. Dex and I have talked a few times since our hospital run-in. And now some stupid part of me decides it would be a good time to take him up on his offer to visit him at work.

I can't believe I'm about to go inside a strip club.

But Dex told me to stop by whenever I wanted. That I could surprise him. His way of telling me he had nothing to hide. That even if I showed up unannounced, there was no chance I'd ever catch him in a compromising position.

Does going to his club tonight signal that I don't trust him?

Truthfully, I just want to see him.

And yet, I don't text him to warn him that I'm here.

Instead, I park in the front of the building with the other customers. But then I'm frozen. I sit in my car, staring at the building in my rearview mirror. I shouldn't do this.

Annoyed with myself, I blow out a breath and open my car door. My heart pounds wildly. Am I really setting foot inside a strip club by myself? I'm like a rabbit willingly hopping into a fox's den.

I run my hands over the sides of my wide-legged black trousers and check the buttons on my deep gray silk blouse. My red heels click softly over the pavement. Under my arm, I'm carrying a black clutch with only my ID, some cash, and lipstick. My keys and phone I keep in my pockets.

Only one or two guys are waiting to go inside. I hold my head up and try to act like I belong here. I scan the parking lot as if I'm supposed to meet a friend and I'm checking to see if they've arrived. Too bad I'm not as good of an actress as my little sister. I probably just look like I got lost on my way to traffic court.

The man at the door is easily the size of a mountain. Dark brown skin, long locs, and a tight black T-shirt stretched over his chest. He's wearing a black leather vest similar to Dex's but without all the patches for decoration. I'd love to get a look at the back to see if it has the Lost Kings MC logo on it.

Lord, the man's arms are bigger than my thighs. I'd feel quite safe working here knowing this man is at the door, deciding who gets let in and who's turned away. His severe expression shifts when his gaze lands on me. He shines a bright smile.

"Evening. What's a pretty girl doing here all by herself tonight?"

I open my mouth to say I'm here to see Dex. But wasn't the element of surprise the whole point?

"I'm, uh, meeting someone," I stammer. That's not really a lie, right?

He narrows his eyes, silently assessing me. "Why don't you sit yourself at the bar until your friend arrives." He phrases it as a suggestion but in his deep, rumbling voice it sounds more like an order.

"Sure."

"Don't forget to tip the girls," he warns.

Tip them for what? "I won't."

His gaze slides over me one more time. Not in a creepy, salacious way. More like he's still deciding if he should let me in or not. Maybe he's worried I'm the wife of a customer here to cause her husband trouble.

"Anyone bothers you, ask for Malik," he finally says. "I'll take care of 'em."

"Thank you."

He jerks his head toward the door. "Go on."

I hold out a twenty to cover the door fee and he shakes his head. "No cover for ladies."

"Thank you, Malik," I say as I pass by him.

I enter a short, dark passageway. A coatroom on my left. Another man sitting on a barstool right in front of me. He raises his eyebrows but nods and lets me through without saying a word.

The throbbing music pulses through my feet as I step into the main

298

area of the club. Lots of neon lighting, flashing lights. About half the tables and chairs have customers.

On stage, three girls whirl around shiny poles. I had no idea the stunts they're performing were even humanly possible and I stand there staring like an idiot until someone bumps into me.

"Sorry," I mutter.

The girl scowls at me but continues walking to one of the tables where she promptly sits in a customer's lap.

Bar. Yup. I should get out of the way.

A tall blonde behind the bar stares at me. "First time here?"

"Yup."

She flicks her gaze over me in a dismissive way. "What can I get you?"

"Lemonade?"

She nods and a few seconds later passes a cold bottle and plastic cup to me. Guess I'll be pouring my own drink. I perch on a stool at the end of the bar where I can place my back to the wall and let my gaze loose, searching for Dex.

There he is. My eyes pick out his familiar shape. He's standing with his back against the same wall I'm currently leaning on all the way on the other side of the club. Arms crossed over his chest. Serious scowl in place. He's facing the stage, but his attention seems to be the men seated around it rather than the girls working the poles.

I tug my phone out of my pocket and send him a quick text.

Me: Why are you so damn sexy wearing that scowl?

A deeper frown creases his forehead. He lifts his head and slowly searches the room. His gaze finally lands on me, and the scowl melts off his face. Surprise, tenderness, and concern all seem to flicker over his expression.

Affection bubbles up inside me.

Eyes on me, he marches through the crowd, dodging dancers, waitresses, and customers until he's standing in front of me. So close, he bumps into my knees.

"Firecracker." His lips twist into a smile. "What're you doing here?"

I shrug even though embarrassment prickles over my skin. "You said I could visit at any time."

"I did." He rests his hand on my thigh and leans into my space. "Wasn't sure you'd actually come, though."

Oh God. With his intense eyes, low voice, and warm breath against my ear, I could come right *now* in the middle of this alien environment from his presence alone.

"How'd you get in?" he asks.

"Uh, the front door?" I awkwardly point toward the entrance.

One corner of his mouth lifts. "Aren't you sneaky." He slides his hand from my thigh to my hip. "Were you okay?"

I nod quickly. "Malik was nice to me. Although he seemed a bit suspicious about why I was here."

He rumbles with laughter. "That's what we pay him to do."

I touch his leather vest. "His vest is kind of like yours, but I didn't see the same patches." I tap my finger under his Lost Kings MC patch.

He flicks his gaze down to where I'm touching and I snatch my hands away. "Sorry, am I allowed to touch your vest?"

He grabs my hand and brings it to his lips, dusting a kiss against my knuckles. "You're allowed to touch anything on me, firecracker." He presses my palm against his chest to demonstrate.

Something tickling at the back of my mind says this is a big deal. Didn't I read somewhere that you're not supposed to touch a biker's patches? We lock eyes and whatever I might've read doesn't seem important anymore.

"You just made my night a thousand times better," he says, leaning in to press a kiss to my forehead. "And to answer your question, Malik's still a prospect, so he doesn't have all his patches yet."

I can use the context clues to figure out what a prospect is. "How is that mountain of a man not fully patched?" I ask.

"Takes more than size," he answers.

"I'm kidding. Sort of."

"We call the patches 'colors,'" he says.

"Colors," I repeat. *Easy enough to remember. They're colorful.*

A hard clack from the front of the club draws my attention to the stage. One of the girls is holding her body in a horizontal line away from the pole. She makes a wide "V" with her legs and snaps them together, knocking her high-heeled platform shoes together.

"Dear God," I mutter, resting my hand on my stomach. "I can't even imagine the core strength it takes to do *that*." The physics of the movement alone hurts my brain. And yet, the woman swings her body upside down and repeats the foot-clap movement. All while making it look effortless. My breath catches in my lungs, waiting for her to spin herself right side up and safely return to the stage. A few seconds later, she does, executing a number of drops and graceful spins before landing in a split at the bottom of the pole.

Men cheer and throw money at her. She crawls seductively over the stage to collect the cash and that's when I lose interest in the performance.

"That takes a lot of…athletic skill," I say to Dex.

His gaze briefly shifts to the stage, then back to me.

"The pole work," I clarify. "Seems insulting she has to crawl around on the stage after performing such complicated moves."

He tilts his head. "Not a lot of people recognize the skill it takes."

"*People* or male customers?" I arch a brow.

His lips quirk. "Good point." He glances at the stage again. "She was a finalist in last year's national pole fitness championships."

"Wow." I blink a few times. I had no idea pole fitness championships were even a thing. "That must be a big draw for your club."

He shrugs. "I don't know how many of our customers keep up on the world of pole fitness."

The dancer has moved on to removing what's left of her minuscule red lace outfit, which seems depressing and banal after the earlier part of her performance.

"She should be in the Olympics, not showing her tits and bits to greasy strangers," I say.

Dex bites the inside of his cheek, like he's trying not to agree with me. Or trying not to laugh. I can't tell.

"Have I mentioned how happy I am to see you?" he says instead.

I curl my fingers in his shirt, tugging him closer. "Yes, but I don't mind hearing it again."

He kisses my cheek, lingering for a moment. "I am."

Even though his attention is mostly focused on me, every few seconds, he turns his head to scan the room, checking out the crowd.

"Do you need to get back to work?" I ask. After all, I did ambush him, and I understand he has responsibilities.

"I should check on a few things." He squeezes my hip. "Are you okay here? You can sit in my office if this is too much."

Except for the bartender and the waitresses coming and going, the bar area is empty. Most of the customers are focused on the stage or enjoying visits from the dancers working the room.

"I'll be fine here." I pick up my lemonade and take a sip.

He nods, then leans over and slaps his palm against the bar top. "Willow!" he calls out.

The blonde bartender whips her head around and hurries over to us with an eager-to-please smile on her face.

Geez. Do all the girls ask how high when my man tells them to jump?

"What's up, Dex?" she asks in a how-may-I-help-you voice.

My, my, look how friendly and chipper she is now.

He curls his arm around my shoulders, affectionately pulling me to his side. "This is my girlfriend, Emily."

My heart stutters. He's introducing me to the people in his life as his *girlfriend*. I'm so lost in the childish pleasure of the official title that I miss the rest of their exchange.

Dex rubs his hand over my back and whispers in my ear, "You're sure you're okay here?"

"I think so."

He chuckles. "I'll check in with you in a bit. Just let me make my rounds."

"I'm fine," I say with more confidence. I don't want him worrying about me when he's supposed to be working.

He nods once then strides into the middle of the room. He stops and talks to another man large enough to crack a skull or two. A woman in an almost see-through silver two-piece...swimsuit? Bra and panties? I'm not sure what to call what she's wearing, but the look is completed by six-inch silver platform boots that hug her calves and end below her knees. Maybe her costume is supposed to be sexy alien hunter or something.

"How long have you and Dex known each other?" Willow asks me.

"Huh?" I tear my gaze away from astronaut girl talking to my man and meet Willow's amused face.

"*Guurrrl*, if you're going to be with him, you better get used to *that*." She nods at the girl still yammering at Dex.

"I'm...I'm not worried about it," I say with a whole lot less confidence than I intended. "I know it's his job."

"Mmmhmm." She gives me a skeptical side-eye. "They're always up in his business."

I reach down and gather my fuck-off attitude. "I'm only worried about it if he's up in *theirs*."

She snorts and ducks her head, resting her forehead on the bar for a second, her thin shoulders shaking with laughter. "If only you knew how ridiculous that concern is."

"What's that supposed to mean?" I ask.

"Dex doesn't date strippers, or muffler bunnies, or...anyone that we know of."

Muffler bunny? Never mind, I can figure that one out on my own.

"Date? Or fuck?" I lift my eyebrows. "Because they're not one and the same."

She nods once. "I don't keep track of his dick." She spears me with an icy look. "I've never ridden it either, in case you're wondering."

"I wasn't, but thanks, I guess." I thought Dex said I'd like Willow. Why is she being such a megabitch?

She's still studying me in a bug under a microscope way I don't care for. "You showing up here unannounced, kinda says you don't trust him," she says.

A spike of annoyance pokes at me but I brush it away. "It's none of your business, but Dex said I could visit him whenever I wanted. So I did."

"Okay." She holds her hands in the air as if she's putting away her bitch claws for the night.

Silver space cowgirl saunters over to the bar, hips swaying in a way that captures every man's attention. A long, thick curtain of black hair falls over her shoulders and down her back. Her perfectly made-up face belongs on a beauty blog of "best application" examples. If I'd brought Serena with me, she probably would've tried to chat the dancer up for tips on her fabulous false eyelashes.

Assuming she's coming this way to drop off a drink order, I turn back to the bar and sip my lemonade. I need some ice, but I'd rather eat an entire lemon—rind and all—before I ask Willow for anything.

Space cowgirl stops right next to me. Bracing her hands against the bar, she leans over to murmur something to Willow. I try not to notice her breasts overflowing the cups of her silver top from my peripheral vision.

"So," she snaps.

My body stiffens at the sharp tone so close to my ear. Is she talking to me?

The dark-haired beauty flicks her gaze over me in a dismissive, bordering on angry, way. "Who are you? Dex's sister?" She spits out the questions like nails.

I drop my gaze to her hands and the purple talons that I'd rather not have raked over my face. She could scoop out my eyeballs with those nails.

"I…" My voice breaks on a squeaky high note. Where did all of my fuck-off go?

"Serenity." Willow leans over the bar and snaps her fingers in the girl's face. "Watch how you talk to our guests."

Serenity? Someone needs a better stage name. Nothing about this one says calm *or* tranquil.

"Well, who's this little Raggedy Ann bitch then, Willow? Sittin' over here lookin' like she's from corporate or somethin'."

That's a…lot of insults to unwrap. *Raggedy Ann?* I touch the ends of my hair. Did I go too red this time?

Screw this chick.

"If I was from 'corporate,'" I pause to curl my fingers into bitchy little air quotes, "do you think insulting me would be a good idea?"

"What?" she screeches.

"Don't make me get Malik in here to throw you out," Willow warns.

"We don't need no more dancers," Serenity says. "We got enough." She rakes her dismissive gaze over my body. "No one's looking for the uptight experience, either."

Uptight? Me?

Willow slams two bottles of what I guess is soda on the bar. "Take your order and go."

Serenity casts one more suspicious look my way, grabs the bottles, and sashays away.

"Sheesh," I mutter.

"That's a good preview of what you'll get up at the clubhouse," Willow says. "If you make it that far."

What is this, a reality dating show where all the women fight over one guy?

"I've already met a few of the old ladies," I mutter. Maybe it was a mistake to come here. "None of them behaved like her."

Willow pauses and squints at me. "You have?" She tilts her head. "How long have you known Dex?"

I glance at the rest of the club, searching for his comforting presence and spot him all the way on the other side talking to another bouncer. "A little while. My best friend is engaged to one of his brothers."

Her eyes widen, like she's rethinking her earlier cattiness toward me. "Oh."

Should I have introduced myself to her as Grinder's old lady's bestie? That sure would've been a mouthful.

Business at the bar picks up. Dancers, or waitresses, I can't tell, stop by with orders for Willow. Some study me with curiosity but none of them speak to me.

After about half an hour, I'm ready to go. None of the other dancers who've taken the stage are as impressive as the one who did all the pole tricks. I watch Dex here and there. Talking to customers, the bouncers, and the dancers. He seems so...different in this environment. Tense. No, maybe that's not the right word. Focused. Definitely not the relaxed, easygoing man I'm intimately acquainted with. It really seems like just a job to him. One that he takes seriously.

I sip my lukewarm lemonade and check the time.

Someone touches my back and leans into my space. Dex presses a kiss to my cheek. His familiar woodsy, soapy scent wraps around me. A faint trace of something chemical and coconutty follows his comforting scent. Cheap body spray from one of the dancers who took a moment to rub up against him?

"Sorry that took so long," he says.

I force a cheerful smile. "It's okay." I pick up my cup and finish my drink. "It's time for me to head home, though."

"Libby have rehearsal tonight?" he asks.

I nod. "Her friend's mom is supposed to give her a ride, but I still want to be home when she gets there."

"Sure. Let me walk out with you." He lifts his hand, waving to Willow some sort of gesture that must mean he'll be right back.

The stool at the entrance is vacant but Malik's still outside the door.

His mouth slides into a sly smile when his dark eyes land on us. "Meetin' someone, huh?"

Heat sears my cheeks.

"Malik," Dex says, "this is my girlfriend, Emily."

"I'll remember you next time," he says.

Dex frowns slightly, then shakes it off and we continue to my car. "You gonna be all right?" he asks.

"Driving home? Sure. I do it every night." I rest my hand on his shoulder. "You've got a full plate in there." I still don't love it. But I understand better now.

"A lot of moving pieces to keep things operating smoothly," he says. "Most nights it's not hard."

"But you never know which nights will be the difficult ones."

His lips curve into an appreciative grin. "Exactly."

I lean up and press a quick kiss to his cheek. He stops me from pulling away with an arm around my waist, holding me against his chest. I tip my head back, staring up at him.

"Give me an actual kiss and I'll let you go," he says just loud enough for me to hear above the traffic noises.

I turn my head. We're standing out in the parking lot by a rather busy road.

"No," he rumbles. "Eyes up here. On me."

That's the only warning he gives before crashing his lips into mine. I gasp in surprise and he strokes his tongue against mine. Any concern about drivers getting a peep show go *poof*. Liquid heat shoots straight between my thighs. I slide my arms around his neck, lifting myself closer. He tastes sweet like butterscotch candies with a hint of smoky burnt caramel, and I can't get enough.

His arms tighten around my waist, holding me like something rare and precious. The kiss consumes everything around us. He's hard against me and I have to fight the urge to press my leg to his hip and climb on him.

He groans against my mouth. "Emily, how am I supposed to send you home now?"

My eyes blink open. "You sure know how to give a girl a proper send-off."

He hugs me to his chest. "And you know how to get me hard as steel in ten seconds flat," he says against my ear.

"I noticed," I murmur, a surge of feminine pride rising in me.

He releases me, but still keeps one arm at my back. "Go. Before I do very indecent things to you in this parking lot."

He pulls my door open and I lean up to give him one more quick kiss before sliding into the driver's seat.

"Text me when you get home." He ducks down into my open car door.

"Okay."

"I'm gonna watch you go." He winks at me and presses his hand to the front of his jeans. "I need a minute."

Laughter bubbles past my lips. "Sorry, not sorry."

His smile widens and he closes my door. I slip on my seat belt and reverse out of my parking spot. I watch him in my mirror, pleased that I gave him a kiss he won't soon forget.

Or you just gave him a hard-on, then sent him into a building full of beautiful, flexible, naked women for the rest of the night.

CHAPTER THIRTY-EIGHT

Dex

THIS IS the second time Emily's left here that I wanted to ditch everything and chase her home.

What the fuck is happening to me?

I wait until her car leaves the parking lot, then head inside, her sweet minty taste still lingering on my lips.

Willow waves to me from the bar.

I stop. "What's up?"

"This came for you earlier." She hands over a cream-colored letter-sized envelope with a return address for what looks like a law firm.

"For fuck's sake, what now?" I rip open the envelope and scan the letter.

Well, hell, the guys I roughed up in the VIP room made good on their promise to sue us. *Fan-fucking-tastic.* Can't wait to tell Rock that one.

Willow leans over the bar to get my attention. "I'm not sure if Emily mentioned it, but Serenity was a real bitch to her earlier."

Tension gathers in my shoulders. Just what I don't need. Serenity's another one of Loco's girls. If I fire her, he's going to annoy the shit out of me about it. "How so?"

"Exactly what you'd expect from these catty little bitches who want to sink their claws in you." She curls her fingers into a tight "C" shape and swipes it through the air. "Emily seemed startled at first but she handled it okay."

"And what did *you* do while Emily 'handled' it?" I ask with a pointed stare. Emily shouldn't have had to deal with any bullshit. I asked Willow to look out for her.

She blinks rapidly. "I told Serenity to knock it off."

I grunt in acknowledgment.

"When'd you start seeing Emily, anyway?" she asks with more judgment in her tone than I care for. "You've never mentioned her."

Willow and I talk—about friendly, work-related stuff. I don't get into personal details with her...or anyone, really. "Am I supposed to advise you when I'm seeing someone?"

"What? No." She shrugs. "I just thought it was kind of shitty that she ambushed you like that. Sneaking in here and all."

I frown and step closer to the bar, not liking the tone or the words coming out of Willow's mouth. "How, exactly, did she *sneak* in the front door?"

"Well, I—"

"What goes on between my old lady and me isn't your concern, Willow." She's been around the MC long enough to know better. "Remember that."

"Okay." Her voice quivers. "I'm sorry."

Shit. She better not have thrown attitude at Emily. I loved having her visit me tonight. And I want her to start socializing with the MC, not be afraid to visit the clubhouse.

I move through the club as unobtrusively as my big body, the clustered tables, and packed customers allow. An upbeat, positive energy seems to be flowing through the air. It isn't always this way and can change in an instant. I check in with our guy manning the VIP rooms and glance at the monitors. Each room is occupied. Good for business. Is it too much to ask that it stay this way until closing?

As I emerge from the hallway, I catch Ravage and Bricks waving to me from the other side of the club. Avoiding getting too close to the stage and the eager men surrounding it, I make my way over to them.

"What's good, brother?" Bricks greets me with a fist bump.

"What're you doing here?" I ask, pleased to see him.

He jerks his thumb over his shoulder at Rav. "This clown said you needed extra hands." He holds his hands in the air and waves them in front of my face. "So here I am."

I tilt my head in the direction of my office. "Let's sit down for a second and catch up. I can't hear shit out here."

They nod and follow me to the office. With the door closed, a good portion of the noise is muffled. I glance at the screens showing different areas of the club before sitting down behind the desk.

"Wouldn't you rather be home with the family?" I ask Bricks.

He scowls at the question, throws a glance at Ravage, then shrugs. "My kids are with their mom." He pulls a sour face at the mention of his ex. "And Winter keeps bugging me about having another kid."

"So?" Ravage asks.

Bricks throws him a mind-your-business scowl. "I'd rather avoid that argument tonight."

Ravage's eyes widen and he bites down on his lip, like he's dying to razz Bricks but somewhere deep down realizes this isn't the time.

Honestly, I'm not sure what to say either. "Sorry, brother."

He shrugs again. "We have enough kids to keep track of. Deacon and Lisa are getting older, so she says they can help out, but I'm not cool with turning them into built-in babysitters. And Caleb's just getting to the point where he's a cool little dude. I don't want to deal with a baby again."

Rav's held out as long as he could. "I thought Mexicans liked big families?"

Bricks reaches over and smacks the back of Rav's head. "For the last fucking time, I'm Puerto Rican."

"The fuck is wrong with you, Rav?" I rub my fingers over my forehead, fending off a Ravage-induced headache.

"What?" Rav grins and points his thumb at Bricks, like they're partners in crime. "It's our thing."

Bricks rolls his eyes. "The shockingly stupid shit that comes out of your mouth is *not* 'our thing.'"

"You sure you wouldn't rather go home and talk things out with her?" I ask Bricks, ignoring Rav.

"No. I'm running out of ways to sneak on a condom," Bricks says.

I hold up one hand. "That's more than I needed to know."

Rav leans toward Bricks like he has confidential information to share. "You should always keep your shit wrapped anyway. Chicks can put a hex on you if they get a sample of your spunk."

Bricks looks from Ravage to me, like we're playing a joke on him. "What the fuck?"

We should know better than to try to have an adult conversation around Rav.

We're saved by someone knocking on the door.

"Come in!" I shout. "Please, God, come in," I mutter under my breath.
Rav stands and opens the door. Kyla peeks her head inside.

"I, uh, I'm done with my shift. Can someone walk me out?" she asks.

"Yeah." I curl my finger at her, motioning her into the office.

She darts a nervous glance at the three of us. "What? Did I do
something wrong?" she asks.

"Naw, looks like you're doing everything right," Ravage says with a
long, slow, creepy gawk.

She flashes a relieved smile. At least Rav's pervy stare isn't sending her
screaming from the room.

"Jesus," Bricks mutters, planting his face in his palm.

"Ravage." I snap my fingers to get his attention. "Move out of the way."
I curl my fingers at Kyla again.

She takes a few tentative steps toward my desk.

"Everything okay?" I ask. "At home."

"Oh!" A genuine smile flickers over her face. "Yes. I'm still staying at
Willow's, but it's going great. She's been super cool about everything."

At least Willow can do one thing I asked. "Stan hasn't bothered you anymore?"

Surprise widens her eyes. She really never figured out I paid her
boyfriend a visit? That's good. "No," she answers. "I blocked him from
everything, though. Deleted all my social media too."

"Good. Glad to hear it." I cock my head. It still might be better to get
her out of the area. "You ever want to travel? See other clubs? We've got a
place in Tennessee. They're always looking for new talent."

"Oh, I...don't know if I want to start over new somewhere I don't
know anyone."

I didn't mean to make it sound like I was permanently banishing her.
"Well, it's always an option if you want. We've got other places too."

"Thank you."

"Rav, can you walk her out, please?" I ask.

He magically slips into professional mode, opening and holding the
door for Kyla. "You got it."

"Rav?" I call in a low voice before he steps out.

He turns to me with a raised eyebrow.

"Wait a sec out there. Make sure no one follows her or anything."

"Yeah. No problem."

Bricks shakes his head after they leave. "How is he a fuckin' clown one
minute and Mr. Manners the next? Gives me whiplash."

"It's a curse."

"Don't you mean gift?"

"No. I don't."

We both share a laugh.

"Shit, I've missed you, Dex," he says. "Where the fuck you been hiding, lately?"

"Who's hiding? I see you in church every week."

"Yeah, but you haven't stuck around afterward to bullshit with everyone. Been missing Thursday night dinners too." He pauses and cocks his head. "Although maybe *I* need to start skipping family dinner nights. I think that's what's giving Winter baby fever."

I choke down my laughter and try to remain in supportive brother mode.

"I should kick Teller's ass," he continues.

"Why just him?" I ask, not following his logic. "Murphy and Heidi just had a baby. Grinder and Serena just had one."

"It's the twin thing. Charlotte's having twins." He rolls his eyes. "I never knew Winter had an obsession with having twins before."

"I'm pretty sure Teller didn't plan it that way," I point out. "Wait until the babies get here and she sees how much work they are. Maybe that'll change her mind."

He slaps his palms together prayer-style and closes his eyes for a few seconds.

Ravage returns, closing the door behind him. "Got her out of here safe, boss," he says, dropping into his chair again. "You're not still talking about babies, are you?"

"Yeah, we were talking about you," I say.

"The biggest baby," Bricks adds.

Rav jumps out of his chair. "Well, I'll let you two sync up your cycles, check your fertility windows, or whatever the fuck. I'm gonna go work the floor."

"Don't forget your G-string!" Bricks shouts after him.

Rav throws up his middle finger, then slams the door.

Shaking his head and grinning, Bricks turns my way. "I never get tired of messing with him."

"Eh. He's been helping out a lot here. I probably shouldn't hassle him so much. You definitely should, though." I flash an evil grin. "At every opportunity."

His shoulders shake with laughter, then abruptly stop. "Did I hear right? Inga stopped by here?"

I let out a heavy sigh. Somehow, I'd managed to forget about that. "Yup. Wanted to waltz right on stage like nothing ever happened."

"She had balls approaching *you*."

"Karma loves fucking with me. Must be all the evil shit I've done."

"What're you talking about?" Bricks stares at me slack-jawed. "You're the best of us, brother."

"You kidding? All the people I've fucked up…or sent to the demon's dinner table, as Jigsaw might say. That's a heavy karmic tax."

Bricks is shaking his head before I even finish, a serious frown crossing his face. "Fuck that. You know how many good things you've done for people? Little things that make a huge difference? You're always there to help a brother out when he needs it." He jerks his thumb toward the door. "Kyla looks like she's had a hundred pounds lifted off her shoulders since she got away from her boyfriend. I feel shitty that I never bothered to figure out why she always looked like a frightened little mouse around here."

"You haven't been working here that much since she started," I point out.

"Don't be dense, bro. And stop feeling guilty."

"I *don't* feel guilty. Sometimes I think *that's* the problem. The lack of remorse." No crime I've committed or body I've buried could ever dig a deeper hole in my conscience than losing my wife and daughter.

"God will judge us, brother. Until then, keep doing what you know is right." He thumps his fist over his heart. "In here. Not what people out there tell you is right." He points a finger toward the door.

I love my brother and what he's saying comes from a good place. So I don't bother telling him that there is no God. Just the universe and its imperfect wisdom.

CHAPTER THIRTY-NINE

Dex

I PROBABLY SHOULD'VE SENT EMILY a text letting her know I was stopping by. It's late. A school night for Libby. I don't want to disrupt their lives but the need to see Emily burns in my chest. Kissing her has been on my mind since she left Crystal Ball.

Unlike some of my brothers, I've never modified my exhaust system to make it louder. Even so, at this hour, the whole neighborhood will hear me coming. I slow the bike as I turn onto her street and basically coast into her driveway.

Lights from the living room shine through the slivers of curtain. Hopefully that means I didn't wake her up.

Outdoor lights pop on, nearly blinding me as I walk to the front porch. The overhead light blinks to life and after a few seconds, the front door creaks open.

"Dex?" Emily whispers.

"Did I wake you?"

"No." There's a click as she unlatches the screen door.

I open it and slip inside.

"What're you doing here?"

"I missed you."

The corners of her mouth turn up. "You just saw me a few hours ago."

"It wasn't enough." I lean down to kiss her, but she ducks to the side.

"Hang on." A heap of black metal flashes in her hand as she skirts around me. She stops at the antique-looking entryway table that I've never given much thought to, and slides open a long, slim drawer, revealing a biometric safe about the size of a shoebox.

A million thoughts race through my head as she presses her thumb to the keypad, unlocking the safe, and stashes a small black pistol inside. She shoves the drawer closed and faces me.

"You always answer the door gun-in-hand?" I ask.

She cocks her head as if it was a dumb question. "Don't tell me guns bother you?"

I snort. "No." I step closer, resting my hands on her hips. "In fact, I'm very turned-on by a woman who's ready to protect herself."

She huffs a soft laugh and leans into me. "Of course you are."

More serious now, I stare into her troubled hazel eyes. "I didn't mean to scare you, though."

"I thought it was you, but I wasn't completely sure."

While I tried to make light of it, I'm bothered that she feels so unsafe in her own house that she keeps a gun by the door. "I hope I didn't wake Libby," I say.

Emily turns toward the stairs. "She's all the way at the end of the hallway. Farthest from the road. I doubt it."

"Good." I pull her closer. She tips her head back and I press my lips to hers. She sighs, her body melting against mine.

"I'm happy you're here," she whispers against my lips. "Just in case that wasn't clear."

I release her for now, turning to shrug out of my cut. Heat hovers around me like a cloud. Emily must set the temperature high at night. Or I'm chilled from the long ride. I unbutton my flannel and pull it off too.

"You can keep going," she teases.

I flash a lopsided grin. "Not until you earn it."

"Ooo." She fans her hand in front of her face for a second. "Hey, are you hungry? I made chicken and broccoli for dinner and there's a lot left over."

I'm about to say I don't want her to go to any trouble when my stomach rumbles. "Yeah, if you don't mind." Besides, I need something to do so I can keep my hands off of her for a few minutes.

"I wouldn't have asked if I did." She turns and gestures over her shoulder for me to follow.

In the kitchen, she quickly dishes a generous portion of chunks of chicken and bright green broccoli onto a plate. "I don't have any rice," she says. "We had cauliflower rice with it and there isn't any of that left."

"Looks good the way it is."

She throws me a grateful smile.

"You think I'd show up unannounced and demand you cook for me?" I ask.

"No. Doesn't mean I don't want you to be happy, though."

"I'm just happy being in your aura, Emily."

She side-eyes me. "I never pegged you for an *aura* kind of guy."

Amused, one corner of my mouth slides up. "I don't enjoy being put in a box."

Her smile fades as if she's worried I'm mad or something. "Sorry, I didn't mean it in a bad way."

I reach over and capture her hand. "Relax, I know what you meant. You don't have to censor yourself around me. I'm hard to offend."

"Well, I don't want to brag," she flashes a cocky grin, "but I'm kind of an expert in shoving my foot in my mouth."

I know she's trying to lighten things up with a joke but I can't do it. "I like you, Emily. You. Just the way you are."

"I like you too," she whispers.

I lean over and kiss her cheek. "Good."

The microwave sings a few notes to let us know it's done. Emily pulls out the plate, some silverware, and napkins and sets everything on the table in front of me. I dig in while she grabs two cans of seltzer from the fridge.

"Thank you." I pull out the chair next to me. "Sit with me."

"Of course." She drops into the chair and pops her can open, taking a long sip.

"This is good," I say, stabbing into another chunk of chicken. I'm hungrier than I realized and force myself to slow down and not shovel in food like an animal.

"Thanks. How was the rest of your night?"

"Told you." I swallow and take a sip of seltzer. "Spent it missing you."

The corners of her mouth twitch, like she thinks I'm full of shit and she's trying not to laugh.

I set my fork down and slide my hand over hers. "Willow told me one of the girls was snippy with you. I'm sorry about that. I should've warned you that might happen." I touch my temple. "Wasn't thinking."

She studies me for a moment, then takes another sip of her drink.

"They seem to feel that they hold some sort of proprietary interest in you."

"*They?*"

"Willow wasn't as friendly as you led me to believe she'd be." She shrugs. "Sorry. Not trying to complain. Or tattle. She said girls at the clubhouse would act even worse than that Agitation chick."

"Agi-who?"

"Oh!" She grins. "*Serenity* didn't seem to suit her personality, so I've renamed her in my head."

I burst out laughing. That was definitely not the response I expected.

And it's one of many reasons I like Emily so much. She's full of surprises.

"I told Willow I already knew some of the brothers' wives and *they* didn't behave that way," Emily says. "That seemed to shut down Willow's attitude."

Fuck. Willow's always gotten along with everyone. Why would she give Emily a hard time?

"She's not someone you've..." Emily lets me finish the question for myself.

"No. Never. Willow's a friend of the club and works for CB. That's it." I chew on another piece of chicken, trying to think of something else to ease Emily's concerns. "Actually, I think she's seeing one of the brothers but no one really knows for sure."

"It's not a big deal." She seems to shake off the memory of the conversation. "So how was the rest of your night? You didn't have to teach anyone the meaning of 'no touching' again, I hope."

"No. All good vibes tonight." I set my fork down. "Bricks—one of my brothers—popped in with Ravage to cover me. I haven't seen him in a bit, so I got to catch up with him."

She tilts her head, studying me. "You were in a club with naked women and instead of watching, you stopped to have a conversation with a friend you presumably see at 'church' every week?" Disbelief coats the question.

"Brother, not friend," I correct. "And yeah. He had some stuff on his mind."

"Is he okay?" she asks.

My chest squeezes. She's met Bricks maybe once for five minutes, but concern still resonates in her question. "He's fine. His girlfriend wants to have another kid and he doesn't. I guess she thinks his older kids can help out and he's not cool with that." I reach over and rest my hand on her leg. "Made me think of what you told me about *your* parents."

She glances at the kitchen door as if she's afraid Libby's on the other side, listening in.

"I'd never say that in front of your sister, Emily." How dense does she think I am?

"That's not what I was worried about." She glances down at her lap and rubs her hand over mine. "I was thinking how last week you came over banged up from kicking a customer's ass and tonight you're all kindness and sensitivity."

I tickle my fingers over her thigh. "I'm a mixed bag." Fuck, I don't want her to have the wrong idea about me. "I don't go deliberately looking for trouble." *Not always.*

"But if it finds you, you don't run away."

She gets me. "That's a good way to put it," I agree.

After confirming I'm done, she stands and clears the table, rinsing off the plate, but leaving it in the sink.

I come up behind her and wrap my arms around her waist, resting my chin on her shoulder. "What's wrong? You seem troubled."

"I'm sorry if it seemed like I was trying to sneak attack you at work."

"Huh?" I slip my hands to her hips and turn her to face me. "I told you to come see me anytime." I stroke my knuckles over her cheek. "I get that it makes you uncomfortable. And I want you to understand I have nothing to hide. You have an open invitation to *sneak attack* me whenever you want."

"I really like you," she whispers.

Fear thumps through my chest. She doesn't sound happy about it. "I like you too." I cup her chin, tipping her head. "It was brave of you to stop in. By yourself."

"Definitely the last place I thought I'd ever find myself." A tight smile curves her lips. "Agitation said I looked like I was from the corporate office."

One corner of my mouth quirks. I tease my fingers under the hem of her shirt until my knuckles brush against her stomach. "I liked that blouse on you. Couldn't stop thinking about taking you home and undoing those buttons, one by one."

She lets out a nervous laugh. "In a club—"

I press my finger against her lips. "Do *not* say any variation of 'with all the naked dancers, you thought the blouse was hot.' Don't question me when I tell you something. Understand?"

Her eyes widen. "Is this?" she mumbles, and I remove my finger from her lips, allowing her to finish. She slicks her tongue over her lips. "Phew, for a minute, I thought that was a blink once for yes, two for no situation."

"It will be if you keep arguing with me every time I tell you something."

She pulls her shoulders back and lifts her chin. "I wasn't arguing. More like, *clarifying.*"

I grip her waist and lift her onto the counter, pressing my body between her knees.

"You want clarity?" How do I express this without sounding like I want to tattoo *property of Dex* on her forehead? "How's this? If I actually prayed to any higher power, I couldn't ask for anyone more perfect than you."

I absently tug on the ends of her hair.

She tilts her head and presses her lips against the palm of my hand. "I'm not a natural redhead."

"Huh?" I stop and stare. "I'm not talking about your *hair*, Emily." I rough my hand over the top of her head. She squeals and bats my hand away.

"I'm just saying, this," she flips her hair over her shoulder, "is salon bought. Celia is a genius with color."

"Dye it purple. I don't give a fuck," I growl. How'd we end up here? I was trying to tell her something serious. Ah, fuck. Maybe *that's* the problem. "Am I getting too intense, too soon, for you?" I ask.

Her smile fades. "No. I think you're pretty perfect too. I just don't want you to think I'm...I don't want to end up disappointing you."

Whoever made her feel this way needs to be smacked with a fucking hammer. "You could never disappoint me."

"Don't be so sure."

Why is that peeved lilt to her voice such a fucking turn-on? Even when she's frustrating, I want to fuck her senseless.

"So, buttons, huh?" She hooks a finger in the neckline of her sweatshirt and tugs. "I'll have to remember that."

Frustrated, aroused, and amused in the space of ten minutes. This woman's a fucking rollercoaster.

And after so many years of not feeling much of anything, I really enjoy the ride.

CHAPTER FORTY

Emily

"YOU KNOW WHAT, SMART-ASS?" Dex presses his hand between my le[...] cupping me through my pajama pants. "I already suspected you might no[...] be a natural redhead."

My puff of laughter turns into a squeak of surprise as he grinds the heel of his hand right over my clit. I inhale a quick, shaky breath. "Oh, yeah?" I aim for a breezy tone, but it's negated by the moan that follows.

With his free hand, he tugs the drawstring of my pants loose. Staring into my eyes, almost as if challenging me or asking for permission, he slips his hand under the waistband and glides right over my center.

He squeezes his eyes shut and groans. "No underwear. Soaking wet. Fuck."

His fingers slide though my wetness, teasing and testing. Taking his sweet time gently working me up.

"Dex," I whisper urgently, curling my fingers in his shirt. "Not...not here." I glance at the kitchen door, and then the back windows that we've never bothered to cover with curtains or anything.

He presses his forehead to mine. "Where?"

Damn, he knows I'm hesitant to go upstairs because of my sister. And respects it. How can he have that feral look in his eyes but still be so understanding? I'm ready to melt into a puddle at his feet.

I slide off the counter, standing on shaky legs and take his hand, pulling him around the edge of the long counter, to the right and into the small laundry room off the kitchen.

I'm behind on laundry and hurry to throw a basket of clean, unfolded towels on the floor.

Dex growls his approval and boosts me onto the washer. "Very nice." He slips his fingers in my pants and tugs. "Lift up."

I can't do it fast enough. One of my socks slips against the washer. A rush of cold air glides over my lower half as he yanks my pants off, tossing them aside. I yelp as the cold metal touches my bare butt.

"Shhh." He holds a finger against my lips.

"It's chilly," I whisper.

"I'll warm you up." He taps the edge of the washer. "Put your feet here. Let me see that pretty pussy."

I squint at the overhead light. Why'd I have to get such a bright bulb?

"Emily." Dex's low, firm tone can't be ignored.

My eyes snap to his. Slowly I place my feet where he wants them, leaving myself exposed.

"Perfect," he says, curving his hand over my sex. He drags his middle finger between my lips, drawing my wetness to my clit and rubbing softer than I'd think a man his size was capable of.

My breathing turns to short, ragged gasps.

"Good."

I can't tell if he's asking a question or making a statement, but I nod furiously.

He leans down and kisses my cheek. "Take your sweatshirt off," he whispers against my ear.

I can't find my way out of the sleeves and pop my head out of the neck hole fast enough. Dex uses his free hand to pull it off the rest of the way. My hair crackles with static electricity and I don't even care that it's probably sticking straight up.

"No bra either?" He nods with approval. "I should stop by at night more often."

I want to say *yes* but I can't seem to form any words.

He slides his hand into my hair, gathering it into his fist. The movement knocks me backward and I lean against my elbows, spreading my legs even wider.

"That's it. Goddamn you're beautiful like this."

I stare up at him with desperate eyes. He tugs on my hair, reminding me he has me tethered in place, and slowly works two fingers inside me.

The pleasurable prickles over my scalp, combined with his fingers working in and out of me at a steady pace and the intensity in his eyes, pushes me right to the edge.

"Dex," I whisper.

He nods. "Show me how much you like my fingers in your tight little cunt. Go off for me."

I squeeze my eyes shut, willing the waves of pleasure to wash over me. He doesn't move faster or even harder, but somehow pushes *deeper*, curling his fingers and stroking a spot that makes my toes tingle.

I open my mouth, a silent scream climbing up my throat.

"Good girls come nice and quiet," he whispers, then seals his mouth over mine, swallowing my cries. Desperate to hold onto something, I curl my fingers over his shoulders as the orgasm explodes inside me. Dex lets out hums and noises of encouragement while he shatters me into a million happy little pieces. He slips his fingers out, rubbing and petting me as if trying to give me every last bit of pleasure possible.

He releases my hair and pulls back. "Noisy little firecracker, aren't you," he teases.

I reach for the bulge in his jeans. "I can think of a way to keep me quiet."

An enthusiastic sound rumbles out of him, that I take as a *yes*. Boneless, I slide off the washer, landing on the floor like an overcooked noodle. I reach for the pile of clean towels, grabbing one and kneeling on it. Every cell of my body's still singing with happiness. I kneel up and grab his belt, half pushing, half turning him toward the washer. His butt hits it with a soft, metallic thud and he lets out a low chuckle.

"Easy," he whispers.

Naked on my knees in the laundry room isn't someplace I thought I'd find myself. But this man seems to have a knack for nudging me out of my comfort zone.

He slips something out of his pocket and sets it on the dryer. I'm too busy eagerly working his belt loose to see what it is. I want to drive him to the same heights of pleasure that I just experienced at his hands.

The energy around us shifts. He brushes my fumbling hands aside and undoes his pants. I lower the front waistband of his boxer briefs and he inhales a sharp breath. He strokes his thick cock in one of his big hands, his eyes on me the whole time.

"You want this?" he asks.

"Yes."

"Show me."

I kneel up straighter, bracing my hands against his muscular thighs. Good God, he's so strong everywhere, and yet so gentle when he handles me, except the few moments I need him not to be.

Feeling encouraged by his watchful gaze, I wrap my hands around the base of his erection and close my mouth over the head.

"Oh, fuck," he breathes. He drops one hand to my head, massaging my scalp. "I replay that afternoon in the truck in my head all the time. And your mouth is even sweeter than I remember."

I tease my tongue along the sensitive underside. "Then I'm a bad girlfriend for not doing this again sooner."

He groans with satisfaction as I slowly take him in my mouth again, while twisting my grip.

"God, yes," he grits out. His thighs tremble.

I smile, pleased at the effect I have on him.

"You like that?" he asks.

I hum an affirmative noise. Feeling extremely greedy, I want to swallow him whole. I suck as much as I can into my mouth, savoring his raw, salty essence. So caught up in tasting him, I forget to move my hand. A spurt of salty liquid pools on my tongue and I moan louder, sucking him harder, as deep as I can.

"Is that as much as you can take?" he asks.

My body freezes, afraid he'll try to push past my limit.

"Emily?"

I nod.

He rests his hand at the back of my head and pulls away, then slowly returns, not going past the point of discomfort. He does this several more times, never giving more than I can handle.

My heart races, my thighs still shaking from earlier.

Dex lets out a deep, guttural groan and tugs on my hair, pulling me off him. "Come here." He lifts me off the floor, setting me on the washer again.

"What're you doing?" I ask, reaching for him.

He tears into a condom and rolls it on without answering. I'm *so* on board with his change of plans. Desperate to have him inside me, I draw my feet up and scoot to the edge.

"Good girl," he praises in a gravelly rasp. He steps between my legs and lines himself up with my entrance.

"Oh God," I chant a few times as he pushes inside me. I sob from the intense pleasure. The angle must not be right for him. He pulls me precariously close to the edge and onto his cock, powerful arms keeping me secure.

"Help me out," he grunts, then digs his fingers into my ass.

I hook my hands over his shoulders for leverage and wrap my legs around his waist, working myself up and down his full length. Much like he's my own personal naughty ride at an X-rated playground.

The position still feels precarious but exhilarating. Any fear that he might drop me disappears. The zing of friction hits me different, forcing me to focus on chasing more of the sensation. Eyes glazed with pleasure, Dex leans in and presses a sloppy kiss to my mouth.

"Keep going. Just like that," he murmurs, our shallow breaths mingling in the tight space.

I flex my thighs and move my hips faster. Rolling, pulling, pushing, and moving in any way possible. Dex digs his hands into my flesh and bounces me harder on his cock, as if holding me in the air hadn't taxed his strength one bit. He'd been allowing me to play and now he means business.

"You're so good. So, so good." He punctuates each word with a hip thrust. "Look at you."

His gruff words pitch me into the abyss. My body contracts, desperate whimpers clawing their way out of my mouth. Dex swallows my sounds with a greedy kiss.

Beads of sweat roll down my forehead. Slowly, I stop moving my body but still cling to him, breathing hard.

He doesn't give me a break, though. Rough hands guide my legs down. My toes barely touch the tile when he spins me to face the washer. One hand presses between my shoulder blades, bending me over the machine. The cool metal is a welcome relief to my sweaty skin.

He jerks my hips up and fills me in one thrust. I yelp and scratch the washer, searching for something to hang onto as he pounds into me from behind.

The washer rattles and bangs, making more noise than anything else we've done. His hands tighten around my waist.

"Fuck," he groans. His body quakes, cock jerking inside me. He stumbles forward, pushing even deeper. After a second or two of heavy breathing, he wraps his arms around my waist. He presses his forehead against my back. His lips glide over my skin with slow, reverent kisses, leaving goosebumps.

He kisses my shoulder one more time, then groans as he pulls his weight off me.

"You okay?" he asks.

"I'm glowing and satisfied." I flash a dopey grin.

He chuckles. "Same."

While Dex puts himself together, I glance behind me, searching for my sweatshirt. The washer's knocked sideways. Dex follows my line of sight.

"If we broke it, I'll fix it," he promises.

As if I'm worried about my washer at the moment.

I curl my fingers in the hem of his T-shirt. "I've never violated a household appliance like that before."

He presses his hands to my cheeks and tips my head back. The relaxed, content expression on his face somehow makes the afterglow burn even hotter. *I* did that for him.

"Thank you." He kisses my forehead, then pulls away. "I didn't come over expecting you to feed and fuck me, just so you know."

My heart stutters. He's really worried I'll think that? "I didn't think so." I wrap my arms around him. "But I'm very happy to do both any time you want."

He returns the embrace. "I don't know if I can walk right, woman."

Shaking with laughter I pull away and run my hands over his arms, up to his shoulders. "You're so strong. I can't believe you held me up that long. I hope you can move tomorrow."

"I'll be fine."

Above our heads, there's a soft pitter-patter. Libby going to the bathroom? I stare at the skewed washer, then the ceiling. "Shit."

"We're standing under Libby's bedroom, aren't we?" he asks.

I bite my lip and nod. "She sleeps with one of those white noise machines. Maybe she didn't hear us."

"Sorry, I didn't realize." His mouth twists into a grin. "Or expect to be so *loud*."

It's not his fault. It's mine. I know better. This is why I'd sworn off dating. I have responsibilities and can't afford the luxury of spontaneous laundry room fucks.

Libby said it didn't bother her if Dex slept over. But sleeping over and being subjected to listening to us fuck like bunnies are two different things.

"Em?" Dex touches my shoulder.

I stare up at him. He hands me my pants and sweatshirt, concern and questions flickering in his eyes.

I'm so screwed. I wasn't supposed to fall for this man so hard that I forget all of my responsibilities.

How selfish am I for wanting to keep him anyway?

CHAPTER FORTY-ONE

Dex

I'M DRIFTING HALF-ASLEEP and half-awake. Too worn out to drag my out of Emily's bed and go to my apartment like I promised.

"No," Emily moans, jolting me fully awake.

Her body thrashes, one elbow catching me in the ribs. Not wanting to startle her, I gently rest my hand over her shoulder, turning her my way.

"Em, baby, it's okay," I whisper.

"Libby, Libby, Libby, where are you?" she whimpers. "Noooo, Libby. Please. Where are you?"

What the fuck's going on? I know how much Emily cares about her sister and worries about her but the raw anguish in her voice seems more sinister than sisterly.

"Emily," I say a shade louder. "Libby's right down the hall. She's safe."

"Noooo," she whimpers, arms reaching into the darkness. "Come out. Come out. Where are you?"

"Emily." I curl my arm firmly around her waist and drag her against my body. Her agony feels like a living, breathing thing between us. "Shhh, you're okay. I've got you. Everything's okay," I reassure her over and over.

She lets out a scream and thrashes. Tears stream down her cheeks.

What the fuck do I do? Let her go? Shake her awake?

The bedroom door creaks open.

"Em?" Libby whispers.

Well, this just took an awkward detour.

Bright light floods the room, searing my eyeballs.

"Oh, shit!" Libby shrieks. "Dex, I didn't know you were here."

Darkness descends, and I blink my eyes open. Colorful dots still dance in my vision.

"What's happening?" Emily slurs. "Why's the light on?"

"I heard you calling for me," Libby says from the doorway. "Another nightmare?"

Another? This happens often?

"Yeah," Emily mutters. "Sorry."

"All right. As long as you're okay..." Libby stands there for a moment. I'm frozen with my own indecision. "Sorry, Dex," Libby whispers. "You've got her?"

"Yeah," I rasp. "I'll make sure she's okay."

Libby nods once and closes the door with a quiet snick. Her little feet scurry over the hallway's hardwood floor all the way back to her room.

Emily groans and sits up, rubbing her forehead.

"Damn it," she mutters.

"Hey." I rub my hand over her back and up to her shoulder. "You all right?"

"I'm fine," she whispers. "Give me a sec?" She tosses the covers aside and slips out of bed. She pauses at the nightstand and opens a drawer, grabbing a pair of shorts and shimmying them up, under her T-shirt. "I'll be right back," she says over her shoulder.

Concern eats at me. The pain in her voice still lingers in the air. But what am I supposed to do? Follow her to the bathroom? Force answers out of her that she's not ready to give?

I sit up, stack some pillows behind me, and grab my phone, checking for messages.

A picture from Z of his son riding a tiny quad with his dogs, Ziggy and Zipper, following closely behind.

Z: Start 'em young.

My thumb hovers over my phone, as I contemplate a response. Nah, better not text him in the middle of the night.

Ravage: CB is dead. Closing early.

I'm not as concerned about waking Rav, so I respond with "good call."

The bedroom door swings open and I set my phone down.

In the weak lamplight, I study Emily's pinched expression. "Are you all right?" I ask.

"Embarrassed more than anything." She stands at the edge of the bed and picks up the blanket like she's about to slip between the sheets, but she ends up twisting the fabric in her hand instead.

"You don't have anything to be embarrassed about." I pat the mattress. "Come here."

"I mean with Libby." She waves her hand in the air. "Finding you here...*Again*."

I'm not quite sure what to say. I'm sure as fuck not leaving when she still seems so rattled.

"Well, she was surprised to see me, so I guess that means she didn't hear us before," I say, hoping to ease at least one of her concerns.

A smile flickers over her lips, so quick I almost miss it and she nods.

Finally, she crawls into bed. When she's close enough, I wrap an arm around her waist and haul her over my lap. "That's better." I brush her hair off her cheek. "Talk to me."

To my relief, she relaxes, resting her cheek against my chest. She curls her body against mine. I hug her tighter and rest my chin on the top of her head.

"This is nice," she murmurs. Her warm breath ghosts over my skin. "Thank you. I...I'm sorry."

"There's nothing to be sorry for."

She rubs her hands over my arm, as if she's trying to reassure herself I'm still here.

"Tell me what your nightmare was about." Maybe purging it from her memory will give it less power.

Her body stiffens, like a cat about to leap from danger.

I keep the circle of my arms around her tight.

"I can't talk about it right now," she whispers. "Just hold me."

Those three little words wrap themselves around my heart and squeeze. "You got it." I kiss the top of her head.

I won't push. Not tonight.

But eventually, I'll unlock all of her secrets and help her fight the monsters lurking in her past.

I WAKE a few hours later and ease myself out of bed. Emily's sound asleep and I take a second to appreciate her sprawled out, face turned to one side and cheek pressed to the sheet. After the night she had, I can't bring myself to do anything to pull her from sleep. She should always look so peaceful.

I tug on my jeans and quietly slip out the bedroom door.

Downstairs, in the kitchen, I find Libby sitting by the window, quietly spooning mouthfuls of cereal. Feeling like a burglar who's been caught, I stop mid-stride.

Libby flashes an easy smile. "Morning, Dex."

"Hey, kiddo." What time does she leave for school? Does Emily drive her? Why don't I know these things? "You need a ride to school?"

Her eyes widen with interest. "On your bike?"

"Uh, yeah." I swish my arms through the air like a giant bird. "I can't fly you there."

She chuckles, then tilts her head. "I don't know if Emily will let me ride on a motorcycle."

Good point. I probably should've cleared that with Emily first. By sixteen, I already had my first motorcycle—had laid it down too. But Emily seems to keep Libby a bit sheltered and it's not my place to interfere.

"You need anything for breakfast?" I don't know why I feel so compelled to do *something*. Obviously, Libby's capable of feeding herself.

She holds out her bowl and gives her spoon a slow, sarcastic tap against the side.

Smart-ass.

"That's all you're gonna eat?" I ask. "Don't you need brain food or something?"

"Sheesh, you sound like Emily." She sets her bowl in the sink. "My friend's picking me up," she says, answering my earlier question.

"The speed racer?"

She rolls her eyes. "Yes."

"Does Emily know?"

"Yes, Officer Dex."

"Funny." If only she knew how off the mark *that* is. "What time does your sister usually get up?"

She shrugs. "Usually she's up with me, but I'm headed to school early to work on the sets before classes start."

"Any idea what she likes to have for breakfast?"

"Why?" she singsongs. "You planning to make her breakfast in *beeeed?*"

Oh boy. This one's a handful. I bite my lip to stop from laughing. No need to encourage her. "Maybe."

"If she has time, she makes eggs." Libby wrinkles her nose. "If not, she'll toast a bagel or something and eat it on her long drive to work." Libby slips past me. "She drinks tea, not coffee."

"Tea. Got it." I glance at her empty hands. "You're not bringing anything to school?"

"My backpack's out there." She tilts her head toward the living room.

"What about lunch?" Why am I acting like her fucking dad or something?

"You sure are nosy." She lets out a dramatic sigh. "I'll buy from the cafeteria."

A car horn blasts from outside.

"That's my ride!" Libby backs into the kitchen door, bumping it open with her elbows. "Bye, Dex!"

"Have a good day," I call after her.

The front door slams shut a few seconds later. Laughing and shaking my head, I pick up a teakettle from the stove and fill it with water. After I light one of the burners and set the kettle over the flame, I realize I'm still smiling.

337

CHAPTER FORTY-TWO

Emily

THE WHISTLE of my teakettle pulls me down the stairs. Libby sent me a text that she went to school early, so it has to be Dex in my kitchen?

Delicious smells tempt my nose when I near the kitchen door. I push it open.

And stare.

No man should look that good in yesterday's clothes. Barefoot in my kitchen. Cooking eggs?

"What's happening here?" I rasp, my voice still scratchy from sleep.

He glances at me over his shoulder and smiles. "Breakfast. You're familiar with the concept, right?"

I swallow hard and blink rapidly to clear my vision.

When's the last time someone made me breakfast? Libby tosses a bagel in the toaster for me once in a while, but that's about it.

"Libby said you make eggs if you have time." Dex frowns. "She didn't specify *how* you like them, though."

"You talked to Libby?"

"Saw her before she left for school." He easily tips my cast iron frying pan to the side as if it doesn't weight twenty pounds, and scrapes a pile of fluffy eggs onto a plate. "I hope scrambled works for you."

"It does." I drift closer to the counter and rest my hand on his back. "Thank you."

The toaster dings and two pieces of toasty peasant bread pop up.

Quick as a cat, Dex yanks one out, drops it on my plate, smears butter on it and sets the other slice on top. Exactly how I would do it.

"Sit," he says, gesturing to the table.

"Wait." I sneak my hand under his T-shirt, grazing his warm skin.

He flinches. "Your hands are cold, woman."

"Well, I woke up all alone."

He turns and takes both of my hands, rubbing them between his larger, warmer ones. His amused expression slides into something more serious. "You didn't sleep well. I wanted to have breakfast ready before you have to leave for work."

"Will you judge me too harshly if I say I already called in sick today?" I stretch my arms over my head and yawn.

His gaze drops to the sliver of stomach bared by my shirt lifting.

"I've never admired you more." He curls his arm around my waist and pulls me closer, dipping down to kiss my neck, my cheek, and finally feathers the softest kiss over my lips.

"I could get used to this." I press my hand flat against his chest.

He pops one more kiss on my cheek, then hands me my plate.

"Since I didn't get a lot of sleep," I say, "I really *do* feel a bit under the weather." I haven't taken a sick day in years. Why do I feel so damn guilty?

"Go. Sit." He gestures to the table with a spatula. "I'll be right there."

At the table, I find wedges of lemon laid out in a neat row, a glass of ice water, and a small bowl with sections of oranges and whole strawberries.

"Wow. You really dug deep in my fridge."

"Don't be mad." He throws me a teasing smile. "I tossed out anything growing fur."

Laughing, I cut my toast into eight neat little sections. "Did Libby seem okay?"

"Yeah." He sets his plate on the table and sits next to me. "I think I annoyed her with all my questions, though." Amusement colors his words. He seems to be more charmed than offended.

"Like what?" I bite into a piece of toast.

He glances over at my plate. The corners of his mouth curl up as he stares at my toast pieces. I push some his way. "I usually only eat one slice," I mumble.

"Noted." He slathers extra butter on one of the pieces and takes a big, sexy bite.

340

"I asked her if she needed a ride," he finally answers. "She wasn't sure you'd let her on my bike."

"You'd do that?"

"What? Drop her off at school?" His eyebrows pinch together. "Yeah, if you need me to."

"Thanks."

He stares at the kitchen door. "I should make sure she has her own helmet, though."

"Shoot. That reminds me, I still have your friend's helmet." I press my hands to the table and push my chair back.

"Relax." Dex circles his fingers around my wrist. "You've had it this long, a few more days won't make a difference. I'll get it back to him."

He has a point. I pull my chair in and take another bite of my eggs.

"I should take you to buy the right gear one of these days," he says. "Gettin' warmer."

"You seem to ride all the time."

He nods once. "It forces me to focus on the road ahead, instead of letting my mind wander...places."

By the distant, almost haunted look in his eyes, he's not talking about anywhere pleasant.

CHAPTER FORTY-THREE

Dex

AFTER BREAKFAST, I clean up the mess I made of Emily's kitchen. "So what do you want to do on your day off? You feel like taking a ride to Fletcher Park or something?" I ask.

Her nervous gaze darts to the door. "I called in sick. What if someone sees me?"

She really is a good girl down to her soul. "Anyone who might see you should be at work themselves, right?"

"Oh." Her face brightens. "That's true."

"You have a leather jacket?" I ask.

"I do. It's more dressy than functional."

"That's okay. Wear some thicker jeans and boots with a short heel if you've got them."

"I think I have something that will work."

If I follow her upstairs, there's no way she'll be getting dressed any time soon. While she's figuring out what to wear, I find my way into the laundry room. My wallet's still on the dryer and my dick's getting hard remembering last night.

The washer's still sideways. I squeeze behind it and check that we didn't knock any hoses loose.

"Dex?" Emily calls.

That was quick.

"Back here."

I stand and pull myself out of the tight space, then straighten the machine, lining it up with the dryer.

"Doing some laundry?" she asks from behind me.

"No, smart-ass. Just checking we didn't break it last night."

I turn and find her watching me with surprise and curiosity. She tied her hair into two short braids. A hint of a blush creeps over her cheeks. Is she remembering how the machine got moved in the first place? Good.

"Is this okay?" She holds out her arms for me to inspect her outfit.

Thick purple plaid flannel shirt with another shirt underneath, dark denim jeans, and a pair of black leather lug-soled boots with a short but chunky heel.

"It's great."

She follows me into the living room. While I'm putting on my boots, she slips into the closet and returns with a black leather jacket full of flashy gold-toned hardware. It'll work, though.

"A bit dated and tacky, huh?" she says.

"Nah, it's fine."

"It was my aunt's." She slips her arms into the jacket. It's a bit big but will serve its purpose. "I think she went through a biker chick phase in the early nineties."

"Looks good on you. Grab the helmet." I curl my hand around hers. "Let's go."

Outside, she stops and stares at my bike for a second.

"Would you rather take your car?" I ask.

"No."

She quickly mounts the bike behind me and wraps her arms around my waist. "Where are we going?" she asks.

The few places I'm familiar with in Johnsonville either aren't open at this hour or won't be of interest to Emily. "Is Fletcher Park okay? Views should be nice today."

"I haven't been there in years." She hugs me tighter. "Sounds perfect."

Emily

Dex is right. Riding forces my mind to remain focused on the present. I bet if I was the one steering this monster machine it would be even more acute.

Speeding along the Thruway is exhilarating and terrifying in equal measures. The pavement rushes beneath our feet and I force myself not to think about what it would feel like to make contact with it at this speed. Dex handles the bike with expertise, reassuring me with each movement.

Dozens of scents fill my nose. Oil, gas fumes, the pungent stench of cow patties. It's all so much more intense.

He takes an exit I'm not familiar with and winds the bike through back roads, gradually taking us up the mountains and into one of the back entrances to Fletcher Park. Some sections of the park are still closed this time of year. But the gates to the Overlook parking lot are wide open. Dex passes through and steers the bike to the upper-level lot, stopping at the far end, away from all the other vehicles.

My legs quiver as I gingerly extract myself from the seat. I unstrap the helmet and Dex takes it from me, hanging it off the handlebars.

"You all right?" he asks.

I must look as unsteady as a baby giraffe. Willing my legs to stop shaking, I stand straighter. "That was a long ride."

"Aw, that was nothing." He curls his hand around my thigh and drags me closer. "A mere warm-up ride."

My gaze nervously bounces around the parking lot.

"Emily. No one's paying attention to us," Dex says in a low voice. "Eyes over here."

How does he always manage to sound firm enough to make me do what he asks but still so gentle that I never have the urge to tell him to fuck off for being so bossy?

He lightly squeezes where he's holding my leg. "Were you okay? You didn't try to crack my ribs this time."

"You make it seem safer than it probably is."

"Riding has its risks." He releases me and gracefully swings his leg over the bike. He leans in and kisses my cheek. "But lots of rewards too."

Yeah, like the big, tall, sexy reward standing right in front of me.

"Where do you want to go?" he asks.

I smooth my hands over my hair, checking for strands that escaped their braided prison. "Can we walk along the wall and check out the view?"

"Absolutely." He takes my hand, and we start down the gentle slope of the sidewalk that runs alongside the low stone wall designed to keep people from falling off the cliff.

I stare out into the distance, making out the shapes of several buildings. "You can see Empire from here."

"I always liked this view." He lifts his chin toward another area of the park straight ahead. "Friends of mine got married over at the gazebo area. And my niece and Vapor got married up here too."

Why does my heart kick up a little tap dance the second Dex mentions weddings? Is it the affectionate, respectful way he talks about his friends and family? Or is it the sudden vision I have of meeting him in front of a judge while I'm decked out in a white dress?

And maybe hoping he's having a similar thought?

Am I out of my mind? I haven't contemplated getting married since I was eight years old and spent an afternoon in my mom's closet trying on her wedding dress and veil.

Dex gives mind-blowing orgasms and cooks me breakfast one day and suddenly I'm picturing committing the rest of my life to him?

"It's a beautiful place to have a wedding." Oh great, now he's going to think I'm throwing out a hint. "I have a friend who got married over by the waterfalls on the other side of the park," I hurry to add.

"I think I know the spot you're talking about."

"Do you, um, ever want to get married...again?" I blurt before my brain can put a stop to my bumbling question. *Why, why, why did I ask him that?* He's never even told me how his wife died.

His hand tightens around mine. I don't dare turn my head to check out his expression.

Casual. Easy breezy. Just act casual.

"I don't have anything against marriage," he finally answers.

He doesn't ask me a similar question.

CHAPTER FORTY-FOUR

Dex

Do I want to get married again?

I haven't given it a lot of thought since my wife died. I had my chance. I blew it. End of story.

I don't deserve another shot. The only person I'm responsible for now is myself. Well, that's not true. The club's my family. I'll protect my brothers with my life. But that's not the same responsibility as being a husband or a father.

Maybe I need to end this now. Before my stupid ass gets any ideas that I *deserve* to have a future with this woman.

And yet, I can't even let go of her hand.

If I allowed myself to go there again—promise to love, honor, and protect Emily for the rest of my days—and then somehow lost her...I couldn't live with myself.

Besides, Emily comes with her own obligations. I can't be responsible for protecting her *and* Libby.

Who are you kidding? You were ready to drop Libby off at school and hand her lunch money a few hours ago.

My mind's screaming at me to come up with another topic—anything will do—quickly.

"The view is so pretty, you almost forget how dangerous it is to get too close to the cliff," Emily says.

If that isn't the best metaphor for my life right now.

"Those warning signs have been up here for as long as I can remember," I say. "But I think at least one or two people go over the side every year."

We continue to where the sidewalk ends. A dirt path follows the edge of the woods, leading to another section of the park. "Do you want to keep going?" I ask.

"No, this is good." She turns and pulls out her phone, taking a few photos.

"Can I take one of you?" I ask, holding up my own phone.

"Can we take one together?" she counters.

"Sure." To fit both of us in the picture, I hold the phone out a good distance.

"Those big strong arms make a handy tripod," she mutters.

I crack up right as I hit the button.

"My eyes are closed," I say. "Let me take another one."

"I like that one, though. Keep it," she says.

I'm not sure what she likes about it. I look like an idiot. She's adorable, though. Half smiling up at me, like it brings her joy that she can make me laugh.

I take another. Then lean in and kiss her cheek. "Good?"

"Aw, you caught that one too." She points to my screen. "Will you send those to me?"

"You want the one with the doofy guy who has his eyes closed?" I tease.

"Hey." She curls her fingers in my shirt and tugs. "My guy is fine as hell."

The thrill of satisfaction burns through my veins. I love that she thinks so. She's the only woman whose opinion has mattered to me in a long damn time.

I lean down and kiss her. "The feeling's mutual."

She stares up at me in this sweet, honest way that burrows into my chest. "I'm really glad you called in sick."

A faint smile ghosts over her lips. "Me too." She tugs on my hand. "Can we sit and admire the view for a minute?"

We don't go far. She climbs up onto the highest part of the stone wall overlooking the entire valley below and sits down. I sit right next to her, sliding my arm around her waist to keep her secure.

She inhales deeply and closes her eyes. "This is nice up here. I know

Johnsonville's a small city, but it always feels old and…dirty or something, you know?"

"I know it's old and there isn't much out there. Never thought it was dirty necessarily."

"Not the good dirty." She nudges me with her elbow. "Like, *polluted* dirty. From all the old factories that used to be out there. Water quality testing is what I do for a living, remember?"

"Ahh, right." She never talks about her job all that much. "Why stay, then?"

She shrugs and stares straight ahead. "I can't make Libby change schools when she's so close to graduating. But once she's done, I want to sell the house and just…I don't know. Roam free?"

I'm extremely familiar with the desire to roam. "You should."

She hums a disbelieving noise. Like it's only a pipe dream.

"How'd you sleep last night? You know, after?"

She doesn't move or say a word. She might have even stopped breathing.

"After I scared the shit out of you?" she asks.

"You didn't scare me. I was worried about you." I hesitate. Maybe this isn't the best time or place to have this conversation. "I got the impression from Libby that you have nightmares a lot?"

She snorts out a soft noise of disagreement. "I used to. Not so much lately."

"Can I ask what happened to your parents?" I search her face, seeking any sign she's uncomfortable talking about it. Who am I kidding, there will never be a comfortable time to have this conversation.

Sadness tugs the corners of her mouth down and she sighs. "It's a really unpleasant story."

"You don't have to tell me if you don't want to." I tip my head back, staring up at the deep blue sky. "But maybe talking about it in the bright light of day now, will keep the darkness away later."

She slants a look at me. "Are you a biker or a poet?"

Prickly. She's so, so prickly when I probe too close to her pain. It's easy to recognize it because I'm the same fucking way.

I have no business prodding her for answers when I don't want to share the darkest parts of my own past.

But the terror in her voice last night still follows me today. Maybe talking about it with someone unconnected to her past will help. I doubt she discusses it with Libby. She wouldn't burden her sister with whatever demons chase her in her dreams.

She swallows hard as if she's gathering her courage.

Such a brave woman.

"They were killed in a home invasion," she answers in a voice devoid of emotion. "Two guys broke in. My dad shot one of them." Her body turns to stone. Her eyes stare straight ahead, focused on a violent past, not the beauty of the valley below.

She takes a deep breath and continues, "I was out with friends. Deep into my 'party girl' phase."

"Where was Libby?"

"Home in bed. Thank God they didn't find her."

She squeezes her eyes shut and gasps for air.

"Breathe, Emily." I hug her to my side. "You're okay. I'm right here." *Why'd I have to do this to her now? Here of all places.*

"I got home and the front door was open." She pulls away from me, her voice dropping into an emotionless monotone that chills my blood. "My dad was a cop. He never left anything unlocked."

She clutches her stomach as if the memory brings a wave of physical pain. "I knew something was wrong right away. I walked in and...and..."

Jesus Christ, she found her parents' bodies? "It's okay, Emily. You don't have to continue if you don't want to."

But it's as if now that she's opened this door to her past, she has no choice but to walk through it.

"Libby. Oh my God," she whispers. "I was terrified they...they...hurt her too. Or took her. I couldn't find her at first. Everything was so silent. I'd never felt a silence like that before. I searched the house, so afraid I'd run into the killers or find her, her b-body." She squeezes her eyes shut again and a tear rolls down her cheek.

No matter how much her pain's tearing me apart, there's nothing I can do to erase those memories for her. It's my question that pushed her into this dark place, so it's my responsibility to help her through the pain.

"She's safe now, Emily," I remind her.

She nods but still seems caught up in the memory. "She wasn't in my parents' room, or her room. I crawled under her bed, her closet, the tub in the bathroom. No Libby," she sobs, and I tighten my hold on her.

"It was cold that night. A breeze came from my room. I grabbed a gun from my dad's closet and crept into my bedroom. The window and screen were wide open. I was so scared she fell out of the window or something. But when I looked outside, I didn't see anything."

Libby's safe at school. But I still find myself holding my breath as Emily weaves her story.

"I kept calling for her and...nothing. No response." She takes a deep breath. "Finally, I opened my closet. My laundry basket was overflowing. This pile of blankets." Her brow furrows. "I hadn't left it like that. I found her hiding under all that stuff. Skinny little arms hugging her knees."

I let out a long, slow, relieved breath.

"She was...blank," Emily continues. "Nothing. No expression. Didn't answer me. Or say a word. I...I...had to make sure she was even breathing and then I...I..."

"Did they hurt her?"

"No. But..." Emily grazes her fingertips over her cheeks. "She had blood splattered on her face, in her hair, on her nightgown."

"How'd that happen?"

"She couldn't tell me. Not that night. But later. Later," she repeats softly. "She told me. She heard a noise and snuck downstairs."

A pained smile stretches across her lips. "She did that a lot when she was little. She hated being told to go to bed, so she'd sneak downstairs and listen in on whatever my parents were doing or try to watch whatever they were watching. Sometimes I'd find her asleep in the hallway and I'd carry her up to bed before my parents found her." A quick smile flashes over Emily's lips then vanishes. "That night, I was out with my friends, so I wasn't there to find her and tuck her into bed."

"Wait a second. Are you saying she saw your parents get..."

"Murdered." She squeezes her eyes shut. "When they shot my mom, I think..." Her voice trails off, but she sweeps her hands toward her face, silently explaining how the blowback left Libby covered in blood.

How the fuck is Libby so...*normal* now?

"She ran and hid in my closet," Emily continues. Her lips twist with sadness and pride. "But first she opened the window, so if they came looking for her, they'd think she ran away."

Jesus. Christ. "Smart thing to do at such a young age."

"I know," she whispers.

"Did they find the guys?"

"One was dead in our living room. So *he* was easy to find." Dark humor laces through her words. "The other one wasn't too bright. They caught him a few days later."

"Where's he now?" I growl. *Please let it be a prison where my club has a connection.*

"In prison." She casts a suspicious glance my way. "Don't even think about trying to get revenge on my behalf or anything. I *want* him to spend the rest of his life rotting right where he is."

Already, she knows me too well.

"Why did they do it? Was it a robbery gone wrong?" I've done a lot of bad shit but shooting a mother and father in front of their little girl—that's straight up fucking *evil.*

She laces her fingers together and squeezes, like she's praying for strength. Pink colors her cheeks and she drops her gaze to her lap. "I... don't even know..." A harsh sob tears out of her throat.

"It's okay." I curl my arm around her shoulders, drawing her closer, and kiss the top of her head. "It's okay," I murmur. "That's enough."

"No." She pushes away and pulls her leg up, turning to face me. "It's still hard to believe sometimes, that's all. He was dirty. My dad. A dirty cop. I guess he was working with these guys and they thought he stole money from them. So they broke in to get it back. They must not have expected my dad to be locked and loaded in the middle of the night."

Something about her assumption doesn't sound right. I don't think Emily's lying, though. It hurt her to admit that her father wasn't a good guy. But the story still feels *wrong.* Only the dumbest fuck of a criminal would show up to a shady cop's *home* and fuck with his family. The smarter move would be luring him somewhere remote and torturing the information out of him. Or so I've heard.

"Who told you that your dad was a dirty cop?" I ask.

Emily chews on her bottom lip, clearly uncomfortable with the question. "His best friend. His partner. They went to the academy together. He told me at my parents' funeral." She lowers her voice. "He said he covered for my dad so Libby and I would still be entitled to survivor benefits."

I'm certainly not an expert on the law, but that sounds shady as shit. What kind of man says that to a grieving daughter? At her parents' funeral, no less. "Why the fuck would he sully your father's memory at their funeral?"

She blinks. "It was such an awful time. At first, I chalked it up to grief over losing his friend. Or that he just wanted to assure me that we'd be taken care of. But later when I thought about it, I wondered." She closes her eyes for a few seconds. "I never told my aunt. It would've killed her even sooner to learn her little brother was a criminal."

My gut says her dad *wasn't* a criminal at all. But I have no basis for that theory and what's the point, anyway? This happened years ago. So, I keep my opinion to myself.

The father's friend, though. Maybe it *was* grief talking. Or maybe *he* was the dirty cop, and he pinned his crimes on Emily's dad. No wonder she thinks her dad killed the guy who cut her.

"He wrote to me a while ago," she says. "That's the last time I had a nightmare."

"Who? Your dad's partner?"

"No. His killer."

A lightning bolt of rage splits my vision in half. I take a breath, willing calm into my body. But it's not easy. My fascination with Emily hovers like a violent cloud, ready to rain terror on anyone who threatens her or Libby's safety.

Fascination? No. What I feel for Emily is more than interest or affection.

Deeper, in a place I thought I'd buried under concrete, I recognize it's *love.*

And that's the only thing in this world that scares me.

CHAPTER FORTY-FIVE

Emily

AFTER BARING my soul at the park, I'm worn out. Dex and I hike through a few trails in silence. As if he knows I need distance from the place where I shared the worst parts of my past. But I can't go home yet. I haven't decided if it was a relief to share all of that with him or not.

"I think I'm getting a blister," I say as I finish limping down a steep trail behind him.

He stops and surveys the area. "I don't think we're far from the bike. You want me to carry you?"

"What? No." But after a few more steps, he crouches down in front of me.

"Arms around my neck," he orders.

"Dex, you can't possibly carry me that far."

"Sure I can." His lips curl into a cocky smirk. "I skipped the gym today. You'll be doing me a favor."

"What bullshit," I grumble as I circle my arms around his neck. I'm so afraid I'm going to hurt him somehow but he's steady as he hooks his arms under my legs and lifts. I squeal and wrap my arms around him tighter.

"That's my girl. Hang on."

People we pass on the trails smile at us. One of the park rangers asks if we need assistance but Dex brushes him off.

The last part of the hike includes a set of old, wide stone steps sunk into the side of a steep hill. "You can set me down now. The parking lot's right on the other side of those trees."

"I got you," he insists, his grip remaining strong on my legs.

He takes each step with care, obviously trying not to jostle me too much. And damn, he's not even out of breath by the time we reach his bike.

"That was an...adventure," I say, strapping on my helmet.

He curls his arms, flexing for me with a silly grin until I burst out laughing. "Come on. Let's grab lunch. I know a place."

About an hour later, we walk into a pub near Johnsonville.

"I've passed this place a bunch of times," I say to Dex. "But I've never eaten here."

"A friend owns and runs the place. So, if the club's out this way, we try to stop in and throw him some business."

As we step in the front door, I recognize the friend he's referring to. Remy came with Dex a few times over the summer to mow my lawn. The first time, I thought I caught him flirting with Libby and read him the riot act. Amazing he came back after that.

"You should've told me it was Remy," I whisper. "I don't think he's my biggest fan."

Dex chuckles. "That's not true. You're an attractive, unmarried woman. He's a fan."

Unmarried.

I curl my arms around his and press my breasts against him. "Unmarried but not available."

He leans down and kisses me. "Definitely not."

"Tongues to yourself!" a guy calls out.

Dex chuckles and pulls away.

Remy grins at us from behind the bar then points to a sign next to a row of liquor bottles. *Tongues to yourself* is spelled out in tall white letters on a black background. "Number one rule."

"Since when?" Dex jokes, walking quickly up to the bar and slapping Remy's outstretched hand. "How've you been, brother."

While they catch up, I glance around at the small, empty restaurant. Now I understand why Dex tries to give him business when he can.

"Sit anywhere you want," Remy says. "I'll bring over a menu."

After we place our orders, Dex slides his hands across the table and covers mine. Warmth from his skin seeps into my chilled bones. Not a chill from the ride—Dex had given me a pair of gloves to wear. This was a deeper cold that sprang from memories, freezing everything in its path.

"You must think I'm a real mess, huh?" I say after I can't stand another second under his watchful gaze. "I've told you about all these shitty guys I've dated, my parents…"

On paper, I don't sound very dateable.

He scowls. Not the regular annoyed-with-the-world-in-general scowl that's kinda sexy on him. A deep, frustrated, at-his-wit's-end expression that snaps my mouth closed.

"How does any of that make *you* the mess?" he asks.

I shrug. "The common denominator is me?"

"No it's not. It's rotten people who like to hurt others." He closes his eyes for a second. "Fuck, Emily. I admire the hell out of you for living through all of it. Taking care of your sister the way you have. Experiencing something so *traumatic* when she was so young…that would fuck a lot of people up for life. But she's such a sweet, funny, *normal* kid. That has to be *your* doing."

"Me and lots of therapy," I mutter.

He lifts an eyebrow. "Who got her the therapy?"

"My aunt sent both of us," I answer. "But I kept taking Libby after she died."

"You're a good sister."

Not that good. Maybe if I'd been home that night, instead of out partying like a bratty teenager, I would've found her hiding in the hallway. I would've carried her into her bedroom like I'd done so many times before and read her a book until she went to sleep. It would've spared her the trauma of seeing her parents brutally killed. I could've hidden in that closet with her, keeping her safe. Instead she slipped into a near catatonic state to deal with what she saw.

"Emily?" Dex glides rough fingers over the back of my hand. "What did the letter say?"

"Huh?" I blink and focus on his handsome face. His brows knit together in curiosity and concern. *The letter.* I force myself to try and remember. "It was a while ago." I curl my hands into fists so tight my nails bite into my palms. "I kept it in case Libby wants to read it one day."

"That's probably good. What did he want?"

I close my eyes, trying hard to remember the tone and intent of the letter if not the exact words. "Sort of an *I'm sorry*. That he had a shitty beginning but he takes responsibility for what he did." I pause, trying to recall the last part. "I think he wanted me to visit him?"

"No fucking way."

"That was my reaction."

A waitress stops by to drop off our sandwiches.

"Can you bring a small bowl of lemon wedges, as well," Dex asks.

"Sure." She glances at me. "Anything else?"

I stare at my grilled ham and cheese, suddenly ravenous. "I'm good. Thanks."

Dex waits for me to take a bite before slicing into his hot turkey sandwich smothered in gravy. The waitress returns with my lemons and leaves without a word.

"Thanks for remembering that," I say to Dex, picking one up and squeezing it into my water.

He dips his chin in acknowledgment.

I bite into the buttery, crispy bread and gooey cheese. My eyes close in comforting satisfaction. I munch on one triangle of the sandwich and take a few forkfuls of coleslaw while my mind turns the letter over.

I set my fork down with a clink against the plate. "He said something about giving me the truth of that night and that he wanted to apologize in person."

Dex's fork is halfway to his mouth but he sets it down. "What truth?"

"I don't know." I poke my fork into the coleslaw, stirring the soggy cabbage and carrots. "It was pretty straightforward." I lower my voice. "I don't need to hear from his mouth that my father was a criminal. If that's the truth he wants to give me, he can choke on it."

Dex nods thoughtfully but doesn't comment.

"Does that make me a coward?" I ask.

He reaches over and squeezes my free hand. "You're brave as fuck, woman. Don't ever doubt that."

"Thanks."

He stares at me for a few beats, then releases my hand. "I'm sorry I made you talk about it today."

I take a deep breath. Something inside me feels different. I can't tell if it's good or not, yet. I haven't talked to anyone about my parents' murder in a long time. "Thank you for listening."

"Thank you for trusting me," he says in a low voice that barely reaches me.

I trust him more than I've ever trusted anyone.
My chest throbs with something else I can't say yet.
Love, love, love.
"I do trust you," I whisper. "A lot."
Please don't make me regret it.

CHAPTER FORTY-SIX

Dex

WRATH: *Church. ASAP.*

MC life is supposed to be about doing whatever the fuck you want, whenever the fuck you want. But it's also about respecting the brotherhood. Doing what's required to maintain the good of the whole MC, not just meeting each individual brother's selfish needs. In some ways the codes and rules we live by are stricter than any civilian law we claim to rail against. But they're *our* rules.

After what Emily shared, I hate leaving her alone in this big, old house.

I slip my phone in my pocket. The urge to pretend I didn't see the text demanding I get my ass to church is damn tempting.

Cell service *is* shitty out here.

No. That's a coward's action. Not mine.

"Do you want to come up to the clubhouse with me?" I ask Emily, pulling her body against mine and leaning on the back of her couch.

"Now? Tonight?" She pulls her phone out of her pocket and checks the time. "I can't. Libby will be home soon." The corners of her mouth lift. "And I need to get to bed early so I can actually go to work tomorrow."

Shit. I'm ready to ask her to quit her job and spend all her days with me. I've never *liked* spending so much time with anyone. By now, I'm usually ready for solitude, a break from the burden of conversation or expectations. But I feel none of that restlessness with Emily. I just want more. More time with her. More *of* her.

Don't get used to it.
"You have to go?" she asks.
"Wrath wants us for church."
Her eyes widen. "I thought you guys only met on the weekends."
"Yeah, but if something important comes up, we get called in." *Fuck.* Wrath wouldn't have sent the text without a good reason. My lack of urgency or concern should be a warning light flashing bright in my brain.
But it's not.
What the fuck is wrong with me? Women aren't supposed to come before the club. Especially one who isn't patched. Not wanting to leave my girlfriend alone with bad memories isn't a good enough excuse to skip a meeting with my brothers.
As if the universe wants to toss me a bone, Libby whirls through the front door. I blow out a relieved breath. At least I won't be leaving Emily *alone.*
"How was rehearsal?" Emily asks.
"Ah-may-zing!" She tosses her coat in the closet, kicks off her shoes, and hurries into the living room. Her eyes widen and a big grin stretches across her face when her gaze lands on us. "Dex! You're still here."
Emily chuckles and shifts herself out of my arms.
"You're going to come to the play, right?" Libby asks.
"Wouldn't miss it," I promise.
"Oh, Em. I'm gonna stay at Linda's Friday. We're getting up early to work on sets Saturday and I know you like to sleep in on the weekends."
Emily frowns. "What's her parents' situation again?"
"Uh, her mom's single. She's a nurse at Johnsonville Memorial. Brother's a bratty little twerp."
"Who's going to drive you to the school Saturday?"
Libby glances away for a second. "Her mom."
"What if she gets called into work?"
"Mackenzie will pick us up."
Emily grumbles but agrees. "Or you can call me for a ride."
"Whatevs," Libby says. "How many people fit on the back of your bike, Dex?"
"Uh, one." I wrap my arm around Emily's waist.
"Em, can Dex give me a ride to school on his bike?" Libby asks with excitement in her voice.
I'm not touching that one. Not my place.

"Uh…" Emily's gaze darts between her sister and me. "Yeah, that might be fine one day. You need the right helmet though."

Libby fluffs her hair and seems to reconsider.

"I gotta head out." I try not to notice the look of disappointment on Libby's face. What does it say about me that I'd rather stay and listen to their back-and-forth instead of sitting down with my brothers?

Nothing good.

Emily slips her hand in mine and walks outside with me. I'm trying hard not to be a possessive dick, but I really want to toss her on the back of my bike, feel her holding me tight for the whole ride, and then tie her to my bed at the clubhouse.

"Thank you." Emily loops her arms around my neck.

"For?"

"Today. Everything. Just being you."

"You're welcome." I lean down and brush my lips against hers. "I hate going. You know that, right?"

"I'm trying to be nice about it because I know it's important." She pulls me down for another kiss.

"How would you feel about coming up to the clubhouse this weekend?" I ask. "I can pick you up after work Friday. We'll stay over. Do the whole family breakfast thing Saturday morning. Sounds like Libby will be at her friend's, then busy with her play."

"Family breakfast, huh? That sounds…intense."

"Not at all. Half the time it's brothers clowning around and our president threatening to throttle them."

Say yes, firecracker. Say yes.

"Yes. I'd like that."

"Good." I wrap my arms around her waist and lift her in the air. "I'm a very happy man now."

She touches her fingertips to my cheek. "Good." She traces a line between my eyes and across my forehead. "As sexy as I think you are when you're scowling, I love seeing you smile."

Her voice, so low, sweet, and sincere punches a hole through my chest.

I love her. That's what this is.

I set her on her feet. "I only do it for you."

"Good. You're much too handsome to flash that smile at anyone else but me."

Jesus, she makes me laugh. "I'll talk to you later."

"All right." She takes a step back. "You better get going. If it's something important, your club's going to be mad you didn't get there sooner."

"This better be good," I grumble at Wrath when I walk into the clubhouse.

"Nice of you to show up," Wrath answers in his deep, pissed-off rumble. Arms crossed over his chest, he pushes away from the wall next to the war room. "This is your party, motherfucker."

My party? "What the fuck does that mean?"

"We waitin' for Downstate?" Ravage asks as he paces in front of the bar.

"No," Murphy answers, "This is strictly an Upstate matter. Rock didn't want to wait around for them to get up here. If we need to, we'll fill Z in on Saturday."

Murphy's over on the corner sectional with Heidi and their girls. My gaze travels to the other couch where Charlotte's stretched out with her feet resting in Teller's lap.

"You all right, Charlotte?" I ask.

She slowly turns her head and rubs her hand over her very pregnant stomach. "I'm sprawled out on the clubhouse couch in the middle of the afternoon in front of everyone." She wildly waves one hand toward Ravage and Stash. "These babies have stolen the last shreds of my dignity. No. I am not okay, Dex."

Yikes. Kinda wish I hadn't asked, now.

Heidi presses her fist to her mouth. Laughter that she tries to disguise with a discrete cough spills out. "You have no idea how much more dignity you're going to lose when those babies come shooting out of you."

"You, be quiet." Charlotte points a finger at her sister-in-law. "Keep your horror stories to yourself."

"I'm trying to help!"

"Go help elsewhere, little sister," Teller says.

"Charlotte, you look more radiant than ever," Ravage says.

Teller narrows his eyes, waiting for Rav's inevitable punchline.

"But," Rav continues.

Here it comes.

"Can we have a…moratorium on more babies for at least a year? I feel like one of you ladies has been pregnant for like, the last four years or something."

"Yes, Ravage," Heidi says in the same patient voice she uses with her daughters. "We'll put our procreation plans on hold to accommodate your sensibilities."

"Thank you, Little Hammer." Ravage dips his chin in Heidi's direction. "It's much appreciated."

Heidi rolls her eyes.

The door opens behind me and I step aside.

Rock walks in, sweeps his gaze over the living room, and nods to Wrath.

"Did Hope come with you, Uncle Rock?" Heidi asks.

Rock must be in a mood. He takes a sarcastic look behind him, then stares at Heidi for a second. "She's at the house." His gaze shifts to Charlotte and concern wipes the irritation off his face. "You all right, Char?"

"Yes, but I might need you to come over and help your son lift me off this couch before you all sit at the table."

"I got ya, Charlotte," Wrath offers.

Rock jerks his head toward the war room. Most of the guys follow him inside. I stop to say hi to Heidi and Alexa.

"How's the baby doing?" I ask Heidi.

"Bit-bit!" Alexa squeals, yanking the blanket off her baby sister's carrier.

"Shhh," Heidi reminds her daughter, pressing a finger to her lips. "Bit-bit's sleeping, remember?"

Alexa pouts but doesn't bother her sister again.

Knowing some of the girls are here tonight, I kind of wish Emily *had* been able to come with me. Or maybe it's a good thing, in case all the talk of babies would've scared her away.

I step into the war room and take my usual spot.

A few minutes later, Murphy and Teller round the table and take their places. I nod to Bricks on the other side, while Ravage, Stash, Hoot, and Birch all take their seats.

Behind me, the door shuts. Wrath drops into his chair on my left.

Great, let's get this over with.

I glance at the clock on the wall across from me. Malik and Blue will be opening the doors to Crystal Ball soon. I'll need to haul ass there as soon as we're done.

Every one of us focuses on Rock at the head of our table.

"Thanks everyone for coming in on short notice. I won't drag this out. Loco wants us to come out to the diner and sit down with him soon," Rock says, throwing a weary look around the table. "He's bitching about MC business happening in Ironworks. Anyone know what the fuck crawled up his ass?"

Teller curls his lips into a dismissive smirk. "Ironworks is *our* territory now. We can do whatever the fuck we want there."

"Agreed," Rock says. "We have a vested interest in keeping him happy, though."

Something about Ironworks nags at me. I can't think of any official business, though.

"How are his girls doing at CB?" Wrath asks me.

"Fine." I run over the list of Loco's girls working for us. "Serenity might need to go. She copped an attitude with Emily the other night—"

"Whoa. Hold up." Murphy slashes his hands through the air in a flag on the play sort of gesture. "*Your* Emily? Why was she at CB in the first place?"

"Yes, *my* Emily," I snap.

The table goes silent.

I shift in my seat, not thrilled that my personal life's been opened up at the table like a book for everyone to read and highlight their favorite passages. I glance at Rock, hoping for some mercy. But he tilts his head, as if he's waiting with his own emotional highlighter.

"I think we're all here to discuss something more important than my love life," I grumble.

"Dex has a *loooove* life, everyone!" Stash shouts. "Holy shit!"

"I thought he was already engaged," Hoot smirks. "To his hand."

"Har fucking har." I flip my middle finger at him.

"This was totally worth coming up here for church tonight," Bricks says.

Birch perks up. "She's the quiet chick who wears the long dresses? Serena's friend?"

"For fuck's sake," Wrath snarls. "Can you guys gossip later? We actually have real shit to discuss."

"Thank you," I mutter.

"Sorry," Murphy mouths from across the table.

"Is Serenity the one who hit on Grinder?" Teller asks.

"Oh, fuck." Ravage cackles like a deranged woodpecker. "That was some funny shit."

"A brother's adjustment to life on the outside isn't entertainment," Rock says. "Have some fucking respect."

That wipes the amusement off Rav's face. "You're right. Sorry."

How Rock's managed to put up with our bullshit for all these years without blowing a hole in one of us is beyond me.

"Yes, that's the one." I close my eyes and laugh. "Although, after the other night, Emily has decided Serenity's name should be *Agitation* forever more."

Rock chokes on a laugh. "So, she handled herself okay?"

"Yeah." I shoot a glare down the table at Sparky. "Willow was kinda rude to her. I had to remind her of her place."

Sparky's eyes bug. "Why are you telling me? She's *your* employee."

"I think Willow's just tryin' to look out for you, bro," Stash says quietly, throwing a scared puppy look my way.

"Well, I'm a big boy. I can take care of myself."

Wrath scratches his beard like he's thinking through something, which is unnerving on its own. Wrath usually doesn't hesitate to say what's on his mind. "I can't believe I'm going to ask this, but why'd you have your girl visit CB before the clubhouse?"

I roll my head his way and nail him with a you-should-be-ashamed-of-yourself stare. "Seriously?"

He shrugs.

I glance at Rock who tilts his head as if he's also interested in the answer.

"Fuck. It wasn't intentional." I lift my chin at Rock. "I told you she wasn't jazzed to find out I manage a strip club."

"Not exactly every woman's dream," Teller says.

"Thanks, Professor Wiseass." I grit my teeth, hating to do this in front of everyone. "I told her she could stop in and visit whenever she wanted." I aim my glare at Rock since he hasn't attempted to steer us back on track. "I wanted her to understand that no matter when she shows up, she'll never find me getting blow jobs in the broom closet or bending someone over my desk."

Rock clenches his jaw, but a grudging sort of respect tilts the corners of his mouth. Were his pre-Hope antics a shitty thing to throw in my president's face? Sure. But if he'd put an end to this whole conversation a few minutes ago, I wouldn't have had to stoop so low.

"Wait." Ravage raises his hand to get my attention. "How come no one ever told me closet blow jobs and desk sex are an option?"

"They're not," I growl.

"I mean, it was *never* an option," Wrath says with a shit-eating grin. "But *some* folks think the rules don't apply to them."

Rock side-eyes his best friend. "I really miss Z sometimes."

"I think we all do," Murphy agrees.

"All right." Rock sits up. "We've gotten a bit into the weeds here."

"A bit?" Hoot walks his fingers over the table in front of him. "Prez, we've stomped over the weeds, through the garden, and fallen into a pit of quicksand."

"Thanks for drawing us a map," Rock says in his least thankful tone.

"Loco," Wrath prompts, attempting to corral us again. "What's crawled up his ass?"

"And why doesn't he want us to meet at the whorehouse?" Rav asks.

"Do you *have* to call it that?" Sparky moans.

"Whore-dorms?" Rav shrugs.

"Whoredom." Bitch and Hoot snicker and smack each other like they came up with something clever.

"I liked it better when you two sat down there and kept your mouths shut," Wrath says, pointing a finger at Hoot and Birch.

"Same," a couple of us mutter.

"Loco specifically asked for Dex to attend," Rock says, ignoring everyone else. "So I assume it's about one of his girls. It was the 'business in Ironworks' that threw me."

"Why didn't you lead with *that?*" I ask.

He glares at Murphy, then Wrath. "Someone derailed us."

"I was concerned for my brother," Murphy protests, throwing a hand in my direction.

"I'm just nosy," Wrath says without a hint of give-a-fuck.

Rock nods. "Truest thing you've ever said, brother."

I wrack my brain trying to think of any issues with the girls. "Desna's been an asset."

"Fuck, yeah, she is," Ravage groans.

Rock shoots a shut-the-fuck-up glare at Rav.

"Could Loco be pissed Rav's perving on his girls?" Wrath asks.

"Hey! I don't perv."

"You're the *definition* of perv," Murphy says.

Rav's saved my ass a few times recently. I should at least make an attempt to defend him. "Rav's been nothing but professional with Loco's girls," I say. "At least when I'm around," I add, just in case.

"Thanks." Rav frowns at me. "I think."

"The girls all like him," I say. "And trust me, they're quick to complain." Rav nods like an idiot.

"I bumped up Desna's hours, though," I continue. "She wants to get out of Loco's place before he talks her into escorting again. She's trying to finish school."

"Ah, okay." Rock nods. "That could be it."

"Fuck him," Wrath growls. "He can't ask us to give his girls jobs, then be pissed at how we do it."

"Agreed." Rock looks at me again. "Anything else more specific to Ironworks?"

Something tickles at the back of my mind again. "Uh, that guy Vapor and I paid a visit to—the one who knocked around one of our girls—he lives in Ironworks. I fucked him up pretty good. Left him breathing, but still." I frown. "That was a while ago, though. And it's really none of Loco's business."

"All right." Rock slaps the table and finally seems satisfied. "That seems like two promising possibilities. If it's something else, we'll figure it out at the meeting. Who's coming with us?" He slants a look my way. "Besides Dex."

Fucking great. On Rock's radar isn't someplace I ever aspire to be.

"I'm in." Wrath lifts his hand in the air. "Might as well get some burgers out of it."

Teller raises his hand next. "I vote we *all* go. If Loco's gonna waste our time with petty bullshit, I say all of us should ride into his parking lot and scare the piss out of him."

"You're the one he's scared of," Murphy points out.

Teller grins. "I know."

"Jigsaw freaks him out too," Ravage says. "He heard about his finger necklace."

"I'll ask Z if his guys want to ride with us." Rock's face settles into a savage grin. "Grinder makes Loco nervous too."

"So, this is mandatory?" Sparky asks.

"*Mandatory* is such a strong word," Wrath says.

"That's a yes," Stash mutters to Sparky.

Murphy lifts a finger to get Rock's attention. "I'll reach out to Loco and see if I can get more info. Maybe try to settle it over the phone."

"I'd appreciate that," Rock says. "Thank you."

"I'll ask Malik if he's got any idea what this is about," I offer. "But I've gotten the impression Loco's been freezing him out lately."

"Good," Wrath mutters. "If we're gonna patch him in, we need to know where his loyalty lies."

"That's a problem for another day." Rock slaps his palm against the table. "Thanks for coming up, everyone."

After that broom closet dig I made earlier, I'm risking a throat punch from Rock by sticking around. But I have to let him know about that stupid lawsuit.

I wait until most of the room clears out and then approach Rock. "Can I bend your ear for a moment, Prez?"

He steps away from the table. "Sure. What's on your mind?"

Fuck, I'm embarrassed to tell Rock this. But it's not like we didn't get served lawsuits when he ran the club or when Z was running it. "We had an incident at CB not that long ago."

He raises his eyebrows, indicating he's listening and I should continue.

"Two customers put hands on one of the girls in the champagne room. Malik saw it on the cameras. Got me to back him up." I run my hand through my hair. "I worked one of 'em over more than probably necessary before throwing him out." I rub my hand over my jaw. "Although he got in a few shots of his own."

"And?" Rock prompts. None of this is shocking. It's part of running a strip club. Not something I'd waste his time with unless there was more to the story.

"He's threatened to sue the club," I explain. "Got a letter from some law firm, so I think it's official now."

Rock snorts, dismissing this as a non-issue. "Forward it to Glassman's firm. One of the attorneys there can handle it."

"Sorry. You know I hate causing the club trouble."

He tilts his head, studying me for a moment. "You've never once in all the years I've known you caused the club trouble."

"I'm sure that's not true."

He raises an eyebrow. Silently asking if I'm disregarding his word.

"Thank you, Rock." I clear my throat. "Uh, I'm sorry about that closet/desk comment earlier. I shouldn't—"

"It's the truth. We're fine, brother."

"Th—"

"Although," he says slowly, cutting me off, "if you *ever* say something like that in front of Hope, I'll throat punch the fuck out of you."

My mouth opens and closes a few times. "I'd never do that."

"She's well aware of things that happened in the *past.*"

"Understood." Time to pivot away from *this* topic. "I'm bringing Emily up Friday night. I think we'll stay over, let her get the full effect of family breakfast."

"Good." He turns toward the open war room door and a wry smile turns his mouth up. "At least there's a fifty-fifty chance she *won't* walk in on an orgy in the champagne room these days."

The reminder of Inga spending an afternoon running a train in our clubhouse is the last thing I needed. Not that she's the only woman who's come up here and tried to fuck every single brother in one night. That event was one I was involved in, and I'd rather forget it ever happened.

"You can always visit the new clubhouse if you want to give her *that* MC experience," he adds.

"Thanks, I'll pass." I cock my head and dare to ask my next question. "Did all that shit bother Hope? She handled it so well in front of us."

He puts his hands on his hips and takes a deep breath. After his earlier warning, I'm flirting with death by asking. But he seems to be carefully considering the answer. "Yes and no. She already had an inkling from doing some legal work at Crystal Ball." He coughs and glares at me. "She'd met Inga too. Got an idea of what she was all about."

He pauses, regret flashing across his face. "The girls who hassled her up here, though…I should've warned her better."

"Trinity was always quick to look out for her."

"She was," Rock agrees. "By the way, if you want to transition away from Crystal Ball, that's fine."

How'd he get there from what I was asking? "I ain't gonna let my woman run my life, Prez."

He doesn't laugh at my stereotypical biker response. "I'm serious. I did it. Z did it."

"Priest moved Z downstate," I argue, as if he needs the reminder.

"I just want you to know, you're not tied to managing Crystal Ball forever." He lifts his chin toward the door. "You've been a big help to Rooster getting the security company off the ground. You can—"

"That's only for the summer concert season, though." As much as I love being on the road with Rooster and Shelby when she's touring, traveling somewhere new every day, visiting our brother charters across the country, and partying with the popular country singer Dawson Roads, I'm not sure it's enough of a contribution to the club to make that my full-time thing.

"We have the funeral home now, too," he suggests.

"That's Teller's action. Besides, on a day-to-day basis, I think Jigsaw has made it clear *he* plans to park his ass there so he can drool over Margot."

"I don't have enough work to bring you on full-time at the shop—"

"Rock, I'm a decent mechanic, but I don't have the skill for that detailed custom work."

He nods. "Well, there's always our lovely porn production company. Z has more work there than his guys can handle." He glances down and shakes his head. "Although, I doubt Emily will think that's an improvement."

Spending my days playing bodyguard for amateur porn stars or monitoring their websites sounds like a circle of hell I'd like to avoid. "No thanks."

"What *did* she think of Crystal Ball?" Rock asks.

He's not asking for her assessment of our business plan. "Uh, she was impressed with the girls' pole tricks and disgusted by the tip collecting part."

He rumbles with laughter. "I think she'll do fine here."

I'm praying to the universe that he's right.

CHAPTER FORTY-SEVEN

Emily

I'm giddy but anxious about accompanying Dex to his MC's clubhouse this weekend. Even though I'm hesitant to bother Serena with something so insignificant while she's adjusting to motherhood, I can't think of anyone else who can offer advice.

After she details all the cute things baby Lincoln has done today, I share my dilemma.

"So, be honest with me." I take a breath. "How big of a deal is this, Serena?"

"For Dex? Pretty big," she answers without hesitation. "They have two clubhouses now. So, if he's taking you to the one out in the woods, he's serious. It's more like family and friends of the club only these days."

"So, I won't encounter any wild biker orgies?"

"I wouldn't go *that* far." She chuckles. "You may still see things you can't unsee."

"Are you and Gray going to be there this weekend?" I'd feel a hell of a lot better with Serena there to stop me from embarrassing myself.

She lets out a loud yawn. "I don't think so. I'm not ready to take Lincoln around that many people yet. Gray might be up there for church, but I'm staying home."

Damn. "Okay."

"You'll be fine. The girls are all really nice." She's quiet for a few seconds. "Trinity is the wife of the SAA. Don't tell her I said this," she lowers her voice as if the club might have her phone bugged, "but I kind of think of her as the enforcer for all the ol' ladies. She might grill you a little."

"Wait, aren't *you* an enforcer's old lady too? Is that what *you* do now?"

"Me?" Her musical laughter tinkles over the phone. "Hell no. Trinity's been with the club for a long, long time, that's all. She's protective of the brotherhood. Once she's confident you'll be good for the club, she'll be your biggest supporter."

"Huh. Okay." *Beware of pretty blondes trying to extract information from me.*

"Hope's really sweet," she continues. "She comes off as laid-back but she's perceptive. She used to be a lawyer."

"That's the president's wife?"

"Yup. And you know Charlotte from her wedding."

"I barely spoke to her." I was so nervous I barely remember anything from that beautiful day.

"She's nice. You know Lilly from planning my baby shower. If Z's there this weekend, she'll probably be there too."

"I like her." She'd had a *lot* of ideas for Serena's baby shower. Saying we planned it together is probably a stretch. Lilly did most of the work.

"Heidi's the VP's wife," Serena says in a more serious tone. "And the treasurer's sister."

"Let me guess, she's also protective of the club and will probably grill me?"

"Not *grill* you. But she'll definitely size you up and report back to Murphy." Serena chuckles like this is all normal.

"Do you swear I'm not being lured into a cult?"

"Do you like Dex?" she asks, ignoring my question.

Oh my God, it really is a cult and she's trying to break it to me gently.

"I do. A lot," I answer seriously. "Maybe more than like him."

She *squees* into the phone.

"Yikes. Settle down." Why'd I have to admit that to her? "My ears are bleeding now."

"Sorry. Look, Emily, these guys are Lost Kings for life. If you love Dex, you'll have to learn to love the club too. They're a package deal."

"Um, I'm not like permanently bound to this cult just because I visit their super-secret clubhouse, am I?"

She doesn't laugh at my weak joke. "No, Emily."

"What should I wear?" I ask, wanting to move far the hell away from the *love and cults* topic.

"Well, if you're riding with Dex, wear whatever he suggests. Some of the girls bring another outfit to change into when they get to the clubhouse. Wear something nice. But not too revealing. You want to make Dex proud but not feel like he has to gouge out his brothers' eyeballs if they stare at your cleavage for too long."

What have I gotten myself into?

"You realize I'm offended on several levels here, right?" I ask.

"They're not the most...modern thinkers." She sighs. "But the men are deeply respectful and protective of the women they care about."

I've definitely gotten that vibe from Dex. "Well, I do usually say some of the most dangerous men are the ones who loudly proclaim to be feminists."

She bursts into giggles. "Yeah, *none* of those guys are going to tell you that."

"All right. Wish me luck."

"I'll check in with you over the weekend."

"Thanks. And let me know when you're ready for me to come down and spend time with you and the baby. Libby really wants to meet him too."

"Aww, thank you." Her voice falters. "It's a *lot*. I'm still figuring it all out. But I'll have you guys come down soon. Promise."

Should I be more insistent? I've been so wrapped up in my blossoming relationship, I don't feel like I've been paying enough attention to other important areas of my life.

CHAPTER FORTY-EIGHT

Emily

MY CONVERSATION with Serena didn't exactly settle my nerves about the trip.

Friday morning, I help Libby pack a bag for her sleepover. Then I pack my own bag.

"Where are you going?" she asks, standing in my bedroom doorway.

"Dex wants me to visit his MC's clubhouse. Uh, introduce me to his friends."

Her eyes widen with interest. "Are you going to be hanging out with Shelby Morgan?" Her voice lowers to an awed whisper.

Libby was still awestruck from meeting one of her favorite singers at Serena's baby shower.

"Uh, I'm not sure if she'll be there. Serena mentioned she's been back and forth from Tennessee while recording her album or something."

Her face screws into a pout.

"Libby," I say as gently as possible. "I'm kind of nervous about this. The club is...family to Dex."

"But you've met a lot of them before."

"This is different." I aim my big sister stare at her. "You have a big weekend of set-building and chilling with your friends, don't you?"

"Ugh, no one says 'chillin' anymore, Em." She snorts in disgust and walks away.

"Well, I still say it," I mutter, listening to her clomp down the stairs.

When I find her in the kitchen a few minutes later, she seems more cheerful. "I forgot to tell you I got an eighty-eight on my math quiz yesterday."

"That's great! So, the study sessions with Troy are helping." I'd been wondering if they were working or flirting but couldn't think of a way to ask that wouldn't tick off Libby.

Her cheeks turn pink.

Must resist urge to tease her.

"Yeah, he's really good at explaining stuff," she says. "Better than our teacher, for sure."

"I'm proud of you, puddin'. You've been putting in a lot of hours on the play and still improving in your other classes. That's not easy."

She ducks her head. "Knock it off. It's not a big deal."

I drop it but I'll have to think of something to reward her. She chatters about classes and the play the whole drive to school. I pull into the drop-off area and put the car in park.

"Hang on," I say.

"Em, I gotta go." Her hand hovers over the car door handle.

"Call me if you need anything. I won't be that far away that I can't come get you. You have Dex's number too, right?"

"Yup."

Much to Libby's mortification, I'd spoken to her friend's mom earlier in the week, so I'm confident Libby will be fine. But I can't help the worry settling in my stomach.

"You gotta let me fly out of the nest once in a while, sister bird." Libby presses her thumbs together and wiggles her fingers like bird wings. "I'll text you. Promise."

I wait and watch her fly up the stairs to the front doors of the school. Someone honks behind me and I resist the urge to flip them off.

I don't know how I'm going to slog through work today. I almost feel like calling in sick again and asking Dex to pick me up early.

THE SUN'S rapidly setting as we ride to the clubhouse. With so many tall trees, darkness descends rapidly, but enough light remains to enjoy the twilight mountain views.

The ride seems both long and over too fast. Dex is right about riding helping the mind focus on what's in front of you. With the pavement rushing below us, I spend more time worrying about my odds of dying than whether or not I'll embarrass myself in front of Dex's club tonight.

I wrap my arms around him even tighter as we pass through a high, metal gate. A big Buddha statue greets us as we pass. I wasn't expecting *that*. An impressive, wide, paved driveway leads up, up, up a hill.

A mammoth log cabin-type building appears to the right. "Wow."

"Not what you expected, huh?" Dex shouts over his shoulder.

"Nope." Even though Serena told me the clubhouse looked like a fancy log cabin, I'd pictured a run-down old warehouse with a cracked parking lot.

He follows the gentle curve in the driveway around to the front of the building. A wide parking area extends the length of the front of the clubhouse. Large garages and a building that looks like a smaller version of the clubhouse stand at the end of the parking lot. Several neat trails cut through the woods surrounding the place. Bright floodlights on the corners of every roof illuminate the area.

Dex backs the bike into a line of other Harleys across from the clubhouse. Once he shuts off the engine, the steady thump of music from inside the clubhouse makes its way to us.

"Full house?" I ask.

"Yeah. Most of us live up here, so it's usually busy on the weekends." He waits for me to get off the bike.

I stand staring at the forest and inhale the crisp, fresh mountain air. "Wow, this is really pretty."

"Thank you." He stops and follows my line of sight as if appreciating the view for the first time in a while. "We were lucky to find the place."

He points to one of the paths leading into the woods. "A few brothers have built houses on the property."

"Wow, really?"

"Z likes to joke that we're building a prepper compound." Dex chuckles. "I guess he's not wrong."

"Z's the one you said moved to your downstate club?"

He nods quickly. "He started construction on a house before the move, and then decided to finish it so he and his family have a place to stay when they're up here."

Damn. That must cost a fortune. But it's a rude comment, so I keep it in my mouth. *Now, if you remember to do that this weekend, you'll be golden.*

"I'll take you for a walk around the property tomorrow, if you want."

He curls his hand around mine. "Word of warning. Everyone's gonna pounce on you. You've already met some of the old ladies a few times. They've been looking forward to seeing you."

He wiggles his fingers, signaling I should hand him my backpack.

"Really?" I shrug the pack off and hand it to him.

"My brothers, though..." An exasperated smile twists his lips. "They're gonna enjoy razzing my ass."

"For bringing a girl home to meet the family?" I tease.

His smile fades. "Exactly."

"I can handle them." I reconsider my answer, remembering some of the things I've read about biker clubs. "No one's going to, like...try to hit on me to test my loyalty to *you*, are they?"

He stops and considers the question for longer than I expected. "No one should do that here."

That's not exactly reassuring.

I shift my gaze to the clubhouse. "Willow won't be here, will she?"

"I'm not sure. But I had a few words with her after you visited CB. She won't throw that attitude again."

"Oh, great." *I knew I should've kept my mouth shut.* "Now she probably hates me."

"No, she just needed to understand you're important to me."

"Aww." I squeeze his hand and try not to melt into a puddle at his feet.

"I wouldn't bring you here, otherwise." In a lower voice, he adds, "Never have before."

I don't know how to interpret that but before I can ask, the screen door squeaks open and a beast of a man thunders down the stairs.

"Look who it is."

Dex takes a step back. "Don't you fucking dare."

Apparently, his brother interprets the warning as a challenge. He wraps his giant arms around Dex and lifts him in the air.

"Motherfucker," Dex grunts.

He sets Dex down as quickly as he picked him up.

"Emily," Dex rests his hand on my back, "this asshole with no sense of boundaries is Wrath."

"How could I forget." I hold out my hand and for a second, it disappears into his large one. "Please don't pick me up. I like my ribs where they're currently located."

"I wouldn't dare." Wrath presses his hand to his chest, like he's offended I'd suggest such a thing. He returns his attention to Dex. "I'm running home to help Trin with something but we'll both be here later."

"Great." Dex slants a sarcastic look at him. "Thanks for the update."

"Have fun, Emily," Wrath calls out as he jogs into the woods.

"Why did that sound ominous?" I ask.

Dex shrugs. "Everything he says is ominous."

I turn and check to make sure we're alone, then lean up on tiptoe to whisper in Dex's ear, "Serena said his wife is kind of like your female SAA here."

Dex snorts. "That's probably true. Trinity's a good woman. Been with the club for a long time."

"But she's not a member? Just a brother's wife?"

"Right. She's vital to the club, though. And a good friend."

I peer up at him, curious about the catch in his voice.

"Not that kind of friend," he says, shaking his head. "I've known her a long time, that's all."

Now I'm even more nervous about being grilled by this woman and I haven't even set foot in the clubhouse yet.

Inside, a wall of heat rolls over me. Dex helps me take off my coat. He opens a door to a cavern of a closet and hangs it inside.

Is that a gun safe in there?

Dex closes the door before I get a good look.

A thin cloud of pungent smoke hangs in the air.

"Sexy Dexy! You've arrived!" someone shouts from across the room.

"Jesus," Dex mutters.

Now that our arrival's been announced, men in leather vests just like Dex's crowd around us. A few hug him as if it's been a while. Some of the bottom patches on the backs of their vests read *Downstate NY*.

A tall, scruffy biker leans into my space. "Welcome, Emily." He picks at the air around my head as if pulling cobwebs out of my way. "If you're in need of a social facilitator or emotional regulator, I'm your guy."

I blink, unsure of how to respond.

He waves his arms in an arc over my head. "You brought an aura of anxiety with you."

"That's enough, Sparky." Dex presses his hand to Sparky's chest and gives him a gentle shove.

But there's something charming about the way he noticed that I'm anxious and offered something to help me cope. I catch his hand. "Thank you, Sparky. I *am* nervous and you already made me feel better."

He aims a blissed-out smile at Dex. Then sticks his tongue out.

Soft, feminine squeals of delight echo from the hallway, accompanied by the sharp clicky-clack of heavy-heeled boots.

"Dixon!" Shelby shouts, plowing into my boyfriend and giving him a fierce hug. "I've missed ya."

Dex's mouth curls into an affectionate smile as he returns the hug. "You just get back from Tennessee?"

She pulls away and tips her head back. "Is that yur way a sayin' I sound more twangy or somethin'?"

"Nope." He holds up one hand like he's about to swear on a holy book.

Shelby hugs me next. "Good to see ya again." She glances behind me. "I'm guessin' Libby didn't come with ya?"

"No, but she was jealous and wanted me to say hi to you."

"Aw, next time maybe."

"Hey, brother." Rooster holds out his hand to Dex, then pulls him in and slaps his back. "It's been a minute."

"Were you guys out on the road?" Dex asks.

"Little bit." Rooster curls his arm around Shelby's shoulders, and she leans right into him.

"Emily." Dex takes my hand, pulling me closer. "You remember Rooster?"

"I do. Best beard in the house."

He dips his chin at me.

Sparky looms behind Shelby and taps her shoulder. "What do you call a stoned king?"

Shelby grins. "That's easy. Your *high*ness."

"Christ," Rooster mutters. "Not this again."

"Rude." Shelby slaps Rooster's stomach.

"Where's Jigsaw?" Dex asks.

Rooster glances over his shoulder. "Prowling around here somewhere."

"I'm surprised he came here with us instead of going to the new clubhouse," Shelby says.

Rooster grins. "I think he wanted to witness everyone giving Dex shit."

"Great, can't wait to see him." Dex slaps Rooster's shoulder and pulls me further into the clubhouse.

Shelby squeezes my arm as I pass her. "We'll chat later!"

"Okay."

Then she's swallowed by a sea of people I don't recognize and Dex doesn't stop to talk to. He pulls us to the side of the room and stops by a large set of tall, wooden double doors. "That's our war room," he says against my ear, "so when I say I'm heading to church, that's where I am."

"Am I allowed to see it?"

One corner of his mouth slides up. "Another time."

A large sectional couch takes up the entire back corner of the grand room. I recognize Lilly and feel a pang of regret that Serena isn't here tonight. She notices me and waves, which draws the attention of her husband who jumps up.

"Dex! Finally, ya fuck," he shouts. "What took so long to get your ass over here?"

"It's crowded, in case you didn't notice. How many of your guys came?"

Z's gaze skims the room behind us. "Everyone."

Lilly reaches me and pulls me in for a hug. "Serena said you'd be here tonight." Her gaze flicks between Dex and me and her full lips curve up. "I'm happy to see you two together."

Embarrassed, I turn my head. "Thanks."

"Come." She curls her hand around mine. "Let them catch up."

Dex nods for me to go ahead. He's still dragging my backpack around and I offer to take it, but he shakes his head.

A few couples are on the couch. And a…throuple? Three people at the far end are entwined and engaged in things I probably shouldn't be staring at. Lilly pulls me down onto the couch next to another couple.

"Hope!" Lilly taps the woman's leg, which is hanging off the lap of a huge guy currently trying to give her CPR, I guess?

"Huh?" Hope blinks.

Lilly tilts her head in my direction.

"Oh! Emily." Hope tries to stand but her husband's arm clamps down around her waist, keeping her in his lap. Laughing, she reaches over and shakes my hand. "I'm so happy you're here!" She turns and nudges her husband. "Rock, remember Emily?"

"I do." He nods at me. "Glad Dex finally brought you up."

"Thanks." A nervous smile flickers over my lips. The man's eyes alone are intimidating.

I fan myself with my hand. "It's crowded. Dex made it sound like it'd be a quiet night of board games here."

Hope and Lilly laugh and share a knowing look.

"Not so much," Hope says. "I'd say let's go to the dining room, but I don't think it's any quieter in there." She gestures to a long corridor on the other side of the house.

Lilly pulls her phone out and checks the time. "I should go relieve Heidi soon," she says to Hope. "I think she was looking forward to a few hours away from the baby." She glances at her husband who's still talking to Dex at the end of the couch. "Sorry, Emily. We're a bunch of boring moms with early bedtimes now. If you'd met us a couple years ago, we would've partied all night with you."

"Speak for yourself," Hope teases.

"I don't know about that," I say. "Unless Libby's sleeping over at a friend's house or something, I don't really get any nights off."

Lilly flinches as if she's worried she offended me.

I shrug. "It's okay. She's older now, so I get a little more time to myself."

"Do you have any other family?" Hope asks.

"No. It's just the two of us."

Hope and Lilly share another one of those looks.

"She's always welcome here," Hope says. "Well, maybe not tonight. Thursday nights and Sunday afternoons are good. Wrath won't open the gates for anyone who isn't family."

"How old is she again?" Lilly asks.

"Sixteen."

"Oh, I thought she was younger for some reason," Hope says. "Heidi started coming up here when she was around sixteen."

Rock taps Hope's leg. "Heidi started *sneaking* up here when she was sixteen," he corrects in his deep, rumbling voice.

Hope shakes with laughter. "Okay, that's true."

My phone buzzes in my pocket and I pull it out.

Libby: Stuffing our faces with Oreos. Hope ur having fun too! Tell Dex I said hi!

A picture of Libby holding a stack of cookies in her mouth shows up under the message.

Laughing, I tap out a quick message, then tuck my phone away. "Sorry, it was Libby."

Dex stops in front of me. I tip my head back—way back to see his face. He stares down with wide, questioning eyes. I nod quickly to let him know I'm okay.

"Prez." Dex leans over and taps his knuckles against Rock's. "First

Lady," he nods to Hope. "First *ladies*." He grins and leans down to kiss Lilly's cheek.

"It feels like I haven't seen you in a long time, Dex," Lilly scolds.

"How's Chance? He over at the O'Callaghan compound for the night?"

"Yup. All the little ones are with Uncle Murphy and Auntie Heidi."

Dex straightens and lifts my backpack. "I'm going to stash this in my room. You want to come up with me?"

"Sure."

Lilly lightly touches my arm. "If I don't see you again tonight, we'll talk in the morning."

"Sure."

Dex offers his hand and pulls me up off the couch. He keeps holding my hand but tucks me behind him, slowly guiding us over to an L-shaped staircase. On the first landing, an older motorcycle is on display. The entire wall on the right side is full of framed photos. Lots of bikers proudly wearing their Lost Kings MC vests. Men riding Harleys. Road trips. Visits to what looks like other Lost Kings MC clubhouses. Several weddings. Men standing with their backs to the camera with the back patches on display and what looks like a concert venue in the background. Babies in tiny Lost Kings MC onesies. Toddlers wearing their own vests. It's a photo album laid open for everyone to see the love and shared experiences of the club.

Dex stops when he realizes I'm rooted in place. "Are you okay?"

"Sorry. This is…impressive." I touch the frame of one of the pictures. "Is this you?"

He stares at the photo for a few seconds. "Yeah. Patch-in party. It was a…weird time for the club."

Huh.

He grips my hand again and continues up the stairs. Moans and groans come from our left. A guy I haven't met yet has his back to one of the doors. Not one, but two girls are kneeling in front of him, taking turns swirling their tongues over his huge, *pierced* cock.

I don't want to stare, but it's kind of hard not to.

Dex glances at them and shakes his head. "Your room is right there, for fuck's sake," he growls.

The guy gives us a lazy smile. "Almost made it."

"Christ." Dex grips my hand harder and pulls me to a door on our right. "Sorry," he mutters.

He slips a key into the lock and pushes the door open, ushering me inside.

"I've never seen a pierced penis before," I blurt.

"Fantastic." Dex's face contorts into a grimace. "I'm thrilled to be responsible for showing you your first one."

His sarcastic tone should be a warning to drop it, but I'm still so shocked my brain won't stop sending words shooting out of my mouth. "Doesn't that hurt?"

An amused scowl spreads over his face and he hooks his arm around my waist, yanking me against his hard body. "I don't know. I've never had the urge to ram a piece of metal through my dick." He kisses my cheek. "But feel free to stop wondering about my brother's anatomy any time now."

Heat flames over my face. "Sorry, I didn't—"

He slams his mouth over mine, swallowing my apology. I melt into the kiss, forgetting all about piercings and penises.

"Emily, curiosity's normal," Dex whispers against my lips. "As long as you didn't want to *join* them, there's nothing to apologize for."

He kisses me again. "But I hope it didn't interest you too much, because I really don't want to put any holes through my dick."

I laugh and tickle my fingers along his jawline. "Please don't mess with perfection."

His hold shifts to my waist and he turns me around. "Welcome to my room at the clubhouse."

The room's a simple, homey square. Slightly larger than your average hotel room. A king-sized bed with a rough-cut lumber frame takes up most of the floor space. A similar style of dresser stands against one wall. A nightstand next to the bed. A reading chair, lamp, and small bookshelf in the corner.

He sets my bag in front of the dresser.

"Bathroom's in there." He points to the right.

I hadn't noticed the closed door. The dark wood seems to blend into the walls.

"Are we returning to the party?" I ask.

He lifts one shoulder. "Up to you."

The closed bedroom door doesn't do much to muffle the sounds of the party downstairs—or the obscene noises from the hallway. But it's easier to hold a conversation in here.

"As much as I enjoyed meeting people, I've been looking forward to spending time with you," I say, hoping he feels the honesty in my words. It's only been a couple of days since our hike at the park, but I've *missed* him.

He brushes his knuckles over my cheek, pushing my hair out of the way. "Same, firecracker."

Dex

"Can you give me a minute?" Emily asks.

"Sure."

She leans over and swipes her backpack off the floor, carrying it into the bathroom with her. Curiosity flows through me, but I stop and take off my boots and hang my cut in the closet.

The party was more than I expected. Too loud and crowded to hold a conversation for long. I liked Emily hanging out with Lilly and Hope, though. And I loved how sweet she was with Sparky. His quirkiness didn't seem to faze her one bit.

The bathroom door clicks behind me.

"Dixon." My given name in Emily's low, husky voice lands in my chest.

I turn and find her leaning against the wall with one arm stretched above her head and one hand on her hip, like a classy, modern pin-up girl. *Skin.* So much creamy skin visible. She stripped down to nothing but a dark green lacy bra with cups so sheer I can make out tight pink nipples and panties so fucking tiny, they barely hide a thing.

"Turn around," I rasp.

She goes up on her toes and executes a neat spin.

"You ride in that little green floss?" I ask, stepping up behind her.

"Not yet," she says over her shoulder.

Fuck. I fit my hands into the dip of her waist, sliding them down to her hips. "You bring this up here for me?"

"Well, the bra I was wearing earlier, but yes, I put the panties on with only *you* in mind."

A simple thing, but fuck do I like that I'm on her mind when she's doing something simple like picking out her clothes. I flex and squeeze my fingers into her hips, loving how soft and pliable she feels under my hands.

Desperate to touch more of her, I slide one hand under the flimsy triangle of satin barely covering her skin. Her body tenses, ever-so-slightly. I cup her throat with my free hand, stroking my thumb against her pulse and gently bend her back against my body.

"Let me show you how much I like this." I don't wait for an answer, just push my fingers lower, groaning when I slide against her slick skin. "Open for me."

She inches her feet apart and swallows hard, her throat working against my palm.

"Good girl."

She whimpers as I slide my two fingers lower, not entering her, just lazily exploring, dragging her wetness to trace firm circles around her clit.

"Dex," she whispers.

"Shh. Let me enjoy touching you."

That must offer reassurance. She rolls her hips, rubbing herself against my hand.

"That's it," I encourage. "Show me what you like."

"I..." Her eyebrows pinch together.

I stop the circling motion and form a "V" shape with two fingers, slowly sliding them on either side of her clit, pressing harder on each downward stroke.

She gasps and raises up on her toes, pushing her upper body against my chest and grinding herself against my fingers.

"That's it," I whisper, kissing her cheek. "Let go. Be as loud as you need."

"Dex," she moans. A wave of higher-pitched whimpers flow past her lips.

I coax her through the orgasm until she's limp in my arms. She tilts her head back and blinks up at me.

"I'm buying these panties in every color they come in." Her words come out slightly slurred and fuzzy.

I erupt with laughter and release her, patting my hand against her ass. "Come shower with me."

Under the harsh light in the bathroom, she seems shy again. Until I strip off my T-shirt. Then, she steps closer, pressing kisses over my chest. Somehow, I work her bra loose with one hand and unbutton my jeans with the other. With her clinging to me, I twist the shower spray on, and fumble out of my pants.

"Get these off." I hook my fingers in the soaked satin panties and tug. She's quick to shimmy out of them and kick them aside.

I half lift, half carry her into the shower, stumbling forward until her back hits the wall. I lift her to kissing height and seal my mouth over hers. Her fingers rake through my hair and over my shoulders.

The hot spray of the shower rains down on us. Her desperate kisses, her wet skin slipping against mine, and her legs hugging my sides as I keep her pinned to the wall shatter my self-control. My hips punch forward, sliding against her dripping pussy. *Fuuuck* that feels good. She whimpers and tightens her hold around my neck, opening her mouth wider, devouring and licking. Just as hungry as I am. My cock slides against her again, finding home, squeezing into her tight heat.

Panting, I drop my forehead against hers. I'm drowning in the desire and surprise warring in her eyes. We drop our gazes to where we're connected. My bare cock driving into her.

"Em," I rasp, closing my eyes, memorizing every sensation.

"It's okay." She kisses and licks my neck.

No, no, no. I need to savor this. Not in a tight, slippery shower where I can't fully concentrate on her because I'm trying not to slip and crack open my skull.

I reach over and shut the water off, groaning as I pull out of her.

"Bed. Now." I push open the shower door so hard it hits the wall with a clang. Emily clings to my arm, following behind me, both of us dripping water everywhere.

I toss her on the bed, and she lands with a little bounce and scoots back until she's up against the pillows. With her feet against the comforter and legs spread, she's way too tempting. I all but dive at her, fastening my mouth over her clit and sucking hard.

"Oh, fuck!" she screams and clutches the comforter, balling it up in her hands.

"In a minute," I mumble against her soft, slippery flesh.

She lets out these sharp little sounds, somewhere between gasps and hysterical laughter.

Her hips shoot off the bed and I clamp my hands around her thighs, holding her down.

"Dex. Oh fuck." She writhes and thrashes as much as my grip allows. "Please, please, let me come."

I growl a sound I hope she interprets as *yes, please come on my face, right now.* I can't take my mouth off of her to say the actual words, though.

"Oh, oh, oh. Right *there!'*

I flick my tongue against her clit again and again.

"That's good, that's good," she whispers, her body relaxing against the bed.

She curls her hands around my neck and gently tugs. "Come kiss me," she whispers.

"Happily." I kiss my way up her body, stopping to tickle her belly button with my tongue and to kiss and suck the soft skin of her hips, where I'm almost positive my rough, grasping fingers left bruises.

My hands palm her breasts. Fuck, they fit perfectly. I swipe my thumbs over her hard nipples, lightly pinching the tips until she moans, "Please."

She tilts her head back, offering her neck. I slide my tongue over the long column of her throat. Drop kisses along her jawline, and finally take her mouth.

"Mmm," she moans against my lips.

The mattress dips and shifts as she lifts her legs, wrapping them around my waist. Again, my bare cock's rubbing up against her slick pussy.

"Em, look at me."

Her eyelids flutter open.

I flex my hips, slipping inside a fraction. "I'm good, I swear."

Her eyes widen as what I'm saying sinks in. "Me too."

"I haven't gone bare with anyone...without a condom since..." My voice chokes off.

Not since—

No. Not going there now. No.

Emily. Emily. Emily.

"I'm right here." Emily runs her fingers through my hair, pushing it back and out of my face. "And neither have I."

I groan, the pleasure so intense it borders on pain as I slide all the way without stopping. My breathing freezes. *Fuck.* I haven't been this close to blowing my load this fast since I was a teenager. I don't dare move, waiting until I gather some control.

"Dex?" She lifts her hips, the friction pushing me to the edge again.

"Don't move," I groan. "Don't you dare fucking move."

She moans in my ear, which is almost fucking worse. Those sexy damn noises she makes are like feathers stroking over my back, right down to my balls.

I slide my hand between us, pinching her clit. Her body jerks. I flatten my fingers, rubbing in slow, exaggerated circles. Her breathing picks up, warm puffs of air hitting my cheek in short bursts. I drop my forehead and she lifts her head to softly rub her nose against mine.

Suddenly, coming isn't the only thing I'm in danger of doing too soon.

As if she hears the words beating in my chest, she opens her eyes and stares into mine.

"I love you," I whisper.

Her inner muscles lock up around me and my vision swims. Then she presses her hands to the sides of my face, and slowly slides her tongue along my bottom lip.

I open to kiss her again, but she touches her lips to mine, stopping me. "I love you too." She breathes the words against my parted lips as if she's trying to send them into my soul.

For a few seconds neither of us move.

One of her feet slips against the back of my thigh and she moans as she lifts it in the air. I push forward again.

Her eyes squeeze shut and she lifts her other leg higher. "Dex," she whispers.

"You close to going off again, firecracker?" I press my lips to the side of her neck.

"Yes, so close. And I'd love that big cock of yours to join the party." She bucks her hips.

I growl, sinking my teeth into a sensitive spot below her ear.

She moans and lifts her arms over her head, lacing her fingers together and pressing her breasts into my chest. Something about the way her back arches and the vulnerability of the position triggers a primal part of me I haven't made contact with in years—if ever. I clamp one hand over her wrists, pinning her in place.

Excitement sparks in her eyes.

I skim my other hand down her side, gripping her hip. Then, hooking my forearm under her thigh, I spread her open wider. I slowly pull back, then thrust in hard.

She lets out a soft grunt.

"You like that?" I lean down and ravage her lips, while driving into her again and again. "You like being pinned down?"

"*Fuuuck*," she moans, stretching out the word. "Yes."

"You can scream as loud as you want here, firecracker." I switch things up, slowing my wild, frantic pace. "No one's gonna notice."

"Fuck me harder," she shrieks.

"All right. *Someone* might notice," I laugh.

She laughs with me, the sound vibrating right down to my dick.

"Jesus Christ," she huffs. "Whatever you're doing...don't stop. You're hitting...something. So good."

I want to fuck her every which way. Make her come in every position I can twist her into. But I need her to go off one more time for me.

"More," she gasps.

I release her wrists and hook my arm under her other leg. Oh, fuck yes, that's good.

"Shit!" She presses her hands to my chest and curls her upper body off the bed. "Right there."

Her legs quiver, the sensation starting at her hips and curling her toes. Tears leak from the corners of her eyes. I trace their path with my tongue.

"You're squeezing me so damn tight." I bend to take her nipple in my mouth, sucking hard.

She screams. Giving her permission to be as loud as she wants must've unlocked something in her. She's *loud*. The sound of her letting go triggers me and I add my groans.

"Holy fuck." I press my lips to her forehead but can't move. My heart thuds like a drum, blood roaring through my ears.

Finally, I find the strength to roll to the side before I crush her.

I curl my hand around hers and we stay side by side, just breathing for a few heartbeats.

She rolls toward me, curling her body against mine. Her ticklish little fingers stroke my chest and down my abs. She kisses my side and I flinch.

"Why you trying to tickle me when I'm too spent to defend myself?" I tease.

"I'm not. I was trying to *thank you*." She places another ticklish kiss close to my nipple. Her fingertips travel up my ribs. "Your body is magnificent, and you know how to use every single inch of it." She flips her fingers in the air, one by one, like she's trying to count something. "I didn't know it was possible to orgasm that many times in a row."

Now, *that's* something I don't mind hearing. My lips twitch. "Told you I'd turn you into a screamer."

Outrage shines in her eyes and her jaw drops. "I won't be able to show my face downstairs."

"Why? No one's gonna care. Or even know who was making all that beautiful music."

She drops her forehead to my side, her shoulders shaking with laughter. "My throat does feel a bit raw."

I lift my chin toward the small refrigerator near my closet. "Give me a second. I've got some water and stuff in there."

Groaning as I sit up, I cup one of her knees and lift her leg, admiring the sticky mess coating her thighs.

"You look absolutely feral," she whispers.

"I am. Stay put." I release her leg and slap my palm against her ass, stopping to squeeze. "Fuck," I mutter.

She chuckles softly and the covers rustle behind me.

I grab a bottle of water from the fridge, then return to the bed where she's stretched out like a damn centerfold, her soft eyes watching my every move. I unscrew the cap and hand her the bottle.

"Be right back."

She nods and takes a quick sip.

I take a few seconds to clean myself up in the bathroom, then return with a washcloth for her.

"What are you doing?" she asks.

"What's it look like?"

She gasps when I brush the washcloth against her skin.

"Too much?" I ask.

A wrinkle forms between her eyebrows. "My bits are feeling… sensitive. But not opposed to more action." She flashes a wicked smile. "I don't think you're prepared for what you've unleashed."

"Firecracker, I'm more than ready."

Emily

A door slamming in the distance jars me from sleep the next morning. Dex's heavy arm rests over my stomach, his hand somehow wedged between my thighs.

Possessive, even in his sleep.

Or did we fall asleep in the middle of sex? There was a lot of it. Slippery sex in the shower. Sleepy sex in the middle of the night. Will I even be able to walk today?

He mumbles something as I gently slide out of bed. Clothes? I brought something to sleep in. No idea where it ended up, though.

In the bathroom, I dig through my backpack, searching for my toothbrush. My fingers hit the hard little case and I pull it out. Next, I find a pair of underwear and a tank top.

Minty fresh and partially dressed, I return to the bedroom a few minutes later.

Dex has rolled to his back, the sheet barely covering him, but he seems to still be asleep. I take a second to admire the relaxed, peaceful expression on his handsome face.

Birds singing outside the window draw my attention. I hook my finger in the fabric shade and pull it toward me, peeking outside.

Oh wow. From the second floor, I have a good view of the rolling green mountains stretching beyond the clubhouse's parking area. I count the roofs of at least three different houses dotting the property. And is that a children's *playground* over there?

The loudest chirping seems to be coming from a bird feeder hanging on a tree near one of the garages. I recognize Sparky's tall frame tossing handfuls of birdseed on the ground.

"What a beautiful view to wake up to," Dex rasps.

I drop the shade into place. "You're the one who has a pretty view out this window."

"Mmhmm." He crooks a finger at me. "Come here."

The mountains can wait. The sexy man calling me over can't. But still, I take my time closing the distance between us.

He sits up, throwing his legs over the side of the bed and closes his hands over my hips when I reach him.

"That's better." He stares up at me with appreciation in his eyes. "Goddamn, you're a gorgeous sight first thing in the morning."

I lift my hand to smooth down any wild hair, but he captures my wrist to stop me. "I said what I said."

Placing my knee on the bed beside him, I climb into his lap, shamelessly rubbing myself against him. He shifts his hands to my butt and falls back against the bed.

"You sure are a morning person." I grind myself against him a little harder to emphasize what I mean by *morning person.*

He groans and closes his eyes. "I'm an *Emily* person."

"Goodness," I tease, kissing his bristly cheeks. "How are you hard as a brick but still so sweet?"

He bucks his hips up, toppling me against his chest. Instead of helping me wriggle out of my underwear like I was hoping, he kisses me and rubs his hand over my back. "I'm so glad you're here."

The raw sincerity in his voice undoes me. "I'm really happy you wanted me here." I sit up so he can see the teasing on my face. "I have to

398

tell you though, last night was one of the most chaotic 'meet the family' experiences I've been part of."

He rolls me underneath him and places kisses along my collarbone. "I don't want to hear about any other experiences," he murmurs against my skin.

"What I meant...what I'm trying to say," *ohmygod, he's so distracting*, "is that I like your family a lot. Even your strange and scary brothers. But I don't feel like I got to meet everyone. Or talk to them as much—"

"Give it time." He licks and kisses my neck, hitting every sensitive spot. "Everyone was on their best behavior when we showed up. Who the fuck knows what went on after we came up here?"

If that was best behavior, I don't want to know what bad behavior looks like.

"Mmm." I lift myself up so I can kiss his lips. "Some exquisite orgasms happened up here."

Like that's some sort of switch, he stops the gentle kisses and teasing licks.

"Emily, look at me." He frames my face with his warm hands against my cheeks. "I love you."

My heart squeezes.

He said it again.

"I know I said it last night," he continues. "But I need to say it when I'm not half out of my mind from having my bare dick in your tight, hot pussy for the first time."

Laughter trickles through me, but tears prickle my eyes. *Why?* I blink them away.

He braces himself on his forearms and looks down at me. "Why are you crying?"

"I'm not." I sniffle. "I love you too." My heart, everything inside me, quivers. "I'm actually scared of how much I've fallen in love with you."

"Why?"

"Because...whenever something good happens, something bad follows."

"Emily, baby. That's the ebb and flow of life, isn't it?"

"No. I don't know. Why does it have to be that way?"

"It just is." He kisses my forehead. "But I love you. And I want to spend all my time showing you how much."

"Okay." I smile up at him. What does that mean, though? His life is *here*. With his club. I could sense how much he's been missed lately.

Because he's been spending so much time around me. I can't ask him to move in with us. Even if I could, would that be fair to Libby?

"Emily," he rumbles. "Where'd you go?"

"Right here," I answer.

"No, your mind's working overtime." He kisses my forehead. "Just stay in this moment with me."

"There's nowhere else I want to be."

All those questions can wait.

CHAPTER FORTY-NINE

Emily

"Is THIS OKAY?" I hold up a thin, purple V-neck sweater, mildly annoyed with myself for asking Dex to approve my outfit. But what if the women dress up for breakfast and I look sloppy next to them?

"I like you in purple," he says, which doesn't really answer my question.

"I mean, should I wear something nicer? I brought a blouse and skirt." They're probably both wrinkled from being stuffed in my backpack, though.

"Em, no one cares. Everyone's laid-back here." He blinks as if he's trying to remember something. "Pretty sure some of the girls get together for yoga before breakfast and show up in whatever they wear to that. Or pajamas."

"Oh." I paw through my bag again. Did I bring leggings?

He pulls my backpack away and holds out his hand. "Do you want to hang that up in there?" He nods to his closet, then the skirt and blouse I'm still holding.

He peers into my open bag. "You brought a lot for an overnight. Do you want to leave some of it here?"

My heart flutters but then my stomach churns. "I wasn't sure what would be appropriate to wear. I didn't bring all this stuff so I could move in or anything."

His jaw clenches. "I want you to be comfortable here. Leave whatever you want."

I hand over the skirt and blouse.

"Thank you," he says in this sexy-sarcastic way that should be annoying, but it's too hot.

After placing my outfit in his closet next to a row of neatly hung shirts arranged by sleeve length, he stalks to his dresser, yanks open the two top drawers, scoops everything out of the first one and drops them into the second.

He holds out his hand again. "Give me whatever you want to leave here."

My gaze shifts from his determined face to the now-empty drawer. "You're taller. You should keep the top drawer."

At first he frowns, then he shakes with laughter. "It really doesn't matter, Emily."

"Well," I glance around the room, "I'd say I'd leave the green set here, but the panties need a good trip through the washer and I'm not even sure where they ended up."

He jerks his thumb over his shoulder. "There's a washer and dryer on this floor."

"Oh. Convenient."

He cocks his head, still waiting.

"Okay, okay." I grab my backpack and tip it upside down, spilling everything onto the bed. My cheeks flame. I really did overpack.

I grab a black cotton bra and panty set, a long-sleeved T-shirt, a tank top, and a pair of black leggings. *Hah!* I knew I'd packed them.

"Here." I turn and hand him the items.

He nods his approval.

"Oh, here. These too." I hand him a pair of thick socks.

"There, was that so hard?"

"I feel bad, I haven't asked you to leave anything at my place," I admit.

"The apartment I'm staying at isn't that far from your house. We're in the middle of nowhere here," he explains. "Although, the girls are usually helpful at rounding up stuff if anyone needs it."

Someone pounds on Dex's bedroom door. "Downstairs in ten!" they shout.

"The fuck?" Dex growls.

Whoever it is continues pounding on doors and making the same announcement up and down the hallway.

Shouts of "fuck off" and loud groans can be heard outside our room.

Dex grabs his phone and checks his messages. A deep frown creases his brow.

"Everything okay?" I ask.

"Not sure. We were meeting at eleven anyway. Don't know why it suddenly got moved up."

I finish getting dressed, grab my phone, then follow Dex out of his room. We join a few of his rumpled, bed-headed brothers in marching down the stairs.

A bunch of people seem to be clustered near the doors Dex said belonged to their "war room." Some of the women I met last night are with them.

Shelby's eyes widen and she runs over to hug me. "Mornin'!"

"What's going on?" Dex asks Rooster.

Rooster glances at us and shakes his head. "Still waitin' for Rock, Murphy, and Z to get here."

Dex blows out an annoyed breath but doesn't say anything.

Sparky ambles up to us, his long, baggy jeans trailing over the hardwood floor.

"Was that you I saw feeding the birds at the crack of dawn?" I ask.

He lifts his head and stares at me, like I caught him doing something naughty and I'm tattling to his parents.

"Wait a minute?" Wrath gasps and joins our circle. "Sparky was outside in the daylight? Willingly?"

"Sorry," I mutter to Sparky.

He shrugs it off. "I like the birds. Their music brings harmony to the home."

"Their shit brings out my need to slap you around when it lands on my bike," Wrath warns.

"It's good luck," Sparky insists.

Shelby steps up and taps a finger against Sparky's chest. "I've got a good one I've been saving up for ya, Sparky."

He waits with a hopeful expression, similar to a basset hound under the dinner table, waiting for you to throw a treat.

"Why can bees handle their liquor?" Shelby grins and rocks back on her heels.

Sparky scratches his head. "Because they only get a little buzzed?"

"Damn." Shelby actually stomps her foot. "Thought that'd take you more than two seconds."

Sparky grins and lifts his chin at Dex. "Hey, did I tell you about the new strain I'm developing?"

"No," Dex answers with a cautious note in his voice.

"Don't ask," Wrath warns.

"I'm mixing laxatives and weed. Guess what I'm calling it?" Sparky presses a fist to his lips like he's trying to swallow the answer.

Dex inhales a slow, patient breath. "Shits and giggles?"

"Aw, man." Sparky tips his head back and presses his hands over his eyes. "Did I already tell you that one?"

"No," another biker says. "It's obvious as fuck."

"Bet you weren't expecting 'botany for the insane' this morning, were you?" Rooster asks, smiling down at me.

"That was not on my Bingo card," I agree.

"No one will ever believe ya if ya try tellin 'em hanging out with the Lost Kings Motorcycle Club is ninety percent sex jokes and weed puns," Shelby says.

"If weed puns are a sin, I'll see you *inhale*," Sparky giggles into his hands.

Shelby shakes with laughter. "Cute."

"Wait, what's the other ten percent?" Sparky asks.

Shelby shrugs. "Sex on pool tables? I've been to a bunch of ya'lls clubhouses now. Ain't seen one of ya use a pool table for its intended purpose yet."

"That's the appeal," another bearded biker says. "Fornicating on objects not meant to see that kind of action."

Rooster slides a slow look at his friend. "Fornicating? Really?"

I laugh and press myself close to Dex's side. "They're right. This is not at all what I expected."

Rooster's friend moves in and rakes his gaze over me. "I missed you last night."

Dex holds me tighter. "Jigsaw, this is Emily. Emily, Jigsaw is the RC at our downstate charter."

"Oh! Dex's job," I blurt out.

Jigsaw flicks an amused glance at Dex.

"Be nice, Jiggy," Shelby warns.

"I'm always nice, songbird."

"Debatable," Shelby mutters, cracking up the guys.

"Oh, there's Trinity," Shelby shouts, jumping up and waving her hand wildly. "Dex, can I borrow your girl?" Shelby asks, gripping my arm in a tight hold that suggests she won't accept no for an answer.

Rooster hooks his finger in the hood of Shelby's sweatshirt, dragging her backward. He leans down, whispering something in her ear, then plants a long, lingering kiss on her lips.

"For fuck's sake," Jigsaw moans. "She's gonna be ten feet away."

Without coming up for air, Rooster throws out a hand, hitting Jigsaw in the chest and shoving him into Sparky.

"Clowns," Dex mutters to me. "I told you."

I loop my arms around his neck and lean up to kiss his cheek. "You're wrong. Your brothers are *way* more entertaining than clowns."

"That's what I'm sayin'!" Shelby squeals and pats my shoulder.

"Better looking too, right?" Jigsaw asks, smoothing a hand over his beard.

"Absolutely."

Jigsaw gives Dex a smug smile.

"I'll take good care of her," Shelby promises, finally managing to pull me away from the guys.

We meet up with Trinity near what looks like a bar area. A few guys are sitting on stools, sipping coffee. I run my gaze over the bikers already in the clubhouse, checking if Grayson's here.

"Look, Trinity!" Shelby announces. "We finally got Emily here."

Finally? I didn't realize they'd been waiting for me to make an appearance.

Trinity flashes a quick smile. "Sorry I missed you last night."

"That's okay."

"Come on." Trinity urges us down a long, wide hallway. "Did anyone give you a tour of the clubhouse?" she asks over her shoulder.

"No, it was already kind of packed when we got here," I answer.

She slows her rapid steps and points to a swinging door on our right. "Bathrooms. We keep pretty much any feminine items you might need stocked in there."

"Uh, good to know. Thanks."

Trinity nods and continues walking, slower this time. "This used to be the champagne room." Her lips tilt into a sly smile. "We use it mostly for yoga now."

Shelby snorts. "The unholy things that happened in there last night had nothin' to do with yoga."

"Seriously?" Trinity sighs. "Damn. I thought we finally won that battle."

"Ravage ain't playin'," Shelby laughs.

Shaking her head, Trinity continues. Another hallway branches off to our right. "Laundry room's down there. Gym. A few rooms for people who live here full-time."

She slaps her hands against the right side of a double-swinging door and leads us into a cafeteria-style dining room, big enough for a college dormitory. A bigger, more official looking bar runs the entire length of the back wall. A large coffee station is set up there now. Vibrant murals of the Lost Kings Motorcycle Club's logo decorate the walls.

Trinity points to the bar. "Coffee's over there. Serena says you're a tea drinker? There should be hot water and tea bags too. The selection isn't great but if you let me know what you prefer, I'll try to have some on hand," she says, as if she expects me to be here often.

Such a simple thing, but her words wrap around me like a hug.

"Kitchen's through here." Trinity marches ahead and pushes open another swinging door.

Heat rolls over us. Someone's been cooking and baking.

"Wow," I mutter, staring at the industrial appliances in the large space.

"Lots of bikers to feed," Trinity laughs.

"I guess so."

Trinity introduces me to a few girls I don't recognize and I'm so overloaded, I immediately forget their names.

"Heidi," Trinity says. "You remember Emily?"

Heidi turns away from one of the ovens and waves. "Hey!"

"Grab whatever you want and relax," Trinity says, gesturing to a long kitchen table. The window above it seems to look out on the front parking area, giving me a view of the garage. Lilly's at the table, so I take a chair next to her.

"Morning." She yawns.

Trinity sets a mug of hot water and a handful of random tea packets in front of me, then sits at the other end of the table.

"Am I wrong, or is this earlier than usual?" Lilly says to Trinity.

"Definitely earlier," Shelby says, dragging a chair in between Lilly and me.

Trinity shrugs and sips her coffee.

"I just hope they're not riding out after church," Heidi says, dropping into the chair next to me. "Swan and I baked like a billion muffins."

"A billion and one!" a tall, lithe woman shouts from the other side of the kitchen.

"Is that possible?" I ask. I rode here with Dex. Now I'm anxious about being stranded here all day long. "They just take off?"

"Sometimes," Lilly says.

"Dex said they had, like, emergency church or something the other night. Can there really be another emergency already?" I try to make a joke out of it but snap my mouth shut when I realize Lilly's staring at me.

"Did they have church during the week?" Lilly asks.

Shelby shrugs. "Rooster didn't say anything about it."

A cloud of dread drifts over me. Like I'm almost certain I just stepped in a pile of dog poop but I'm afraid to look down and discover I ruined my shiny new shoes.

Heidi picks at the label on the bottle of juice in her hands.

Trinity stares at me like she'd like to superglue my mouth shut. Then shifts her gaze to Lilly.

"I think it was something concerning one of Upstate's businesses." Trinity twirls a finger in the air. "Not something they'd bother Downstate with."

Oh, fuck.

Lilly's husband is the president of the *downstate* charter. Shelby's man is the downstate VP, right? Everyone seems so close, I didn't think the distinction mattered.

Someone should've handed me an organizational chart or maybe even a family tree when I walked in.

Lilly accepts Trinity's answer with a casual shrug.

No big deal, right?

I sip my tea and try to study Trinity from the corner of my eye.

The enforcer's wife. Dex's friend. *Oh, shit.* Is she going to tell the guys about my blunder?

CHAPTER FIFTY

Dex

EVEN THOUGH WE were all called into church earlier than expected, my head's still upstairs with Emily. Letting her leave with Shelby hadn't been easy. I'm confident she can hold her own with the other women but the abrupt shift in our morning leaves me unsettled.

I fucking told her I love her. My heart jumps, reliving the moment. I never expected to feel this way again.

Christ, I'm acting like a teenage girl about to flip open her diary and doodle a bunch of hearts around Emily's name.

Now's not the time.

Focus.

Did Loco agree to a meeting time? Most of Downstate was here anyway, so it'd make sense if we were meeting with Loco today. Not sure that called for all of us to sit at the table earlier than normal, though.

My brothers are more boisterous than usual as we wait outside of the war room. I scan the living room several times. Except for Rock and Murphy, every Upstate brother is here. Z seems to be the only missing member from Downstate.

I elbow Jigsaw's side. "You get a hint about why we're here so early?" Jigsaw's so far up Rooster's, his VP's, ass, that he must know something. *My* VP doesn't seem to be anywhere in sight.

He glances at Rooster, then leans in close enough to hit me in the face with a minty wash of whatever the fuck toothpaste he used this morning.

"Digger went to the big highway in the sky. Priest's calling all the charters to talk about arrangements."

Holy fuck. "Shiiiit."

"Yeah."

Wrath opens the war room doors and shouts for us to get our asses to the table. Brothers are rowdy, loud, and don't seem to be aware of what happened.

While everyone's taking their seats, Wrath hands Rooster an older, triangular-shaped speaker, something you'd expect to find in a boardroom, not a biker clubhouse, and Rooster places it in the middle of the table, checking underneath for wires. Wrath checks a burner phone and sets it in front of Rock's chair.

The volume in the room drops a notch. Behind me, Wrath and Rock's low voices seem to be working out something. Z slaps my shoulder on his way to his chair.

Grinder drops into the chair next to me. "How you doing, Dex?"

"All right. Serena and the baby come up with you?" Emily would probably feel a lot more comfortable with Serena here today.

"Not today." He slides a look down the table at Z. "Plannin' to head home when we're done here. Unless Z needs me to stay."

"All right." Wrath's hands slap together louder than a clap of thunder. "Settle the fuck down."

Rock walks to the head of the table. Head up, shoulders back, stone-faced, but he still looks like he's carrying the weight of the world. Instead of sitting in his chair, he curls his hands over the back of it and sweeps his stony gaze up and down the table.

"Thanks for coming to the table earlier than usual and in an orderly fashion, everyone." He taps one finger against the chair. "We had some unfortunate news this morning. Digger, the former president of our Deadbranch charter, passed away yesterday."

Murmurs go around the table. Digger was mostly well-liked throughout the organization and in the larger MC community. He probably should've retired as president a few years ago, but otherwise was a decent guy.

"What are we doing for him, Prez?" Bricks asks.

Rock's hands tighten on the back of the chair. "Well, Priest's going to call in a few minutes and let us know. But Digger wore that president patch for a long time and was a brother even longer. Even though he retired the gavel not that long ago, the whole organization's going to show him the respect he earned."

I take that to mean we all better get comfortable with a trip to Deadbranch in the near future.

As much as I love my club, danger surrounds MC life. Not every brother makes it to Digger's age. A president's life expectancy is even shorter than the average outlaw biker's. So the desire to show our respect by celebrating Digger's life will be strong.

I'm going to have a lot of work to do to get ready for this trip. It'll be my first major club ride since I stitched this road captain patch onto my cut. I glance down the table at Jigsaw, three seats away. He dips his chin as if he's thinking the same thing. At least *his* first trip as RC was a low-pressure vacation both of our charters took to Texas together. Everything about *this* visit to Deadbranch will be intense.

As much as I'd like to take Emily with me, it's not an option for an event like this. Not this soon in our relationship.

The burner phone rings. All the chatter and questions cease.

Rock answers. With his free hand he motions for Wrath to do something with the speaker.

"You've got both New York charters at the table, Priest," Rock says once everything's working right.

Priest clears his throat, the sound exploding through our long, narrow room. Rooster jumps up and adjusts the volume. He waits, his hand suspended above the speaker until Priest begins talking, then sits.

"Morning, everyone. I'm sorry to be the bearer of bad news. But yesterday we lost our good brother Digger, outta the Deadbranch charter. As a lot of you know he was president for a long time, only handing the gavel to Squiggy a couple months ago."

"We're all really sorry to hear this," Z says.

"That you, Zero?" Priest asks.

"Yup."

"If y'all would identify yourselves before speaking, that'd be best," Priest says.

Bricks catches my eye from the other side of the table and makes a face I interpret as, "I ain't saying shit." I nod to indicate that's my plan too while Priest's on the line.

"Now, just so we're all on the same page," Priest continues, "Digger was loved and known in the MC world, not just our organization."

Priest pauses but none of us say a word.

"I've been working hard with law enforcement from Nashville to

Deadbranch to arrange a proper memorial service without them busting our nuts." Priest's voice holds a weariness I haven't heard from him before. "More than any other time, I *need* each and every charter on their best behavior. If you've got any crooked arrows, you best set them straight. If anyone acts up, it makes all of us look bad. Not just Lost Kings but every single motorcycle club in this country." Priest spells it out as if we're not all aware of this and it's the first time we've heard this lecture.

"We can do all the toy runs and charitable events in the world," Priest continues. "But if we have an incident, that's what folks will remember about the Lost Kings. Media and law enforcement will talk about nothing else."

"Understood," Rock says, glancing at Wrath. Rock will depend on him to keep us in line.

I lean to my left and hold out my fist, tapping Wrath's leg to let him know I've got his back. He flicks his gaze down, one corner of his mouth turns up, and he taps his fist against mine.

Priest isn't finished with his lecture. "It may not seem like it, but this is bigger than our national event or any rally we attend. We're negotiating to hold the memorial service at the Dashport Center."

Rooster sits forward and mouths "what the fuck" at the speaker.

"We'll have to agree to metal detectors at each entrance. Anyone causing trouble will be removed immediately. There will be severe consequences for misbehavior." Priest stops for a long, noisy breath. "You're responsible for each of your members and guests, Rock."

Rock's jaw clenches. Probably a good thing Priest's all the way in Mississippi.

"Don't get twisted, Rock," Priest says as if he can see Rock's reaction. "I'm having the same conversation with each president. Same goes for you, Zero."

Z rolls his eyes. "Got it, Priest."

"Rooster." Priest's voice turns warmer and almost fatherly. "I expect you to step up here. Set a good example for your brothers from all over."

Rooster's eyes widen to half-dollar size. "Uh, yeah. Of course I will, Priest." He quickly scans the table. "We don't have any bad apples. New York won't be a problem for you."

"That's what I want to hear." A loud clap fills the air, like Priest's closing the book of notes he's been reading from. "All right. I'll get in touch when we have a firm date, but I'd say it's going to be within the next month, so start making any arrangements with your families and businesses now."

Murphy and Wrath frown at each other. They've got a third business partner at Furious Fitness who isn't affiliated with the MC. Still, it's hard to make arrangements for coverage when you don't know the fucking dates you'll be gone.

I glance at Ravage and Bricks. They're who *I* go to when I need coverage at Crystal Ball. Guess it'll be Malik's time to shine. Might need to pull in Remy or Griff to help with security while I'm gone. Working at the strip club's always been a hard *fuck no* from Vapor, but maybe I can ask him to help out at Furious.

"Got more calls to make," Priest says. "Looking forward to seeing everyone. Thank you for your time."

"Thank you," Rock says.

Everyone around the table mutters a "thanks," "goodbye," or "see you soon."

Rock stands and swipes the phone off the table, flips it closed, and tosses it in a drawer. He returns to his seat and rests against the back of the chair, closing his eyes for a few seconds. Wrath gets up and unplugs the speaker, wraps the cord around it, and stores it in the closet.

"Sorry, Rock," Rooster's gaze slides between our two presidents, "Z, I didn't mean to overstep."

Rock holds up a hand to halt Rooster's apology. He's never held grudges and certainly not over petty stuff. "I think your assurance helped end the call, so for that, I thank *you*."

Rooster drums his fingers against the table. "Not sure how I feel about him specifically calling me out, though."

"Yeah." Murphy glances at Rock and smirks. "Should I be offended or something?"

A hint of a smile flickers over Rock's face. "No, be thankful."

"It's just because you've been down there recently," Z says to Rooster.

"I hope that's all it is," Rooster grumbles.

"He saw my pretty face plenty," Jigsaw says. "I was right by Rooster's side—"

"You mean up his ass?" Murphy asks.

"Look who poured himself a cup of extra-strength fuckwad this morning," Jigsaw sneers in Murphy's direction.

To take some heat off Jiggy, I raise my hand. "I spent plenty of time with Priest too. Don't take it personally."

Z's mouth twists into a devilish smirk. "I think Priest likes Rooster because of the *celebrity* he can bring to the club's name."

"For fuck's sake," Rooster grumbles, sliding his hand over his face.

"We've got you, brother," Wrath says. "No one's letting Priest use Shelby for publicity."

Damn, Wrath's awfully protective of Shelby. I hope like hell that's going to extend to Emily one day.

"Do you guys realize how big the Dashport Center is?" Rooster asks. "That place holds expos, trade shows, and smaller concerts. What the fuck is Priest planning?"

"Shelby ever play there?" Z asks.

"Not with Dawson, that dude sells out arenas." Rooster shakes his head. "But holding a memorial service there is fuckin' wild."

"Maybe he's doing it there because they can handle the extra security needs?" Hustler suggests.

"All right," Rock says in a louder voice meant to capture our attention and shut our collective mouths. He bangs his gavel against the table to quiet any lingering chatter.

"Obviously, this is a mandatory run," Rock says, casting a glance around the table. "No excuses."

"Uh, boss." Sparky raises his hand.

"That includes *you*," Rock warns before Sparky can even ask his question. "You need the miles."

We're all required to ride a certain number of miles every year to keep our patches. As road captain, I'm the one who should be keeping track of that. But the math is simple. Sparky never leaves the basement, so it's not exactly shocking that he's coming up short.

"You're between crops, aren't you?" Wrath asks Sparky.

"Well, yeah." He glances at Stash. "But the dark energy of a funeral? I don't want to bring that home."

"You're paying respects to a brother," Rock says in the kind of voice you'd use on a kid who's afraid to sleep without a night-light. For some reason, he's always had infinite patience with Sparky.

"How is it dark energy, Sparky?" Rooster asks in a similar gentle tone. "We're celebrating the life of a brother. Giving him a proper send-off into the next life. That should bring all of us good karma."

Jigsaw side-eyes his best friend. "You start reading Tarot cards with Shelby? Gonna be jacking off with crystals next?"

"That sounds painful," Stash mutters.

"What Rooster said." Z points at his VP, ignoring the rest of the chatter. "Respect for our fallen brother is good for our combined karma." Sparky frowns but doesn't utter another complaint.

Grinder sits forward and lifts a finger to let us know he has something to add. "This might not be my place to say, but as much as Priest might prefer the spectacle of us all in attendance at his little lovefest, we *need* some brothers to stay behind. Sounds like the whole damn world's gonna know every Lost King in the country will be in Tennessee at a certain time. Leaves us vulnerable at home."

"Grinder's right," Wrath says. "If Priest's working with law enforcement to plan this, word will spread. Our clubhouses, businesses, and everyone associated with our club will be unprotected."

"Uh, won't *we* be at risk if we're all in the same location at once?" Murphy asks. "What if the ATF decides they'd like to end their MC problem once and for all and drops a fucking bomb on the stadium?"

Everyone stops and stares at Murphy. He doesn't flinch. He's serious.

"I don't know that we're so important the government wants to risk civilian casualties just to wipe us all out," Z says.

"Uh, maybe you should dial it back on the action movie watching, Jason Statham," Rooster says.

"Please." Murphy lifts his arms and flexes his muscles. "I look more like Channing Tatum than Jason Statham."

"Nah," Wrath says. "Papa Smurf maybe."

"Discuss who's gonna play you in your Lifetime movies later," Rock says. "We're not done here."

He searches the table, checking to see if we have any more brilliant suggestions. When no one speaks up, Rock continues, "Grinder and Wrath are right. A lot of people knew Digger. Word will spread about this event."

"Not everyone is a fan of the LOKI nation," Butcher adds.

I suppress the urge to chuckle. We don't have charters in every state. We're hardly a *nation*.

"Is anyone worried Priest might try to use this for his documentary bullshit?" Jigsaw asks. "Or live stream it?"

"Fucking hell." Z rams his fingers through his hair. "Priest hasn't mentioned the documentary again but who the fuck knows with him."

Rock stares at Teller. "I want *you* to stay home."

"What?" Teller scowls and sits forward. "Why?"

"Because no one cares about the treasurer," Murphy says.

"Because I *said* so." Rock glares at Murphy, then Teller. "I want an officer *here* to watch over the compound and the ol' ladies."

Teller glares at the table. It's gonna take a minute for him to move to acceptance on this one.

Grinder shoots a look at Z. "You need your SAA with you. And you know damn well after fifteen years, Priest's gonna expect me to be there."

Irritation ripples over Z's expression. Knowing him, he was planning to have Grinder sit this one out since he has a newborn at home.

"You're right," Z says slowly. "Serena and the baby can stay with Lilly at our house."

Grinder lifts his chin at me. "She's been wanting to visit Emily."

"Emily's welcome to stay at our place too," Z offers.

"Thanks, brother." I'm not sure how Emily will feel about me asking her to pack her bags and move in with someone she barely knows while I'm away for who knows how long, but I appreciate the offer anyway.

"Our place is big enough," Murphy says. "And they'd be safest up here."

"Clubhouse is gonna be empty," Ravage points out. "Girls can take over the whole damn place if they want."

Considering Rav loves to bitch about all the changes the girls have made to not only the clubhouse but the club itself, I find his offer pretty damn funny.

"Careful," Stash warns. "We'll be coming home to candles and pretty pink fuzzy furniture all over the place."

"I like candles," Sparky says.

"All right." Rock holds out his hands. "Make your housing arrangements later. We're not done here."

"Fuck, Rock." Teller gestures to the drawer where Rock tossed the phone. "Priest's going to think I'm one of the misfits you had to leave at home."

"He'll understand that I'm trusting you to take care of things here." Rock's voice sounds patient, but the shut-the-fuck-up glare he drills Teller with says volumes. "He'll be leaving someone he trusts at home too."

Murphy leans over and says something against Teller's ear and the two of them share a quick laugh.

"Do we know *how* Digger actually died?" Grinder asks.

"Probably a heart attack," Rooster says. "Anyone ever have a meal with that man? He never met a piece of meat he didn't want to dip in batter, fry, and shove down his cake hole."

Jigsaw squeezes his eyes shut and shakes with laughter. "Mean. But true."

"Maybe one of the customers his dancers were rolling shot him," I suggest, leaning forward to nod at Rooster. "I still can't believe that clusterfuck hasn't somehow bitten the whole organization in the ass. Priest owes you more than a few empty compliments for discovering that mess."

Rooster nods. "I keep waiting to see something about it in the news one day."

"No point in speculating," Rock says. "I'm sure we'll find out at the funeral. Let's worry about conducting ourselves appropriately." He pauses to scan the table, meeting each of our stares.

Rock's gaze lands on Z last and Z nods. "No one from New York is going to cause any problems or dishonor our patch in any way." Z's statement feels more like the warning you'd give a group of rowdy frat brothers before taking them to the opera.

"A funeral for one of our presidents is *not* the place to confirm all the lies law enforcement likes to spread about us," Rooster adds.

"Other local clubs will be there to pay their respects," Grinder says. "Digger moved in the MC world for decades. He knew a lot of people. All beefs need to be set aside."

"Deadbranch getting this same lecture?" Hustler asks.

Z's frosty glare settles on his treasurer. "I've spoken to Steer."

"We're going to support our Deadbranch brothers, conduct ourselves like men worthy of wearing this patch, and celebrate Digger's life. That's it," Rock says.

"Like him, love him, disagree with him or whatever, Digger was a loyal brother for a lot of years," I say, nodding at Rock. "We all respect that."

Murmurs of agreement go around the table.

"We're not there to hook up, either," Z adds.

"Easy for you to say when you've got a hot as fuck ol' lady," Butcher mutters.

"Watch yourself, fucker," Z warns. "I haven't decided who's staying home, yet."

"Yeah, don't threaten me with skipping the funeral, Prez," Butcher sneers.

"Watch your fucking mouth." Grinder's deadly tone settles over the table like poison mist, silencing everyone. "Fuck around elsewhere. At this table you speak to your president with fucking respect, or I'll yank out your goddamn tongue myself."

Butcher holds up both hands, his nervous gaze darting between Z and Grinder. "No disrespect intended. I go where Prez tells me to."

"Good to know," Z answers with enough sarcasm to make Butcher squirm in his chair.

Rock taps his knuckles against the table. "All right. Whether you want to admit it or even recognize it, having a brother die—no matter his age or health status—puts us all on edge, questioning our own mortality. It's only human nature."

In another life and different circumstances, Rock would've been a great psychiatrist.

"The long ride to Deadbranch should help give all of us some clarity and settle down before we get there," I say.

Rock nods at me. "Exactly." He scans the length of the table one last time. "All right. You're free to go. Z and I will let everyone know when we get dates and times from Priest. I'm sure we'll have a few more sit-downs about logistics between now and then."

The volume of chatter increases as everyone stands and starts discussing the ride.

Teller must still be smarting over having to stay home. He and Rock move away from the table, talking to each other in low voices.

Murphy fixes his troublemaking eyes on the two of them and stands.

"Don't," I warn.

The mischief melts from his expression. He nods at me and leaves with the others.

I approach Rock and Teller slowly, assessing their interaction.

Rock squeezes Teller's shoulder and Teller nods. Since things look civil, I join them.

"Do you want me to give Malik a heads-up that most of the club will be away?" I ask Rock. "Or just tell him I'll be out of town?"

"Have him call me if anything comes up," Teller says. He's not as sullen as he was at the table, but annoyance seems to linger in his expression.

I rest my hand on his shoulder. "You'll never forgive yourself if Charlotte goes into labor early or something happens with those babies." My voice drops to a dull rasp. "Trust me. You're needed here more than you're needed to wish Digger a bon voyage into the afterlife."

"Thanks, brother." Teller nods once. "Appreciate that."

"I'll kick Murphy's ass if he needs it," I promise.

That finally makes Teller laugh. "Perfect." He taps Rock's arm with his fist, then mine, and heads out of the war room.

Rock watches him leave with an unreadable expression. When we're alone, he settles his gaze on me. "Thank you for that. I didn't want to spell it out for everyone at the table. But there's no way I'd drag him down to Tennessee right now."

I get it. Most bikers will tell you the club comes above everything else in a biker's life. But it's a lie. Or it should be. "He can't be a good brother if his body's on the road, but his heart is here."

"Exactly."

"You think you'll have Hope and Grace drive down with Trinity or something?"

"I haven't had a chance to talk to her about it, yet." Rock shrugs. "Honestly, I don't think any old ladies should go. It'll be boring for them."

"How do you feel about riding down to Virginia, and meeting with Ice's crew?" I ask. "Then we can all ride to Deadbranch together. I know it's a longer route but—"

Rock must approve, he cuts me off before I finish offering alternatives. "No, that's a good idea. We can ride home whatever way's quicker, but I think three charters from the East Coast riding in together is a good showing. I'll give Ice a call later and run it by him."

"I'll map out a few routes just in case and when you give me the go-ahead, I'll touch base with Boots about the ride." I have a good relationship with Virginia's road captain, so it should be an easy conversation. "I'll run it by Jigsaw today."

"Thank you, Dex. That's a big help." He slaps my shoulder. "Emily doing okay up here?"

Heat creeps up my neck. "So far."

"All right. Better go get her before she's overwhelmed by everyone."

"Thanks, Prez."

Outside of the war room, Jigsaw's waiting for me. "Let's get you ready to pop your road captain cherry," he announces.

"I don't know what to say to that, Jiggy."

We walk down the hallway to the dining room together, discussing the ride and the possibility of meeting up with Ice's crew.

Once I step into the dining room, I tune Jiggy out. My gaze roams over the crowded space, searching for Emily.

"Boy, you're already pussy whipped, aren't ya?" Jiggy says.

I roll my eyes at him.

"Looks like your girl's with Shelby." He lifts his chin toward the end of one of the dining tables. Emily's sandwiched between Shelby and Heidi. She's smiling but tight lines of tension frame her mouth.

"Figures you can spot Shelby from across the room," I say, just to be an asshole.

He doesn't care, though. Just gives me a shit-eating grin and makes his way to the breakfast buffet.

Emily's eyes find me as I walk over to her. Relief softens her expression. She says something to Shelby, pushes her chair back, and hurries to meet me.

I curl my arm around her, hugging her against me. "What's wrong?" I ask low enough no one will overhear.

"Nothing. You were gone for a while. Then the others came back and you weren't with them..." Her voice trails off as if she's worried she said too much.

"Just stayed to talk to Rock for a minute." I kiss her temple. "No big deal."

"Oh. Okay. Heidi said her brother is usually the one who's detained after church."

"Yeah, it's a running joke around here. He runs his mouth all the time." She must not have realized Heidi was kidding.

"Oh." She covers her mouth with her hand.

"Relax." I rub my hand over her back.

Someone's hand lands on my shoulder and I turn to find Wrath's serious face.

"Meeting with Loco's set up for later this afternoon." He flicks his cold eyes to Emily and back to me.

For fuck's sake.

"Yeah, all right. I got it," I say. Fucking *knew* Loco would set that meeting up at the most inconvenient time.

Emily watches him walk away, then turns to me. "I need to get home anyway." She pulls her phone out of her pocket. "I forgot about a report I need to finish and send."

"Do you need me to take you by your office?"

She shakes her head. "No, I have all the numbers on my computer at home." Finally, a smile brightens her face. "I knew taking that sick day would haunt me later."

I blow out a relieved breath. She's not making an excuse to get out of here, she actually has shit to do.

"I could try doing it on my phone, but the signal's been spotty up here." She squints at the small screen. "And it's a pain in the ass to input the numbers on this thing."

"No, I get it." Disappointment stirs through me but I push it away.

I have what I wanted the most out of this weekend. Emily spent time around my club. I told her how I feel about her, and she feels the same.

I really can't ask for more.

CHAPTER FIFTY-ONE

Emily

RIDING AWAY from the clubhouse leaves me conflicted. I have to get home. Part of me wanted to stay but I'm also relieved to have an excuse to leave. Everyone is so close, I felt like an outsider. After my earlier mistake, I didn't want to open my mouth again around the other women and risk saying something else I wasn't supposed to say.

Dex pulls into my driveway and shuts off the engine. Should I invite him in, or does he need to leave right away?

I thought this trip brought us closer but for some reason, now I feel farther away.

"Emily?" Dex swings his leg over his bike and stands in front of me. "What's wrong?"

"Nothing. Can you come in, or do you need to go right away?"

A brief frown wrinkles his forehead, but he nods. "I'll come in."

Gee, don't sound so excited about it.

Why do I feel as awkward as the first day he gave me a ride home from work?

Inside the house, I set my backpack at the bottom of the stairs so I remember to take it up with me and unpack it later.

When I turn around, Dex is right behind me. He rests his hands on my hips and walks me backward until the back of my foot hits the wall. I lean against the cool surface and stare up at him.

"What's wrong?" he asks.

"I wish you'd told me what I should or shouldn't say around your club. I hate feeling like I'm going to do something wrong."

He tilts his head in a questioning way, but I don't have anything to add.

"Em, you have to give me more information. I doubt you said or did anything wrong. Everyone liked you."

"Is that what you talked about in church for so long?"

"What?" he snorts and steps back. "No." He stares at me for a few beats. "A brother...the old president of one of our southern charters passed away. Our national president's organizing a big memorial service. Attendance is mandatory. So there was a lot to discuss."

"Oh." My mouth stays open, but I don't know what else to say. "I'm sorry about your brother."

"Tell me what you think you said that you shouldn't have?"

I shrug. "It's stupid."

"But it's bothering you." His stubborn tone says he expects an answer.

"I just mentioned something about how you guys had church the other night. And Lilly seemed surprised. I forgot she's part of Downstate. Trinity looked pissed. I didn't know I wasn't—"

"Hey, hey. It's not that big of a deal." He cups my cheek. "Z's probably being looped in right now. Downstate was supposed to come to that afternoon meeting with us."

"Oh." Well, now I feel dumb. "I just don't want to say the wrong thing and make them hate me when I know how important the club is to you."

"Emily." He drops his forehead to mine. "That means the world to me. You have no idea."

Having him so close, pressing me against the wall like this, sets me on fire. My breathing turns quick and shallow, but I try to act like nothing has changed.

"Please don't take this the wrong way," he says. "I have a lot of love and respect for Lilly, Trinity, and all the ol' ladies. But as much as I love them and it would make me happy if you get along with them, *my* opinion's the only one that matters. So, if Trinity didn't like that you said something in front of Lilly, I really don't give a fuck."

Part of me wants to be offended—I'm not sure why. The other part of me is relieved. And a tiny sliver of myself is annoyed that I crave his approval so damn much.

"If it *was* a problem—which it's not—then it'd be something Wrath and I would work out, not you," he adds.

"But…then I'd be getting you in trouble with your club. And I don't want that." Reacquainting myself with my backbone, I stand straighter. "You really need to give me a Lost Kings' organizational family flow chart or something."

A slow smile spreads over his face and laughter rumbles out of him. "I like that idea. I'll bring it to the table."

"What? No, don't do that. I'll figure it out. Serena will help me."

He brushes his lips over my cheek. "I love you, firecracker."

The heat licking my skin returns hotter than before.

"I'm glad you want to talk to Serena," he says. "But I'm concerned she made you *more* anxious by telling you whatever she said about the girls."

My need to defend Serena cools my desire for him. "No she didn't." I narrow my eyes and put some heat into my words. "And don't forget she and I were friends way before *your* club entered *my* life."

His mouth twitches like he's trying not to laugh. "Noted."

"I did have a nice time. Until I felt like I showed my ass. And then you were gone for so long."

He brushes my hair off my shoulder, his fingers tickling over the sensitive part of my neck exposed by the V-neck of my sweater.

My breathing stutters. I wish I'd chosen a bra with some padding. My nipples are harder than diamonds, probably poking through the thinly knit sweater.

"Sorry things were chaotic up there. I thought you'd be more comfortable if Downstate was around, since you've met Lilly and Shelby." He drops one hand to my waist, squeezing in that demanding, possessive way that makes my heart pound.

Without another word, he leans down and feathers his lips over mine. My mouth opens and I slide my hands into his hair, pulling him closer. His lips glide against mine, so slow and soft for the longest time.

I moan into his mouth and that seems to crank up the heat between us. He grabs my other hip and yanks my lower half into him. He leaves a demanding trail of hot, wet kisses along my jaw, down to my neck.

"Emily."

The rough desire in his voice snaps my eyes open.

"I want to make love to you before I have to leave."

If those aren't the sweetest words to grace my ears. I tighten my arms around his neck and drag him closer. "Yes, please, yes," I whisper in between kisses.

He lets out a deep, tortured groan and attacks the button of my jeans.

"I love that sweater on you but take it off. Now," he says without shifting his gaze from where he's tugging open my zipper.

I yank the sweater off so fast it isn't even funny, dropping it somewhere on the floor.

"Good girl." He kisses all my newly exposed skin, dipping lower to bite the tips of my nipples through my sheer lace bra.

"Oh God."

He growls an affirmative noise but doesn't take his mouth off me. His hands slide into my pants, and he shoves them down over my hips. "Get these off."

I don't even know how I do it without dislodging his mouth, but finally my jeans hit the floor and I kick them away.

He kisses a trail from my breasts to my mouth. I tighten my arms around his neck, wanting his body pressed to mine as tightly as possible.

"Em," he groans like he's starving, his hands clutching my butt and lifting me.

Eagerly, I wrap my legs around his waist, gasping when he presses his erection against me. "Please. Not here. Take me upstairs."

He rumbles an unhappy sound but lifts me high, holding me securely while he turns us around and moves to the stairs.

"Hang onto me."

I nod frantically, burying my face against his neck. I try not to distract him as he navigates the staircase.

Finally, he turns to the side, using his elbow to push my bedroom door open. As soon as we pass the threshold, I reach out and slam it shut.

He drops me on the bed, and I stare up at him. Our eyes lock as he quickly sheds his clothes.

My mouth waters at the sight of him. I slide to the edge of the bed and wrap my hands around his erection, dipping my head to taste him.

"Oh, fuck that feels good, baby," he murmurs, resting one hand on the back of my head. "A little more, then I need you in that bed."

I lick and suck, taking as much of him as I can.

"Fuck." He gathers my hair in one hand and pulls me away.

I swipe my hand over my mouth and smile up at him. "How do you want me?" I roll over to my hands and knees, glancing at him over my shoulder. "Biker's choice," I tease.

"You're really poking the bear today."

"No, I want the bear to poke *me*."

He snorts with laughter and shakes his head.

I swish my hips from side to side. "Like this?"

He grabs me by the hips and drags me to the edge of the bed. Instinct brings my chest flat to the mattress, arching my back and tipping my butt higher.

"Fuck," he groans, and yanks my panties out of his way. His rough hand teases between my legs. "You're so wet." He slides one finger between my lips, gently working it back and forth. "Are you ready for me?"

"Yes," I whisper urgently, curling my fingers in the comforter.

I inch my legs apart and arch my back even more.

His cock prods my entrance and I wiggle my toes in anticipation.

Holding my hips in a firm grip, he slowly pushes inside, groaning with pleasure the whole way.

My mouth opens, no sounds coming out as I adjust to the shocking invasion. Every other time he's made sure I came at least once or twice. Excited or not, he's a lot of man to take.

"Em? You okay?" He pulls back a bit.

The slow slide and drag feels so good, but sharp at the same time. "Yes. Go slow. Just like that."

He murmurs something I can't quite make out and rubs his hand over my back. "Relax for me."

I stretch my arms out to the sides.

"That's nice," he says as he slowly starts sliding in and out. "You're so fucking beautiful from every angle."

I moan and pant, the sharpness from his deep thrusts melting into a blissful tension in my center. "Oh, that's good." I press my hands against the mattress, lifting myself to all fours.

"Yes," he groans, gathering my hair and tugging. He snaps his hips harder and faster.

God, he's good at this. Tension builds but not quite enough to send me over the edge.

"Can you come like this, Em?" he rasps.

"I…I…don't know. It feels good, though, so don't stop."

After a few minutes, he slowly pulls out and throws himself onto the bed next to me. "Up." He taps my leg.

Slightly disoriented, it takes me a second to throw my leg over him and line myself up. He rests one hand on my shoulder, slowly guiding me down his length.

He sucks in a breath through his teeth. "That's so good. This is perfect." His hand slips from my shoulder to cup one breast, then clutch my hip and finally rest on my thigh. "Show me what you like."

Where do I even start?

I experiment with moving my hips back and forth. "Oh." That's good. I lean back, resting my hands on his thighs, and move my hips faster.

"Good girl. Ah, fuck, that's so good." He snuggles his hand between my legs, rubbing his thumb over my clit.

"Yes, yes. Do that," I whisper desperately.

I flex my thighs, working myself up and down harder and faster.

"So, so good, little firecracker," he mumbles.

"That's it," I chant, so, so close to the edge. The tension snaps, pleasure bursting from my center and out. I keep grinding myself against him, enjoying every last flutter and spark.

I slow my wild bucking and tip my head down to see his face.

Eyes hazy with desire. Teeth biting his bottom lip. He barely seems to be holding on. I rest my hands on his chest, shifting my legs, and he groans.

His hands clamp down on my hips. The hazy look in his eyes turns into wild need. "Stay right there," he rasps.

As if I'd go anywhere.

His powerful legs tighten under me. Holding me tight, he thrusts up into me hard and fast.

"Oh fuck, that's good," I gasp, my voice vibrating from the power of his wild thrusting.

He unleashes a deep, breathless roar of satisfaction, squeezing his eyes shut. "Fuck." He thrusts up hard once more, and I feel his release deep inside me.

Completely spent, I fall on top of him. He bands his arms around me, holding me tight and kissing the top of my head. "You're like my queen up on her throne when you're riding my cock like that."

I chuckle softly against him. The sweetest things come out of his mouth. "I felt like I could rule the world. That's for sure."

Little aftershocks work over my body. I twitch my hips against him and he groans. "You're gonna have to give me a minute, if you wanna get on this ride again."

I lift myself off him and stretch out against his side, throwing my leg over his. He sneaks his arm underneath me and I cuddle up closer. My eyes close. Warm, swoony afterglow wraps around me. "I could go to sleep just like this," I whisper.

"I could look at you all night."

I open one eye and find him watching me. "I suppose we should get up. I need to run to the bathroom."

"Kiss me first."

Laughing, I lean toward him and drop a quick kiss on his cheek.

His fingers slide over my body as I sit up.

"Good thing I'm spent, or I wouldn't let you leave the bed."

I walk over to my dresser and pull out a clean T-shirt. Remembering how he cleaned out an entire drawer for me at the clubhouse, I stare at my packed top drawer. I can put this stuff somewhere else. I've been meaning to get rid of some extra clothes.

"Dex?"

"Hmm?"

"If you want…um, you can have this drawer." I run my gaze over his beautiful, perfect naked body. "To leave like pajama pants or whatever."

He sits up in one graceful motion. "Okay."

"Good." I shove the drawer closed and hurry to my bedroom door. "But get dressed now. I'm not sure what time Libby's coming home."

His rumbling laughter follows me into the hallway.

CHAPTER FIFTY-TWO

Dex

THE SCENT of Emily's skin taunts me as I ride back to the clubhouse. wanting to leave her is becoming a problem.

By the time I pull into the clubhouse's parking area, almost everyone's outside. They're not quite ready to leave yet, so it's not like anyone was waiting for me. Still, my skin crawls from my brothers' scrutiny. I stop my bike in front of our smaller garage, not sure where in the formation Jigsaw and I will ride today.

I can't find Jiggy outside, so decide to search for him in the clubhouse.

"Where'd you run off to?" Z asks, blocking my path with a hand on my chest.

"You learn that from Grinder?" I ask, sweeping my arm up to dislodge Z's hold on me.

He laughs. "Yeah, probably. Where were you?"

"I had to take Emily home, not that it's your business."

He pats my cheek. "Everything is my business."

Whatever. "Are we ready to go?"

"Just waiting on Rock."

"What's new."

He chuckles, then turns and raises his hand, signaling to Murphy that he should join us.

Murphy ambles over. "I couldn't find out anything about what Loco wants. Were you able to talk to Malik?"

Shit, I completely forgot. "No, I haven't seen him since the other night."

Murphy shrugs. "Probably doesn't matter. He enjoys yanking Rock's chain, so he woulda called a meeting no matter what."

"It's enough to make you wish we could go back to the old days of dropping off shipments to his minions down by the river," Wrath says, holding his arms out wide. He glances at me. "Where's your girl?"

I narrow my eyes. "I had to bring her home. Why?"

He slides a look at Z, then shrugs. "Barely got to see her, that's all."

"Barely got to *terrorize* her, you mean," Murphy says.

Wrath nods once. "That too."

"You will *not* be terrorizing Emily for any reason," I warn. "I'm not fucking around."

A blank expression settles over Wrath's face. Should I be antagonizing our enforcer right now? Probably not.

Jigsaw joins us, resting his arm on my shoulder, like he's leaning on a post.

"When did we all get so touchy-feely around here?" I grumble, shrugging Jigsaw off of me.

"Let's move out," Grinder yells as he moves toward the front door, pointing like a flight attendant showing us where the exit is.

"About time," I mutter.

Jigsaw hangs back with me. "You want to ride at the front of the line or bring up the rear?" he asks.

"Rear is fine." That way I can easily watch my brothers and hopefully park somewhere I won't get hemmed in at Loco's.

Rock pats my back as he passes by.

Corralling both clubs goes quicker than I expected. Fifteen minutes later our entire pack thunders down the clubhouse driveway. We go slow easing onto the main road. These back roads are too narrow for all of us to ride side by side, so we end up in one long chain until we hit Route 155 and can change it up. Pride flows through me at the way my brothers seamlessly roll up next to each other. Jigsaw and I are the only ones riding without a partner. He's all the way at the front of the line and I'm by myself at the back.

An evil glee prickles through me as we reach Loco's place. Teller was right, Loco's going to shit himself when all of us ride into his diner's parking lot.

Emily

After Dex leaves, I wander into the kitchen and pour a bowl of cereal. I need to keep my strength up to handle Dex.

I reach for my phone but it's not in my pocket. Where the heck did I leave it? I hope it's not at the clubhouse.

I finish my cereal and set the bowl in the sink, then search for my phone.

My attention's drawn to my backpack and the pile of clothes scattered in the hallway. *Oops.* Dex and I had gotten so carried away, I'd forgotten about them.

I pick my jeans up off the floor and shake them.

Something heavy clatters to the floor. *Great.* Found my phone. Hope I didn't crack my screen.

I lean over to pick it up and the screen flashes with a missed call. Shit. Did Libby need a ride? I glance at the time. She should've been home by now.

The phone dings and buzzes.

I flick the screen on. Not broken. That's good.

A line of text messages and missed calls appears on the screen.

My blood runs cold.

Between the time we left the clubhouse and now, Libby tried to text me a bunch of times.

Libby: Em, can you come pick me up?

Libby: Yoohoo! You said you'd come get me.

Libby: Is everything okay?

Libby: Mac's giving me a ride.

My heart thunders against my rib cage.

In between the texts are several missed calls from Libby and a few from a local number I don't recognize.

Damn. I feel like shit. Too busy screwing my boyfriend to answer my sister when she needs me. I'm going to owe her big.

I dial her number. It rings and rings, then goes to voicemail.

"Sorry I missed your texts, pudding. Cell service was spotty out there. I'm home now if you still need a ride."

I disconnect the call and stare at my phone.

It lights up with an incoming call. Again with the number I don't recognize. It better not be one of those damn places trying to sell me an extended car warranty.

"Hello?"

"Is this Emily Walker?" Ice cold fear snakes through my stomach.

"Yes, who's this?"

"Are you the guardian of Liberty Walker?"

My legs shake and I stagger forward, bracing my hand against the wall. "She's my sister. What's going on?"

"Ma'am, your sister has been in a car accident. She was brought into the Johnsonville Emergency Room. We've been trying to reach you."

Tears slide down my cheeks. "Is she okay?"

"She's stable. But we need you to—"

"I'm on my way right now."

CHAPTER FIFTY-THREE

Dex

Loco's still standing outside the front doors of his diner, staring at the rows of Harley-Davidsons neatly lined up in his parking lot. Right out front where all the potential customers passing by can get a good look at the patch-wearing bikers standing next to the machines.

The faces of the few customers inside the diner stare out the windows at us.

I fight the urge to laugh.

Murphy steps up next to me, his shoulder brushing mine. "This is gonna be fun."

Rock turns, his steely gaze landing on me. He jerks his head, indicating Murphy and I need to get our asses to the front of the line.

"I think he just wants you," Murphy says, giving me a quick shove forward.

"Dick," I mutter.

Loco seems to have recovered from his shock. He holds one of the front doors open wide. "Rock, you're rolling a bit deep today. What's with the entourage?"

Rock's eyes widen, the picture of outlaw innocence. "It sounded important, Loco," he says in a sarcastic, *I'm just trying to be helpful* way. "So, I brought everyone to make sure we'd meet your needs."

Loco swallows hard. "Perhaps I was, um, unclear. I really just needed to speak to you and Dexter."

"Dex," I correct.

"I figured big man might join you." Loco nods to Wrath. "But, uh, I didn't expect both clubs. Hey, Z, Rooster, Murphy, Teller." He nods to my brothers one by one. "Not sure we got enough seating for all y'all."

"Don't mind sittin' at the counter," Grinder says, brushing past Loco to go inside.

It's a smaller, old-fashioned diner. Loco's upgraded it a few times, but most of those improvements focused on the basement, which is basically one long murder chamber.

A few minutes later, we're crowded into the diner, taking up the empty booths and all but a handful of stools at the counter.

Loco, Rock, Wrath, and I are at a booth in the back corner. Well, Wrath's at the stool across from our booth keeping an eye on us while he waits for his cheeseburgers. Murphy and Teller are on the two stools next to him with their backs to us.

Loco's gaze keeps straying to his civilian customers who hurry through their meals. Finally, he seems to relax a notch. He sits back and spreads his hands out wide.

"First, I got mad respect for your crew, Rock. Want to get that out of the way first."

Rock glares at him.

"Now, I know you all claim Ironworks as your territory and all," he says in a way that suggests he disagrees. "And I been helping you hold it down for a while now."

"With varying degrees of success," Rock says.

Loco frowns.

"Well, I gotta say, it don't make me look too good when one of my constituents is beaten half to death in my backyard and I don't know nothing about it."

"Constituents?" Rock raises an eyebrow and glances around. "You running for mayor now?"

"Yeah," Loco answers with an equally sarcastic tone. "Mayor of Pussy Town, New York."

Teller—or Murphy, I can't tell—snorts but neither of them turn around.

I'm getting tired of all the posturing and bullshit. "You talking about that piece of shit Stan Elliot?" I ask.

"That'd be the one," Loco confirms.

"What's your relationship to him?" Rock asks.

"He's an occasional customer. But that's not why I wanted to sit down. He went to the cops about the spa treatment you gave him, Dexter."

"Spa treatment?"

He waves my question away with a frustrated huff. "Code, motherfucker. Look where we at."

"What about it?" Rock asks, ignoring the outburst.

"Well, how the fuck am I supposed to have your back in Ironworks, if I don't know what you all's up to?" He jerks the lapels of his suit and then settles into place, sort of like a rooster sorting his ruffled feathers. "Luckily Stan went to one of the cops in my pocket and he brought it to me."

"He I.D. me?" I ask. "Did he say it was a Lost King?"

"Yeah! Why the fuck you think you're here?" he shouts.

"All right. They puttin' out a warrant on me?" I ask. Fuck. I don't actually care if I get picked up. It's Vapor I'm worried about. But so far, Loco hasn't mentioned that he knows there were two of us.

"No. Fuck, no." Loco slaps the table. "You think I'd let that happen? I made it go away."

Ahh, I see where this is going.

"Are you shitting me?" Rock growls in a low, furious tone. "You dragged me out here to shake me down?"

Loco touches his chest as if he's deeply offended. "Dragged?"

"What do you need, Loco?" I ask.

Rock slants a look at me, like he wants me to shut up.

"The way *I* see it," Wrath rumbles, lazily swiveling from side to side on his stool, "taking care of shit like that is part of our arrangement that allows you to keep running *Pussy Town* in our territory."

Jesus Christ. This is getting way out of hand.

"Rock," I say, trying to humble myself. "This is my fuckup. I didn't think it would bring heat down on one of our partners."

Rock's eye twitches at "partner" but Loco nods and seems less irritated.

"I just like a heads-up," Loco says. "Help me to help you. That's all."

"How much?" I ask.

"Well." Loco scratches his chin. "It cost me about five K to make this go away."

Rock glares.

"I'm not asking to be reimbursed." Loco holds up his hands. "Just forewarned."

"It won't happen again," I say. "He's a piece of shit who hurt one of my dancers, though. It needed to be done and I only had a short window of time to make the visit."

"Oh." Loco sits back. "Well now. That changes everything. I figured it was an MC business spat. But you's just protectin' one of your girls?"

"Yes," I answer. "He sprained her wrist, fucked up her shoulder, and fuck knows what else."

"How she supposed to ride the pole like that?" Loco asks.

"Exactly," I say.

"All right then." The strained atmosphere seems to dial down a notch. "You know how I feel about that shit, Dexter."

I nod. At least we see eye-to-eye with Loco about something.

He strokes his hand over his cheek. "My girl Minnie says you been taking good care of her too."

"Yeah, that one brought us a lawsuit," I say. Rock shouldn't care that I'm disclosing this. Loco needs to understand we have unexpected expenses too.

"That gonna cost you a fuck lot more than my bribe to Ironworks' finest."

"No shit," Rock says.

Loco sits back, placing his hands flat on the table. Like suddenly he's rethinking this "urgent" meeting.

My phone buzzes in my pocket.

We're still face-to-face with Loco, so I ignore it.

"Now that we've taken care of business, how about we all eat?" Loco says. "Burgers sound good?"

"I don't know." Rock sits back and runs his hand over his stomach. "I'm trying to limit my red meat intake. Let me see a menu."

I swallow down my laughter. Rock's watching his diet like he's turning in his Harley for a Vespa.

"How's the corned beef and cabbage?" Murphy asks over his shoulder.

"Oh, y'all about to clean out my kitchen." Loco points two fingers at his eyes, then sweeps them in our direction. "I see you."

My phone goes off again.

"Just get it, Dexter," Loco says.

I pull out my phone and check the screen.

Missed call from Peanut.

Missed call from Peanut.

Missed call from Vapor.

Peanut: Uncle Dex, I got a call about Libby at Johnsonville Hospital. Is that your girlfriend's sister? Call me.

"I gotta go." I shove the phone in my pocket and slide out of the booth.

"Everything okay?" Loco asks.

"No." I meet Rock's surprised eyes. "It's...something happened to Libby."

"Go, go," Rock says. He lifts his chin to someone behind me.

Behind me, Loco asks Rock, "Dexter got a girl now? Good for him."

I'm out the door before I hear his answer.

CHAPTER FIFTY-FOUR

Emily

"LIBBY WALKER, WHERE IS SHE?" I slap my hand against the front desk at the hospital, startling the woman behind the desk. "I got a call she was brought into the ER. I'm her legal guardian."

"Libby?" She frowns and taps at her computer.

"Liberty, sorry," I say. "Walker."

"She's been moved to critical care now. Turn—"

"Wait, the person I spoke to said she was stable."

A doctor in green scrubs and a white coat greets me, taking me to another part of the hospital.

"What happened?"

"As far as we can tell, your sister was in a vehicle with two other girls. Another driver ran through a stop sign. Hit the driver's side. Your sister's very lucky."

I blow out a breath. *Lucky means she's okay, right?*

"Can I see her?"

"She's out right now but you can sit with her."

"Wait, what?"

The doctor lists several injuries. I can't keep track. *Why wasn't I there?* A broken arm and bang on the head seem to be the worst of it.

I'm still not prepared. My baby sister. Swallowed whole by a white hospital bed. White sheets. White blankets. White cast halfway up her left arm. White bandage around her head. Her skin so pale.

Except for the red blood all over her face.

My stomach lurches, my vision narrows, throwing me back to the night I found my parents. The night I found Libby in the closet covered in blood.

"Her face." My voice quivers. "What happened?"

The doctor steps closer, frowning at my question. Did she already explain?

I'm caught. Unable to shake off the grip of the past.

"...windshield shattered...safety glass...scratches will heal...looks worse than it is." The doctor's voice drones on and on.

Scratches. Not blood spatter.

I fall into a chair by her bedside.

"I'm so sorry, pudding," I whisper.

Guilt tumbles over me like blocks of ice.

I should've been there.

She shouldn't have had to get a ride with a friend. One I know damn well isn't a safe driver.

Instead of being there when Libby needed me, I was at some stupid motorcycle club in the middle of nowhere. Worried about my own selfish needs, *again.*

Rage consumes me until I'm ready to throw something out the window.

I sit there staring at my sister. Completely still on the outside.

Coming apart on the inside.

I don't know how long I'm sitting there seething when a nurse bustles into the room to tell me there's a man here to see Libby. He's insistent. But he's not family, so they won't let him past the front desk.

It has to be Dex.

"No, he's not family," I whisper.

I'm the only family Libby has. And I abandoned her today. For a man. Something I swore I'd never do.

Anger wars with my self-loathing and I don't know which one will win.

"I'll take care of it," I assure the nurse. "Will she be okay?"

She nods and checks Libby's vitals.

I walk through the corridors of the small hospital almost in a trance.

Dex's voice reaches me before I see him. Arguing with someone in the lobby.

I stop.

446

If I wait, I won't have to do or say a thing. Security will probably escort him out.

I'm so furious, the security guard might be the better option for Dex.

I step into the lobby.

"Emily!" Dex's relieved voice somehow makes me feel so much worse. "What happened? Is Libby okay?"

"No, she's not."

He wraps his hand around my arm. "Where is she? What can I do for you?"

"Leave."

"What?" He recoils as if I'd slapped him.

"Leave. You need to go."

I can't stop seeing the scratches on my sister's face. How much they look like the blood on her face the night our parents were killed. I close my eyes, trying to separate the two events. But the memories return with a swiftness bordering on violence.

Finding Libby huddled in the closet.

Skinny little arms wrapped around her knees.

Speckles of dried blood splashed across her cheeks, nose, and forehead. So much blood, for a second, I thought she'd been shot too.

I wasn't home to protect her that night.

Just like I wasn't there when she needed me today.

CHAPTER FIFTY-FIVE

Dex

NOT THAT LONG AGO, I swore I'd never set foot in another hospital.

Once again, I feel responsible for the suffering of someone I care about.

I shouldn't have pushed Emily into going up to the clubhouse. I should've waited. I've known all along she comes with responsibilities. Responsibilities I was all too happy to ignore to satisfy my selfish need to have Emily to myself for a few hours.

"Not every relationship is meant to last forever," she whispers in a cold, monotone voice. "I can't do this."

She turns her head, staring down the long hallway.

"Emily." I curl my hand around her arm, trying to force her to look at me.

"Please." She sniffles. "I can't do this now."

"All right." The sinking feeling in my stomach intensifies. "I'll wait out here."

"No. I can't do *this*." Emily's jagged voice slices into me sharper than any knife. "With you. I should've been *home* in case she needed me. What was I thinking? She sent me a bunch of texts, and I missed them because I was with *you*."

The air in my lungs turns to ice.

"Please go," she says in a louder voice.

The security guard who'd been hovering since I walked in, eyeballing me like he planned to call the cops if I breathed in the wrong direction, steps up to Emily.

"Miss, are you all right? Is this man with you?"

"No." She looks anywhere but at me. "No, he's not."

"All right, sir." He holds out his arm, blocking me from Emily. His other hand goes to his belt. "You need to leave now."

Emily turns and walks away, leaving me with Officer Death Wish.

Is causing a scene going to get me what I want? I can easily knock this guy out and chase Emily. She took a left at the end of the hallway. I'd find her.

But what good does that do?

Will it help Emily? No.

Will it help Libby? Also no.

I stumble outside into the cool night. Under the harsh yellow parking lot lights, my bike waits for me.

Should I go to Emily's house? I don't have a key. What am I going to do? Sit in her driveway until she comes home? Then ambush her after she's had a hellish night?

Questioning everything, I straddle my bike and head to the only home I've known for the last sixteen years. My club.

When I finally get there, several bikes are parked out front. I glare at Grinder's. Why the fuck didn't he go home?

Hoping to avoid him, I pull my bike into the garage.

The fucker knows me too well. He's waiting inside.

For some fucking reason, Jigsaw and Rooster are also with him.

"What happened?" Grinder asks, stalking over to me.

I don't even know what to say. Grinder has all but threatened to dismember me if I did anything to hurt Emily. I did something far worse, I hurt Emily *and* her sister.

"Emily and I broke up." I don't have the words or energy to explain.

"Broke up?" He stares at me. "I thought you told Rock something happened with Libby? Is she okay?"

"I don't know," I grit through clenched teeth. "Emily wouldn't tell me what happened. She just broke things off."

Her cold, detached voice and flat expression haunted me all the way here.

"What the fuck do you mean she wouldn't tell you anything?" he shouts.

"She broke up with me, then asked me to leave, so I left."

"What do you mean you just *left?*"

"Are you senile?" I'm losing patience with the repeated questions. I haven't even processed what happened myself, let alone prepared a speech for Grinder's nosy ass. "She told me to leave. My options were go voluntarily or be *thrown out* by security. I didn't think the second option would make the situation better for Emily."

"Bro, how was any of it *your* fault?" Rooster asks.

"Because she was *here*," I gesture toward the clubhouse, "instead of *home* when her sister needed her."

Grinder's oddly silent. I glance over and find him tapping away on his phone.

"What are you doing?" I snap. "Stay out of our business."

"Not everything's about *you*, Dixon. I want to know if Libby's okay," he mutters.

"What hospital is she at?" Rooster asks. "You want me to run out there and check on them?"

Why does his selfless offer make me feel so much worse? "I don't know, brother."

Jigsaw scratches his head. "I still don't understand why she blames you?"

Did she actually blame me? Not exactly. Emily's hardest on *herself*. Jesus, the answer's so obvious, it stabs me in the chest. She blames herself for not being there the night her parents were killed. She wrongly carries all the blame for everything bad that's happened to her and Libby. "A lot of bad shit's happened to them. Emily's the only person her sister has," I answer quietly. "She's...hard on herself."

Grinder tucks his phone away. "Serena's calling her to find out what's happening."

That's just fucking great.

"You need to turn your ass around and fix this," Grinder warns, stepping into my space.

"She's the one who broke it off, not me. She was really fucking clear that she was done with me," I warn, in case he gets any ideas about breaking my bones. "I hope you're happy for pushing me into this with all your *rusting or riding* bullshit. She turned my fucking heart inside out."

I'm so fucking miserable, I don't even give a fuck about all the embarrassing words flowing out of my mouth.

Jigsaw approaches us slowly, hands tucked in his pockets, thoughtful expression in place. "Easy, Dex," he says. "Look at it this way, not every storm is meant to wreck your world. She opened you up to the possibility of being with someone again. That's a big step for you, right?"

He's talking about Emily as if she's already been erased from my life.

"I want to be with *her*." I stop and replay what Jigsaw actually said. He wasn't around when my wife died. I glare at Grinder, confident that's where Jiggy got his one-sided info. "Must you gossip to everyone about my business?"

Ignoring my hostility, Jigsaw clutches my shoulder. There isn't a trace of his usual humor on his face and that somehow makes what he's saying even worse. "Some storms clear a path for you to start a *new* chapter of your life. You'll get through this and come out stronger on the other side."

Rooster must be concerned I'm about to grab a wrench and beat his best friend to death. He grabs Jigsaw's shoulder and pulls him back. "Enough."

Jigsaw doesn't know how wrong he is. Emily *is* the new chapter of my life. She's not a storm. She's the sunlight that brought me back to life. A once-in-a-lifetime kind of woman that I'm not letting go of without a fight.

Dex and Emily's journey concludes in
Agony to Ashes (Lost Kings MC #23)

THE LOST KINGS MC WORLD READING ORDER

Sometimes I'm asked how my other books fit into
the Lost Kings MC World.
Here is a loose chronological order.
https://books2read.com/rl/LOSTKINGSMCWorld

1. KICKSTART MY HEART (HOLLYWOOD DEMONS #1)
2. BLOW MY FUSE (HOLLYWOOD DEMONS #2)
3. WHEELS OF FIRE (HOLLYWOOD DEMONS #3)
4. RENEGADE PATH (LOST KINGS MC WORLD)
5. SLOW BURN (LOST KINGS MC #1)
6. CORRUPTING CINDERELLA (LOST KINGS MC #2)
7. THREE KINGS, ONE NIGHT (LOST KINGS MC #2.5)
8. STRENGTH FROM LOYALTY (LOST KINGS MC #3)
9. TATTERED ON MY SLEEVE (LOST KINGS MC #4)
10. WHITE HEAT (LOST KINGS MC #5)
11. BETWEEN EMBERS (LOST KINGS MC #5.5)
12. BULLETS & BONFIRES (Lost Kings MC world)
13. MORE THAN MILES (LOST KINGS MC #6)
14. WARNINGS & WILDFIRES (Lost Kings MC World)
15. WHITE KNUCKLES (LOST KINGS MC #7)
16. BEYOND RECKLESS (LOST KINGS MC #8)
17. BEYOND REASON (LOST KINGS MC #9)
18. ONE EMPIRE NIGHT (LOST KINGS MC #9.5)
19. AFTER BURN (LOST KINGS MC #10)
20. AFTER GLOW (LOST KINGS MC #11)
21. ZERO HOUR (LOST KINGS MC #11.5)
22. ZERO TOLERANCE (LOST KINGS MC #12)
23. ZERO REGRET (LOST KINGS MC #13)
24. ZERO APOLOGIES (LOST KINGS MC #14)
25. SWAGGER AND SASS (LOST KINGS MC #14.5)
26. WHITE LIES (LOST KINGS MC #15)
27. RHYTHM OF THE ROAD (LOST KINGS MC #16)
28. LYRICS ON THE WIND (LOST KINGS MC #17)
29. DIAMOND IN THE DUST (LOST KINGS MC #18)
30. CROWN OF GHOSTS (LOST KINGS MC #19)

...and many more to come!

AUTHOR NOTES

I hope you enjoyed the beginning of Dex and Emily's story! Dex has been waiting for so long, it was fun to finally get inside his head.

Rust or Ride was such a difficult story to write. Dex has been a large part of the series since the first book, but we've never been inside his head. I realize some people expected details about his relationship with Swan or other things, but since they weren't relevant to Dex and Emily's story, I didn't see the point. While MC romances tend to bend this rule, in general romance readers aren't big fans of details about the heroe's past relationships, and honestly, I just didn't see the point. And the book was long enough without adding chapters and chapters of a relationship that doesn't matter. Inga, on the other hand, it was just too irresistible to have her return. Dex has thoughts he really wanted to share about what Inga did to the club. And of course, ever since More Than Miles, Dex has been dying to share his feelings about Axel with someone. Why wouldn't it be Hope?

Spending time with Dex at Crystal Ball, did seem important to me. Since we knew Emily would have a problem with him working there, I wanted the reader to experience Crystal Ball through Dex's eyes—that he's kind but professional. He's ruthless about offering protection but when the girls are overly friendly, he makes it clear he's not interested. He doesn't offer friendly ass-slaps or spew cheap compliments. He's all business. And I loved having Emily visit, because I don't think we've had any "newbies" at Crystal Ball since Hope. And we learned that Willow isn't as sweet as we think she is!

In fact, experiencing *all* of this through Emily's eyes was fun for me. While Shelby was new to the MC world, she's younger, focused on her singing career, and a bit more carefree. Emily is older and responsible for raising her teenage sister. She's hard on herself for choices she made in the past and constantly trying to achieve some impossible version of sisterly perfection. I'm fully prepared for people to be hard on Emily, everyone's always harsh on the heroine. Emily can handle it.

xo
   Autumn

ABOUT THE AUTHOR

Autumn Jones Lake is the *USA Today* and *Wall Street Journal* bestselling author of over thirty novels, including the popular Lost Kings MC series. She believes true love stories never end.

Her past lives include baking cookies, bagging groceries, selling cheap shoes, and practicing law. Playing with her imaginary friends all day is by far her favorite job yet!

Autumn lives in upstate New York with her own alpha hero.

www.autumnjoneslake.com

facebook.com/autumnjoneslake

goodreads.com/autumnjoneslake

pinterest.com/autumnjoneslake

instagram.com/autumnjlake

bookbub.com/authors/autumn-jones-lake

tiktok.com/@authorautumnjoneslake

Made in the USA
Monee, IL
05 March 2023

29245036R00267